BLUENESS

The Aquamarine Sea Series

Karen Stensgaard

All rights reserved. Published in the United States by Sandefur Metz Publishing Company, Philadelphia, Pennsylvania, USA.

ISBN 9780999219720 (ebook)
ISBN 9780999219737 (paperback)

Books by Karen Stensgaard in The Aquamarine Sea Series:
~ *AQUAVIT*
~ *BLUENESS*

For more information, please contact the author through her website: karenstensgaard.com.

~ DEDICATION ~

To my friends, family, and fans,
Who enjoyed my first book and asked for more.
And to my furry cat friends,
Who kept me company while I wrote it.
And for anyone who has ever felt blue.

~~~

~ BLUENESS ~

Blueness is the quality or state of feeling blue, sad, and down in the dumps.

The color blue, often associated with the sky and sea, provides a beneficial calming effect and symbolizes truth, intelligence, and confidence.

Aquamarine, a pale bluish gemstone, is believed to protect travelers at sea, ward off laziness, and bestow energy.

~~~

~ INSPIRATION ~

"The Victoria is said to be the finest boat on the P. and O. Line, still it could not be more unsuited for the trip. It is very badly planned, being built so that a great number of cabins inside are absolutely cut off from light and air. It is a compliment to call them cabins as they are really nothing more than small, dark, disagreeable, and unventilated boxes."

From Elizabeth Jane Cochrane's memoir, *Nellie Bly's Book: Around the World in Seventy-Two Days,* published in 1890. Ms. Cochrane was one of the first American women investigative journalists. Despite some competition, she unexpectedly won and beat Phileas Fogg's fictitious 80-day journey in the novel, *Around the World in Eighty Days*, and met the novelist, Jules Verne.

~~~

"I have watched patients stand and gaze longingly toward the city they in all likelihood will never enter again. It means liberty and life; it seems so near, and yet heaven is not further from hell. Do the women pine for home? Excepting in the most violent cases, they are conscious they are confined in an asylum. An only desire that never dies in the one for release, for home."

From Elizabeth Jane Cochrane's memoir, *Nellie Bly's Book: Ten Days in a Mad-House,* published in 1887. Ms. Cochrane wrote an account of her voluntary undercover visit to Blackwell Island's Lunatic Asylum. Her expose resulted in New York City distributing another million dollars annually to better care for the poor unfortunates.

~~~

BLUENESS

1 ~ *First Night at Sea*

"You have got to be kidding me." I looked around puzzled at the sight of my small dark cabin on the old clipper sailing ship. This was my new 'home away from home' for up to three months.

I raised my oil lantern illuminating the room in a golden haze. My travel agent lacked a cruise brochure, so this was my first look and downright discouraging. I frowned at the holes forming in my bucket list voyage from Denmark to Hong Kong.

"Are you sure this is my cabin?" I switched to Danish so Uffe Petersen, my young cabin attendant, would understand. He carried another old portable lamp to show me around.

Uffe said, "Yes, M-M-Madam Jensen."

Maybe his stutter would disappear once he got to know me. I stomped my feet on the wooden floor to warm my legs. My mandatory re-enactment costume needed some extra layers against chilly Northern Europe in November.

I reached along the wall next to the door for the light switch and felt something unusual. With help from my lantern, I stared at a strange metal bracket. With a click, Uffe latched his lantern into it and reached for mine.

I handed it over hoping this didn't mean what I feared. "No electricity? Only lanterns?" Clipper ships ruled the seas in the nineteenth century, but this was 2016. Small sailboats had electricity.

He looked solemn while still holding my lantern. "Yes, Madam Jensen."

A sudden whoosh of wind from out on the deck lifted my 1860-style hoop skirt as if someone had thrown it up to hide underneath. My long hair twisted around my face and eyes temporarily blinding me.

The bed's headboard rattled against the wall until the door slammed shut with a deafening bang. I nearly jumped out of my skin but instead bumped into Uffe.

"Sorry," I shouted, while I pushed my hair from my eyes.

Uffe stumbled with his lantern. Luckily, he regained his balance and held on preventing a disastrous fire at sea. He shivered and wiped his brow. "From the wind," he said. As if to reassure me that a ghost didn't cause this.

Halloween pranks ended last month, but I smiled at his polite self-control. "Hate to disappoint you and the rest of the gang, but I don't believe in the paranormal."

Uffe pointed to where he stored my carpet bag suitcases on top of some old trunks. After studying my plain cabin, I took a deep breath to stay calm. This must be a storage room for an initiation ceremony for newcomers. Any moment now, someone would yell surprise, and show me my real cabin.

"Uffe, please, not so formal. Can you call me Kat? It's short for Kathryn or Katrine in Danish."

He didn't respond but nodded. Uffe was an unusual Danish name for a teenager, but it suited his role on this old ship.

"Can you understand my Danish?" I had been so excited to settle into my cabin. Now I grew worried. This must be a language issue.

"Your accent is d-d-different."

"I am an American, but I was an exchange student in Denmark for a year. My husband was Danish." With the crew and ship from Denmark, I was prepared to speak Danish all the time. Unless they got into technical stuff or nautical terms, I would get by.

"*Javel.*" Uffe used an unusual but polite Danish term that meant he understood.

An ache in my gut told me this cabin was no joke. I considered complaining and yelling, but I didn't want to scare poor Uffe. Based on his general behavior and stuttering, he must be nervous. I was the first passenger to board and the only woman on the ship until England.

Now I regretted not checking into my cabin before we left. But the captain let me watch our dramatic departure. With the ship powered only by sails, my dreams had come true. Our night-time departure, including sailing past Hamlet's Kronborg Castle, was unforgettable.

"Will your h-h-husband join us in England?" Uffe asked.

"No, he died last year from cancer."

He looked down at his shoes. "So, sorry."

"Thanks. I am trying to move on with my life and starting with this adventure." I winked at Uffe, and he smiled.

"Are family meeting you in England?"

"No, flying solo on this one. All the way to China." I grinned at my bravery. Despite being an experienced world traveler, I was new at making all the decisions and arrangements. But I was determined not to wait around to find a travel buddy.

"My last cruise was also from Copenhagen. We sailed through the Norwegian fjords on a mega-ship. Have you gone there, Uffe?"

He shook his head.

I smiled remembering a wacky snowball fight in the Norwegian mountains in May. That was our last vacation together. My husband, Axel, splurged for a deluxe cabin with a private balcony - the exact opposite of this place.

I surveyed my surroundings again. My cabin included the basics - a bed, a small table, and a chair. An oversized armoire for a closet filled the corner of the room along with another bigger chair, and a squatty dresser. Two long wooden trunks stood against the walls. A single tiny porthole adorned the wall. Nondescript and plain furnishings were what I expected and completely acceptable.

The ship rocked, so I softened my knees to absorb the movement and remain balanced.

"Where is the bathroom?" I only saw the one door where we entered the cabin.

"B-B-Bathroom?" His nervous stutter was back in full force.

"Yeah, you know, the toilet."

"Madam, I mean Kat, here." In a few short steps, Uffe stood by the small table with his lamp. He raised the top of a wooden chair stationed against the wall to show me.

In one giant stride, I stood next to him and stared down at the dark hole in horror. This toilet lacked a handle or flushing mechanism.

He showed off a poorly disguised porta-potty. On top of the low dresser, he pointed to a metal bowl and pitcher. The makeshift sink apparatus fit snug into a wooden frame to prevent them from falling.

"That's not a bathroom. How d-disgusting!" I could barely speak from stress. "I can't have that in my room. This can't be hygienic. What if it leaks or falls over?"

Uffe shrugged his shoulders but didn't respond.

My panic grew. I threw my hands into the air and moaned. An experienced sailor in New York City told me all these old sailing ships had been modernized. I wanted the romance of the sails and the wind and didn't mind reimagining the days of old without electronics. But I never dreamed this meant no electricity or modern plumbing.

I didn't expect or want upscale benefits like a fitness center, pool, or a hot tub. But I couldn't function without my daily hot shower. On the rare occasions when my apartment building in New York City had plumbing repairs, I showered at the gym across the street.

Uffe shuffled his feet and struggled to speak. His stutter got worse, and his words were unintelligible.

The ship rocked, and we almost fell. I slumped down on the bed, and Uffe braced himself against the small table by the wall. He pushed his hair out of his eyes.

I hated to overstress Uffe but not having a real bathroom was a deal-breaker. Now I understood why my travel agent in New York City who sold me this cruise lacked a brochure.

I should have insisted on more information. But I was in a rush to leave town and start my once-in-a-lifetime vacation while I had some time off between jobs.

I moaned. Should have, could have, won't help me now.

"Where do I take a shower?" I never expected a bathtub since cruise ships had small bathrooms. But all had showers.

Sadly, I received only a blank look. I twisted my windblown hair into a temporary knot eager to control something.

"You know, a shower for taking a bath?" A community bathroom for all these men must exist somewhere.

Uffe shook his head and didn't respond.

"Great. Here I am on this ship for months without a real toilet or bathroom. Utterly fantastic."

I propped my head on my hands to figure out what to do. My blonde hair fell out of the loose bun, but I ignored it to stay focused.

I consented to wear an 1860-style costume for this odd re-enactment cruise. But never in my wildest dreams did I imagine living as they did back then for months. My long-awaited break from an unbalanced work-life routine in Manhattan hit its first major snafu.

Only the officers and crew were on board, so there was no one else to compare notes on the accommodations. The other passengers won't board until our first port of call in England three or four days from now.

"This is a joke. Right? An initiation ceremony for new passengers?"

I yearned for a shy grin from my cabin attendant as if he only had to play this game a few more minutes.

"Are all the cabins like this?"

"I b-b-believe so Madam Kat." He sat on the small chair with a grave expression on his face.

My stomach ached with the realization I might be living without a real bathroom for months. This cabin wouldn't even merit a half star rating. Employees on a cruise ship had better accommodations.

I racked my brain for a solution like analyzing an internal audit issue at work. From many trials and even more errors, I had learned to go to the most senior person to save us all the extra aggravation.

I didn't want to scare or offend Uffe. He wasn't to blame for this mess.

"Uffe, please tell the captain I must discuss this with him. This cabin isn't what I expected. I can't live like this." Lower level staff like Uffe lacked enough authority or information.

"This is a t-t-top quality cabin."

I shook my head. "This most definitely is not top quality. Please tell the captain to stop by when he has a free moment."

I might have to wait hours to see him and switch cabins We were sailing around the northern tip of Denmark past Sweden and Norway towards England powered only by the wind.

Earlier on the deck, the captain had said, "The Kattegat is a shallow sea and perilous with stony reefs and shifting currents." He had urged me to settle in for the night.

Uffe hung his lantern on another hook and left in the darkness. The poor guy might be upset, but he will thank me later for saving us both a lot of time and trouble.

Sitting on the bed, I remembered Annette, my Danish travel agent liaison, and her parting words of advice. "Your first port is about three days away. Get off there if you don't like it." But that would destroy my exciting, adventurous plan to see more of the world by sea.

Some unconvinced friends at home predicted problems. They said, "Your vacation sounds too extreme. Not your kind of trip, Kat. Do something easier."

But all those non-believers were wrong. I was tougher than they realized.

One of my managers long ago used to compliment my persistent auditing style. He had said several times, "You're tenacious. Digging like a pit bull and sinking your teeth into tough issues."

Finding solutions to issues was part of my daily existence. And, I'd never give up without a fight.

2 ~ A Witchless Wardrobe

While I waited for the captain, I leaned back on my elbows on the tan-colored bedspread. The ship creaked and rocked in a soothing motion while the lanterns cast everything in a dim yellow light.

Stretched out, I scrutinized the wooden ceiling. My cabin had every imaginable shade of brown with nothing on the walls or floor to break the monotony. The Pantone Color Institute experts in New Jersey would have a field day with all this brown.

The cabin reminded me of bruised and rotten fruit and even worse, cat poop, not more pleasant browns such as chocolate and coffee beans. Everything looked like genuine wood without any plastic or other artificial materials.

If only I hadn't agreed to follow their stupid rules and left my electronics behind. Just a few hours into my first digital detox, I was already suffering from withdrawal. If I had my phone, I might still be in range to call or email the travel agency. But long-term, without a power outlet, I couldn't charge them anyway.

I experienced a different tinge of grief. Minus my phone, I wouldn't see my screensaver of Xena, my four-legged soulmate. But I had a Xena photo I used as a bookmark, and I dug around to find it.

Inside some old classic novels packed in my bags, I found two photos. Xena, my tabby cat, made my heart ache for a moment, and I gave her face a quick kiss. I stuck her picture back inside Emily Brontë's *Wuthering Heights*, confident I'd soon move to a better cabin.

The other photo was of Axel, my former husband. His condescending smirk tempted me to tear up his picture. Instead, I stuck him back in the appropriately titled book *Great Expectations* by Charles Dickens. Now I knew not to expect much from the men in my life.

Another re-enactment rule was only to bring books published before 1860. Dumb requirements begged to be broken, so I had snuck on board a more recent book. But I was too stressed to read.

After about fifteen minutes, I paced around the perimeter of the cabin touching the walls. This could be one of those escapism games with a secret button to open a hidden door to a real bathroom. But if there was a way out, I couldn't find it.

My carpet bags lay on top of one of the wooden trunks. I unbuttoned them to confirm my smuggled toiletry bag, and modern-day clothes made it safely. To follow their weird rules, I'd leave my period costume on for now.

I pulled out an old cashmere sweater, rubbed the warm wool against my cheek, and put it on. Moths had created small holes, but I had patched them up as best I could with my rudimentary sewing skills. Recently, I'd sworn off buying any expensive clothing to save money. My failing business tore a hole in my nest egg.

Glancing around my bare-bones cabin, here was proof you get what you pay for. This discounted cruise was a bargain. In my quest to save money for a longer trip, I had gone too cheap.

I opened the metal latch on the other trunk and peeked inside. It held towels, linens, and extra period clothes provided as part of my vacation package.

I raised my long skirt and loosened the ties around my waist to release my hoop petticoats. The metal ring made an angry clank when it hit the ground. I stepped over it and said, "Good riddance," to the empty room.

The wide hoop skirt had made it impossible to pass through the cabin's narrow doorway. I lifted my long dress above my knees and tilted it to the side to enter the cabin. Besides the dress code policy, the officers and staff were friendly and seemed laid back.

My friends were right. This crazy idea to go on this odd cruise was stupid and impulsive. When I finally return home, I will be exhausted, run down, and dirty. I sat on the bed and stared at the floor as it gently rocked.

I could have afforded a fancier cruise for a few weeks on board a modern mega-ship somewhere. Right now, I'd be warm and afloat in the Caribbean Sea. The picture before me was vivid and tantalizing. My legs were stretched out on a lounge chair with a piña colada in one hand while serenaded by a live band playing Jimmy Buffet songs.

But I'd be surrounded by people I wanted to avoid - couples and even worse, honeymooners. Besides, where was the challenge and true adventure on a trip like that?

By starting in Denmark, I'd crossed one more nagging reminder from my to-do list: scattering Axel's ashes in his homeland. And, I didn't have much of a choice. My small audit consulting business closed last week, and this ship was the only one leaving Denmark in November for an exotic destination.

I threw my undergarment layers, including the miserable hoop skirt and petticoats, into a trunk and slammed the lid shut. I needed to convince the captain to limit the fancy dress code ordeal to weekly formal nights.

After grabbing a towel from the trunk, I poured some water from the pitcher into a bowl. I dipped a corner into the cool water and wiped it against my forehead to freshen up after a long grimy day.

A small mirror hung above the sink, and a wild-haired person stared back at me. I looked unhinged and menacing. No wonder Uffe made such a quick getaway. I dragged a comb through my hair. Refreshed and more presentable, I studied my options.

Over by the dresser, a wide armoire closet dominated one corner reaching up to the ceiling. Could the armoire hide a secret passageway to a real bathroom? Wherever it went, I was ready. I flung open the doors and pushed aside the loaner period clothes hanging in my way. After I climbed inside, I had a bit of space to spare and felt along the back for an opening. The armoire's back paneling didn't give, but I was just as stubborn.

I tapped on the back panel to find the pressure point and opening. The wood was solid and not supplemented with thin veneers or particle board. I knocked harder, but still nothing.

The ship rocked to the side again, and I stopped to listen. Once we rounded Northern Denmark, we would enter the North Sea. The captain had warned me the waves would be rough.

I couldn't fall with the clothes supporting me in this cramped area, so I continued searching.

"Come on, open!" My knuckles ached, so I slammed my palm against the back panel.

A man called out in Danish, "Kathryn, what are you doing?"

Hidden in the armoire, I froze, wondering what to say. This armoire might be an antique and valuable. Fortunately, my hammering had not damaged it.

This meeting was not starting well. I needed to be in a position of strength, or an equal when dealing with a senior guy like the captain.

I pushed wisps of hair behind my ears, straightened my dress costume, and poked my head out from behind the hanging clothes. The captain and Uffe stared at me - their strange new passenger.

Speaking Danish was now becoming second nature. One plus from practicing and memorizing their lingo for my annual vacations in Denmark.

"Thank you for coming. I was checking the strength of the armoire." I avoided making eye contact eager for this lame excuse to pass inspection.

"Is it strong enough for your purposes?"

"Yes, sir. It is." I climbed out of the armoire, shut the door, and faced him. With his height towering over me by about a foot, I craned my neck to look him in the eyes.

The captain's blond hair shone in the lamplight, and he chuckled. His tall, uniformed presence in my small cabin was intimidating, but at least he had a sense of humor.

I placed my hands on my hips to look as forceful as possible. I cleared my throat to begin telling him my litany of problems with this cabin.

Uffe peeked out from behind the captain and stared. Captain Madsen placed his hand on Uffe's wavy hair as if petting a huge dog.

"Kathryn, Uffe said you were displeased with the cabin and wanted to discuss this."

"Yes, I do. This cabin is not acceptable. I mean it is, but I expected a bathroom with a real toilet. One that flushes." Under the captain's intense scrutiny, I stumbled over my words and somehow forgot what to say. "And you don't have electricity either."

The captain sighed and brushed some lint from his suit.

"This is a commercial sailing ship, not a luxury hotel. As such, we do not require newfangled equipment. Your booking agent should have been explained all these matters."

He stopped for a moment at what must be an obvious look of distress. "In the morning, you may see the other passenger cabins. If you find one more to your liking, you may move elsewhere. However, this is one of the nicest."

His Danish language was rapid and formal with an unusual dialect. When I translated his response, I was speechless. My run-down cabin wasn't a joke.

The ship jolted throwing me off-balance, and Uffe landed on the floor. The captain grabbed my arm to keep me standing, reached around, and with one hand pulled Uffe to his feet by his collar.

The captain chuckled amused by our antics. "Kathryn and Uffe. Your first night and our accommodations are all new. You shall adapt and gain your sea legs soon enough."

I sat on the bed to keep from falling again. This conversation had led nowhere.

"Now if there is nothing more, I must hurry back to the bridge. The waters around the north of Jutland can be turbulent."

I sighed not wanting to argue further. "Sure." Exhausted, a yawn escaped. I chose to be here on this ship. Scraped from what must be the bottom of a bucket list. For now, I would have to make the best of it.

"It is late and past midnight. You should rest after a busy embarkation day, Kathryn."

"Okay, Captain Madsen." My enthusiasm fizzled out from the shock of my current situation.

"You may call me Captain Mikkel. I know it is unusual. At sea, we are an extended family."

I nodded. If I got to know him better, I might suggest my nickname, Kat.

"Please do not forget to turn off the lamps before going to bed. The most critical rule on the ship. Come along, Uffe."

Uffe took a lantern from the wall, opened the door, and stood at attention. "*Farvel og god nat*, M-M-Madam Kat."

I repeated his Danish farewell and good night greeting.

Before shutting the door, Captain Mikkel said goodnight.

Over his shoulder, he added, *"Faites de beaux rêves."*

French? He must mean 'pleasant dreams.' Picasso's famous painting was called *Le Rêve,* The Dream. The door shut so I was finally alone. I had not planned on deciphering French. Speaking Danish would be hard enough.

After rummaging through my stuffed carpet bag, I found my nightgown and slipped it on. I regretted not being more forceful with the captain. I should have refused to stay here and walked out. But where would I go? I would need a key for another cabin.

Three long months were ahead of me with no electricity or plumbing. That explains why the ports of call and dates were all uncertain. Without an electric power supply to load and unload cargo, it would take forever.

Tomorrow, I'll be more prepared, see the other cabins, and find a better one. If necessary, I will search the ship.

Uffe took the lamp by the door, but the second lantern still hung over the table. I jiggled the little metal switch, and to my relief, it flickered and went out. With all this wood everywhere, no wonder they worried about fires.

In complete darkness, I found my bed and climbed under the thick comforter. The bed's mattress was comfy and warm under the thick covers.

Glancing around the pitch-black room, I tried to relax after such a long and stressful day. If the ship had not stopped at a second port north of Copenhagen, I wouldn't be here. I had checked into a real ship, not a hotel.

A tear rolled down my face, and I wiped it away. My husband broke my heart the first time with his cancer diagnosis and death. Learning earlier today from his brother how he had planned to leave me for a life in Denmark with his former girlfriend was the final wound deep in my soul.

"Axel, I hope you're happy now. You wanted Denmark, and now, you got it." Where was he exactly? His ashes could have floated in the current and ended up near Germany, Poland, or Sweden. Or, he may have sunk to the bottom of the muddy shoreline north of Copenhagen.

I curled my legs up to my chest under the warm comforter. Despite everything, I'd never forget the good times we had together. After twenty years of marriage, he would always be part of my life.

To forget about this crummy room, I hummed the upbeat song, *Always Look on the Bright Side of Life* from the Monty Python film. I had not seen a clock or radio in the cabin. Even one that ran on batteries. I stopped humming. There was no bright side here.

The smell of polished wood mingled with the scent of salt water. The bed swayed accompanied by creaking sounds. I closed my eyes and relaxed remembering other cruises.

The faint sound of the sailors' voices mixed with commands from the officers slipped under my cabin's door. Their voices sounded strangely soothing. But I couldn't relax. This was too close to camping and roughing it.

I can manage one night. Tomorrow I'll figure this out, come up with a plan, and things will be back to normal.

3 ~ *Boxed In*

I slid out from my warm nest under the thick layer of blankets to stop the pounding on my door. Some light from the cabin's porthole illuminated my discouraging brown box cabin still unchanged from last night.

This room had seen better days but not during my lifetime. Hadn't they seen HGTV or heard of the concept 'renovate and upgrade'? Even a can of paint and some cheap decorations would do wonders.

I yelled, "Coming," to stop the constant knocking. With my robe still packed away, I hid behind the door and peeked out.

Uffe stood there with another sailor. "M-M-Madam Kat. Good morning." He held a tray. "Here is your breakfast. I can show you the other cabins now."

I opened the door to let him in and shut it quickly to keep out the cold. He had excellent night vision since he found the desk in the faint light from the porthole and placed my breakfast there.

"Thanks, Uffe. I need some help lighting the lantern. I've never done this before." I unhooked the lamp not caring if he saw me in my blue nightgown. A beach cover-up was more revealing.

"Yes, of course, M-M-Madam Kat."

He peeked at me and then the other direction. I guess he didn't expect to see me in my nightgown.

I braced myself against the wall and held the lamp while he struck a matchstick and opened the glass covering to light it. He offered me a set of matches from his pocket.

"Give me about twenty minutes, and I'll be ready." I didn't need extra time for my usual hot shower. The reminder made me want to scream or at least growl.

Uffe nodded and shut the door.

I slumped in the chair famished. My last meal was a late lunch with a Danish friend. He helped me get back on the ship after I chickened out. I doubt he expected this. However, he might be the rugged mountain man type and enjoy it.

The cup of hot tea, rye bread, and cheese were edible but nothing to rave about. The basic menu was the least of my problems. I enjoyed eating but was far from a connoisseur or into the Michelin-starred hype. I craved variety and adventure in food and drink more than anything else. But this situation was a cautionary note for the next time I booked a vacation.

After finding some tissues, I made a quick stop on the portable toilet. Afterward, I poured water from the pitcher into the bowl to wash my hands with the courtesy bar of soap. I washed my face and did what I learned camping in the Girl Scouts. Wipe your underarms and crotch. There was no way this would work long-term.

After I unpacked my toiletries, I washed my hair as best I could in the shallow bowl with limited water. I needed another pitcher with hot water. This was serviceable for a few days, but I didn't feel clean or awake. Brushing my teeth worked fine without a cup of water.

I debated pulling on my comfortable jeans and a sweater, but not before the captain gave his okay to break the re-enactment rules. I slipped back into the long dress I wore yesterday minus the impractical round hoop.

Uffe knocked, and when I opened the door, I froze.

"Man, it's cold." I squeezed my arms against my chest and pulled on a sweater coat before following him.

"Passenger cabin number two," Uffe declared with a flourish of his hand and invited me inside.

I hoped for newfangled electricity, but he had to use his lantern to illuminate the room. This cabin was not one iota different except for my clothes and mess.

We went to the next cabin and another. At the fourth and last one, I didn't bother entering but peeked in from the doorway. Why would anyone play such a mean trick?

"How could they expect anyone to live like this? It's so damn uncivilized." The chilly wind blew hard so Uffe couldn't hear my string of complaints.

I scanned the water surrounding the ship in dismay. How could I reach the travel agency? Even if the rules allowed me to bring my cell phone, we had sailed too far from shore, and by now, we were out of cell phone service.

If Axel were here, he'd laugh at my stupidity and go along

with it. He'd argue, "This is better than being dead." Barring some painful days from cancer, he was upbeat most of the time. But his real feelings were a façade like this damn ship.

"Madam Kat, would you like to swap c-c-cabins?" Uffe lingered politely waiting.

"No. I am going back to my damn cabin."

I jammed my hands in my coat's pockets to get warm and felt a plastic bag. I pulled out a bag of Danish licorice. I'd traded my modern polyester filled down coat for my travel agent's more time-period appropriate sweater. Annette must have left it in her pocket.

"Do you like salty licorice?"

"Salty licorice?" He said it twice as if he had never heard of such a thing. My Danish was rusty but not that bad.

"You know. Licorice with the salty flavor that most Danes love?"

He didn't respond as if considering his options. I liked licorice but couldn't abide the salty stuff. They even had salty licorice-flavored chewing gum.

"Here, all yours. If you don't like it, give it away. Or throw it overboard to the fish."

He accepted the plastic bag with small black chunks of licorice, put one in his mouth, and mouthed a thank you. At least someone on board was happy.

Listless in my cabin, I was at a loss. My schedule at home was always jam-packed. Beyond the porthole, I reflected on the vast blueness of the North Sea. Those blue colors matched my mood.

My breakfast tray was still on the table, and like in a cafeteria, I should turn it in. Motivated by a real goal, I left to find the kitchen, or what's called a galley on a ship.

I picked up the tray and concentrated on keeping it level since the ship's movements threw me off balance. Sea legs might take years to develop. I passed some sailors on the way and said good morning in Danish but didn't linger to prevent dropping anything. They nodded and said good morning but stared at me. All because of this silly costume from the 1850s. I should wear pants and look like them.

The ship's galley was easy to find since my nose led me straight to the baking bread. I poked my head into a small room lined with barrels. Bags of food balanced on top of each other and leaned against the walls. Wooden benches by the cast iron stove sagged under duress from demanding burdens.

A heavyset man in an apron swung around and grinned. He wiped his hands off and took my tray, placed it behind him, and shook my hand.

"Good morning, Madam Jensen. Welcome aboard. I am Simon Svendsen, the chef and baker. As you can see, not much of a surprise."

He was about my height with a broad grin. A chubby chef was a positive sign.

Simon showed off loaves of bread ready for the oven as proof of his work. "I trust my small breakfast was satisfactory to start your day?"

"Great," and added thank you in Danish. *"Tak for mad."*

Danes said thank you at the end of every meal. Even children thank their parents but only when a meal is over. Once I told my mother-in-law early, after the first course, and she was worried I wasn't eating anything else.

"Please call me Kat. My name is Kathryn Jensen, but I go by Kat."

"Cat? Like the animal? Meow?"

"Yes, it's my nickname. I was always rescuing lost or injured animals and most often cats."

"You should like this."

He crooked his finger to show me something. A small black kitten was sleeping in a little box packed with white towels on the floor.

"We always have a cat or two aboard."

I nodded, but this was a first. Cunard was the only cruise line I knew that allowed animals on board. But pets were isolated in separate caged areas with strict visiting hours.

"Adorable. What's her, or his, name?" I crouched down to pet the kitten.

"Her, I think. No name. Not yet. Perhaps you would do the honor?"

The fur was baby soft, and the small kitten opened her eyes. As if not wanting to leave her dream world so soon, she shut them again and turned away.

"I would love to. I will think of a something perfect for her."

"She is worn out. Her first night aboard. She wandered the entire ship."

"She's curious about her new home like me."

"Are you hungry? Lunch will be served …" He stopped to look at a pocket watch hanging from a small hook on the wall. "In about an hour."

"No, I can wait." I had nowhere else to go, so I sat on a stool next to his work table. The galley was cozy, warm, and light as opposed to my blah, cold, and dark cabin.

"Can I help?" I hoped I wouldn't regret my offer after recalling my friend Kathleen's warning. She was convinced I would be on permanent kitchen duty.

"Help?"

"With the cooking or …" I was slow at peeling vegetables and visualized bags of potatoes surrounding me. Danes ate potatoes as part of most of their meals. Boiled with brown gravy was the most common and my least favorite version.

"Oh, no, no. Some crew members assist with those duties."

A sailor walked in but stopped in his tracks when he saw me. Simon introduced me to his assistant Henrik Dalgaard, and we shook hands. He was the sailor at my door this morning with Uffe.

"A cup of tea or coffee, Madam? I mean Kat. You are English, so tea?"

"I like both, but I prefer coffee in the morning. I'm an American."

"Not from England?" His eyes grew round in surprise.

"From New York City." I was proud of my new hometown.

"You have had a long journey to board our ship."

"Pretty easy. A piece of cake." The flight from New York City to Copenhagen via London was uneventful. Even the airplane had better bathrooms despite no shower.

In the pantry next to the galley, Simon showed me some provisions which consisted of potatoes and smoked fish. Marinated herring and pickled vegetables occupied large barrels. Bags of flour, rice, and kidney beans leaned against the walls next to cartons of salt and sugar. Some tin containers of nutmeg and unknown spices filled a shelf next to jars of homemade preserved fruit and relishes.

Simon moved some food around and looked busy. "Excuse

me. I must get lunch ready to keep the crew happy."

Henrik placed a steaming cup of coffee in front of me. I poured in some cream and watched them work while it cooled down.

Simon and Henrik were busy, so after finishing my coffee, I thanked them and petted the kitten goodbye.

I wandered around the ship to see my new home. On a mast, I found a brass nameplate with *Anne Kristine*, the ship's name, and the year 1852. I had expected a modern replica so was in awe this old ship was still seaworthy. Three huge masts towered above with sails furled.

The vessel moved fast, at a clip, and lived up to its name. A fast, sleek clipper ship was what I had searched for. Such a shame the cabins remained so out of date. Next time I would get a brochure and confirm they took the time to install electricity and plumbing. But I bit my lip knowing there would never be a next time.

4 ~ Furry Hope

When I got back to my cabin, Uffe stood outside and spoke to another sailor, but they didn't see me.

"Ah, there you are, Kathryn."

I was surprised to see the captain again. He must be busy commanding the high seas.

"Kathryn, what is this that Uffe said about the other cabins? None are suitable?"

I shook my head. A Danish-English translation wouldn't cause a problem here. "No, Captain Madsen."

"Please call me Captain Mikkel. Unless you prefer to be addressed as Madam Jensen."

In the daylight, his blond hair sparkled, but his face was like tanned leather from years in the sun and wind. He was fresh and clean, and I tried not to stare. I envied his hot shower this morning.

I was astonished to be on a first name basis with the captain but delighted. "Captain Mikkel, I need a cabin with electricity and a bathroom with a flushing toilet and a shower. You know, more modern."

"Kathryn, this ship is modern. To my knowledge, those additions are not found on any clipper ships." His voice was formal and lecturing. He glared at me, and I squirmed disheveled without my daily shower.

"Why didn't the company upgrade the cabins? I know it's supposed to be old, but aren't you taking this too far?" My complaints sounded high-pitched and whiny. This re-enactment had gone overboard and was in dire need of a rescue.

"The *Anne Kristine* was built ten years ago. She's a well-regarded and admired ship. In ports of call, some lodgings include those additions. Here, it is simply not possible."

I wanted to say it was possible, but it was pointless to argue with him.

"Would you care to inspect my cabin? Follow me." He rushed off.

I ran to keep up with him. At least, it would be hard to hide his up-to-date bathroom.

The captain's cabin was a combination of two modest rooms. On a table, there was a medicine chest with bottles of dried herbs and powders, bandages, and a pile of books. I wrinkled my nose at the smell of stale smoke and needed a cabin that was smoke-free.

Fear and Trembling, a book by the Danish philosopher Søren Kirkegaard, lay next to a Bible. A four-foot sword in its scabbard hung on the wall. I imagined him fencing with a sailor turned pirate during an upcoming talent show.

He pointed to some maps. "The second room is my office to track our position, maintain the daily logs, and other duties."

I didn't mind that he, the most essential person, had extra room. The size of the cabins meant nothing. I needed standard up-to-date facilities.

"As I told you, none include separate bathrooms or electricity."

We peeked into the first mate's cabin, and it was about the same size as mine. Captain Mikkel apologized since Oskar Mortensen, the second mate, worked at night and was asleep in his cabin. But it didn't matter. Since their cabins weren't modernized, I ditched my last hope.

Out in the fresh air, Captain Mikkel gazed at the sails and the water. He pulled out his pocket watch. "Satisfied?"

Up close in daylight, he lacked perfect movie star features. His nose was too broad, and he had narrow eyes. Still, it all blended together to make him attractive.

He wanted an answer and not an assessment of his face. I nodded. "Thank you for showing me around." I was still in denial about no real bathroom with a shower and no electricity on board.

"Uffe, please escort Mrs. Jensen back to her cabin. And in an hour to the dining room for lunch. If you wish to join me for lunch."

I nodded to agree since it beat eating alone. I trudged along following Uffe counting the days left before Hong Kong.

Goldie Hawn in the film, *Private Benjamin*, joined the military and expected a resort with swimming pools. Instead, she got a basic bunker. But this was my vacation, and I didn't sign up to be in the military.

Even on a Navy ship, there'd be standard toilets and showers. I wanted to shake my fist at the sails, but a few crew members walked by and nodded. I forced a smile to be friendly.

My DNA won't let me give up without trying. But could I live like this for months? My fears before boarding focused on being the only woman and having to work in the galley. Nothing compared to this.

I had three or four days to decide before our first port of call. I emptied my carpet bags into the wooden trunks and the armoire. Unpacking didn't take long since I liked to spread my stuff out to see it. My hotel rooms were always a mess, and friends teased me about it. I didn't see the point when it was so temporary.

With time to kill before lunch, I explored the ship, got some exercise, and built those sea legs. Sailors climbed among the white sails in the masts and rigging like monkeys.

During my walk, I repeated the nautical terms for locations. "Left, port; right, starboard; front, bow; back, stern." Some men cleaned or swabbed, the port side, so I avoided that area to not get in their way.

I nodded a greeting to everyone I passed while walking to the bridge area at the back of the ship. Aft, not back, I reminded myself.

I rattled off the locations fast going clockwise, "Bow, starboard, stern, port." They had not conducted the standard emergency drill yet. If they yelled a direction, I wanted to head the right way. I was the oddball who memorized designated exits wherever I went.

Captain Mikkel and First Mate Lars waved hello. They stood on the bridge behind the wheel to watch the sails and sailors from a raised platform. The crew worked on the deck and overhead on cross-beams adjusting the sails based on the officers' instructions. They climbed so high and fast it was disturbing to watch them.

A small cannon pushed its short snout through a narrow hole over the water. I squatted down to touch it. A shadow came over me.

"Expecting pirates?" I asked First Mate Lars.

He slapped his leg in jest. "Ha! A funny one. It is used for signaling."

"Cute." I rubbed the cannon and started to stand but stepped on my hem, tripped, and fell to my knees. I accepted Lars' hand to get back to my feet.

He said, "I must leave," and gestured to the left.

"Back to port?" I wanted to impress him with my nautical vocabulary.

"Port?"

"That side of the ship." I motioned that direction.

He shook his head. "We say larboard. Brits say port."

I paced by the railing in a loop and adjusted my chant to practice counter-clockwise and back again. "Bow, port-larboard, stern, starboard. Fore, front; aft, back."

The chill from the wind worsened, so I headed back to the warmth of my cabin. When the bells rang for noon, Uffe reminded me it was lunchtime and explained the bell system. Every four hours a bell rang, and the crew members assigned to the larboard and starboard watch switched over.

The bells continued 24/7 to my dismay. I didn't hear them last night - another significant advantage of being a sound sleeper.

"Back and forth every four hours?" How did they manage that around the clock schedule?

Uffe nodded. "B-b-but our captain allows two four-hour shifts to be combined to rest."

"So generous of him," I said unimpressed. I had experienced long work days and slave labor bosses. My job often lasted at least ten hours plus a commute.

I followed Uffe to the ship's dining room. A huge table covered with an embroidered tablecloth occupied most of the room. Eight upholstered fabric chairs stood next to the table with four more scattered in the room. A place setting for two awaited, but the captain hadn't arrived.

Henrik, the chef's assistant, said, "What would you like to order?"

Without a written menu, I had to ask what they had, apart from the freshly baked bread that smelled so heavenly.

Henrik's right eye was cloudy, and he held his head at a

slight angle watching me from his left eye. I looked at him again ignoring his injured eye.

He didn't appear to notice my concern. "Soup and *smørrebrød*." This meant 'butter-bread' and referred to open-faced sandwiches. Danes smear real butter on their bread instead of mustard or mayonnaise.

I was hungry and ordered soup, an open-faced cheese sandwich, and tea. Henrik carried in a tray loaded with different meats and cheeses, so I could make whatever I wished.

I remembered their unwritten rule: one piece of meat, fish, or cheese per slice of bread. When I was eighteen, I was an exchange student for a year in Denmark. First, I attended a Danish language school for three weeks and made a submarine sandwich from the lunch buffet. No one had mentioned this rule to us, and our teachers scolded me in front of everyone.

Captain Mikkel arrived at the same time as my soup. He devoured a few open-faced sandwiches with a beer. I preferred iced tea, but it wasn't popular in Europe. Alcohol at lunch made me tired, but he explained the alcohol content was watered down. I should order several after how today had gone. I was officially on vacation, even if it didn't feel like it.

Captain Mikkel ate faster than I did. "Are you getting what you need and settling in?"

I nodded still not pleased but tired of complaining.

The captain was not one for small talk, and my usual energy to keep the conversation going was gone. "Excuse me. I must return to the bridge."

I ate my open-faced sandwich alone in silence. The food wasn't worth raving about. At least, I won't gain too much weight without a gym on board.

I selected some newspapers from a side table for something to read. Everything was old and dated in October or early November 1862. The news from the past was fascinating. I was impressed that they had gone to the trouble of making copies of these old papers. Most of the articles discussed Denmark and King Frederick VII, England and Queen Victoria, and the Civil War in the Divided States.

At that soul-crushing time, the Confederacy was winning

the war and expected to win. Thank God, they didn't. If only the Founding Fathers had outlawed slavery right from the beginning, so many lives would have been saved, and so much pain and misery averted. All wars were so depressing. I tossed the papers back on the sideboard.

The more reminders about 1860, the angrier I got. As if I would forget what was happening in 2016. This cruise was turning into a colossal mistake. They took this re-enactment and 1860 authenticity too far.

This twist presented me with a brilliant idea. The bathrooms and new stuff must be below deck for the men. TV's and showers must be in the hold.

Henrik began to clear away the food and dishes. I could wait to ask Uffe, but why bother the poor boy?

"The captain said I could see the library located downstairs. Can you show me the closest stairwell?"

He nodded. I didn't want to disturb the men in their private part of the ship. Most were busy working and avoided eye contact.

Henrik led the way to a stairwell, but down in the hold, my hopes dissolved. He carried a lantern to light the way. The nasty smell of tobacco hung in the air trapped below deck.

"Where is everyone?" Usually, sailors walked about the ship.

"Sleeping or working."

Henrik knocked on a door.

The door opened, and Uffe stood dressed in his clothes from this morning. His eyes were half-closed, and he stifled a yawn.

"M-M-Madam. What –?"

Henrik interrupted. "She would like to see the library, Uffe."

"No, sorry, I changed my mind. Not now." I had lugged two months-worth of books on board last night.

"Henrik, I would like to see the more recent stuff. You know the bathrooms and TV's?"

"TV's?" Henrik said.

Uffe rubbed his eyes trying to wake up.

"Oh, forget it. The bathrooms."

Henrik nodded. Finally, I was getting somewhere. He strode down another hallway with Uffe and I trotting behind him.

Henrik moved quickly so his vision must be unaffected by his injured eye.

He opened an unlocked door to what I prayed was a contemporary bathroom. I was okay with sharing with the guys. He ushered us in, but my heart sank. Barrels, crates, and racks wedged tight with bottles occupied the storage room.

Henrik pointed to a tin basin in the corner. "This can be put in your cabin."

I stared in disbelief at a vintage bathtub disconnected from any water pipes. The air in the room was stuffy and smelled of sweat and other unpleasant odors I didn't want to identify. Heat radiated from inside my body trying to find a way out, and I took off my sweater coat to cool down.

"Oh, forget it. You win." Without waiting for my male escorts, I hurried back to the stairwell. As I climbed the stairs, I said under my breath, "Unbelievable. Such a stupid game."

Sweat rolled down the side of my face as I made it to the top rung. I would fit in and be sweaty and disgusting in a few days.

"Madam Jensen." I feared it was the captain and couldn't face another lecture.

Some of my instructions last night mentioned rule number two: do not go into the hold. Right after rule number one: do not burn the ship down with a lantern or cigarette.

To my relief, it was Simon, the friendly chef. "I couldn't find you, Henrik." Simon tapped him on the shoulder.

"The Madam asked to see the bathtub and –"

"Please, call me Kat. I can't handle anymore Madam's."

"Ah, yes. Kat, you only need to ask Uffe or any of us, and we shall deliver it. The hold is not a place for a lady."

I was about to quip back that I wasn't a lady, only a woman or an old girl, but they looked so serious.

"All right. Tomorrow I would like to take a bath, please." I started to leave but remembered. "Simon, I figured out a good name for the kitten. Esperanza."

"A perfect name indeed."

I thanked Henrik and said goodbye. I wanted to soak in their ancient bathtub, but I lacked the energy and craved time alone.

Esperanza meant hope in Spanish. Something I badly needed. Besides, Plan C was an awful name for a cat.

5 ~ *Going Sideways*

The bells rang for 2000 hours signaling 8 p.m. and dinnertime. They rang out every four hours to notify the sailors what time it was and when to change shifts. Another archaic tradition easily solved by wearing programmable watches. I'd heard them all day and hoped I could sleep undisturbed tonight.

I wore a prettier outfit but didn't bother with the hoop skirt. On a ship with these narrow doorways, they were impractical. I had no clue how women dressed back then managed. At any rate, my last-minute outfits from the dressmaker in New York City's Chinatown got some use.

Captain Mikkel stood and welcomed me to dinner without a hint of irritation. He wore his captain uniform and looked handsome, but unapproachable in an 'I'm official and out of bounds' way.

What came to mind was how unfair women had it. Men only needed one nice suit, and they're ready to go. Women's apparel was another story.

I sat in the assigned chair and spread my skirt around my lap. Getting into position in a formal 1860 costume was a chore. The captain was a gentleman and helped push my chair closer once I was situated. The table was set for three. Who else was coming for dinner?

Two wine glasses with multiple forks and knives straddled my plate. Along the top of my place setting was a spoon for dessert, so a long meal lay ahead.

Life on board was dull. Light from the lamps clamped to the wall didn't work well for reading in bed and watching TV wasn't an option.

"Second Mate Oskar Mortensen will join us. I believe he is close in age."

The captain sounded like a matchmaker. My last blind date was a disaster, and I had sworn to never go on another.

Pretty blue and white patterned plates were on the table. I turned one over and confirmed they were from Denmark's famous Royal Copenhagen factory.

"Pretty dishes." Especially for a run-down ship, I wanted to add.

"Only the best for my passengers," he said smiling.

His opinion of 'the best' missed two significant details - modern plumbing, and electricity. I ignored his comment to stop dwelling on my horrible situation.

"Can I wear more modern clothes? These dresses aren't that comfortable or practical."

"You may wear what you wish. Your dress is pretty. The color of the sea around the Canary Islands. You shall like it there." My outfit was a shade of blue turquoise and my favorite color.

I considered telling him I might disembark in England, but I had a few more days to see if I could handle roughing it. I expected him to say something, but he remained silent and stared at me and the table.

"The ship's name is ..." I tried to remember.

"*Anne Kristine*. After my mother, Anne Petersdatter, and my wife, Kristine Andersdatter."

They both had the old Scandinavian-style names for women rare today. Petersdatter meant the daughter of Peter and Andersdatter, the daughter of Anders.

"A beautiful name for a ship."

"She is a powerful lady and deserves a superior name."

For a second, I thought he referred to his wife or mother, but he meant the ship. At least he didn't call her a she-devil.

"Are they in Copenhagen?"

"Yes, north of there. In the cemetery."

"Oh, sorry." I regretted asking and changed the subject. "And your sister? She couldn't come?"

"Correct. My sister, Nicoline, had to remain in Denmark. She shall marry soon."

He frowned. Either he didn't like her fiancé or being stuck with me without his sister. But there was nothing I could do to change either one.

"So that is why she couldn't come on the voyage."

He nodded. "Nicoline wanted to meet you. All her plans were for naught." Captain Mikkel snapped his fingers for emphasis. I hoped, for her sake, it would be a happy marriage. With more luck than I had, remembering Axel, my deceitful husband.

"Nicoline bought some clothes for you to use. They are in your cabin. Your uncle requested we –"

"Uncle? What uncle?" Only my parents knew about my unusual cruise. Why would an uncle get involved?

"Your Uncle Maxwell with a Scottish last name. Mac something. I shall fetch his letter for your review later."

I wanted to find out more about this mysterious uncle, but Oskar entered apologizing for his delay. He was unusual for a Dane with pale skin, reddish hair, and dark green eyes.

After our introductions, Simon recited each course from the unwritten dinner menu with finesse. When he finished, Simon winked at me. "Shall I translate to English?"

"Not for me. Thanks."

Simon wiped his brow with an exaggerated motion signaling his relief. I laughed at his comic antics, and Mikkel and Oskar watched me and smiled.

They both raised their cocktail glasses and made a toast to welcome me on board. I started to clink glasses with them, but Danes don't do this. Instead, I lifted my glass and made brief eye contact with each of them before taking a sip.

The mysterious cocktail was a hazy reddish-black color. At first, I longed for a shot of aquavit which meant 'water of life' in English. My fascination with an old ship on the label of aquavit is what got me into this mess. All bottles of aquavit nearby should hide from my wrath.

I inhaled a pleasing scent of anise and berries and sipped the rest. The aftertaste had an unexpected licorice flavor. Like this ship, appearances can be deceptive.

"What was that?" I asked.

"The King of Denmark aperitif." Captain Mikkel grinned. Like most Danes, he was proud of his small country.

"What's in it?"

Oskar recited the ingredients. "Pernod, black currents, and water."

Licorice-flavored Pernod was not my favorite, but Oskar retrieved the half-full carafe from the sideboard and topped up our glasses before I could stop him. The wine glass was ornate and delicate with etched crystal.

"Now to toast King Frederick VII. If he avoids another war

with Germany, so much the better."

I hesitated but I was against warmongers, so I swallowed it with a smile. The second one tasted better. My body temperature went up a degree or two, and everything looked more promising.

My date, Oskar, was super-friendly and an easy-going guy. Since he worked the night shift and slept during the day, I wouldn't see him much.

Oskar said, "Like the vampires, I roam about while you sleep." He flicked his tongue over his lips and in an ominous voice said, "Best to keep your door locked just in case."

Straightaway, I made plans to sleep in and join him during the more mysterious nighttime. I giggled fascinated and inspected his teeth. They had a light-yellow stain, and his face was pale from a lack of sunlight. Oskar was like the red-haired boy next door. Nothing at all like a scary vampire.

I was eager to chat about vampires and tell some ghost stories, but Mikkel said, "Cease, Oskar. You will give Kathryn nightmares."

Slasher and horror movies weren't my thing, but imaginary vampires and werewolves didn't scare me at all.

"Please call me Kat. My nickname. Kathryn sounds like I'm in trouble." Oskar agreed at once, and the captain chuckled but said he would.

"Oskar, you remind me of my husband's good friend. The best man at our wedding."

"I consider that an honor." Oskar tipped an imaginary hat. "What is the name of this honorable gentleman?"

"John Lundbeck. He died years ago from AIDS."

"AIDS?"

"Yeah, tragic. Much too young. Johnny was only in his thirties."

"I shall try my best to fill his shoes." Oskar smiled but looked uncomfortable. This conversation reminded me of the sad fact. I had lost not only my husband but a good friend.

~~~

Back in my cabin renamed 'the box,' I massaged my stomach to soothe it. Our upscale four-course meal turned into one course with more alcohol than eating. The wind increased, and my dinner companions had to return to work. Eating alone wasn't much fun, so I had left.

I rolled on my belly fearing the worst. The ship rocked wildly, and the safest place was in the middle of the mattress. I turned off my lantern worried it might fall. Fighting the waves was enough without a fire to add to it.

In the darkness, faint figures floated near the ceiling. A wicked half-goat half-man with a pitchfork chased a rabbit with big feet like a kangaroo.

My stomach lurched along with the ship in a sudden drop. I regretted not taking some bread with me to soak up the alcohol. Tomorrow I would stash some emergency supplies in my cabin and take my chances with the mice that poor Esperanza hunted.

I could make a dash for the galley, but Captain Mikkel was adamant when he left. "Stay inside your cabin tonight. I have enough of a burden with this gale."

What if the food was packed away? Raiding the fridge was another one of those American traditions that Danes frowned upon.

The ship stopped rocking, and everything became calm. My mouth went dry - a bad sign of too much alcohol and not enough food. Staggering over to the toilet, I raised the seat, but the potent odor almost floored me. I can't. Not here.

I forced myself to swallow and stopped my reflexes from kicking in. The ship was still, and I rubbed my stomach to feel better. My hand dropped away when inner knots grew, and a sickening queasy feeling took control.

The best remedy had been learned the hard way after choppy boat rides to scuba diving sites. Stay in the fresh air and stare at a fixed point on the horizon. Here in the North Sea, I won't see the shore, but there might be a star or the moon to focus on.

I slipped on some shoes and snatched Annette's dark sweater-coat but hesitated at the door. The captain said to stay inside. But the thunderstorm was over, and a rush of water entered my throat. The supernatural images on the ceiling moved closer. I couldn't stop now and pushed open the door.

The deck was eerie and empty like on a ghost ship. Our masts were bare while we bobbed around. Where did everyone go? To my relief, in the distance, some mariners carried sails.

Bright stars packed the sky and swirled around with a life of their own. They created an unusual dance I had never seen before. I held the railing, closed my eyes, stretched back, and took a deep breath. I expected the fresh air would soon calm my stomach.

The ship made a slight rocking motion, and another stronger one, as the wind built up. I couldn't hold back anymore and bent over the railing retching everything I had into the water below.

Some sailors shouted to each other from the other side of the ship. They raised the sails about a foot but pulled them back down. The rain began to come down in torrents. The squall came back harder with more fight for another round. We must have passed through the calm eye into the thick of it.

As if a full bucket of water had spilled over me, I shivered from the cold. The rain was a piercing cold shower and not the warm one I missed this morning. I ran to get back to the safety of my cabin and much-wanted box. The soggy and wet wood was slippery, and it went sideways.

I reached to grab something, but there was only air and nothing to hold. I fell slamming the deck and slid. I tried to stop moving, but my wet shoes couldn't get any traction. I clawed my fingernails into the hard-polished wood, but it was impossible to get a grip and hang on. My head ached from hitting the wooden deck, but I ignored the pain.

The rain mixed with ocean spray whipped against my body blinding me. I wiped the water from my eyes and saw the dark walls signaling the cabin area. Despite knowing how bad my odds were to reach it, this was a life-and-death situation, so I had to try. I crawled forward but slid further back.

If I fell overboard, I would die in a few minutes without a life preserver. Worst of all, no one would see me, a tiny creature in the vast North Sea.

My feet pressed against the wooden barrier that circled the main deck. This might hold me unless the waves tossed the ship further on its side. Rain jabbed through my clothes like needles. Exhausted and aching, I couldn't focus, worry, or think.

6 ~ *Clawing My Way Back*

Propped up in bed in my lovely and safe brown box, I studied the tray of goodies Uffe deposited on my lap. Dying of thirst, I sipped the hot tea and took a bite of a sandwich. My appetite was slow to kick in.

The ship still rocked, but not like last night. No wonder I was seasick after all this. My cabin's kaleidoscope of brown was like a comfortable old pair of socks. Not to show anyone, but cozy.

Uffe sat next to me. A faint light came through the porthole, and I had glimpsed light from the doorway.

"What time is it, Uffe?"

"1600 hours. You slept all day."

"Wow. I guess so." 1600 hours was 4 p.m. Not that there was much to miss. The ship had nothing planned for passengers to do.

My white nightgown was prickly, so I undid the top set of buttons squeezing my neck. I touched the bandage wrapped around my head, but Uffe cautioned me not to remove it.

I couldn't remember getting to my chocolate-colored room or changing clothes. My memory after falling was gone.

I surveyed my broken and ragged nails. In some places, my fingertips were red from clawing into the wooden surface. I reached over to my nightstand and squirted some hand cream into my palm. I caressed the buttery cream into my injured hands and fingertips.

"How did I get –"

The door opened, and the captain watched us. Uffe stood at attention, and the captain took Uffe's seat.

"Uffe, I must talk to Kat alone. Wait outside for a moment, please."

Uffe left, and I yearned to go with him. I knew I was in trouble.

"How do you feel?" Captain Mikkel peered into my eyes as if not trusting what I would say.

"I'm better. Thank you." I moved the tray to the side of the bed. "Sorry about last night. I should have stayed in my cabin."

"Yes, you should have."

I feared he had noticed I had broken another rule by sneaking on board a modern plastic tube of lotion. I hid my creamy and slick hands under the bedspread.

"What are you hiding?"

"Nothing." To prove it, I rubbed some lotion off my hands and put them on top of the bedspread.

"What happened to your hands?" He lifted my left hand to examine it.

"I tried to stay on. I needed claws."

He shook his head and put my hand back on the bed as if it might break.

"Would you like anything else from the galley?" He stood and took out his pocket watch to check the time.

"More tea and water would be great."

He opened the door and asked Uffe to bring me some ginger beer.

"Beer?" I was about to turn this down, but on second thought I could use a stiff drink after last night.

"It is weak and safer than water. Ginger is helpful for dizziness. Now I must check your injury."

He unraveled the bandage on my head and moved my hair around. The light from the lantern warmed my head. He was so close I could smell his strong cologne masking a touch of sweat.

"Why did you go out in the storm? In gale winds?"

"I thought the storm had stopped. I felt sick and the room … I had to get fresh air." I didn't want to mention the weird images, and how I couldn't stay trapped inside with them.

"You have a dark red mark on the side of your head. Does it hurt?"

"No, not a thing. I am hard-headed." I was proud of my ability to bounce back.

He sighed as if annoyed. "I did not touch you yet."

"Well, what are you waiting for?"

"Is there something you need to attend to?"

Did he mean the toilet? "No, but I just want to … ow!"

"You see, it is a bad bruise. You are not as tough as you

think."

The captain wrapped the bandage back around my head. "In a few days, you should be fine but be careful. Do not wander about on your own until you are fully recovered, and I say so."

I nodded and stared at my strange nightgown with long sleeves, embroidered pink flowers, and green leaves. The material was thick and stiff and must be one of the loaners from the captain's sister. I didn't want to wear her hand-me-downs or freebies, but I couldn't switch now.

"We must speak about last night. As your captain, I am always responsible for the welfare of the ship and all on board."

"Sorry. You said I should stay in my cabin. This is my fault, so I'm responsible."

"You are for not following orders. My obligation extends even if I am asleep and the officers decide to act contrary to my wishes. And when we are in port, regardless of whether I am aboard."

Mikkel paused. His 24-7 sense of duty sounded extreme. I stared at the unmoving porthole not sure what to say.

"You must promise to follow my orders for your sake and the others. You put us all in peril. If you were more seriously injured or had fallen overboard ..." He ruffled his hair with his hand still watching me.

I focused on my food tray wishing I could hide under it or a mouse would make an appearance. "I will be better about following your orders."

"Not merely better. If you cannot obey orders, you cannot remain on my ship. Passengers are not exempt."

Captain Mikkel studied my tray still loaded with food. "You must eat more. We shall not serve a formal dinner tonight. There is too much work to do after the squall."

"No problem. I have plenty of food. Simon is a great chef."

He took an envelope from his pocket. "Here is the letter from your uncle, Maxwell McIntosh. You may read it, but I must retain it with the ship's records."

I grasped the beige envelope wondering who this mysterious uncle could be. First, I had to know what happened last night. "How did I get back here? The last I remember was being in the rain."

"Stefan Lauritsen found you. He was anxious about carrying you to safety."

"Anxious?"

"He did not want to hurt you. He secured his line around your waist to protect you. The waves pounded the ship and rushed over the deck. Another sailor fetched Oskar, and he carried you here."

"So, I guess ..." Embarrassed, I didn't want to say more. Oskar took my clothes off and put on my nightgown.

"Your clothes were soaked through. To prevent pneumonia, I re-dressed you in private. I can assure you nothing untoward occurred."

"Sorry." I looked away mortified.

"Do not fret. What remains important is your recovery and following orders. I must leave for the bridge. Good night, Kat."

As soon as the captain left, Uffe brought me a cup of hot tea and a small brown bottle of ale. I sipped my drink and pulled a wooden cork out of the bottle. The beer was weak and room temperature, but I liked ginger. This herb in capsule-form helped prevent nausea on many boat rides to scuba diving sites. I sipped the beer but put it down to unfold the strange letter.

The letter to the captain was on my travel agent's letterhead. It included the standard dull legalize terms for my voyage that I had read and signed in Copenhagen. But an atypical section grabbed my attention, and I read it twice.

> *I am entrusting my niece, Kathryn Jensen, in your care as a gentleman and experienced captain. We paid a generous sum to cover the journey to Hong Kong, China. This includes reimbursement for personal items she needs while on this journey. A to-be-determined bonus payment is payable upon her arrival in Hong Kong and a satisfactory report.*

Mr. Maxwell McIntosh signed the letter. I didn't know anyone named McIntosh. MAX was the acronym for my travel agency, *Maximum Adventure to the Extreme*. On the way to board the ship, Annette, my local travel agent said,

"The computer is named Max, and he found your requested cruise on an old clipper ship."

Uncle Max must be a machine, not a real person. Programmed with AI, artificial intelligence, he must think he is a real person or want to act like one.

Like a computer programmed with sophisticated algorithms for high-frequency trading on Wall Street, Max devoured shipping data from all over the globe. Max could comb through the details faster than human travel agents to find my offbeat ship and itinerary. And now, he was communicating with the captain via a typed letter.

I laughed at the absurdity of the situation and finished my ale. I put the letter back in its envelope. I guess Max didn't want to ask Aunt Siri to coordinate with the captain on his behalf.

My head ached, but I sighed in relief. The travel agency must be concerned about my well-being. I turned off the lamps and lay on my left side to protect my injured head and rest.

~~~

My door creaked. For a few seconds, I stared at the round porthole and the doorway wondering where I was until the memory of my worn-out cabin returned.

"M-M-Madam Kat, it is Uffe. May I enter?"

Uffe carried a tray and didn't make eye contact. I still wore the thick nightgown but pulled on a robe to make him more comfortable.

"Your breakfast."

"Thanks." Distracted, I wanted to finish the short story Oskar dropped off last night. The small four-inch square novella was the Dracula precursor, *The Vampyre, a Tale*. Lord Byron had urged his house guests to write a ghost story, and Mary Shelley contributed her famous Frankenstein novel. Dr. John William Polidori, Lord Byron's physician, published this story, the first vampire tale, back in 1819.

Yesterday's delivery and papers concealed my desktop, so Uffe put the tray on the bed next to me. I lifted the covers to see what goodies he had brought me.

"Hey Uffe, please stop with the Madam. Just call me Kat." The Danish word for Madam and Mrs. was *Fru. Fru Kat* sounded even worse.

"Kat?"

"Yes, you remember. It's short for Kathryn or Katrine."

"They told me to call you M-M-Madam."

"Well, please don't. You make me feel old, and I'm not ready. If you have a moment, sit here and join me."

I slapped the bed eager for some company. I wasn't hungry. In the middle of the night, I devoured everything left from yesterday. I passed him a piece of bread with jam not accepting a no.

He devoured it in a few quick bites with jam dribbling down his chin.

With my napkin, I dabbed his messy chin and laughed.

"Can I meet your father today?"

He glanced around the room as if bewildered.

"When I'm more presentable, of course."

"My father ... he is d-d-dead."

"Oh, Uffe. I am so sorry. Is your brother or another relative on the ship?"

"No, my mum and family are back in D-D-Denmark."

"Are you going all the way to Hong Kong?"

He nodded smiling. This was hard to believe. Uffe was so young and alone. I might be older than his mother.

"Uffe, you should be in school." I spent a gap year abroad as a foreign exchange student before college. But I attended a Danish college prep school. He would miss six months or more of school if he stayed on board for the return trip.

"I am in school." Uffe sat up higher with a slight swagger. "I am a seaman apprentice on the Anne K-K-Kristine with the kind Captain Madsen." His sleeves were several sizes too long, and he rolled them back up.

Kind? How could they take such a young boy from his family and school? "How old are you?"

"Thirteen."

I gasped. Uffe looked young, but that was incredible. "You are a brave young man to be here on this old ship."

Uffe's eyes met mine for a second, but he didn't say anything.

"We can watch out for each other. I can be your big sister while I'm here."

This was all temporary since I had decided to get off at the next port and spend a few weeks in Europe before flying home. For the next few days, I would convince the captain he should be in a real school.

"I shall look after you, Kat. Your husband is in heaven with my father. They would approve."

"In heaven?" I shook my head. "My husband was an atheist, like so many Danes. If he is there, it's an accident."

Uffe looked down as if worried about his dad. The whole concept of heaven and seeing people you loved and lost was enticing. Like crossing the Rainbow Bridge and finding my cat Xena and other pets. A place you'd love to go but without a ticket to get there.

"Don't worry, Uffe. Your father must have been a believer in God, so he is there. Waiting for the rest of the family. But not too soon. You have another eighty years ahead of you here on earth."

"Eighty years? I should not last that long. Do you believe in God and heaven?"

"I am still stuck in the middle. Since I haven't had to choose, I'm agnostic. I would like to believe, but I haven't been convinced. Not enough proof."

"There is proof in the B-Bible."

"Not enough for me. But who knows? Maybe one day I will turn into a believer."

"We have church services on Sunday."

I hated to tell him we should arrive in Southampton beforehand. "If I am on board, I shall attend and perhaps be convinced."

He smiled at the idea of having saved another lost soul and started to clean and straighten up clothing.

"You don't need to work so hard to bring me things or clean my cabin. I like to see everything, and it gives me something to do."

My cabin was in its typical disarray. Clothes lay in piles on top of the opened wooden trunks. My toiletries covered the dresser in a random mess near the makeshift sink. Organized chaos I called it.

He smiled and nodded in relief.

"You must call me Kat. All right, little brother?"

Uffe jumped up to answer the door. Simon gave Uffe a basket.

Simon said, "Glad to see you are better. You gave us all a fright."

He could try to join us, but my cabin was small for three people. Simon stood in the doorway and motioned for Uffe to open the basket. A sweet meow arose from the blanket, and Esperanza stuck out her black head.

Simon said, "Thought you might like some company."

"Oh, how wonderful. Little Essie, short for Esperanza."

I lifted the small kitten and placed her on my lap to pet her. "Perfect company."

"Bar one tiny problem." Simon stared at the other side of my cabin distracted by my messy system of organization.

"Problem? Did she get hurt during the storm?"

"Oh no, nothing like that. She has white fur on her stomach."

"That doesn't matter at all. She is beautiful." I kissed her head not wanting her to hear this and develop body image issues.

"For a ship, it matters. We only accept solid black cats."

"Solid black? Why?"

"Mariners are a superstitious lot. It is bad luck. We shall find her a home in Southampton and another black cat."

"Another cat without white fur? How ridiculous. I'll talk to the captain."

On second thought, a new home off the ship might be healthier for little Essie. "We're all safer off this low class, no star floating debacle." I buried my head in her soft fur.

Simon frowned at my insult. "As you will, but I doubt you shall sway him. This is a long-standing tradition and best for the crew and the ship."

7 ~ *A Modernista*

A steady constant wind filled the sails replacing the violent gale from last night. The captain said to not go out alone, but he couldn't be referring to an almost perfect day like today.

My head stopped aching, so I unwound the bandage. After finishing the tale of the vampire, I craved companionship with living and breathing humans.

I picked up my tray and carried it to the galley to give young Uffe a break and set up delivery of the metal tub. My daily sponge bath had become routine, but my back itched from the storm's salt water when I hung on for dear life.

Some of the crew walked by, and I nodded a customary hello. They stared back as if I had a giant hole in my pants or something embarrassing like toilet paper stuck and flying in the breeze. I checked around me, but everything was fine.

Were they just concerned? I refused to be a stereotypical weak female and stay in bed until we arrive in England. I will show them I am tough. I marched onward to the galley and placed my tray on the table.

Simon and Henrik heard me and turned around. Henrik gasped, and Simon said, "Are you in costume today?"

"Costume? Oh no, this?" I curtsied to show off thrilled to be wearing my normal outfit of a black sweater and jeans. "I can't bear another day in a costume. I almost never wear dresses back home."

Simon shook his head and blinked several times.

"The captain said I could. With just you guys on board, why should I bother dressing up every day?"

Simon nodded, still speechless, and Henrik's mouth hung open.

"You don't mind, do you?"

"No, of course not," Simon said chewing over his words. "Wear what you fancy."

"I would prefer what the men wear. Thick sweaters and blue pants."

Simon wore a big white apron and baggy pants. His outfit

wasn't the look I was going for.

"Do you think there are any extras?"

"Extra clothes from the crew?" He said with raised eyebrows.

"Yeah, if there are extras." I didn't count on it. In a few days, my voyage will be over.

"They are allotted some and bring clothing. A sailor's uniform is not proper attire for a young lady."

"Afraid I'm not that young anymore, and who wants to be proper all the time? Oh well." I refused to be a rude and demanding passenger today. "Simon, do you think I could take a soak in the tin bathtub today. Below deck is fine. My skin itches from the storm."

"Certainly. We will bring it to your cabin. The hold is restricted to the men."

~~~

I sauntered to the bridge to say hello to the captain, and some sailors delivered admiring looks. I checked behind me a few times and caught more shy glances.

Lars said, "Are you feeling all right, Madam?"

"Yes, I am, and it's Kat, remember?"

"Ah, yes. Your attire. Did all your dresses get ruined?"

"Oh no. The captain said I could wear modern clothes."

"He did?" Lars scrutinized the water and the sails flapping in the wind and delivered a command to the crew to adjust them.

Lars turned and inspected my outfit from head to toe. "Kat, you are turned out like a man."

"I guess you could say that. I wear this all the time back home. Today I needed a break from those dresses."

Lars was busy and distracted, so I wandered back to my cabin.

I jumped at the knock on my door eager for my soak in a bubble bath. When I opened the door, the captain's face was masklike without a smile.

"What's wrong?" I asked.

"Precisely what I must ask you. I spoke with Lars. He said you visited the bridge. Wandering about at will with your head injury. I instructed you not to, and you disobeyed my orders again."

"Oh that. I feel fine, and it's such a pretty day."

"That has nothing to do with it. Those were clear commands. You cannot ignore them whenever it suits you."

"Fine. I will stay here until we arrive in Southampton. Just give me the word when I can get off. I am tired of all this."

He grimaced, and I imitated his angry expression.

"What are you wearing? Are you changing your sex?"

"Changing what?" He stared at my jeans. "You said it was all right. Did you forget? I asked you at dinner on the night of the storm."

"You suggested modern clothing. Such as more ribbons and bows. Not, not that … a tight man's suit."

He sputtered and ran his hand through his hair. He sank down in my chair and took a deep breath. "Kat, you simply cannot dress like this. It is not natural or proper for a lady of your standing."

"What standing? You all are taking this whole re-enactment too seriously. I dress up in these old dresses, but why does it matter? We are fighting to survive storms. I am sick and tired of looking like an extra in *Gone with the Wind*."

"I cannot comprehend your concerns. When I last visited the United States, women presented themselves as in Europe. Here on this ship, you should appear properly attired."

"Fine." I slumped down on the bed and held Essie close. What a jerk!

"Stand over here in the light so I can see your head."

"What? Not again. I'm fine."

"Kathryn."

I had never heard my name said like that. The bristly snarl came from deep in his gut. Against my will, I put Essie down, walked towards him, and sat on the bed. He flipped my hair around to examine my head.

"You should not have removed the bandage."

"It needed some air."

"Are you a physician now?"

I wanted to quip something smart but bit my lip.

"Your bruise looks better. The blueness is lighter. You should be as good as new in a few days."

"I will be fine. Thanks to Mother Nature." He should get the hint that he had nothing to do with this.

He mumbled something about being hard-headed, but I let it go. He had no idea how persistent I could be.

"Do not worry about me. Focus on getting us to England." I knew this was rude, but I had lost my patience.

"Yes, Madam, I most certainly will."

After he left, I threw myself on my bed wishing I had never come. I will tear up my bucket list and never make another one. Or better yet, burn it in Denmark at the next Saint Han's bonfire with the witches. I was so tired of this re-enactment game. This vacation time warp couldn't end soon enough.

Esperanza jumped on the mattress, sniffed my face, and licked my tears giving me a wet kiss of hope.

~~~

The captain sat at the table reading the paper when I arrived. I was fifteen minutes late, some type of sin, but after the lecture this afternoon I killed time in my cabin until my escort showed up.

Uffe acted flustered, but I took his arm, squeezed his hand, and told him to relax. After my lukewarm soak, I slathered lavender-scented body oil all over. My skin drank it up and stopped itching. With my hair washed, I felt revitalized and powerful.

I wore a gold-colored silk evening gown. For another few days, I could do it. Without a hair dryer, I twisted my damp hair and pinned it back.

The captain eyed my outfit and grinned. I showed off my pretty new aquamarine jewelry and got some more use out of these period clothes.

He sniffed the air. "Did you enjoy bathing? Your perfume is pleasing."

"Lavender. A natural stress reducer." I needed a gallon or two to swim in it.

"Did you rest this afternoon?"

I nodded and put my napkin in my lap to protect my fancy outfit from spills.

"I trust you slept well with the cat?"

"We try to when we can." I envied Essie and her ability to sleep so much.

"Oskar's not coming tonight?" The table was bare and gloomy for just the two of us.

"No, he's resting. We work long hours."

But they made it harder on themselves by refusing to modernize. I should tell the captain my decision and end this.

The captain folded his newspaper and slid it to me. "You might like to read this."

The date was October 1862. "You know, you can stop doing this. Going to all this trouble with the dates. Why bother? We all know it's not 1862."

Captain Mikkel stared at me. "Of course, it's 1862. What else could it be?"

I shook my head not wanting to hear more of this gibberish or waste time arguing.

He stared at me. "Your head injury must be more severe than I feared."

"My head is totally fine. If you want to live in the past for a few months, go ahead. I'm not participating much longer."

Simon stood by to recite the dinner menu and asked the captain about a pre-dinner cocktail.

"Kat, would you like an aperitif?"

"Yes, most definitely. Thank you."

Captain Mikkel didn't do small talk, but with my angry silence, he chatted about the upcoming port.

"We shall arrive in Southampton tomorrow. The tempest sent winds in our favor."

After a short grace, which was rare for me to hear in Denmark, we received the first course. Most Danes I knew weren't religious at all. They only went to church for special occasions such as christenings, weddings, confirmations, and funerals.

The smoked salmon appetizer with dill sauce was delicious. Even if the food was basic and predictable, it was well-made. Simon was talented without any contemporary kitchen equipment.

"What is the next port after Southampton?"

"Vigo, Spain."

I had been there once before on a cruise ship so no great loss. I debated telling Mikkel straight out but hesitated not wanting to spoil the dinner.

"When you were unconscious you called for Charlie. Was he your husband or your son?"

"Charlie? A boyfriend. I never had any children."

"A fiancé?"

"Oh no. Please. We broke up." But remembering Charlie made me miss him. After the last few days, his cruel trick wasn't so terrible.

Captain Mikkel reached over to pat my hand, but I jerked it back. He didn't react but must have noticed.

"We are both childless," Mikkel said.

"I suppose we are, but no regrets."

"Did your husband want children?"

"Nope. We both traveled a lot. Neither of us wanted to commit to raising kids. Now he's dead, and I'm alone, so it's a good thing. It would be hard to be a single parent."

"Perhaps your Uncle Maxwell will arrange another marriage for you."

I choked on a mouthful of wine and fought to keep it down.

"Max? Very doubtful. If he tried it, he'd never hear the end of it."

"You are young. You could try again."

"Even if I wanted children, which I don't, I'm too old. To put it in your lingo, that ship has sailed."

Mikkel contemplated the room as if he wanted to find an escape from such a depressing dinner companion.

"I hope I didn't offend you. You said your wife died in childbirth. How awful. My husband died of cancer, but it didn't happen that fast."

"I am sincerely sorry for your loss. More wine?"

"Please." I wanted the entire bottle. "If I change my mind, I will try to adopt an orphan. Maybe a young girl from India or China."

He didn't respond but must have seen many young children in ports of call. Our conversation switched to more trivial matters like food to my relief. Telling him more of my life story wasn't happening. True confessions were overrated. But my knowledge of nineteenth century politics and stimulating topics for a sea captain was lacking.

When Simon served a tray of desserts, I knew it was now or never. My bad news was timed when he was sidetracked with dessert.

"I am not continuing on to Hong Kong. I will get off in

Southampton. I read Maxwell McIntosh's letter. I'll see he gives you a bonus, but I can't stay on board."

He leaned back in his chair. "Why? Because of the gale? I restricted your wanderings to protect, not hurt you."

"No, not because of that. I can't live like this." Behind the table, I flicked some crumbs from my lap thankful they didn't leave a stain and hurt the resale value of my dress. "Once in a while, but not all the time and ..."

"When we arrive in Southampton, you should see a doctor for your head injury. You have not been the same since it happened."

"No, it's not that. I'm fine really. This just isn't for me." I stood to leave. Not having electricity was manageable. At home, I seldom used a blow dryer, but two months without running water was more than I could handle.

Mikkel stood. "Please allow me to escort you to your cabin."

The moonlight reflection on the water reminded me of that first magical evening when we sailed past Kronborg castle north of Copenhagen. When we both happened to recite Shakespeare. This evening was another one of those strangely beautiful nights in November.

"Do you know the constellations?" He asked pointing out some.

"No, not really." I walked with his arm linked in mine to the railing. I grasped the wooden barrier and arched my back to see the moon and stars. The blinking stars reminded me of fireflies I used to chase in Texas.

Captain Mikkel bent down to whisper in my ear and pointed out the North Star, Cassiopeia, and the Dippers.

The wind increased, and I pulled my borrowed shawl tighter. The evening was so beautiful I didn't want to leave. If we arrive in Southampton tomorrow, this was my last night on the ship.

"Damn, it's beautiful. I will miss seeing this."

Mikkel stared up at the moon. "O, swear not by the moon, the fickle moon, the inconstant moon, that monthly changes in her circle orb, lest that thy love prove likewise variable."

"Shakespeare?"

"Yes, the fair Juliet again. She received much better lines."

Mikkel strolled by my side to my cabin and lingered along the way. "Despite the difficulties, I took pleasure in your companionship. Americans are quite remarkable. Please delay your decision until after you have seen a doctor."

At my cabin's door, I shook my head but smiled to be polite.

"The morning should be calm when we enter the *Strait of Solent*. If it is calm, you may walk about as you wish but please mind the sails and my crew."

Captain Mikkel kissed my cheek. His beard felt like a soft hair brush against my face.

Before I could respond, he walked towards the bridge. He traversed the deck with ease and grace as if his body and the ship were one.

Watching him and the beauty of the sails and the surrounding water, I longed to forget the antiquated ship and all the rules. But one romantic night and a few starry-eyed hours won't end all these difficulties. I had to trust my gut and stick with my decision.

8 ~ *Lost Not Found*

Despite leaving stuff behind, my carpet bags overflowed again. I had dumped all the heavy books, except for my Shakespeare goodbye gift, and the book about Salacia, the reluctant wife of King Neptune. I needed something to read on the train to London.

I left some of my casual costume dresses behind. The cost-benefit to lug them back home to sell on eBay wasn't worth it. The next nutty re-enactor could have them. I also left Annette's torn sweater coat, still damp from the rainstorm, hanging in the armoire.

I considered taking the Chunnel fast train from London to Paris. But I needed to exchange the carpet bags in Denmark for my suitcases, clothes, and electronics. First, to Copenhagen to get my belongings, and second, figure out what to do and where to go.

After I disembark at the cruise ship terminal, I'm heading to the nearest ladies' restroom to switch into jeans. Good riddance was all I could say as I viewed my outfit. All those women in the past had earned my complete sympathy.

With nothing to buy on board, I had no need for money. My purse lay hidden under some extra linens in a trunk. I reached into my bag for my wallet, but it was missing. That was weird. My wallet was the size of a checkbook so hard to lose.

I dumped the entire contents on my bed and panicked. "Damn it. Where in the world is it?"

Besides cash and credit cards, my wallet held my passport and medical identification cards. I bit my lip but tried to stay calm convinced it must be in one of the carpet bags. I dumped everything on my bed to find the elusive wallet without success.

I crawled under the bed, unloaded each trunk, and the armoire piece by piece and item by item. I wanted to scream in a state of panic but could only moan. The only place I didn't check was the throne chair for doing the unspeakable. I mulled it over for a brief second but came to my senses.

I sat on the bed to figure out what happened. The captain must have locked my passport and valuables in a safe. My no-star cabin didn't include an in-room safe.

I threw everything back into the chests, armoire, carpet bags, and purse. Now my cabin resembled the fateful night I first arrived.

It was still too early to wake Uffe or the others. I had tossed and turned all night after seeing the constellations with Mikkel. I couldn't second guess my decision to disembark, so I packed early to get it behind me.

I opened my cabin's door and peeked out. A calm but foggy dampness greeted me. The coast of England was not yet in sight. I strolled to the kitchen galley to get some caffeine and wake up.

Simon counted aloud as he went through his supplies to make a shopping list.

The teapot was full, and I poured myself a cup.

When he stopped counting, I said, "Are you looking forward to stopping in Southampton for local fish and chips?"

He shook his head. "My preference is home-style Danish meatballs, rye bread, potatoes, and gravy."

So much for adventures in fine dining. I squatted with my dress piled around my legs next to the sleeping kitten. "Goodbye, little Essie. I hope you get a decent, loving family."

Anywhere is better than living here on a ship. She will be okay. Esperanza won't have to search the cargo hold for mice anymore. I wanted to take her with me. If lengthy quarantines to bring an animal home from Europe didn't exist, I would.

Ridiculous how a tiny patch of white fur meant bad luck. Just like the superstition about women on board. We'll both leave and let them pine away full of regret.

Cup in hand, I strolled to the railing searching across the water for the United Kingdom's southern coast. Despite an overcast grim sky, I regretted leaving without any photographs of this ship and life on board. No one will ever believe what this was like.

In the distance, a coastline appeared. That must be England. An excited yell came from some of the crew. One sailor said, "Great Britain starboard."

I jumped and squealed from exhilaration and relief. A couple of the crew watched me as if I was a space alien. "I'm happy to see dry land just like you."

They stared in surprise and laughed.

Another ship approached, the first I'd seen, and I trusted they saw her. A maritime collision was not something I wanted to experience first-hand.

I didn't see Uffe and marched to the bridge on a mission to warn them and get my wallet.

When I came close, I overheard Mikkel speaking to someone, most likely Lars. The captain said, "She decided not to proceed further. The cabin and life aboard did not meet her expectations."

I couldn't hear the other man's response.

Captain Mikkel said, "I hate to concede, but you were right. For my sister's sake, I made an exception. And her uncle's offer was generous."

The other man said, "She wore peculiar clothes yesterday."

"Her head wound caused this confusion. We are lucky she survived."

I didn't want to eavesdrop further and started to say something when Lars said, "Bad luck with women aboard. We should abstain."

"I agree. We shall."

Did they just say they changed their policy because of me? They can't be serious. I'll let Uffe get my wallet and be off the ship soon.

I turned to leave before they saw me, but I dropped my teacup, and it shattered. I bent down to pick up the pieces and heard Mikkel's voice.

"Who is here? An early bird. Did you find your worm or lose it?" He laughed at his silly joke.

I wanted to tell him if I found a worm, I would hide it in his breakfast. "Sorry, I broke a cup."

"No matter. Here." He cupped his hands together and took the pieces from me.

"Did you see that ship over there?" I pointed to where I last saw it.

"Our tugboat pilot for Southampton. Steam-powered." He motioned towards a light in the distance.

The coastline was visible, so we would arrive soon.

"We must bring down the canvas. Southampton is a busy harbor."

"Canvas?"

"Another name for sails. Often, we call them sailcloth. And that concludes your maritime lessons."

"No problem. We ran out of time."

"Not if you continue. Only three days to Vigo, Spain. A delightful and amusing seaport."

"I know, but I'm all packed and ready to disembark. I just need my passport and wallet from the safe."

"The safe contains nothing of yours."

"How will I disembark without my passport?" I went into a full panic. I had forgotten my photo ID once for a flight from New York to Texas. The extra procedures for clearance took so long, I almost missed my flight.

"You are listed on the ship's manifest. That is the only requirement."

Cunard's luxury ship, the Queen Mary 2, cleared immigration for passengers on board their vessel. Even if I could get off the ship, I needed my passport to leave England.

"I suppose this means you haven't seen my wallet either?" My chest tightened, and my cheeks burned.

"Your wallet and belongings are likely in your cabin hidden under something." Captain Mikkel pulled out his gold pocket watch. "Uffe should be awake and at your cabin soon. He can assist you."

"Thanks for nothing." I didn't care if he heard me and marched off.

Our arrival was unexciting without any sails aloft as we neared Southampton. A gnarly towboat dragged the *Anne Kristine* by ropes, or what seafarers called lines.

Mentally I retraced my steps to when I had last seen my wallet. I had offered Annette, the local Danish travel agent, cash to pay for the gasoline after ruining her Sunday evening to drive me to the ship.

I must have dropped my black wallet on her car's floorboard, and in the dark, I didn't see it. If Annette found it when she got home, it was too late. My ship, with me on it, had sailed.

Or another worst-case scenario, my wallet fell into the parking lot. The cash was gone with fraudulent credit card charges racked up. Nothing like more complications to further mar this vacation. At the hotel, I will get this straightened out.

I rested against the railing to see the ultimate moment of our arrival. Many of the crew, without having to raise or lower the canvas, stood around nearby to watch.

The city of Southampton should materialize soon. I had been here years before on a cruise, but I always enjoyed watching ships arrive into ports.

A small flock of seagulls flew out to greet us. The sun peeked through the clouds, and the water reflected a deep blue. The dreary gray switched over to a beautiful day building my optimism. Finally, the city materialized in the distance.

I calculated it was six years ago when I last visited. Axel and I spent one night in Southampton before boarding a mega-sized cruise ship for a week at sea. During our brief visit, we toured the *Titanic* museum, dined at historic pubs, and ambled along still existing Roman walls.

Axel surprised me by booking a night at the Dolphin Hotel. He knew I was a Jane Austen fan. The famous novelist lived in the area and attended a regency ball upstairs, but it was a disappointingly drab conference room today.

As the ship neared, I squinted to see better. Where were all the tall buildings? This must be a smaller seaport outside of town.

"No, it just can't be," I said to no one in particular.

The buildings reached only two to three stories high. The busy streets overflowed with people and carriages parking and rushing around. Everything was scruffy, small, and old.

The tug pulled us to a wooden pier. A couple of crew members threw lines to some men standing on the dock to tie up the ship. At least, we didn't need a tender boat transfer. No one paid much attention to our arrival. With her sails down, she was not a showstopper.

"Where are all the cars and trucks?" I stammered under my breath.

People rode on horseback or behind an assortment of horse carts and carriages. The women wore long dresses in the same general style as mine. The organizers must have ring-fenced this village to turn it into an 1860 re-enactment site.

"Welcome to Southampton," Captain Mikkel said to the group of us standing nearby. He should have said, "Welcome to 1860 Disneyland." Before I could correct him, he walked further away to chat with Lars.

"How far are we from the city?" I asked a sailor who stood nearby to secure the lines to the dock.

"The city is right there." He pointed to the streets ahead of us with a few buildings two or three stories high, but nothing more.

He had said, *"By,"* which was the Danish word for both city and town. He must be wrong.

My hands ached from gripping the ship's railing. I feared I would collapse without it. Why would the travel agency, or whoever planned this cruise, go to so much trouble and expense to recreate an imaginary town?

I blinked and shut my eyes not wanting to believe this. There must be a rational explanation.

Uffe tapped me on the shoulder. "Are you all right, Kat?"

In denial, I willed myself not to cry. "The city looks different than I remember."

"I think I shall like England." I had tried to teach him a few words in English, but he stumbled over them. His stutter made it worse.

The crew lowered the gangplank to the pier. How would I manage without any money? This was so unexpected, and I swayed against the railing.

Captain Mikkel said, "Ready to go ashore?"

I stood frozen and unable to move or speak. He watched me with a mix of concern and apprehension as if I was mentally unhinged.

Locals congregated around the ship with horses and wagons. A donkey or mule was dragging a derelict cart. The waterway surrounding our vessel overflowed with small rowboats and men shouting to sell their wares or services. Could this all be part of a massive re-enactment?

"I need to get my luggage." My voice shook.

Uffe trailed behind to help me.

"Goodbye and good riddance, old box." I switched to

English to not offend Uffe and shut the door.

Earlier we traded home addresses, and I assured him I'd send some money or bring him some when I could. He thanked me but argued it was unnecessary. But I would. If nothing else, I keep my promises.

I hugged him farewell since he was staying on board for a while. I would miss him and worried about what lay ahead.

If only I had some cash to buy new clothes. Not only did Uffe continually roll up his sleeves, but his baggy pants were also too long. He shouldn't stay either, but poor Uffe had no choice.

Yesterday, when I had questioned the captain, he said, "Uffe is better off here than in Denmark. I was once a young apprentice. The results turned out well for me."

The captain and first mate stood by the gangway waiting for me to disembark.

I hesitated. What would I find in this town? Where would I go if I couldn't reach my family or friends? What if I couldn't reach Annette in Denmark with the *Maximum Adventure to the Extreme* travel agency?

Uffe refused my help and carried my carpet bags to the pier. When he was back in Denmark next year, I would help him get into a real school. I imagined meeting him and his family, visiting the Tivoli Gardens amusement park and shopping on Copenhagen's picturesque walking streets. I would transform him into a fashionable young gentleman.

With a definitive goal to make a difference in young Uffe's life, I disembarked refusing to look back.

9 ~ Off the Grid

In an antique horse-drawn carriage headed to our hotel, Captain Mikkel said, "We docked at the Eastern Docks built about 1840."

"So long ago?" I murmured in awe. Lars and Simon rode into town with us and didn't seem to notice anything amiss.

People crowded the narrow wooden and dirt walkways on the side of the cobblestone road. They walked dangerously close to the wheels. If I stretched out my hand, I could have touched them.

A smelly horse pulled hard to drag the coach and our belongings into town. Our luggage was on the roof, and the coachman sat on a raised bench in front. The wagon resembled a California gold rush stagecoach from the Wells Fargo's museum in San Francisco.

Mikkel and Lars both wore a black top hat, but Simon had a plain cap. The women wore bonnets, and many of the children had caps. I didn't like hats. If I wore my usual baseball cap, it would look strange.

Except it wasn't just the hats. Everyone was clad head to foot in nineteenth century clothing. This town was like a movie set and an incredibly expensive undertaking.

No one on the pier asked to see our passports or any identification. Arriving in a foreign country without going through immigration and customs was bizarre. We must be in a fenced off area to avoid the standard border crossing procedures.

I asked Mikkel, "Who's staying at the hotel?"

"We both have hotel rooms. I will be back and forth to the ship. An officer must always be aboard even in port. The crew may go into town, but they usually sleep on the ship."

"Unless they want to pay for a hotel room out of their wages," Lars said.

"My officers and men are free to do what they want within reason. If they stay out of trouble."

Simon looked uncomfortable and changed the subject. "Kat,

you must be happy to be on *terra firma* again."

I nodded still distracted by everything around me.

The carriage stopped at the Lyford Castle Inn on Porters Lane a few blocks from the ship. Calling it a castle was a major overstatement. In fact, saying this was a hotel was an exaggeration since it was so small. Nevertheless, the quaint inn had charm and faded elegance. Appearances can be deceptive, and I prayed for an updated hotel room.

Simon and Lars said goodbye. I thanked them and instead of an awkward hug we shook hands.

Mikkel pushed his blond hair back while adjusting his hat. In the bright sunlight, his intense sky-blue eyes distracted me from his weathered face. "Ready?"

I accepted his hand and jumped down and walked ahead of him into the inn eager to find the internet or a telephone. Mikkel spoke with the hotel clerk, and I scrutinized the lobby to see if they had any computers available for guests. A few men sat on overstuffed sofas reading newspapers.

I wandered back to the front desk and stood next to Mikkel.

"We are in luck since our rooms are available. We arrived a day early with the help of your storm."

"My storm? That certainly wasn't mine."

"You were the only one venturing out for the enjoyment of it."

I ignored him and asked the clerk, "Do you have internet or Wi-Fi here?"

"What Madam?"

I repeated my question, but he sputtered around clueless. He dipped his pen in an inkwell and slid it towards me with a blank sheet of paper.

"Never mind." I would find one without his help.

Mikkel didn't comment. I knew he would play dumb and stay in this 1860 re-enactment.

~~~

My hotel room was old-fashioned. But I did a Snoopy happy dance after I flipped the switch for electric lights, turned on the sink's water faucet, and flushed a real toilet. Civilization had finally returned. I searched for a phone but couldn't find one. Oh well. I could make a collect call from a pay-phone.

While I waited to meet Captain Mikkel in the lobby, I asked

another desk clerk about a telephone. My request received another vacant twilight zone look. Another colossal mistake: agreeing to leave my cell phone and laptop behind.

I couldn't complete my first to-do. Call my dad and go over all these problems, including the gory details. He would know how to find my way out of this chaos.

My mom would say, "I knew it. Bad idea. You couldn't hack it."

I jotted down a to-do list on a notepad. First: Find a computer, log in, find my parent's itinerary, and call their hotel in New Zealand. Second: Email or call MAX the travel agency to get my wallet and passport shipped here. Third: Email or call my neighbor, Abby, and get some money transferred here.

Mikkel's voice came from another room. He sat across from another man on the sofa.

"What are you carrying?" The man asked him, and I wondered what we brought from Denmark.

Captain Mikkel said, "Dried bacon and grain alcohol. A few days to unload and a few more to reload with English ale, spirits, and cotton bound for Spain. Cotton is slow with the sanctions."

"Dirty business all that."

"Hate to think about the bloody slave labor. More civilized to outlaw it as we did in Denmark and England. Americans are too headstrong."

His friend laughed and concurred.

When Captain Mikkel saw me, he introduced me to his friend, a Scottish marine captain, and stood to leave.

Captain Mikkel said goodbye to the captain. "Tell the Frenchman if he wants to sail to the continent, we sail in three days for Vigo. One cabin became available."

I sighed in relief. Three nights at the inn allowed for plenty of time to arrange my flight to Denmark or home. The cruise package included my hotel and meal costs in Southampton. Money wasn't an issue yet.

"Kat, did you send telegrams to your friends and family? When will they meet you here?"

"Meet me? Oh, no. I'll find my own way home."

"All the way to New York City?" He shook his head. "I

assured your uncle to deliver you in China. I cannot leave you in England alone."

I didn't want to argue. We turned in our large, cumbersome room keys at the front desk. Mikkel told the desk clerk, "If anyone asks for Captain Madsen, I will be at the hospital."

His last word echoed ominously in my head.

Outside Captain Mikkel scrutinized me from head to foot. "Can you manage a short walk?"

I stopped and stood still. "Sure. Why are we going to a hospital?"

"Your head must be examined. You had a nasty fall. I made an appointment. The sooner it is assessed, the better."

He took my hand refusing to take no for an answer. Southampton, or wherever this was, fascinated me. I was glad to be off the ship and on land again without having to keep my balance or fight the wind.

I stopped to look at a man's wagon selling an eclectic mix of clothes, fruit, and candies. Mikkel grabbed my arm and steered me away.

"You cannot purchase items from these vagabond sellers. If you fancy something, we shall visit an appropriate establishment."

I didn't agree, but it didn't matter. I couldn't buy anything without some cash.

We crossed the street without any traffic signals or crosswalks. Mikkel steered me in between the flux of horse carriages and donkey carts when I stopped to gawk. The crowded road continued up an incline.

Long rows of pale brown buildings lined both sides of the street. Some shops had awnings and signs adding a pop of color to the drab town.

I read the quaint shop signs as we walked by. Draper, cheese-monger, green-grocer, boot-maker, milliner, chemist, baker, clock-maker, bonnet-maker, brewer, and barrel-maker. Interspersed between the stores stood business offices, banks, and taverns. Nothing was modern-day; no phone booths, ATMs, McDonalds, or Starbucks.

The smells of Southampton were overpowering and nauseating. A rancid blend of rotten eggs, urine, sweat, and other scents I didn't want to recognize encircled me. I held my breath until I couldn't and tried to ignore it.

Dressing up in old clothing was one thing, but recreating the smells? Part of the past I had never contemplated and preferred to avoid.

After we left busy High Street, the neighborhood deteriorated to rows of stables, brewers, skinners, and meat packers. I gripped a handful of my petticoats and skirt to lift them above the brown and red stains on the ground. The problems amplified, not only from the disgusting odors but the ever-present dirt.

Dirt coated the roads, sidewalks, buildings, and the clothes everyone wore. My hands and face felt grimy just seeing it. My hem had already dragged on the ground, so it had a light brown stain. I blended in whether I liked it or not.

I wanted to suggest walking back to the inn. We turned and faced an impressive but formidable building. The name, Royal South Hampshire Hospital, and the year, 1838, were carved into the stone. An attendant opened the door. I hated hospitals and stopped on instinct.

"I feel fine. My head hurt a few days ago, but not now."

We stood arguing while people walked around us to enter the front door. Strong men carried in sick and bleeding people of all ages crying out in pain.

"These people are severely injured and need urgent medical attention. I'm wasting their time."

Captain Mikkel took me by the arm and pulled me out of the way.

"You have not been yourself since your fall. I am responsible since it happened on my ship."

"All right. I'll see someone. If this takes longer than an hour, I'm leaving." I had more important things to do.

We went inside the miserable, filthy excuse for a medical facility. I regretted agreeing while we stood in line behind the others. Mikkel didn't seem to mind.

"Doesn't this place look terrible? I'm getting sick standing here. Are you sure you want to stay?"

He studied the area, but his expression remained unchanged. After waiting ten minutes, we were at the front of the line.

Mikkel cleared his throat and spoke formal English with a strong accent. "We made an appointment with Dr. Johnson for

11 o'clock."

The clerk told us to write down our names and sign a sheet and read our names aloud, "Captain Mikkel Kløve Madsen and Mrs. Kathryn Jensen."

We nodded. The clerk didn't pronounce the Danish letter 'ø' in Kløve correctly. This was understandable since the 'ø' was a guttural vowel and almost impossible for foreigners.

The clerk said, "Please follow my boy to room 120." He snapped his fingers, and a kid, about ten-years-old, approached. The clerk gave him some papers.

The boy said, "Sir and Madam, please follow me."

So shocked by the young child, I was speechless and obeyed. Is this one of those 'bring your child to work' days?

The boy opened the door to room 120 and delivered the paperwork to another man who sat behind a desk. I figured the man was his father, but he didn't glance at him or say any kind words to our young guide.

Captain Mikkel thanked the boy for helping us and awarded him a coin.

The doctor's office had a few empty chairs, so we sat to wait. I figured the time would run out, and we would leave soon.

Fifteen minutes later, he ushered us into his office with an adjoining examination room crammed with equipment. Whatever happened, I would refuse any weird treatments.

Dr. Johnson introduced himself. "What seems to be the problem?"

"Three days ago, in the North Sea, we experienced strong gales and severe weather. Kathryn fell and hit her head severely. She's been confused ever since. I would like you to evaluate her present condition."

I decided to set things straight. "I hit my head and had some headaches, but I'm fine now. In fact, I feel better than I have in ages."

I pondered asking if I could borrow his phone. But I didn't see one, and this might cause more problems or delays.

The doctor adjusted his spectacles. "Captain Madsen, I will examine your wife's health."

"Wife? What the –?"

10 ~ Re-Examined

"He isn't my husband. I'm not married." My words came out in a high-pitched screech.

Captain Mikkel nodded in agreement probably horrified about the idea as well.

"You were married?" The doctor asked in response.

"Yes."

"What happened to your husband?"

"He died over a year ago. From cancer."

"Children?"

I shook my head. The doctor shrugged his shoulders and gave me a gown. "My assistant will help you."

Before I could argue this was unnecessary, a young girl said, "Hello, Madam." She didn't look much more than thirteen.

"Thanks. I can manage."

I took the shabby gown while Dr. Johnson and Captain Mikkel went into an adjoining room. With so many layers of clothes to take off, being modest was the least of my concerns. I stood behind the door while undressing to listen.

Their voices were low, but Mikkel said, "She has been confused about where she is and what year it is. She dressed in strange clothes after it happened. A man's attire."

The damn re-enactment game continues. Well, I can play along for a few more days.

Dr. Johnson said, "Head injuries can be fatal or cause lingering problems. Any other health issues or illnesses?"

"Her uncle said she was examined before leaving home and in good health. I was not provided the details."

Scattered pink spots stained the gown that I prayed weren't from old bloodstains. Waiting here, with the sound of crying and periodic screams out in the hallway, was unnerving.

My index fingers pressed on my forehead to find the pressure points that relieve stress and anxiety. But to no avail. I was ignorant of acupressure techniques.

The young girl entered the room, and I couldn't eavesdrop any longer. "Madam, please do not be scared. Dr. Johnson is a kind doctor."

I shook as if freezing but from nerves. Why didn't the doctor ask me these questions? What happened to filling out a damn form?

Was he another actor and part of this game? Why would a run-down hospital not have a phone and a computer? The local medical establishment should pull their license for working in such a backward manner.

Dr. Johnson knocked, but without waiting he and Mikkel marched in. The doctor wrapped an old blood pressure measuring device on my arm.

He glanced at the result. "Good."

Of course. At home, I was a gym rat and worked out whenever I could.

"What is your year of birth, Mrs. Jensen?"

I hesitated. I shouldn't say 1969 if he expected me to play along in the re-enactment game.

"Eighteen … thirty." I tried to subtract 47 from 1862. Doing mental calculations was never my strong suit. If this was 1862, I had cut fifteen years off my age. At least being only 32 years old sounded healthier.

"Who is the queen of our fair country?"

"Queen? In 1862?"

"Yes, not next year." The doctor laughed at his weak joke, but Mikkel didn't smile, and his jaw tightened.

"Queen Victoria."

"Who is your President? For the northern part, I should say."

"Lincoln." Who could forget President Lincoln?

He examined my head, and Mikkel showed him my injury.

The doctor said, "Bruised but healing nicely."

He reached for a scalpel, and I jumped up in a hurry. "What's that for?"

"To clean the wound, my dear. I shall lance it to release any pressure."

"But you said it was healing nicely. There is no pressure."

The scalpel had spots, and the doctor had not bothered to wash his hands or put on gloves.

I stared at Mikkel and pleaded, "This was not part of the deal."

But the doctor didn't put the scalpel down. "When were you last bled?"

"Bled? Never. You know that killed George Washington."

"The President?"

I nodded while the doctor jotted something on his notepad.

"All right. We will not drain it today. However, if there is any swelling, you must return for treatment. Perhaps, Captain Madsen, you could wait in the other room?"

Mikkel fled the room, and the doctor stared at me. "This shall not take long."

The young girl stayed behind, and I was grateful for her company and some protection.

He lifted the back of my gown while I inhaled and exhaled, and he listened with a stethoscope. I balanced on one foot and the other and did a mix of different calisthenic exercises he requested. All easy to do after my grueling workout routine in New York City.

He handed me a book of poetry written by William Wordsworth. "Do you know him? My favorite poet."

I hesitated. Everyone knew Wordsworth, but I would fail any poetry quiz.

"Turn to page twenty-five and read the ballad."

The short poem, just seven verses, was titled *Strange Fits of Passion Have I Known*.

While I read, the doctor leaned his head against his chair and shut his eyes. I continued reading assuming he wanted to ignore his mind-numbing surroundings.

The poem was about a woman named Lucy who was dying. This struck me as a strange choice of poetry for a doctor who must lose patients.

When finished, the doctor opened his eyes. "Lovely. Thank you."

He moved the gown around reminding me of my dermatologist's sun cancer body check. "What occurred here?" He pointed at my thin appendix scar on my right below the bikini line.

"Minor childhood injury." I wasn't about to explain my emergency appendectomy that may have been a kidney stone problem instead.

Goosebumps covered my arms and legs. I tried to hide my

shivering. When the doctor said the exam was complete, relief swam over me. I had avoided the gruesome bloodletting and leech procedures I'd seen on TV.

After he and his assistant left, I sprang into my costume faster than I ever had before. I pulled on my boots when the doctor and Mikkel returned.

"Excellent news. Her physical and mental state are lively and overactive, but fine. Unless she has more symptoms or swelling, she is free to go."

Captain Mikkel took my hands in his but blushed embarrassed at his sudden emotion.

Dr. Johnson beamed as if he had pronounced me free from cancer. He wrote on a slip of paper and gave it to Mikkel. "Take this to the chemist. Three drops once a day and six if the confusion returns."

Captain Mikkel pocketed the note, thanked him, and settled the bill while I fumed in the corner. If the travel agency billed me for this insulting exam or medicine, I would refuse to pay.

Outside Captain Mikkel stopped on the side of a building for some privacy. Others had found it as well since the smell was putrid, but he didn't seem to notice. "Thank you for subjecting to the examination. I am so relieved by the doctor's satisfactory report."

I didn't want to argue, and he was silly to worry so much. My focus was to get as far away from here as possible.

We walked back to the inn. "Didn't you say you are going to London tomorrow?"

His happy look disappeared. "A full schedule of business meetings awaits me. Little time for sightseeing I fear."

"I must go with you. Not to go sightseeing, but to plan my trip home." To avoid angering him, I didn't mention my plan to travel around Europe before heading home.

"It is a crowded and dirty city. I can deliver messages on your behalf."

As if this city wasn't filthy? "I need to go with you to find them." I couldn't waste time with snail mail letters. I needed a phone or the internet.

"Very well."

A man screamed, and we froze in our tracks.

I covered my mouth to stifle a shriek horrified at what lay

in front of me. A grey horse fell while pulling a heavy load on busy High Street causing the wagon and its contents to spill out on the street.

An old man stood over the horse whipping the animal still wearing a harness and bridle. "Get up miserable beast. Immediately!"

People stopped and congregated, but no one did anything.

My adrenaline kicked in, and I crouched next to the horse laying in the street. The horse's eyes rolled back, and his coat was dark and drenched from sweat. The horse's entire body shook as it heaved and tried to get its breath with its legs still moving.

I knelt protecting the horse's head in my lap and shouted, "Are you insane? You are killing this poor horse!"

People around us talked, including high-pitched women's voices, but I couldn't understand them. Mikkel knelt and tugged my arm. I shook his hand away to comfort the horse and wait for a veterinarian. But he seized my arm and hauled me to my feet.

"No, I must stay and help this horse. Go find a vet."

Mikkel didn't let me go. "You cannot do this. This horse is not your responsibility."

I pushed past him and screamed at the horse killer. "You should be ashamed of yourself. Treating a wounded animal like this." The mix of hatred and disgust was so intense I wanted to strike him as he had done to the poor defenseless horse. I lifted my arm to do just that, but Mikkel pulled me out of reach.

The man stopped whipping the sick animal and scratched his head. He scowled in our direction and spat into the street but didn't say a word. This poor doomed horse broke my heart, and tears rolled down my face.

The crowd stood aside to let us by while murmuring and pointing at us. All those weak bystanders should be ashamed. Someone must act to stop this, but no one moved.

Carriage horses still exist for the tourists in New York City near Central Park, but animal welfare groups monitor their well-being. I had never seen this type of cruelty and ached from being powerless. Out of options, I couldn't bear to watch the injured animal die.

Spots hovered on the ground ahead of me. A symptom of not eating anything all day. I accepted Mikkel's arm for help as we walked away. This might have happened in 1862, but the re-enactors didn't need to recreate this misery.

I jumped when a gunshot rang out and froze unable to move.

Mikkel shook his head. "The poor beast is out of his misery."

"He shot the horse? Right there on the street?" I glanced back towards where it happened in shock.

Mikkel nodded.

"Unbelievable. What will happen to it?"

"The carcass will be sold to a rendering plant and boiled in a sizeable vat. The fat becomes fertilizer, glue, and oils. The meat is sold to the poor for food."

I couldn't bear all these details, and the idea of that horse destroyed like this. My knees buckled, and I collapsed. Mikkel caught me right before I landed on the ground.

Bile from my gut moved to my mouth. I moved my head away from him. He stood beside me and held my hair back from my shoulders while I vomited on the street.

Mikkel gave me his handkerchief and pulled a silver flask from his breast pocket. "Take a swig of this."

I clung to it like a lifeline and took a deep sip. The alcohol burned my throat, but I took another to destroy the memory of this painful day.

Mikkel held his flask and after taking a long sip watched me. "Better?"

I couldn't speak but nodded.

We strolled arm in arm along a congested, filthy street. Whatever charm existed in the past was gone. Why bother recreating it?

11 ~ *Homesick*

Mikkel ushered me into The Seven Seas pub, and we stood around waiting for the first available table. He rubbed my shoulder to console me.

"I regret you saw a horse mistreated. But we cannot meddle in matters that do not concern us."

"Inexcusable how that man treated that poor animal." I refused to apologize for trying to help or making a spectacle if that was his problem.

"It happens every day. You see it in Denmark and your United States."

"You might, but I sure don't. Furthermore, that doesn't make it right." My loud voice boomed to stand up for animal rights. Some of the customers seated nearby stared at us.

An old woman wearing a dirty apron caught my eye and frowned. She had seen better days decades ago and limped over to show us to a table. She ignored me and seemed upset since we disturbed her customers and left again.

This place wouldn't merit a D restaurant quality rating in New York City, and I didn't want to dine here. An uncomfortable silence grew between us.

Our too-busy-to-bother-with-us server nodded she was on her way but stopped to talk with other customers. More working-class men filled the restaurant.

"I am not that hungry. Some salad or vegetables maybe."

"You had a healthy appetite for meat on the ship."

"I am not a vegetarian, but I don't want to eat abused and suffering animals."

"How do you not know they are not abused or suffering? I'm afraid that is the way of life."

Animals suffered. I'd seen them packed in trucks on the way to a slaughterhouse. Not long ago, live chickens stuffed into an open eighteen-wheeler had passed me on the highway. Some poor animals were likely dead with their legs in the air.

The alcohol from his flask had warmed me up, but I was light-headed. "What type of liquor was that?"

"French absinthe. An ingredient in the King of Denmark aperitif."

"Didn't absinthe drive Van Gogh insane? When he cut off his ear?"

"Who?"

"Oh, come on. Everyone knows Van Gogh, the famous artist."

"Never heard of him."

"Well, regardless. You should check the label. If it's from the 1800s, it may be made from wormwood. Banned for years."

"I shall look." He ruffled his hair and chuckled as if I made up a story to entertain him.

"You should. The powers that be theorized the wormwood caused hallucinations and made Van Gogh cut off his ear. The beginning of his end." I reminded myself not to take another sip from his flask no matter what happened.

Captain Mikkel leaned forward, reached across, and grabbed my dull table knife. "Just in case. For safekeeping. You need two ears." He was teasing, but I couldn't laugh about it.

Before I was dead from hunger, the waitress came over for our order. I requested a menu, but this annoyed her further. She spun around in her tight uniform, swayed against my arm, and waved to a blackboard behind me.

"You may order what remains in our kitchen."

I stared at the chalkboard, but the squiggly writing was impossible to decipher. She tapped her foot and looked impatient.

Still reeling from situation and unable to decide, I said, "I would prefer a drink first."

"Ale or wine, missus?

"Wine, a white –"

The captain glared at me. "Absolutely not. You must eat something first."

"I don't know what to order."

Mikkel ordered tea for me and a beer for himself. To show he could, while I couldn't. Hours ago, I considered I might miss his company when I was back home. Our first real fight had turned ugly and public. I wiped my eyes with the back of my hand to remove any trace of sadness.

"Do you miss home?" He asked and sounded worried.

"New York City? Yes, I do." Once I got to Denmark for my belongings, I wasn't sure I would stay in Europe any longer.

"Why did you leave? You are far from home."

"I needed a break. A vacation from work and stress."

"I traveled to New York and the States. Several times."

"Oh, really, when?"

He thought back for a few moments. "I visited New York City about ten years ago."

That would be 2006. "I lived there then. We might have passed on the street."

He grimaced. "I doubt it. I did not stay in a refined part of town."

"Where did you stay?"

"The Dry Dock District."

"Where is that?" I thought I'd heard of all the neighborhoods.

"Avenue D by the East River."

"I know that neighborhood. Alphabet City. The hipster area with funky cafés and shops."

"A rough area when I was there."

"Did you like the U.S.?"

"I liked Philadelphia and Boston. New York was crowded. Slave traders ruined the southern ports."

"What?"

"I witnessed some auctions in New Orleans. Something no man or woman should ever be subjected to."

"Oh, come on. It's not like that now. Black lives matter, and I wish everyone got along better. New Orleans is such a fun city and the food. I love Cajun spice."

Mikkel didn't say anything but eyed his pocket watch.

"When exactly where you there? What year?"

"About 1850."

I bent forward. "Mikkel, no one is listening or watching. You can be honest."

"I am honest. Perhaps it was twelve years ago, not ten."

"Oh, right." I was annoyed. He would never stop with the charade. "You know, you can stop with this game. It's just us.

Even if everyone around here is so caught up with it."

Mikkel rubbed his beard and didn't respond.

"I don't see the fascination. This is all so dirty and smelly. A real downer."

Our beverages arrived while I continued my rant. "Look at all the poor people around here. Much worse than the homeless problem today. All these kids running around the streets. They should be in school. Why would anyone want to honor or remember a sad past like that?"

I stared at my stained and chipped teacup refusing to look at him after insulting the whole clipper ship era.

The waitress frowned and demanded our food order. Mikkel pressed me to order.

"Nothing." Tears welled up in my eyes.

Mikkel ordered something. "Bring her the same as my order. Thank you, Madam."

He offered his napkin, but I shook my head. I would be strong and ignore this place.

"I love New York City. Far from perfect but it's the best place in the world. Copenhagen has charm but can't compare."

"I am not in favor of crowded cities. I prefer smaller towns on the water like this one. The sea is my life."

Another thing we didn't have in common. In my case, the bigger, the better, with more things to do. New York City was my adult Disneyland without fences. This café was a rundown roach trap. Here I was trapped in a Disney-style Victorian Frontierland. After being on board a *Pirates of the Caribbean* ship, minus Johnny Depp.

"Well, I can't wait to get to London. Tomorrow will be so wonderful. Can we first stop at the travel agency's office? I need to make arrangements and straighten out my trip."

He nodded without any real enthusiasm. If only he had taken the time and spent some money to modernize. He forced me to reschedule.

"What's next?" I was big on having a plan for the day, especially on weekends with overwhelming options and little time.

"Some shopping and errands. Afterwards, I must see to matters on the *Anne Kristine*. You shall stay at the hotel."

I didn't like his bossy tone, so I didn't bother to make more small talk.

When the food came, it was downright unappetizing. My chipped plate had a piece of undefined meat that smelled bad with boiled potatoes and rubbery beige gravy. I missed my workday salad lunches even if I never had time to enjoy them.

I held my fork ready but put it down again and sipped more tea.

Mikkel noticed I had not touched my food. He said just one word, "*Spis.*" His guttural command got my attention. *Spis* meant 'eat,' and he pointed at my food with his knife.

I cut a piece of the so-called meat with my dull knife. "I'm glad this isn't horse meat."

"I would not be so certain of that."

This possibility made me more upset, but I forced down a small piece. Mikkel said that to punish me and was unnecessarily cruel.

I ate about half the meal but couldn't finish. I slid my dish to Mikkel eager to be rid of it.

He ignored me and my plate while he drank a second beer. He didn't say anything and waived his hand for our bill.

When they exchanged money, I wanted so badly to have some of it I could taste it. I hated walking around without a cent to my name. I always carried extra cash, and now I didn't even have a credit card. None of the store windows said they accepted them, so I needed cash and lots of it.

I didn't dare ask in his present mood. I regretted not taking the rest of my lunch in a take-out container for some of the young kids hanging around. They looked so thin and sad. No one took any food to go.

"Can we give these poor children some money? They look so hungry." As actors, they deserved Tony nominations. "Add it to my bill."

He handed me a few coins. I squeezed the cold metal in my fist reassured. Without a cent to my name, I wanted to keep it, but that was greedy. The coins couldn't be worth much, and these poor people needed it more than I did.

I knelt next to a woman sitting on the ground with a baby in her arms. A young boy stood next to her. They wore clothes that resembled nothing better than rags. Overpowered, I held my breath but slowly exhaled.

I placed the coins in her outstretched discolored palm. Her red eyes looked tired.

"God bless you, Miss."

Why would she choose to re-enact such an awful homeless woman with young children? She must be extremely poor and paid to do this.

I thanked her but had an ominous feeling I needed her prayers.

"Come. The day is wasting." Mikkel pulled me to my feet.

I couldn't wait to escape from this sad and distressing poverty. The pervasive sense of despair beat against me like twelve-foot waves.

12 ~ Letters to Nowhere

Mikkel held my arm so tight it ached. He opened the door to a tobacco store, but I stopped. My clothes would reek of smoke for days.

"Can I wait here?" I held my nose. "The smell."

"No, but you may wait in the shop next door. You need a bonnet and new shoes."

The store next door sold only hats. The last place I would ever shop.

"I don't need a hat. I will never wear it. I lost one shoe in the thunderstorm, but I have more." I lifted my hem a few inches and stuck out a boot to prove it. Spending more money on re-enactment clothes was the last thing I wanted to do.

"Your shoes are fine. All well-bred women wear hats, and it will be cold at night." He shook his head and muttered something about difficult women.

I wandered into the small millinery shop specializing in women's hats, luckily tobacco-free. Everyone, rich and poor, wore them, so they had plenty of demand. But they looked ridiculous.

"Allow me. Very fashionable, Madam." I didn't comment to avoid insulting the sales clerks hovering around trying to convince me. She would have refused to take no for an answer anyway and plopped another hat on my head beaming with pride.

I lifted it off carefully to avoid having to buy damaged goods and the winning entry in an ugly hat contest. I was far from a fashionista but combining beige, green, and pink should be illegal.

The saleswoman snatched it back and adjusted the pink ribbons. As if rearranging them would make a difference. She persisted. Her assistant brought from the back room six more bonnets. They convinced me to sit in front of a mirror this time.

Seeing myself was startling since my hair was a mess. I took a comb from my purse to smooth it down. The subsequent parade of headgear didn't help. All were garish and decorated with over-the-top doodads.

Mikkel entered the shop and picked up one of the worst hats, in pale orange with pink decorations, to help. What was it with the British fascination with weird hats?

"Anything plain? In a solid dark color like black?" I asked the clerk to end my misery.

"Dark? Black is for mourning." She answered as if horrified at the thought.

I was in mourning, missing the days when baseball caps were fashionable and perfect for sunny days. "How about dark blue?"

She hurried to the back and carried in a navy-blue velvet bonnet. Brown ribbons attacked the hat in an all too familiar cabin-colored shade of brown. Why was there this fascination with everything brown? Must be the color of the year for 1862. The sales clerk called it chestnut-colored. Nutty and hideous, but I could remove them. I tried it on, and it fit.

Mikkel glanced at the time on his pocket watch probably glad this was over. "Very pretty."

While he paid the bill, I borrowed a pair of scissors and snipped off all the ugly brown mess to their horror.

We left the shop, and I slowly put on the bonnet reluctant to appear this way in public. But my head was warmer, and it didn't matter since no one I knew would ever see me.

The sun had set. I shivered since my sweater was more decorative than warm.

Mikkel noticed. "You shall catch your death. Where is your coat?"

"I left it on the ship." Not wanting to explain it was torn and still damp from the rainstorm.

He gestured to another shop across the street. "In that case, you must obtain a new one."

"I don't need one or want to waste more money. I'll be fine back at the inn."

"Nonsense. Your uncle made that very clear in his letter. He will reimburse me, and you must not suffer a chill. You are still my responsibility."

He was wasting more money, but it was pointless to argue. We stopped at a few more shops to order a new coat and found some gloves. My hands and head were warm, but I shivered outside in my thin sweater. Off-the-rack outerwear wasn't in stock, but the store promised to deliver it tomorrow.

I was tired, but Mikkel insisted on one last stop. We entered a chemist, also known as a pharmacy, and he pulled out a slip of paper.

While he spoke to the pharmacist, I browsed the shelves and the limited choice of toiletries for sale. A table featured some quaint bars of soap as something new. I studied the ornate label. Dr. Brounstein's castile soap dated from 1858. The soap smelled good and would be a fun memento, but I hated to ask for money.

Mikkel mentioned my name and Dr. Johnson to the man behind the counter.

When the pharmacist went to the storeroom in the back, I pulled on Mikkel's arm to get his attention. "What was that about?"

"The doctor suggested some medicine to calm your nerves. I also need some medical supplies for the ship."

"Medicine for me? I'm fine."

"Yes, I know." He patted my hand resting on the counter. I didn't trust that weird doctor and would refuse to swallow any of his strange concoctions.

Mikkel paid the bill and told the pharmacist to deliver the order to our lodging. The pharmacist called a young boy from the back and passed him the bag with the delivery instructions.

"What? I can carry the bag to the hotel. He should be in school not running packages around town."

The pharmacist inspected me through his frameless eyeglasses balanced on his prominent nose. "Madam, this is his job function. He is fortunate to be employed here."

Mikkel's blue eyes flashed, and the red blood vessels in his eyes were prominent. "Stay quiet. You must not modify the order of things."

As an internal auditor, I'd heard this argument countless times. Everything could use some occasional checking and rearranging. But Mikkel was so angry, I kept quiet. At the inn, I would try to convince Mikkel to give our underaged worker a generous tip.

On our walk back, Mikkel didn't take my arm, and I had to

trot to keep up.

"Do you need to get any new clothes?" I suggested.

"I planned in advance to bring the right clothes with me."

Now wasn't the time to ask how many re-enactments he had taken part in. At last, our hotel materialized at the end of the road. I wanted to barricade myself inside until we left for London.

In the street children wandered around picking up pieces of dirt or mud. "What are they doing?"

"Who?"

"Those children." I stood next to a young girl who had found something.

"Collecting material for tanners. They are called pure finders."

I knelt to see what she put inside a burlap sack. Mikkel grabbed my arm and pulled me to my feet.

"I have never seen pure finders."

"Come." He ushered me away. "You must not touch that waste from a dog."

"What?" Suddenly, it struck me. He meant dog-shit. The streets were so smelly, I had become immune to the scent of urine, and God knows what else.

"Those poor kids." What a miserable job. They must be desperate to do that.

At the inn, we collected our room keys. The hotel clerk gave Mikkel a note.

"I must meet with my local agents. Swear you will not leave. After sundown, the streets are not safe."

"Fine. I will stay here." Where would I go with no money?

"Would you prefer to dine at the hotel or a restaurant tonight?"

I debated my options. I wanted to go to London and end this but didn't want to anger him again. "You decide."

"We shall celebrate your health at one of my favorite restaurants. Please write your letter while I am away."

Locked safely in my hotel room, I sat on the bed and studied my surroundings. The décor was ornate and frilly with a flowered bedspread and matching curtains. A big wooden tub was in the bathroom. Serviceable but it had seen better days years ago.

I unpacked my toiletries and mulled over taking a soak or finding a phone. Somewhere in the hotel, a guest must have a phone hidden away. I could beg to borrow it for one short call.

But the doctor's dirty hands and nails had contaminated my skin, so the tub won. I would solve the communication problems later.

I filled the bathtub with lukewarm water and settled in for a short soak. With some soap and shampoo, I was clean and humanized again. The towels, like so many low-end hotels, were thin and lousy.

Mikkel hadn't said he would take me to London. Tonight, I had one last opportunity to talk him into it. After dressing, I jotted a few quick letters to hand over to Mikkel in exchange for dinner. I chewed on the end of my pen wondering how to start.

I explained to Uncle Max, the travel agent's computer, how I wanted out of this re-enactment journey and to go home. I emphasized how desperately I needed money since I had left my wallet in the travel agent's car in Denmark. I closed the letter by begging for his help to make other plans.

The missing wallet issue was the most problematic. I rubbed my forehead trying to get rid of the painful memory.

While I brushed my hair, I pondered my options. I had paid for an expensive cruise, and the travel agency wouldn't leave a customer stranded. If I can't reach them, what will I do?

The only person I knew in London was Vicky, also known as Lady Victoria Sandford. I met her on the plane last week from New York City. She had invited me to visit her. Now, I might take her up on her generous offer.

I pulled out her pink calling card and wrote her a letter about how my dream cruise turned into a disaster ratcheting up the problems. I asked if I could stay with her for a few days until I made other travel arrangements. I still debated going home or elsewhere in Europe and needed a few days to figure this out.

In both letters, I asked them to contact me at my inn on Porters Lane in Southampton since I was without phone or email access. I swore I would be indebted to them for the rest of my life.

I played around with my hair for tonight's dinner. All the

women parted their hair in the middle pulled back into a severe bun behind their head. I left mine parted on the usual side where it was happiest, but I pinned it back as best I could with some hair clips.

Mikkel knocked on the door looking like a dream date. Instead of his customary captain's uniform, he wore a dark suit with a white shirt and a vest. I wore my plush burgundy velvet formal gown to win him over.

"You look beautiful, my dear."

My hand-sewn designer gown would transform anyone. "Can we go for dinner now? I'm starved."

"Since your coat isn't ready, when I stopped by your cabin, I asked Uffe for help. He found this cape in your cabin. My sister bought it for you."

"Thank you, sir." I took the cape from him, draped it over my shoulders, and curtsied. Madam Gris, the New York City-based creator of this spectacular costume, would approve since a sweater made my outfit look dowdy.

He laughed, bowed, and offered me his arm. "Madam, shall we?"

In the hallway, I caught our image in the oversized mirror together for the first time. We resembled a couple right out of a Civil War film. Nevertheless, in a flash, I'd trade all this to wear jeans and go for fish and chips at a local pub.

13 ~ Date Night

Stereotypical London-style fog descended on the town. I took Mikkel's hand as we left the hotel for our elegant dinner together. Excited about my final re-enactment night, I planned to celebrate the end of this challenging cruise. The captain was eccentric with a weird fascination for a bygone era but harmless.

My corset hung loosely around my waist to give me more room. I'd lost some weight, so I was ready for a delicious feast. Outside the inn, Mikkel suggested taking a hired cab or walking. The commonplace yellow taxicab came to mind, but he meant a horse carriage.

We agreed to walk and headed towards busy High Street. Most stores and shops had closed, but the bars and taverns were active and crowded. The street had a string of ornate lamps making the night look festive. For November, the evening was pleasant, and crowds thronged the narrow streets.

After a few short blocks, Mikkel stopped in front of a hotel. "Here we are."

The building was older than our inn, half-timbered with massive stones, and the style in the sixteenth century. Next to the doorway, a *porte-cochère* let the carriages pass into a protected courtyard. I had seen these before, but this time a real horse carriage turned into the entryway.

A coachman opened a gold-trimmed door, and a wealthy couple descended. I couldn't help but stare. The woman, decked out in a fur coat with a glittery tiara, looked like royalty. In my prettiest evening gown, I was a plain Jane.

Mikkel told a gentleman we had a reservation. His English had a strong accent and sounded stiff compared to his Danish. The Brits seemed to understand his English better than mine, so I didn't bother to help translate.

The maître d' greeted us as if he knew us. An attendant took our coats and ushered us into a formal dining room surrounded by ornately carved wood paneling. Vases filled with colorful flowers adorned elegant tablecloths. Candelabras, lit with real candles, perfected the lavish dreamy atmosphere. Few tables were empty, but there was a reasonable distance between them. Unlike many New York City restaurants, where space was always at a premium.

Today was the most prolonged period we had spent together, and what a day it had been. On the ship, he was busy working and interrupted all the time. Usually, I was proud of my ability to chat with anyone.

What do you say to a sea captain who refuses to get out of character? In this costume and jewelry, I would follow Scarlett O'Hara's lead and worry about it later - either tomorrow or better yet, next week.

We received a leather-bound menu written in elaborate French. The menu was pre-set, so I was free from decision making and ordering in my shoddy French. While I deciphered tonight's lineup, the waiter poured red wine from a clay pitcher into a pewter glass and made small talk with Mikkel in French.

Mikkel raised his glass and made polite eye contact before taking a sip. I did the same and made a silent toast to what lay ahead.

"Your jewelry is beautiful. Aquamarine?" Mikkel stared at my low neckline. I put my hand up feeling self-conscious.

"Yes, it is." I reached across so he could see the matching bracelet and ring.

"Did you know mariners wore aquamarine to guarantee a safe journey? It represents serenity and protection."

"No, I didn't." But for some unknown reason, I felt safer when I wore them. There might be something to that old tale.

The first dish, *Hors-d'oeuvre Russe,* was a deviled egg topped with a sprinkle of caviar and served with a glass of white wine.

"Delicious," I said, and Mikkel nodded. I sat back in my chair savoring the experience and atmosphere ready for more. Next, *pot au feu*, a beef and vegetable stew, arrived with a glass of sherry.

The third course was an Indian curry and coconut milk soup with rice. Despite not finishing my wine, the waiter replaced it with another. Our portions were small but delicious.

Mikkel said our Indian dish tasted strange, so he didn't

finish it. He shook his head, unwilling to believe me when I insisted on how much I liked spicy food. Most Danish dishes were bland after growing up in Texas, engulfed by Mexican cuisine. This meal was the best so far. Simon would be a better chef if he had a larger and more state-of-the-art kitchen.

I sipped my wine to pace myself. I shouldn't get drunk and lose control. "When's the ship leaving Southampton?"

"Friday. We are boarding three new passengers. The cargo should be ready and prepared for departure. You still plan to return home?"

"I think it's for the best."

Mikkel sighed. "Do what your heart tells you. But I suggest you delay your crossing home until the spring. The Atlantic passage is turbulent with storms at this time of year."

I swallowed wine and nearly choked. "I'm not going back home via ship."

"No?"

I was about to clarify via plane, but the server said, "*Sole Waleska.*" Saved by the fish, this was perfect timing to delay answering more questions.

The chef blended the sole with small pieces of lobster in an herbed cream sauce, and another waiter shaved black truffles on top. I savored every bite of what was called the *pièce de résistance*.

"Were you disappointed with my performance or my crew?"

"Oh no. I wanted to be on a real clipper ship, and now I have."

"What about Hong Kong? Your uncle?"

"I don't need to go to Hong Kong. I wanted to leave from Denmark, and your ship was it."

I took another bite of the fish and shut my eyes to savor the subtle flavors. "If Uncle Max is disappointed, too bad."

I could not allow a travel agency's computer to run my life or force me to endure a vacation that wasn't any fun. Men and machines control enough and mandate everything. This past week was a weird but welcome break from pings, dings, and urgent alerts to incessant boring social media posts, emails, and texts. Now I was ready to see and speak with real people more often.

I raised my glass resolved to unplug once a week when I'm home. Mikkel continued eating and didn't smile.

"If you were wondering, I will relay favorable comments about you, your crew, and the officers to Uncle Max." My negative comments focused on the prehistoric conditions. The travel agency should warn people.

He looked relieved. "I shall inquire with the shipping company in London for a partial refund. You were aboard less than a week."

"Thank you. Appreciate it."

"Do you have a European bank account?"

"No. Mine is in New York, but they –"

"You must have a local account to receive a reimbursement."

"Fine. I will open one." And close it when I get my money back.

The next dish was *noisette d'agneau lavallière*. Lamb medallions and artichoke hearts were smothered in a tarragon-scented sauce. They paired the lamb with *Haricots Verts a l'Anglaise*. The plain English green beans were amusing since the French chef was poking fun at the Brits.

"Do you have family or friends in England?"

"No. I will stay in a hotel for a few days and figure things out. I may take the train somewhere else in Europe."

"Not alone, I trust."

"Why not?"

"A woman traveling alone faces too many dangers."

"I am used to being on my own. I don't go out late at night alone or take unnecessary chances."

"You should not travel alone."

A rosé, one of my favorite wines, went with the lamb. Silently, I raised my glass to toast Mikkel in thanks for this special meal.

I considered telling him when I was 18, I was an exchange student in Denmark and left behind everyone and everything I knew. I lived with a local Danish family and went to school for a year. Despite some issues, I made it work and stayed the full year. Quitting was rare, but I had to trust my instincts. I didn't have to stay on this cruise.

"You could afford a reasonable and safe accommodation

here. For perhaps as long as six months."

"Six months? I can't stay here that long." In six months, I would be back at work again after another miserable job search.

A small plate of *petits fours* arrived for the sweet finale. For an after-dinner drink, I ordered a sherry, and Mikkel asked for a cognac.

After all this alcohol, I was tired of eating, drinking, and the whole charade. Liquor made me braver, foolish, or both.

"I know this isn't allowed, but we both know it's not 1862. This is all made up." My words ran together, and I gestured to be clear.

"What year is it, if not 1862?"

"You know."

"No, I fear I do not."

I leaned across the table to whisper. "2016."

He sat back, stared at me, and took a sip of wine. "Why would it be two thousand and …" He paused as if trying to remember

"Sixteen. How should I know?" Tipsy from all the alcohol, I couldn't keep up this ridiculous charade. "One year follows another, and before we know it, it will be 2020, then 2050, and so on. If we don't screw up the environment, the world might make it to 3000."

"My dear, you are fatigued and have overindulged. My sincere apologies."

14 ~ *Rebuffed*

Captain Mikkel was exasperatingly right on both accounts. I had overdone it on the alcohol, so I accepted his hand to steady myself. With my walking wobbly, he suggested we ride in a coach back to the inn.

I shivered outside while we waited. To forget the cold, I scanned the walls outside for an official English blue and white plaque.

Mikkel said, "What are you searching for?"

"A sign that mentions Jane Austen, the writer. She was here once."

Mikkel had never heard of her but helped me in search.

Besides the missing plaque, we couldn't find an available coach. Typical, I fumed, like trying to find a taxicab in New York City on a busy night. Instead of waiting and freezing to death, I suggested we walk back. He offered me a sip from his flask of absinthe, and I knew I shouldn't, but I did.

Mikkel held my arm as we walked back, and I appreciated it. I couldn't see the ground, and this costume didn't help. The sidewalks were not slippery but uneven, and the street lights were dim. The circumference of my hoop skirt kept us about a foot apart.

A woman approached Mikkel as if she knew him and said something unfamiliar in what might be French.

He let go of my arm and listened to her. I waited for an introduction, but he shook his head, took my arm in his again, and we walked away.

"What did she want?"

"She wanted … it's not a proper topic."

"Oh, that."

Footsteps echoed behind us, and out of habit, I turned back to check.

"Ignore her." He increased his pace, and I struggled to keep up in my dress shoes.

Her heels made a loud clatter, so I stopped and turned around. The young woman, less than a foot behind us, looked pitiful. Usually, I would feel sorry for her but not tonight. "Back off. He's with me."

The woman stared at me, shrugged her shoulders, and turned around. Mission accomplished.

Mikkel said, "You must not speak to them. A proper lady does not converse with a fallen woman."

A fallen woman? He must mean a prostitute. I nearly laughed, but she did look desperate and, in a way, fallen, so that was sad.

Mikkel, the never-ending gentleman, escorted me up the stairs and to my room. After the physical exertion and fresh air, I insisted I was okay, but he refused to leave my side. Memories of my last binge with aquavit, the Scandinavian liquor, in New York City came to mind. The well-traveled bottle with a sailing ship on the label gave me the idea for this damn trip.

Mikkel said, "Perhaps now you could provide the letters?"

"I am going with you." He stood waiting, so I opened the door. "They're on the desk." I sealed the envelopes shut to hide my weird comments and requests.

He scooped them up and into his pocket.

"I don't have an address for Uncle Max, but you said you know where he can be reached."

"My shipping company has his information. I will handle my business first."

"Great." I clenched my jaw in worry. What will happen when Mikkel figures out he isn't a person but a computer?

"The other letter is for a friend, Victoria Sandford. She lives in London and invited me to stay with her."

"An excellent solution."

I wanted to open the window for some fresh air but struggled with it. Mikkel stood behind me and pushed it open.

Something moved in the shadows.

"Do you see that? Over there."

"What?"

"A huge man with a horse over there."

"No, I don't see anything."

Did I imagine it? Another reason to shun absinthe. These re-enactors took this too far. I can't wait for London and everything to be back to normal again.

He stepped away from the window and pulled out his pocket watch. "It's late, and tomorrow we shall leave early. Goodnight, Kat."

He bent down to kiss me on the cheek. I turned my head, put my arms around him, and kissed him on the lips. He tasted of tobacco from his earlier cigarette while we waited for the carriage. His short beard scratched softly against my face.

He pulled away, and our eyes met for a moment. He kissed me again, and I pressed my body against him. But we had layers of petticoats and clothing between us. I sunk down to sit on the bed, and he sat next to me.

"My dear, Kat, we should cease." I kissed him again. "A relationship with you is not permitted, nor acceptable."

"Why not? Last time I checked our status, we were both single."

"I am the captain, and you are my passenger."

I reached over to kiss him again, but he moved out of reach. "Don't be silly. I'm not your passenger any longer, and this is a hotel, not your ship."

He kissed me as if this changed his mind. I leaned back on the bed to be more comfortable and convinced him to join me.

"There is just one thing first before –"

"Yes?" His hands on my legs stopped moving.

"When were you born?"

"I am not that old." He kissed me and caressed my legs protected by my skirt. "Provided that worries you."

"No, not yet." I pushed his hands away wanting an answer first.

He leaned over and supported himself on his side next to me. "I'm forty-five." He tucked some of my runaway hair behind my ear.

"What year?"

"1817."

"I don't believe you." I pushed him away and moved over to add space between us.

"Should I lie and say I was born in 1917 or 2017? Which do you prefer?"

"No more lies."

He shook his head and wiped his mouth with the back of his hand as if erasing my kisses. I needed someone to be real and honest. My ex-boyfriend, Charlie, lied to me right up to the moment I left.

"Well, Mrs. Jensen. I regret my date of birth is unsatisfactory."

Mikkel eyed me as if I was a love-starved female teasing him.

"You know, Captain Mikkel. I'm not desperate. I had several boyfriends back in New York City." My voice shook from frustration. No wonder with all the stress today.

He nodded. "As I expected. This was not our destiny. In America, you shall settle down with one of your kind."

"I'm not settling down with anyone. Never, ever. Got it?" I was so angry I spat out the words.

"Sorry to upset you. We must rise early tomorrow. The hotel staff will wake you to ensure you will be ready in time. Goodnight, Kat."

He stood brushing his pants as if dust had gathered in the few minutes he had been in my arms.

"Please dress plainly tomorrow. Leave your jewelry behind. It won't be needed and invites more risk."

His warning was strange. London was the place to look fashionable. I didn't own anything of value besides my aquamarine jewelry.

"I nearly forgot." He took out of his pocket the small glass bottle from the pharmacy. "You must take your medicine now. Three drops."

"No, thank you. I'm just a little tipsy. I'll be ready for London."

"Kathryn, you must take it."

"Let me see it." Mikkel handed me the medicine. As I feared, there was only the pharmacy name and some illegible handwriting. "I don't even know what this is. Do you?"

"No, but the pharmacy does. The doctor prescribed it for you."

"Well, you try it. Let me know how it works out." My adrenaline was winning the battle against the liquor sloshing through my bloodstream. "You should leave now. I'm tired and going to bed."

"I am not leaving until you take the prescribed dose." He sat down on the small sofa and stared at me.

"You are in for a long wait."

I threw a pillow from my bed at his head. He caught it and tucked it behind his back. "Very comfortable. Thank you."

I frowned, but he didn't budge. To the contrary, he stretched across the sofa.

I grabbed my nightgown and a robe, strode to the bathroom, and locked the door. I washed my face and brushed my teeth expecting he would tire and leave. But I didn't hear the door open or shut.

My head ached from all the liquor. I touched my lips remembering his kisses with the light bristles from his beard. Why wouldn't he admit his real birthdate? If he is forty-five, he is two years younger than me, and he was born around 1967.

When I emerged from the bathroom, he still sat on the sofa. "I could force you to take your medicine."

"I will fight you until the end."

"Please. This medicine is for your own well-being."

I shook my head wondering how to convince him to give up and leave.

"Why do you fear this so much?"

"My brother Keith died from a drug overdose. Unless I'm dying, I'm not taking something especially when I don't know what's in it. Your absinthe was enough of a risk."

He rubbed his beard contemplating this information. "Fine. I shall ask the chemist to inventory the ingredients, but in the meantime." He walked my direction with the medicine.

"Forget it." I dodged him. "You don't understand. I had a run in with drug dealers a few years ago. They planned to kill me but make it look like an accidental overdose."

"Oh, Kat, the stories you tell." He stared at me unconvinced but put the medicine in his pocket. My body shook remembering the narrow escape. "Fine. You win. Goodnight."

After he left, I locked the door and stumbled into bed. My body sunk down into the mattress. I yawned and shut my eyes hoping my dreams would take me to a safer and saner time.

The images from a black and white Laurel and Hardy film came to mind. Their famous quote, 'what a fine mess I've got myself into,' looped in an auto-repeat mode while I drifted off.

15 ~ *London Detour*

I threw on my clothes like a pro, despite all the extra work involved with an 1860 outfit. Something I wouldn't miss after today. It took twenty minutes for all the added layers, hooks, and buttons.

My head ached for caffeine after all the alcohol last night. Either coffee or tea would work, but I couldn't call room service without a phone. I opened my door and checked for Mikkel or an employee. The hallway was dark and quiet, and it was still pitch-black outside. I paced in my room eager to return to more familiar, current times and happier days in London.

A knock sounded at my door, and a woman's voice said, "Madam, please prepare yourself."

"Thanks. I'm prepared." That was an understatement. All week I prepared for the best but faced the worst. Today better be different.

I snatched my silly new bonnet and slammed the door to my hotel room. I headed down the narrow stairway in search of coffee and Mikkel. Footsteps echoed nearby, so I stopped midway. "Mikkel?"

"Yes. Coming." He wore a formal suit, but he slumped down as if exhausted. Without caffeine, I'd suffer the same fate soon.

"Is there time for coffee or tea before we leave?"

"No, we must leave now." His words came out clipped and harsh.

A carriage waited, and the coachman held out his hand to help me up the steps inside the cab. Mikkel spoke to the coachman and climbed in behind me but had neglected to offer his hand to help me. He must be still angry about last night. I would buy him lunch in London to smooth things over.

I positioned my skirt on the seat around me to reduce the worst of the wrinkles. "Oh, I forgot my money."

"Did you not say you lost your wallet containing all your

money?"

"I did, but I found some money in an envelope. A goodbye gift. Can I run back and get it?"

"Not now. You may spend it or give it away to the street urchins later."

Mikkel sat across from me but stared out the window. I had to get back on his good side. How without a shilling to my name?

It was still dark outside, and dark clouds threatened rain. "What time is it?

Mikkel checked his pocket watch. "Nearing 0700 hours." Seven o'clock.

"What time is the train?"

"0800 hours." He continued staring out the window.

I couldn't think of anything else to say, so I gazed out the window. London would be a mess if it rained, and my costume would get impossibly wet.

People would stare at both of us but mostly me. Men's suits had not changed as much as women's outfits. My excuse would be we were actors auditioning for a period film.

The carriage stopped, and the coachman opened the door and reached for my hand. I wanted to exchange this oppressive atmosphere for the train and less grumpy people.

I stepped down to a gravel drive and faced a substantial red brick building surrounded by sculptured gardens and not train tracks. The setting was eerie without the normal flow of people in and out of a station.

I asked the coachman, "Is this the train station?" It must be a quiet suburban branch station.

The coachman didn't answer me.

"Mikkel?" He didn't respond and took my arm to escort me toward the building.

"Wait." I wanted an answer before I went any closer. "Is this the train station?"

"No, Kat. You cannot accompany me to London."

"What? Of course, I am."

"You are unwell. The staff is properly trained. They shall watch over you while I am in London."

"No. I must go with you." I turned, picked up my skirt, and sprinted back to the carriage.

"Wait." Mikkel ran after me and grabbed my arm before I could reach it and spun me around. "Stop! Now."

I jerked my arm free and kicked, but Mikkel stepped to the side and avoided it. I stunned him since he stood still for a moment. I knew not to hesitate and ran. The coachman watched while I fumbled with the handle to get back inside the coach. Mikkel leaned against me with his hand holding the door shut.

"Please. This is only for the day. I promise to pick you up as soon as I return. By 1700 hours this afternoon."

"No, please. Don't do this." Tears rolled down my cheeks, and I wiped them away with the back of my hand. I pulled his fingers away to unblock my entrance into the safety of the carriage.

"Do you require aid, sir?" A heavily accented man I couldn't bear to look at asked Mikkel.

"No, I believe I can manage. Kat, will you please turn around?"

I stared at the door and his hand willing this nightmare to end. "No. I just want to go home."

"And you shall. Soon. I promise." Mikkel stroked my arm still whispering in my ear. "A fine and pleasant rest for the day. Much preferable to a noisy, dirty train ride."

I wiped my tears away and turned around. "I like train rides."

He shook his head. "I cannot watch over you in London."

"I will stay on the ship in my cabin. I promise."

Captain Mikkel pressed his hand against his abdomen for a second. Was he reconsidering?

He sighed. "You called her a rundown excuse for a ship. Furthermore, my crew lacks proper medical training and cannot watch over you today. My answer must be no."

"I didn't mean it. It, I mean she, isn't so bad. I just –"

"Come now. It is starting to rain." Mikkel took my hand.

Faint drops, like tears from above, hit my shoulders. My heels sunk into the wet and spongy moss-covered dirt. "I promise I'll stay in my cabin."

The uniformed man and another woman in black approached us, and I let go of his hand.

"Come." Mikkel gripped my hand.

I plodded along beside him towards the ominous dark brick building while he matched my pace. I peeked over my shoulder, and the two employees narrowed the gap behind us.

As we got closer, a complex of buildings appeared and the sign, Hampshire County Hospital.

"A hospital again? I am not sick. The doctor said so."

"Not sick but confused. All this talk last night of 2020. You have been unwell since you fell on my ship."

"I will be fine in London. You won't even know I'm there. I promise."

"I cannot handle my business today and watch over you. I shall deliver your letters and arrange matters with the shipping company."

"Why can't I stay at the inn while you're gone? I'll wait in my room."

"If you left the hotel and were harmed, I would never forgive myself. I have no one else to turn to. This is a well-regarded and recommended facility."

"By who?"

"Dr. Johnson."

"That quack? Wonderful." The raindrops fell faster as if in agreement while the couple caught up and watched us.

"We often experience these issues," the woman said. "A change of mind is understandable." Her voice was smug and haughty.

"There was no change of mind. I never agreed to this. And I'm perfectly fine." I had to make this one-hundred percent clear to these imbeciles.

"Not if you do not know what year it is, my dear." She rolled her eyes and make a weird clicking sound like a sick rooster. The rain fell in full force, and I wished she would melt away with her smart-ass attitude.

I was so angry I glared at all three of them. Before I could figure out what to do, the massive door swung open, and the employees pushed me inside and out of the rain.

The impressive entryway caught me off guard. A grand wood-paneled hall, it had a twenty-foot ceiling full of ornate carvings.

A woman in a white uniform carrying an official notebook took Mikkel to the side.

I couldn't help but look around and admire the overwhelming interior. An ear-piercing scream echoed, and I refocused on the danger surrounding me. The know-it-all woman seized my right arm with hands as strong as a metal vise. The man squeezed my left arm. I pulled to get free, but they held fast and tightened their grip almost cutting off my circulation.

"No, please. This is all a mistake."

I made eye contact to plead with the man and the smarty-pants woman. But they stared at me as if I spoke gibberish.

Thunder boomed, and the lights in the hallway flickered. A smaller but clear sign was on the wall: The Hampshire County Lunatic Asylum for the Relief of Persons Deprived of the Use of their Reason.

"Is this a lunatic asylum for insane people?" I swallowed so hard it hurt, and my legs wobbled. "Please, Mikkel," I screamed. "Don't do this to me."

He didn't respond. Was this because of last night? "I'll take my medicine. Where is it? Give it to me, please."

Torrents of rain slammed against the stained-glass windows drowning out my voice.

Mikkel stood on the other side of the hallway with another uniformed woman and pointed to me. She shook her head and said something to him, but I couldn't hear it. She opened another door, and he took one last look at me and disappeared.

"No." I sunk to my knees paralyzed by fear. Mikkel must have heard me scream and hurried my direction.

The women kneeled next to me and coaxed me to stand up. The man told Mikkel, "Sir, I can assure you. She shall receive our finest, utmost care. A doctor will examine her to soothe her agitation and help with her recovery."

I couldn't hear Mikkel's response and panic overwhelmed me. On my knees, I wanted to crawl away and hide. They escorted Mikkel out the front door. All hope left with him.

"Stand up. You are not a child." My handlers yanked my arms, and the sharp pain brought me to my feet. They dragged me through a small doorway into a long, grim corridor. I lacked the strength to fight or even look back.

16 ~ Not My Kind of Spa

"Bath time, my dear. Strip out of your clothes." A grizzly gray-haired woman barked out these instructions.

My head spun, and I was dizzy and slow to react after swallowing three drops of Dr. Johnson's prescription an hour ago. I kneaded my aching arms from the not-so-friendly escorts into a dressing room.

"Bath?" I perked up. "A hot tub like a spa?"

"Nothing fancy, lassie. Just a wash. Hurry along."

"I had one yesterday. I think I'll pass."

"There are no passes. Everyone must do this." She missed a front tooth and wrinkles crisscrossed her face. Not the best advertising if she portrayed the after-spa look.

"Why?" A faint scream reverberated from the hallway.

"Because we must keep our facilities clean. You must be spotless before you see the doctor."

"Doctor? I don't need to see a doctor." I tried to rationalize with her. "He examined me yesterday and said I was fine. The doctors are so busy with other needier patients."

Another scream and some yelling came from beyond our little room.

"Missy, if you refuse to undress, I must ring for help. Would you prefer that?" She waited with a look of concern.

"No." I studied my options. She stood in front of the only door and exit. I hated to knock her down. How bad can this be? "Oh, all right."

She offered me a thin robe and waited.

I preferred some privacy to undress. My hands shook fumbling with the buttons on my chemise. The old woman made some soothing clucking noises and helped me. I pulled on the robe while she scooped up my clothes from the floor and rolled them up.

"Elegant clothes for a fine lady. We shall store them until your departure."

I had made another huge blunder. I longed for my costume instead of this thin robe for the rest of the day. It was torn under one arm, and a reddish stain traversed a large area near the hem past my knees.

She escorted me into the hallway and took my arm to show me the way. We passed about a dozen rooms with people talking, but some cried.

She unlocked a door. "Here we are, lassie."

A plus-sized solitary tub sat in the center of a white tiled room. I climbed into the empty metal basin while the woman reached for my robe. Completely naked I sat and folded my arms over my chest hugging myself to protect my remaining modesty. The chilly room gave me goosebumps, so I was eager for the hot water. I didn't see any soaps or gels for a bubble bath. Not that I would enjoy them.

The old woman pulled a long rope, and a bell rang. Two young girls unlocked the room, and one put a long rubber hose into the tub.

"Goodbye, lassie."

I nodded to her but focused on the two girls and the wooden bucket with stiff brushes poking over the edge of the tub.

~~~

Wrapped in my robe, I shivered while waiting for the doctor. That had to be the worst freezing cold bath ever, and I had lost the top layer of my skin due to the aggressive brushing techniques. Objecting to their intense scrubbing routine only make it hurt more. I clenched my teeth so hard to not complain that they still ached.

A man in a dark suit entered the room with a female assistant. "Hello, Mrs. Jensen. I'm Dr. Fitzpatrick. Welcome to Hampshire County Asylum." He contemplated his paperwork again.

"I am in an asylum?" Hearing it out loud made it real. "This is all a huge mistake."

He patted my hand, but I pulled back in horror. "Here is your report from yesterday. You saw Dr. Johnson, I believe?"

I nodded and concentrated on answering his questions correctly, so they would realize their mistake and I would obtain a speedy discharge.

"He said you hit your head on a ship. I understand from the gentleman who brought you here that you are confused. You do not seem to be familiar with our customs or know what year it is."

"I was confused, but now I'm fine. It might be from the vintage absinthe I drank." He was young for a doctor and unusual with green eyes and flaming red hair. He reminded me of a mischievous elf, and the women working with him were his trolls.

"What year is it?"

I paused and went with the lie. "1862." Before he asked again, I said, "N-N-November 1862. We are in Southampton, England."

"Excellent. Today is Tuesday, November 11th."

This didn't sound right, but I refused to argue. I boarded the ship on Sunday night. Five nights ago, so this should be Friday.

"On what day were you born, Mrs. Jensen?"

He fumbled with his papers and might be comparing this to what I told Dr. Johnson.

What did I say yesterday? "1830?"

"Are you unsure?"

"No, I'm so cold. It's hard to think." My teeth chattered in support.

"My apologies. Miss Moore, please bring us a blanket. The hydrotherapy is an important part of your treatment."

I arched my back against the cold and uncomfortable wooden chair. "Not when it's freezing."

"We find it helps our patients. Encourages blood flow, Mrs. Jensen. May I call you Kathryn?"

I nodded in agreement to get on his good side, and his assistant supplied me with a discolored blanket. I murmured a thank you and wrapped it around my shoulders.

"Have you been treated before?"

"No, this is all a huge mistake."

"The capable Dr. Johnson believes you may suffer from hysteria. Stand so I can test your reactions."

After following a series of exercises such as standing on one foot at a time and other silly tests, I grew impatient.

"I did this yesterday. This is a complete waste of time. Can I change into my clothes and wait somewhere for the captain?"

Dr. Fitzpatrick scowled.

"You must have other more important patients."

"Please sit, Kathryn. A few more questions."

Unwillingly, I sat on the stiff wooden chair again.

"Mr. Jensen is deceased and no children. Correct?"

I nodded.

"Answer the question."

"Yes."

"Were you ever with child?"

Pregnant? "No."

"Any miscarriages?"

How if I'd never been pregnant? "No."

"Any problems with your uterus and menses?"

Uterus and menses? I paused unsure what he meant.

"Is there a problem with your hearing?"

I shook my head. "What was the question again?"

"Your monthly female menses."

"What about it?" I played dumb since being smart didn't seem to help.

"Regular, scanty, or profuse?"

My periods were slowly ending now that I was 47. But the doctor thinks I am only 32. I wasn't sure how to respond.

"You may have a sluggish womb and illness of the uterus causing hysteria. Treatments could be prescribed."

"Regular. Both are normal. Like I told you, I am perfectly fine."

"Very well." He turned to his assistant. "Miss Moore, please start the treatment. A quarter from each arm."

"What treatment? What do you mean?" But he had left the room, and the young girl and I were alone.

"Do not fret, Madam." She stroked my arm while looking at my veins to reassure me. "You shall feel much better afterward."

"Afterward? I'm fine now." I jumped up and hurried into the next room with the doctor to convince him.

He frowned and signaled for another assistant. "Please help Kathryn with her treatment."

The two assistants closed in.

"No," I shrieked. "Don't you dare touch my arms!"

~~~

I turned over on my right side, but a shooting pain went

through my sore arms, so I switched to lay on my back. I couldn't sleep and pondered the ceiling wondering where in the hell I am now.

"Sleeping beauty, how are you?" An old woman with a hook nose and dark hair laced with frizzy gray streaks stood over me.

I struggled to sit and stay out of her reach. She resembled a deranged homeless person.

"Do not fear, Miss. I am not one of them."

I moved to the foot of my bed, and as far away as I could get without standing up. She sat at the other end of my bed and sighed.

"I am glad you awoke. You slept for hours."

Her hands were empty, and she watched me. The rock-hard mattress hurt my back, and I froze in the thin grey gown that smelled of a sickening antiseptic.

"Where am I?"

"The Hampshire County Asylum."

"Oh." I grabbed a smelly blanket and wrapped it around my shoulders. Mikkel, the untrustworthy captain, went to London and left me behind. But he had promised to pick me up today.

"Not much in the way of accommodation, is it?"

"You could say that again." The dingy room had two narrow twin beds and a white chamber pot in the corner. Disgusting and much worse than my cabin.

The room had no windows. "What time is it?"

"I expect about two in the afternoon." She stood, retrieved a tray from the floor, and placed it on the bed between us.

"Great. I should be leaving soon." My scratchy voice ached from thirst.

"Lovely, dear." I could tell from the way she said it, she didn't mean it. "Eat some food and drink. You shall need your strength to walk out of here. It has been waiting for an hour. Although, it was never hot."

I sipped some lukewarm tea, but the soup didn't look appetizing. "What kind of soup is that?"

"Bone soup. After what you experienced you will need it."

My arms, wrapped in bandages, ached. The last I could recall was the interview with the Irish doctor and fighting when they forced me to swallow something.

"What did they do to me?"

"From the looks of it, they bled you."

"Bled me?"

"Yes, their answer for everything. Cleaning the blood by removing a generous part of it. This happens about once a week."

"Oh no! How insane. George Washington died from that."

"The American President?"

Starved, I tasted a spoonful of the pale brown colored broth, but I dropped my spoon in disgust. "Yeah. He had pneumonia and asked his doctors to bleed him. They took so much it weakened him, and he died. His wife had tried to talk him out of it."

"Smart woman. Like most of us. Hurry and have some soup and bread. When the staff comes, we can request another one. I shall tell them I ate yours."

I handled the hard roll and frowned at the repulsive meal. "I'm really not that hungry."

"You must eat, my dear. Otherwise, the nurses force you with the pump."

"Pump?"

"Yes, it is ghastly, or so I have heard. Dip the bread in the soup, and it will soften up."

To avoid the sinister pump, I gnawed on the soggy bread. Even though the soup tasted disgusting, it helped revive me, but my entire body ached. I moaned and stretched out my legs.

"Did they give you pills or a drink first?"

"A drink."

"Laudanum or possibly chloral hydrate, since it is cheaper. If you do not willingly submit to the bloodletting, they give you some."

I swallowed hard to absorb more shocking news. I had heard of laudanum, a liquid form of opium.

"Have you been here long?"

"About a month. My son promised to come for me. Any day now."

I stood and once balanced trudged to the door with the almost worthless blanket trailing behind me.

Metal bars shielded the door's small opening. I couldn't slip out with the tight mesh of silver and thick bars. I turned the knob and shook it, but the door wouldn't give.

"We are locked in, I hate to say. The nurses check on us to ensure we do not leave."

I rested my head against the bars and hollered, "Help."

Electric shock therapy was supposed to be illegal. If they perform bloodlettings and administer laudanum, I wouldn't put it past them.

"Pipe down, dear. They only come when it meets their schedule. If they hear you, it will not be pleasant for either of us."

"I have to leave. I don't belong here."

"None of us do, dearie. Sit back down and rest." She patted my bed. It didn't take much to convince me that was a better choice.

"You are a Yank, I can tell from your accent. What is your name?"

I didn't respond unsure if I wanted to get to know a crazy person even a kind one. She may be a spy and will report back to the doctor or Mikkel. Best to keep my mouth shut.

"I am Millicent Phillips, but please call me Millie." She extended her left hand, not her right, to shake hands. Our handshake was awkward with my right and her left.

"I am afraid I have not had much company lately. Apologies for my appearance, and this miserable room. My right arm is not doing so well." Her right arm hung limply by her side, and she used her left hand to reposition her hand resting on her lap.

"I am Kathryn Jensen from New York City. My friends call me Kat."

"You are a pretty girl. I expect they will release you soon. I have been here for weeks. My son wants everything I own. But I was smart and hid some away. He will be sorely disappointed when he reads my will."

I was about to say anyone who put me here shouldn't get a dime. But now I would pay everything I had to get released.

Footsteps echoed in the hallway and stopped. Keys jangled in our door.

Two women in matching black dresses with long white aprons came into our room.

"The young princess finally woke up," one of the women

said.

"Yes, and she is hungry. I ate her food." Millie winked at me keeping our secret.

"Millie, stop that misconduct, you hear?"

Millie hung her head ashamed. The scene was so bizarre, I couldn't help but grin.

"What is so funny?" The other woman scolded me and made a tsk-tsk sound. She sat on the bed next to me. "I am Nurse Griffiths, and this is Nurse Hughes." She rifled through her mess of paperwork on the bed. "Kathryn Jensen, let me see your arms."

Nurse Hughes made Millie take some medicine while Nurse Griffiths examined me.

Millie said, "Careful now. Her first time. She needs soup."

"Maybe she won't sass the doctor next time." Nurse Griffiths snapped back. Her pockmarked face, from what must have been a severe case of acne, was unsightly, and I felt sorry for her.

Nurse Griffiths unwound the bandages on my arms. Some of my blood had dried, so the dressing fused to it. This didn't detour her as she ripped it off. I pulled my arms away in pain and watched in horror as the bleeding started again. She reminded me of the wicked Nurse Ratched in the movie *One Flew Over the Cuckoo's Nest*. Any pity for her scarred face disappeared.

As if the onset of blood was all my fault, Nurse Griffiths said, "Now are you going to calm down and follow orders?"

I nodded.

"Take this, Kathryn." She passed me a yellow-colored pill and a glass of water.

I hesitated at the suspect pill in the palm of my hand. "What is it?"

"Medicine to make you well. Doctor's orders."

I put it in my mouth and held it between my teeth while I drank the water and tried to convince her I swallowed it. But she watched me without blinking.

"We do not have all day here. If you get an infection, we must use leeches. Your choice. Now open."

Nurse Hughes finished examining Millie and put her hands on my shoulders, and I was imprisoned between them.

The pill, still trapped between my teeth, was dissolving. They knew this trick, and it soon disappeared.

Nurse Griffiths commanded, "Open wide."

With nothing to hide, I complied.

They didn't believe me. Nurse Hughes jerked my head back and with her fingers searched inside my mouth rubbing her fingers against my gums and under my tongue.

I nearly gagged when three more drops of Dr. Johnson's potion followed this procedure.

I closed my eyes and adhered to their instructions while praying it was only harmless vitamins.

"Nicely done. On to our next patient, Nurse Hughes. Make a note for another bone soup and tea to be sent here."

17 ~ A Thoroughly Modern Millie

The drugs made me drowsy, so I yawned and stretched out on the narrow bed, smaller than an American twin bed.

Millie rested on her bed, and the metal frame made a screeching sound from her movements.

I longed to shut my eyes for some peace and quiet before Mikkel showed up. He owed me big time after this awful day. I would force him to take me to another fabulous restaurant for dinner tonight.

"Do you see a large white rabbit in here, my dear?" Millie asked.

I didn't respond, but she called my name wanting an answer.

"Did you ask if I can see a giant white rabbit?"

"Giant? I didn't say giant. L-A-R-G-E. Large."

"Whatever. Fine."

"Well?"

"What about this large white rabbit?" This dumb conversation had to end. I turned on my side to face the wall. But when I did, my arms cried out in pain, and I feared the bleeding might start again.

"Do you see it?"

"No, should I?"

"Thank you and thank God. My last roommate did."

"She must be seeing things." They shouldn't lock people up for no reason. "You know Millie, I am sane. I haven't lost it. Not yet."

"Me either. Glad to know."

"What happened to her?"

"Poor woman. She surrendered. Left this world to find the white bunny, I suppose."

I tried to sleep, but after the second serving of bone soup, I ached to talk to someone. A therapist, like the one I had seen in New York City after my husband Axel died, might help. All these problems about Southampton nagged at me. I needed to talk it over with someone sane. Millie was a kind soul and not involved in my journey. The lights were dim, and I hid in the darkness.

"Millie, are you still awake?"

"Yes, dear."

"Can I tell you something?"

"Of course."

"I have a really huge weird problem."

"We all have problems."

"This is … well … not like most." I paused considering how to explain.

"I am waiting, my dear."

"You won't believe this. Seeing rabbits is minor."

"Now I am intrigued. You must tell me."

"If you promise you won't say anything to anyone."

"Of course. Mum's the word."

"Great." I didn't know how to start, beside with today. "Here's the thing. What year is it?"

"1862."

"Well, 1862 is part of my problem. Six days ago, it was 2016."

"2016 you say? Quite something. So far in the future. I can see why they locked you up."

"The problem is I'm not making this up. I know about England and what happens after 1862. From books and movies, they don't exist yet, but …"

"Fascinating, my dear. Please resume."

"I have traveled to England many times but not on a ship. I came on an airplane. About a hundred years ago, they built planes. A type of flying machines. They are like automobiles and another invention." I knew this was hopeless. "Never mind, Millie. It's too hard to describe." I flipped on my side to face the wall.

My mattress sagged, and Millie sat next to me and rubbed my back. "Please tell me."

"Today in London I figured it would be different. New and modern like home."

"Unfortunately, not, my dear. More of the same but crowded with bigger buildings. Do you want to be here in 1862? Or would you rather return to your time?"

"I must go back. Or should I say go forward? I can't stay here. Life is much too hard for women. All these clothes, the rules, everything. This was meant to be a vacation for two months on an old sailing ship, and here I am."

"You wanted to go on a voyage on an old ship?"

"Yeah. I arrived in Southampton yesterday ready to cut it short and go home, but everything is old. Like 1862."

"Hmm. This is unusual. Highly irregular but intriguing."

"I know. Even if I manage to sail home, it might be 1862 in New York City. The U.S. is at war, and I don't know anyone alive back then."

"No ancestors or great-great grandparents?"

"None that lived in the New York City area and going to the south where they might be would be impossible. I can't live in the Confederacy. They would never believe me even if I did find them." I pictured walking up to my second or third great-grandparents saying, "You don't know me, but we're related. I'm the daughter of your great-great-great-granddaughter." Nope, not happening.

"Well, you must find another way to get back to your time."

"I know, but I can't figure it out. I should be in London today. This whole charade and re-enactment would end."

She laughed. "You thought it was the year 2016 in London, but still 1862 in Hampshire County?"

"Yeah. Weird, I know."

"Did something happen to the ship to change time? A lightning strike or an outlandish visitor perhaps?"

"No visitor, but a heavy storm. I hit my head, but that's not the problem. I feel fine."

"Can you return to where you boarded the ship?"

"Yes, if I go back to Copenhagen. But the ship is going to Hong Kong, my original destination. The captain thinks I'm ill so while he is in London today, he left me here."

"When you boarded in Denmark, was it your time? The year 2000?"

"Yeah, 2016. I wanted to go on an adventure on a beautiful old sailing ship."

"My dear, you must persist on that same ship to the end. To Hong Kong. When you reach the final port of call, you shall return to your own time."

"You think so, Millie?"

"Yes, I am certain of it. The moment you boarded the old

ship, you physically moved to 1862."

"Millie. I know you mean well. No, no, no, no." I shook my head overpowered by what I feared the most coming true. I had kept pushing away this nagging possibility since I disembarked into the bizarre town of Southampton.

"Oh yes. I am sorry, Kat. That must be what occurred."

"But this is so inconceivable. I don't believe in imaginary worlds or sci-fi. I'm a business-woman used to logic, numbers, and facts."

"Sci-fi?"

"Science fiction and the supernatural. I never even went to see *Star Wars* or *Harry Potter*."

"Harry who?"

"Never mind."

"Please, tell me. This is fascinating."

"Harry Potter is an imaginary English kid, and he became a magician. The books were enormously popular everywhere." I began to mention the movies, but that would be hard to explain.

"Did he move through time?"

"Time travel? I don't think so." Tears rolled down my cheeks now that I finally had to accept that this is what happened to me.

"My dear Kat, you shall be just fine." Millie offered me a cloth napkin to wipe my tears. "Get back aboard, finish your voyage, and return to your time."

"Oh, I don't know. It's a long voyage. I'm not sure I can. What if it doesn't work?"

"It will work, and you can. You are a strong and smart young woman. What else do you need?"

"Maybe you're right. This is just so strange. At home, I dreamed of this ship, and it was bizarre from the very beginning." When I boarded the old ship, I somehow entered the ship's 1862-time zone, and when I get off at the end of the voyage, I will be back in my time. I couldn't hold back my excitement, and I sat up and rubbed my eyes.

"Bless your lucky stars you did not fall back another thousand years to 862. A vile time from what I have read about our history. Viking invaders and assaults. Danelaw was the law of the land, and they controlled a vast area from

London to Chester. And can you imagine life on a Viking longship? A clipper ship is luxurious."

"You are right again." I still hadn't fully absorbed 1862. "862 would be much worse."

She clapped her hands pleased. "Any other problems to discuss?"

I only had to convince the captain to let me re-board the ship. "I'm so astonished you believe me. You are a lifesaver, Millie."

Millie got up and turned a switch to make the oil lamp brighter. She pulled out an old wooden box from under her bed and rummaged around searching for something. She waved a book at me. "This should help you."

She sat next to me on my bed and presented me with an old, frayed book, *The Night-Side of Nature, or, Ghosts and Ghost-seers*, by Catherine Crowe.

"I am a spiritualist. One of the reasons my son placed me here. I suffered from some fatigue and anxiety. Please take this as a token of my friendship. It may benefit you during your long journey."

"Oh no, I couldn't."

"I insist. This book explains the possibility of other worlds. The author, Mrs. Crowe, is a living pioneer of the unknown and famous in Europe and the States. Have you heard of her?"

"No." I never believed in ghosts or hocus pocus stuff. It's illogical and can't happen. Except now I'm living proof.

I opened the book to the first page. The author had signed it with a personal inscription to Millicent Phillips.

"I can't. The author signed it just for you." I tried to pass it back, but she refused so I placed it on her lap.

"Please. I have memorized the contents." She dropped it on my lap. "My address is in the back. I should much like to hear about your journey if you have an occasion to send me a letter."

"Sure, I will write to you. But I'll read the book while I'm here and give it back. If I do get back to 2016, I must travel light."

She laughed and threw her head back. "Yes, very light to travel so many years."

Millie turned off her light, and we both lay in our beds

breathing the rancid air. When I boarded in Denmark at night, the shoreline and harbor were unusually dark. People stood on Kronborg castle's roofline. Captain Mikkel had explained they were soldiers. In 2016 Kronborg was a museum, not a fort.

"Well, Kat, my advice is to make the best of it. Get your fanny back on the ship. And for heaven's sake, do not tell anyone. Not a soul. Do you hear me? Nothing about anything in the future like flying machines. Unless you prefer to stay here. I would live on your ship at any time over this vile and filthy place."

She was spot-on. I must accept this. I can't forget about 2016, but I can keep my mouth shut. I chewed my lip worried. I'm a natural chatterbox, so that won't be easy.

"Rest now, Kat. In a few hours, we will be liberated for dinner."

Scenes from science fiction, time travel books, movies, and television shows ran through my mind like a PowerPoint slide show. *The Time Traveler's Wife* movie was unbelievable.

Outlander was a TV show about a woman's time travel romance with a Scottish hunk from the 1700s. She returned a second time for love, mud, and more mayhem. No way would I ever do that.

At my first opportunity, with or without Prince Charming, I am time traveling back home. I crossed my heart with my finger and whispered the rest.

In Hong Kong, everything should work out, and I tried to relax. But how? Where was the captain? Getting out of here would be hard enough.

18 ~ A Night to Forget

Inside the shabby dining room, a petite grey-haired woman stood right in front of me with her face inches from mine. I stepped back, and with a quick flourish of her hand, she bowed into a polite curtsy.

"Such a pleasure to meet you, my dear Kathryn. I have a nagging message to tell you. But now I cannot hear it with the endless chatter in my head." She stretched her head and neck from side to side.

As if off balance, she tilted against me and mouthed something into my ticklish ear. I couldn't hear her, so she repeated it. "Don't be discouraged or give up. Help is on the way. Try to enjoy yourself on this journey of life." She circled her hands above her head and wiggled her fingers as if tapping into the cosmos surrounding us.

"Thanks, I'll try." I began to ask her name, but someone tapped me on the shoulder, so I turned around.

Millie wanted to introduce me to another friend of hers. By the time I was free, the mysterious woman had vanished.

With a loud clattering, the nursing staff delivered food buffet-style to a long table on the side of the room. Everyone lined up, but the group lacked enthusiasm. Our meal featured a bland stew with tiny flakes of what was said to be chicken, unknown blobs of what once may have been vegetables, and rock-hard bread that could be used as a weapon. Canned cat food looked more appetizing. We washed it down with a watery beer or tea. Too weak for a slight buzz and seconds were unavailable.

Millie didn't eat much but swallowed some soup and stale bread in our room after I begged her. Last night's great meal, still lingering somewhere in my system, kept me alive.

Some of the patients were seeing not just white rabbits but an entire zoo. Our group dinner was beyond sad, but it put my problems into perspective. Time traveling and living on an old ship was nothing compared to life here.

I stopped eating after a few bites to monitor the doorway.

Mikkel should arrive any minute. He promised. As the minutes ticked by, I moved his name to the lengthy list of unreliable men in my life. This time, I faced severe consequences trapped in a nut house. Had he lied and completely given up on me? I couldn't live here. To stop thinking about it, I listened to their conversation centered on the continued dreariness of the asylum and cruel staff.

Many women were eager to know more about me, the only American in their midst. Soon, I grew tired of answering questions and let Millie take over. My unfamiliar accent made it hard for them to understand, and Millie enjoyed being in the limelight.

A piano stood in the corner of the room by some barred windows. "Does anyone play?"

One of the women said, "Not since Mary. She passed on."

Another woman said, "Please play something. I must warn you; it is a rickety old thing."

"I am pretty rickety myself."

I sat behind the battered keyboard and slid my hand across it. Several keys were missing their thin veneer. I tapped a few. The piano was out of tune but should suffice.

Sheet music was unavailable, but I couldn't read much of it anyway. During my childhood, I took lessons and not by choice. My musically talented brother, Keith, preferred the guitar and later encouraged me to play when we infrequently met at our childhood home in San Antonio, Texas.

Usually, I refused to play for an audience with my mediocre musical skills. But bravery and ability were unnecessary to perform in such a decrepit place. Banging on a set of garbage cans, like Bongo Joe did for tourists on San Antonio's Riverwalk, would be a success here.

I bungled along and played a classical number relieved my family couldn't be here to criticize tonight's performance. Beethoven's *Moonlight Sonata* will never be the same again. A few ladies, who must be hard of hearing, clapped.

Everyone applauded after hearing the theme song from *The Pink Panther* film. Since this was their first time to hear music from the 1900s, my mistakes weren't as noticeable.

My audience, starved in so many ways, clamored for more and wouldn't take no for an answer. I racked my brain for another song.

A few months ago, I attended the Broadway musical about Carole King in New York City. I stumbled through some of her songs on the piano at the last family Christmas with my brother Keith. We surprised our mother with songs from Carole King's *Tapestry* album, one of her favorites.

Keith had the talent and the voice, but I knew all the words and would sing along in the background. Mom had musical skills as well. I was the weak link. But they were unable to criticize me tonight. So, why not? I am stuck here, and I'm bored.

First, I stumbled through the song *So Far Away* with just the music, and I sang the words I could remember. This song was a mistake since it was sad and a real downer. A crowd of women gathered around the piano, and Millie sat on the wooden bench next to me.

When the song ended, the room was quiet except for some sniffling. When I had the nerve to look up, some women dabbed their eyes with napkins. To cheer up my discouraged captive audience, I played and sang along as best I could to *Beautiful* another hit from that album.

Afterward, the women clapped and encouraged me. "Such a beautiful song. Another please."

I warned my kindhearted fans. "This next one is better with a full band. You know, guitar and drums, but I'll give it a try."

They nodded and implored me to play more. I sang and played the upbeat song, *One Fine Day.*

Some women called out praises accompanied by all around enthusiastic clapping. I stood taking a break from the uncomfortable, wooden seat.

A half-dozen medical staff, all females and in uniform, entered the room but kept their distance and stood next to the walls. They watched over us, and especially me.

Millie sat on the bench behind the keyboard and tugged on my sleeve to get my attention. "One more. Please, Kat."

After I surveyed our guards, one of the evil ones nodded that this was fine.

"For the finale, I'll do my best with one of my favorites, *You've Got A Friend.*"

After I finished, the women stood in line to shake hands and thank me. All these women had names I would never remember, but the happiness in their tired faces would be hard to forget.

In an emotional high, I almost forgot I was in a madhouse. I had never received so much applause for my lackluster musical skills. My eyes welled up, but I refused to break down in front of my fans or our keepers. The ladies shook my hand, and some hugged me or kissed my cheek. Many women pledged, just like the song, to always be my friend.

The mysterious woman who greeted me before dinner lunged towards me and clasped my hand. "Beautifully played. Do not fret, my dear. I forgot to mention Hong Kong. I should say something about it. Oh, Lordy, I forgot again. So sorry."

"Hong Kong?" How did she know? Millie vowed to keep it a secret.

"If I remember, I will tell you. May I give you a hug goodnight?"

"Yes, of course."

I put my arms around her shoulders and sensed a feeling of calmness by her soothing touch. She smelled fresh, like baby powder, which was unexpected in a place saturated with the stench of sickness, rot, and dirt.

Another woman waiting to speak with me spoke up behind her. "Please make haste, Maxi. We want to thank her for her enchanting music."

Another one cut in between us and said, "Delightful, my dear."

"Is your name, Maxi?" I asked.

"Yes, Maxine, but call me Maxi."

"My friends call me Kat. Pleased to meet you."

The next woman moved around Maxi, and I greeted her while Maxi hovered behind me and got close. "I remember now. In Hong Kong, once you are there, everything will work itself out. You shall be on your way home to your friends and family again."

Millie must have told her. "Thanks for the update. I hope you're right. First, I must get out of here."

A head nurse announced, "Tonight's entertainment has concluded. Return immediately to your rooms."

On the way back to our room, Millie said, "Many suffer

from private maladies or misfortunes without the prospect of release. We are in the better section of this foul madhouse. The other wards are for charity cases and tightly packed with six to a room."

How much worse could it get? I touched my aching jaw from all this stress and searched for a more upbeat topic.

"Do you know Maxi? She's friendly."

"Oh, yes. We all know Maxi. A peculiar woman, but kind. Not all quite together upstairs though."

"She told me not to give up or get discouraged. And she mentioned Hong Kong. Strange unless you told her."

"Not me. We agreed. Mum's the word. She's a habitual drunkard and changes her name every week. A few weeks ago, she was Marlene and before that Madeline. Her names always start with the letter M. She is consistent about that part."

"So sad."

"It gets worse. Maxi is often locked in the seclusion room with padding on the walls and floors. Located in the J block."

Great, just what I needed. Getting encouragement from a loon in a real-life loony bin. Poor Maxi or whatever her name really is. However, kind words are welcome from anyone.

~~~

After returning to our prison cell of a room, Nurse Hughes handed us two unwanted dingy looking nightgowns. I refused to take mine, but Millie snatched both.

"I am not spending the night here. Captain Madsen said he would return this afternoon. He should be here any minute."

"He has not materialized yet, has he? You must prepare for the night."

"He promised to be here today after visiting London. He must be running late. I have a prepaid hotel room to sleep in with all my belongings."

She put her hands on her ample hips. "Kathryn, if half the promises from men were true, I would not be here at this moment wasting time talking to you. Now stop your foolishness. Put on your nightgown and go to bed."

Millie handed me a nightgown.

"You know the rules, Millie." Nurse Hughes pushed her.

"Yes, Nurse Hughes."

"Furthermore, if I hear any late-night gabbing, you shall both receive a dose of laudanum or worse."

"Yes, Nurse Hughes," Millie answered since I refused to answer.

"Kathryn? Clear on our rules?"

"Yes."

"Yes, what?" She dug into my shoulder with her index finger.

"Yes, Ma'am Nurse Hughes." I would call her the Queen to get rid of her.

"Millie, mind she does not misbehave. Ring the bell, if you must." Millie turned to the side and gave me a sly wink.

Nurse Hughes went to the door but turned back as if she forgot something. She had a venomous look and retrieved a bottle from her medical bag. "Sit down Kathryn, and open wide."

"I appreciate it, but it's not necessary, Nurse Hughes." With her disgusted look, I knew she wouldn't listen to reason. Three more drops went down my throat.

The keys clanked in the door locking us in for the night. After her footsteps faded away, I tiptoed to the door and jiggled it. We were doomed. Our tiny locked room grew colder by the minute.

Clad in a stiff and uncomfortable long-sleeved nightshirt, I couldn't sleep. Questions bombarded me. Why did Mikkel lie to me? Damn it! Where could he be? What if he was never coming back? How would I get out of here?

"Please tell me more about the future." Millie kept her voice low so we could listen for threatening footsteps.

"Sure. What do you want to know?"

"Oh, anything. You said you prefer life in the future."

"Absolutely. It is far from perfect. But it's easier for most women. Usually, we are treated more fairly. We don't have to wear fancy dresses unless we want to."

"What do you wear instead?"

"Women can wear pants like men. Skirts can be short. Above the knee."

She gasped. "Pantaloons? Short skirts?"

"Oh, yes. Women can wear short pants showing off your leg. They were once called hot pants."

"Hot pantaloons?"

"Yeah, super short."

She turned her light on and fanned herself as if overheated.

The lock rattled in the door but didn't open. "Quiet down in there and lights off."

I waited for the footsteps to fade away. "Only for the young ones. Not old ladies like us."

Millie chuckled. "I should certainly hope so."

We snickered and tried to stop, but the image grew. Millie's infectious giggle made me chuckle, and we exploded in a cascade of full-blown laughter.

I hadn't listened for footsteps. An annoyed employee unlocked the door and flashed her lantern and big nose into our privacy. "Ladies, what is so funny?"

"Hot pants for women." Millie giggled and slapped her mattress with her uninjured arm.

I threw my head back and laughed. Our watchdog didn't look pleased.

"Shall we use restraints to calm you two down?"

"Oh no. Please." Millie and I said simultaneously. To stifle our laughter, Millie put her hand across her mouth, and I did the same.

At last, the nurse left. We remained still until her footsteps faded away before we spoke again.

"That was a narrow escape. She wasn't kidding." I had given up on Mikkel and was ready to call it a night.

"Just envious, my dear. A hearty laugh is rare here. Those thickheaded simpletons like to throw their weight around. They eat better and have a surplus to throw around."

"Yeah, they sure do." How unfair it all was.

"Poor dear. Something smells rotten in the state of Denmark."

"Yeah, it was rotten. If I had avoided that country, I wouldn't be in this mess."

"You shall get through it. Relax and dream more. Goodnight, dear." And the next sound from her was soft snoring.

I put the foul covering over my head as she had suggested to protect myself from rats or mice scurrying around in the dark. The blanket was terribly small. I had to bend my legs and twist my back to fit under it. I tried to conserve what little warmth existed. My tummy grumbled angrily after today's meager diet.

Tears rolled down my face at the possibility of staying here for weeks or months. I had heard at dinner if someone pays the bill, they keep you here or put you in the dilapidated wing that houses the poor and indigent patients.

Millie's soft snoring continued. I'd had problems sleeping with my husband's loud snoring. But her noises were slight and soothing.

I said a quick prayer, to a God I didn't believe in, so quietly I couldn't hear it. But my final words were to a more likely living deity. "Please, Mikkel. I apologize about last night. You must come back for me. I will die here."

19 ~ The Morning After

My shoulder shook, and an urgent voice said, "Kathryn, wake up."

A bright light shone in my face, and Nurse Hughes dropped a bundle of clothes on my chest. The faintly familiar smell of my perfume was comforting, and I pressed my face into my old costume. This wasn't a costume, but from now on, my regular, daily wardrobe.

"Kathryn, open wide."

My brain was woozy at the unexpected wakeup call, so I did what she demanded. Three more drops of vile, bitter medicine dripped down my throat.

"All that stupid arguing before. How do you expect to get better? Not so bad, is it?" Her screechy voice was as pleasant as nails on a blackboard.

"No, but I prefer coffee with cream in the morning." My throat coughed in agreement.

"A Miss Somebody, is it? You have a visitor. Dress at once! I shall return in ten minutes."

"Is it the captain?" My morning voice croaked from the bitter medicine, but she ignored me and left. I climbed out of bed, pulled off the stained nightgown, and eyed Millie.

She lay in her bed watching me. "Your sea captain is here to take you back to his ship."

"I would love that, Millie. But it's not easy. He doesn't like me very much."

"You can win him over. Your smile is so pleasing."

"Thanks, Millie. I wish you could come with me."

"To Hong Kong? No, thank you." She knew what I meant. "Do not brood over me. My son should be here soon. Maybe today."

"Well, as the Brits say, keep calm and carry on." I buttoned my chemise, but the signal from my brain to my fingers was sluggish.

"What? I have never heard that saying before."

"Never? It's an old saying. Used for all sorts of things. Keep calm and eat chocolate. Keep calm and drink more beer. Might be from World War II though."

"Sounds ominous. A second world war?"

"Unfortunately. The first began in 1914 and the second in 1939. Britain was right in the middle of both. Mainly fighting the Germans. Not everything in the future is so wonderful."

"Regrettable to hear. How long did the wars continue?"

"Before my time, but from what I remember, four or five years. Too long."

She didn't ask how many people died, and I didn't have a number. Way too many would be my answer.

I straightened my clothes while she watched me and thought about the awful events and problems after 1862 that she would never know about. Terrorist attacks, global warming, pollution, contamination, animal extinction, and weird new diseases like AIDS. Living in 1862 for a few months may not be so terrible.

"I think I shall stay in 1862." Somehow, she read my mind.

Millie got out of bed slowly and grunted as if in pain while wrapping a shawl around her shoulders.

"Are you all right, Millie?"

She winced. "As well as this old woman can be."

"If you're hurting that badly maybe you should see a doctor."

"And let them bleed me again? No, thank you."

"What if it's life-threatening? Maybe they won't bleed you."

"Now, my dear Kat, no need to fuss." She forced a smile and pressed her middle with her hand as if to push the hurt away. "I shall be just fine. Once I am at home, I shall write you long, dull letters from 1862." She winked. "I will miss you."

"I'll miss you, too. I promise if I figure out a way to get you out of here, I will come back and rescue you."

"Sweet of you to say, but not at all necessary. Goodbye, dear Kat. I have complete faith in your future. You shall make it back to your own time."

"My motto is to keep calm and get back home."

"I may borrow that Yank saying. Chocolate makes me calm."

"Can I borrow a mirror and comb?" My fingers couldn't comb through my messy hair.

"With my short hair, I do not have one. But there is one in our community water closet. Ask Nurse Hughes to let you stop there."

She walked over with a slight limp that I didn't notice yesterday. "I used to arrange my daughter's hair." She helped set my hair in place with her uninjured hand. "How old are you, dear?"

"Forty-seven but I accidentally said I was born in 1830. Now I'm only 32."

"You look 32. Not in your twenties, but not 47. Adopt that age while you are here. I am 57 and look at me. The years must go easier in the future."

"Anti-aging face products help."

"Did they find the fountain of youth?"

"Oh, no. Face lotions have retinol made from Vitamin A to help prevent wrinkles. The worst thing for your skin is the sun. You know how the skin on your butt stays young."

Millie slapped her leg and laughed. "One small advantage to being here. I never see the sun."

"Sorry, Millie. No one deserves this type of treatment. I will try to get you some money. That should help some."

"Do not fuss about old me. Save your money. You may need it. In a matter of days, I shall be free. Board your glorious sailing ship for Hong Kong, and do not allow anything to stop you."

"I am determined. Hong Kong or bust."

She laughed. "Once released from this godforsaken institution, I shall live in tranquility at my cottage with a pleasant garden for the rest of my days. Magnificently situated within walking distance to an amiable town. The house is in my birth name from my grand-mama. No one, not even my son, can seize that from me."

"Sounds wonderful."

"You are always welcome to visit. For as long as you wish. My address is in the book."

"Thanks. I sure will if I get back." If I was stuck in 1862, a real and scary possibility. But if I returned to 2016, I would never see her again.

We hugged and kissed each other's cheeks. Somehow in this rank environment, Millie smelled sweet, like roses. Nurse Hughes returned and grimaced at our embrace but didn't complain.

Nurse Hughes led me down the dilapidated passageway while I feared more disappointment. But I had changed. This time I held my head high knowing I had friends like Millie and the other ladies.

We stopped outside Dr. Fitzpatrick's office, and she opened the door but waited in the corridor.

My stomach, like a balloon filled with contaminated air, deflated in terror. Behind that door lay nothing but pain and stress. I wanted another door. Any other one would do, and I froze.

"Come now, Kathryn. A gentleman is waiting."

I hesitated worried this might be another mean trick. Would she refer to the captain as a gentleman? Or did she mean one of the doctors?

Last night I had heard so many terrible stories about patients trapped here. On high alert, I entered the room.

Doctor Fitzpatrick sat behind his desk and greeted me as if I was his favorite person in the entire world and had been missing for months.

I forced a smile remembering Millie's advice to smile, smile, and then smile some more.

Millie said, "Keep doing this even when it hurts, and you are convinced your lips will never touch again."

"Here she is. Mrs. Jensen, you look so refreshed. Does she not, Captain Madsen?" Dr. Fitzpatrick said.

A tall man, seated to my right hidden behind the door, stood. I knew it must be Mikkel without hearing a word or seeing his face.

"Mikkel, thank you. You came back. I thought you changed your mind." To elude further disappointment, I had not counted on seeing him today. My voice shook, and my knees were weak.

I hugged him but heard a slight groan and let go. His arm hung in a sling, and a large bruise darkened his right cheek.

"What happened?"

"Captain Madsen's train jumped the tracks. A most

unfortunate occurrence. He is lucky to be alive," Dr. Fitzpatrick shook his head as if to deny it.

"Is that true?" I asked Mikkel ignoring the untrustworthy doctor.

"Yes. I apologize, Kat. I vowed to collect you yesterday, but the accident –"

"Oh, it's fine. I'm just glad you are here." I scrutinized the doctor. "Can we leave now?"

"I discussed your case with the benevolent captain." Dr. Fitzpatrick ignored me and said to Mikkel, "Mrs. Jensen would benefit profoundly by staying here a few more days."

"No, I can't. I won't. Mikkel, please."

Mikkel studied me and looked at the doctor.

"I am begging you. I can't stay here. I'll die if I do."

"Do not be so melodramatic. Sit here, Kathryn. Let us hear what Dr. Fitzpatrick has to say."

I couldn't sit. Staying here one extra minute made me want to turn and run.

Nurse Hughes might be standing by the door, and I wouldn't get far. And where would I go? The ship was my only chance.

A loud crash exploded from out in the hall. Another medical assistant ran in and uttered something into the doctor's ear. He excused himself and left the room with her. Now we had a chance.

"Mikkel, we must leave. Right now. This place is dangerous."

"Here? How?"

I wanted to tell him this was a madhouse and the crazy people were the doctors and nurses, but he wouldn't believe me. "They took my blood yesterday. A lot of it. I will show you the red marks, and when they changed …"

Dr. Fitzpatrick came back into his office, but he ignored us and shuffled through some paperwork. "My apologies. I shall return."

I wanted him to take his time to convince Mikkel to leave. Once I'm released, my focus will shift to getting back on his ship.

"Here, Kat. A small gift from London." Mikkel presented me with a wrapped package with a crunched corner. "The box was damaged in the accident, but the contents should be fine."

I untied the yellow bow and ripped off the brown paper, my customary handling of any wrapped gifts. Underneath some tissue paper, I lifted out a light blue shawl. I wrapped it around my neck and shoulders, touched at his thoughtfulness.

"Practical and matches your pretty eyes."

"This is perfect. Thank you. I nearly froze last night." My attention returned to escaping from this madhouse. "Mikkel, let's go. Immediately. Please." I stood, grabbed his hand, and pulled as hard as I could without hurting him.

He pulled his hand away shaking it. "Sit down. We shall soon." He patted my knee not ready to leave.

"It's filthy here. Some of these people are sick and could be mentally ill. But I'm sane. I promise you. I was confused about the year but not any longer."

The doctor reappeared, but his face was red nearly matching his hair. I gritted my teeth worried about the patients.

"Is everything all right?" Mikkel asked him.

"A minor skirmish. All settled now." Dr. Fitzpatrick thumbed through his paperwork to find the right page. "As I said, Mrs. Jensen, or may I say Kathryn?"

"Fine." He had called me Kathryn before, and this was the least of my fears.

"Dr. Johnson diagnosed hysteria. Many in her category would never survive childhood. She has a sluggish womb with bad birthing hips. You can see for yourself how thin she is."

How ridiculous. How does having babies relate to this? I shook my head and tried to catch Mikkel's eye, but he paid attention to the doctor.

"Kathryn, please stand," the doctor ordered.

"No." I crossed my arms and eyed a dirty spot on the wall behind him.

"Kat, please." Mikkel squeezed my hand to encourage me.

I put my bundled coat, with the book from Millie hidden inside, on my chair, stood, and crossed my arms over my chest.

The doctor stood next to me and uncrossed my arms holding them out from my side. He pushed and prodded against my hips and ribs to illustrate his concerns.

"No wonder I'm thin. I barely had any food last night."

"And why was that? Did you refuse our fine chicken dinner?

I received reports that you had a pleasant evening with the other patients."

"The food was inedible."

"Captain Madsen, the staff reported Kathryn entertained the ladies on our piano. Music and singing. Quite well from what I understand."

"All the patients here are cold, starving, and bored." This place made the loony bin in the film *One Flew Over the Cuckoo's Nest* look like a resort hotel.

The doctor shook his head. "This is a fine institution."

"I would rather be homeless and on ..." I stopped. This might make things worse, but I wouldn't apologize.

"Forget it," I said. Complaining to someone who didn't care one iota was a complete waste of time.

"I must counsel and appeal to your sensibility. Kathryn is ill and much too thin. She should stay here, at the bare minimum, for another week. Captain Madsen, you will find much improvement. Today she is slightly improved. The bath and bleeding helped vastly."

"No, no, no." I shook my head so fast a few stray tears landed on my lap.

Mikkel gave me his handkerchief and touched my shoulder. "I should have bought more in London."

I thanked him and blew my nose in preparation for battle.

"Captain, you can see for yourself. Kathryn is ill and sobbing. It is the hysteria I promise you, and we can best treat it here."

"Absolutely not. I'm fine." I wrapped my arms around my chest to stop shaking from fear. "This is a stressful situation, and I –"

Mikkel interrupted me. "I cannot authorize a longer stay. Since she does not wish it, we shall leave as planned."

Thank you, I mouthed.

The doctor said, "As you wish. First, I must demonstrate a tiny inkling of how much progress she made under our supervision."

My tormentor winked as if we had been on a secret date together. "What is today, Kathryn?"

"1862."

"Come now. The actual date?"

"November 12th, Wednesday, 1862."

"Excellent." Mikkel reached out to hold my hand, and I squeezed it hard.

"And your birth?"

"You want to know when?"

He nodded, but Mikkel hadn't loosened his grip on my hand. I could tell both were eager to hear.

"February 5, 1830."

"Bravo. You see, Kathryn made some progress, Captain Madsen."

"Yes, she has. For that I am grateful. Thank you, Dr. Fitzpatrick."

20 ~ Caught & Released

Outside with the horse carriage and freedom in sight, I ran and sucked in the fresh air as if I'd been underwater for hours. Mikkel ran after me and insisted I stop and put on my coat.

The book from Millie dropped with a thud, and he retrieved it from the ground. "A gift from one of the doctors? Or an admirer?"

"No, from my roommate, Millie. She helped me and became a close friend."

"Usually generous of her." He didn't seem convinced.

"A book is unusual?"

"Yes, they are expensive."

On the way back to our hotel, I looked out the window filled with relief and some remorse. I regretted signing forms to leave since I had never signed anything to enter. Leaving Millie behind hurt, but I didn't see how I could get both of us released. Once I'm allowed back on the ship and figure things out, I will do something about it.

The doctor had recommended a hard bed, no pillow, weekly cold baths, and monthly bleedings. My new diet should consist of bread, butter, dairy, fats, sugars, limited meat, and no fruits or vegetables. And to top it off, no spicy food or alcoholic beverages. He gave the medicine from Dr. Johnson to Mikkel and handed him another bottle of pills.

The doctor predicted I would fall prey to consumption if I didn't follow these rules. I had heard of this illness in a Charles Dickens story. Consumption was a form of pneumonia. That doctor was an idiot, so his predictions were idiotic too.

The only problem was if Mikkel believed him. Mikkel grimaced and rolled his head from side-to-side.

"Are you sure you feel all right? What happened on the train?"

"A terrible accident. Ships are a much safer way to travel." He shut his eyes as if searching for an explanation. "No matter how bad your night was being on the train was much worse."

"I doubt it. That was the worst night of my life."

"You are alive. Many on the train were not that lucky."

"Did people die?"

He nodded. "Death lurked everywhere."

"How awful. Where are you hurt?"

"My shoulder, my hip, and my face ache. Minor injuries. I am sorry I broke my promise. When I reached Southampton, the hospital had closed."

"Never mind. I survived." The asylum beat a deadly train accident. A twisted form of luck had been with me.

"Unfortunately, I do not have good news from London. Your address for Lady Victoria Sandford must be incorrect. No one there knew of her. The shipping company delivered your letter and one of my own to your uncle, Maxwell McIntosh. But, alas, no response."

"Oh well. I didn't think it would be easy to reach them." What else could I say? They didn't exist in 1862. "I made a big decision. I want to continue to Hong Kong."

"Continue?"

"On the *Anne Kristine*. I want to go with you to Hong Kong, as originally planned."

He didn't say anything, and we were back at the inn. "We shall discuss this later. You must be tired."

"I am not that tired. I want my cabin back. I was silly to complain. Please, Captain Mikkel, I must."

The coachman opened the door to the carriage. Mikkel tossed in my lap a small bag with my medicine, jumped out, and walked up the front steps leaving me behind.

I scrambled out of the cabin with the coachman's helpful hand and the bag in the other. I caught up the captain and touched his back to get his attention.

"All right, Mikkel? Can we please go back to the way it was before?"

He refused to look at me. "I do not know if we can, or if you should board again. This is not my sole decision. I must consult with the other officers and consider my men. The voyage takes months, and you would be the only woman aboard. Best that you return home as you planned."

I can't sail to the United States in 1862 with a Civil War going on. What does he mean, he doesn't know, and it's not his decision? He's the captain and in charge of everything.

My head throbbed, and faint spots appeared before me. I slipped as if the floor opened. Could this be the rabbit hole Millie mentioned?

Mikkel caught my arm, kept me from falling, and insisted I rest in my room while he was away. He refused to discuss my request until making his rounds at the ship.

I filled the bathtub with the warmest water possible and submerged slowly to relax. But my mind jumped from one problem to another.

The screams from the madhouse haunted me along with memories of abandoning Millie. Surely her worthless son wouldn't leave her there forever.

The waterlogged bandages hung droopy around my arms, so I removed them. The bleeding didn't start again, and the red marks were healing.

After toweling off, I rustled around in my carpet bags and found Dr. Matteo's goodbye gift. The one I insisted I would never need: my emergency medical pouch. I wanted to thank the two-timing cheat.

I wiped my puncture marks with alcohol pads, smeared on some first aid antibiotic ointment, and attached a band-aid to each arm. A plastic container held my prescription for antibiotics, and I counted twenty-five pills. I debated whether this was critical enough to use some. What beat this? I counted out five pills to take once daily.

I pulled out the envelope with my British money Charlie gave me as a goodbye gift. I lined up the bills on my table and counted 125 pounds, worth less than 200 dollars in 2016 but much more today.

Every single bill referred to Queen Elizabeth II. This currency would never work in 1862. I can't even go to a bank to exchange them. They would refuse and think they were forgeries. But in Hong Kong in 2016, I can use them.

Why couldn't the Brits be like Americans and honor someone from the 1700s like George Washington? Or the five-dollar bill with Abe Lincoln? Ten-dollar bills were adorned with the hunk, Alexander Hamilton. Those oldies, but goodies, might pass inspection.

If only I had some American money. Locals wouldn't be

that familiar with foreign bills. I could blame any slight differences they noticed on the Civil War.

But it was useless to keep contemplating. I had no money and no ship. If I snuck back on board and hid, when we are at sea, *voilà*, it's done. I would charm Mikkel into letting me stay or make myself valuable and needed. Supported against the fluffy pillows on my bed, I was optimistic and relaxed in my towel.

Someone knocked on my door. Still wrapped in my towel, I sleepwalked to the door without a peephole. I opened the door a crack, and a hotel employee handed me a paper bag with more worthless medicine.

The label was illegible, and I tossed it into the trash. But the medicine was real, and it might help someone. So many people of all ages were either run down, sick or both. Some sat in doorways or were slumped over on the side of the road. I pulled the bottle out of the garbage and shoved it in my handbag.

Bright sunlight passed through the curtain, and I pushed it aside to see some old buildings and a church steeple. Not old, I reminded myself, but quite possibly new in 1862.

On such a beautiful day, it was a shame to stay inside trapped in my small room. I had promised Mikkel not to leave, but he couldn't object if I sat in the lobby.

My tummy growled reminding me of lunchtime. Mikkel wouldn't want me to starve, so why not?

21 ~ *Everything's Rosy*

I chewed a cucumber and tomato sandwich with butter instead of mayonnaise in the empty and lonely hotel's dining salon. Piano music filtered in from another room, and I wandered in to listen and found a seat. This instrument was top-notch and flawlessly tuned.

A dark-haired woman sat behind the piano, and a gray-haired man stood next to her turning the sheet music. I didn't recognize the classical music, but the composition was lovely. She was talented putting my modest success last night to shame.

She stopped at the end, and the man and I both clapped. She nodded at me and played another one. When it ended, she said, "Enough."

I walked over to thank her for playing the music. We introduced ourselves, and they said they'd arrived in Southampton this morning.

The pianist, Rosamund Styles, was young and bubbly, and about thirty years old. She was plump, but the perfect specimen and female shape according to someone like Dr. Fitzpatrick.

Albert Bittner looked about fifty and was stout with a German accent. If they were married, they didn't bother with wedding rings.

"Would you like to play?" Rosamund asked while tapping on a few keys.

"Oh no. Sorry. I played last night. I am awful at it. You play so beautifully." Playing for a captive audience who were not one hundred percent functioning was one thing, but she was gifted. I faced an awkward humiliation with no upside. She tried to convince me, but I stayed firm.

Albert said, "I would play my violin if my wrists were not so sore."

"I will so miss playing on our ship." She patted the piano for emphasis. "Mine refused to fit inside my baggage."

"Which ship?" I was curious with so many different ships

in the harbor.

"The *Anne* … Albert, what is the name of our boat? I always forget these details."

"*Anne Kristine*. And the captain would prefer you refer to her as a ship."

"Yes, of course, I will try to remember both. The Scandinavian language bewilders me."

"Are you going on that ship?" I was dumbstruck.

"Yes. All the way to China." Albert's eyes were full of excitement.

"Both of you?" I touched my head unable to fathom this. Rosamund must be the female passenger hinted at by the travel agent in Denmark. Captain Mikkel was wrong when he insisted that I was the only female on board.

"I sailed on that ship from Denmark and want to continue on to Hong Kong."

"Please tell us all about it. I am so curious about what it will be like living on a ship. Shall we sit and have a beverage? What do you say, Kathryn?"

Rosamund was so friendly I would agree to do whatever she wanted. "Albert be an angel and bring us a glass of wine. Do you like wine? It is a wee bit early. Perhaps you prefer tea?"

I was thrilled with the prospect of female companionship. One thing I had learned over the past few days, I could get by with a little help from my friends. "Either one. Wine is great. It's five o'clock somewhere."

"Five o'clock? Oh, I understand." She laughed. "Please call me Rosie."

"You must call me Kat."

Albert stood by waiting for our decision.

"And can we call you Bertie?" Rosie teased him.

"And be confused with the heir to the English throne? Never!"

"How about Al?" I suggested joking with him.

"Like an owl?" He flapped his arms like a bird. "My mother would be horrified. Two syllables: Al-Bert."

"Be a good lad, Al-Bert. Two glasses of wine for the ladies."

Rosie and I sat at a table while Albert went to find a waiter. A few other visitors wandered into the salon.

"I accepted a position as the governess for a senior manager in Hong Kong. He has three young children, my charges." Rosie scrutinized the people around us as if there was a spy in our midst. "Many eligible men there seek wives."

"Oh?" Finding a man was the last reason for me to go to Hong Kong.

"Why are you going to Hong Kong?"

"I had a break from work and always wanted to sail on a tall ship." From the expression on her face, I knew my explanation was flimsy. "My Uncle Max invited me, so I want to visit with him and his family."

"I wonder if my employer knows your uncle? They might be neighbors."

"I doubt it. My uncle is a loner. Not that social." I chuckled imagining an introduction to my Uncle Maxwell, a computer and metal box crammed with wires, chips, and bytes.

"Oh, of course," She patted my hand. "So many men are like that. If only Albert were ten years younger, he would be quite the man for me. We are so lucky to have the three of us together on this arduous voyage."

Albert returned with a hotel employee. He must have overheard Rosie's comments since his face had turned pink.

"Well, there's been a slight complication. I must speak with the captain about it. I'm desperate to go to Hong Kong on his ship." Sharing my problem with a fellow passenger might help.

The waiter set down two glasses of wine and a beer for Albert.

"When we arrived in Southampton, I decided to get off. I changed my mind and asked the captain, but he wants to be sure. I'm waiting to get his permission."

"Sounds reasonable to change your mind. A lady's birthright so I am certain he will agree. I am dreadfully fearful of storms, but I cannot wait to see our ship."

"Our ship is in the harbor nearby. She is stunning but really old."

"Shall we go see her? We have nothing scheduled for the afternoon."

"I am not done with my pilsner." Albert's glass of beer was half-full.

"How many beers are you having?" Rosie punched his arm

to tease him. "We shall wait until we are all finished with our drinks."

"Why are you going to Hong Kong, Albert?" In 1862, this was a significant life-changing journey. You can't board a plane and fly back to London in twelve hours.

Albert took a big sip of beer and cleared his throat. "I woke up a few days ago with a powerful desire for wanderlust. What we call *fernweh* - an ache to be far away. This sudden decision was out of character for me."

"I know that feeling." At last, I had a travel companion who shared my strange desire for an adventure.

"I made a few inquiries in Prague and heard about a ship leaving from England for Hong Kong." Albert held his beer high as if to contemplate its golden color. "I quickly made arrangements to leave my home in Bohemia in the custody of my brother. Packed my violin and some clothes, and here I am. I expect to find an answer or satisfy my wanderlust when I reach the Orient."

"Well, we are delighted you did." Rosie grinned.

Albert continued his contemplation. "As a wise man once said, 'the goal of life is to explore all possibilities whilst you still can.' Travel is part of it. I craved a faraway destination where I do not know the customs or understand the language. Where else but Asia?"

I mulled over warning them about the lack of decent plumbing and electric power. But in 1862, Rosie and Albert wouldn't expect modern conveniences on a ship.

Stay on the script. If it didn't exist or happen before 1862, keep your ultra-modern trapdoor shut.

~~~

With my two new friends in tow, I led the way to the waterfront and the busy pier. The *Anne Kristine's* three tall masts were easy to find. The sun sparkled against the harbor's gently rolling water.

This must be the prettiest day since I had left New York City. Any day would look beautiful after a night locked up in a crazy house. This was close to the euphoric feeling on the day I quit another miserable job.

Along the harbor, we passed other sailing ships and paddle-wheelers. The sailing vessels turned steamers had hideous black chimneys ruining their sleek look. The ominous stacks resembled angry black snakes with ugly, garish heads jabbing a hole from the hold.

I understood why Mikkel resisted adding steam power to compliment the sails. He had said several times, "While I still draw breath, I will never allow anyone to disfigure *Anne Kristine*."

I had read about the unavoidable progress before I left home. Ships like the *Anne Kristine* ended up modernized or abandoned. A lucky few, like the *Cutty Sark* located outside London, became museums. The glory days of the clipper came to a gradual halt when the Suez Canal opened. Clippers couldn't maneuver through those narrow channels.

Once we reached the ship, I was thrilled my lifeline to get back home hadn't disappeared. The steep gangway connected to the pier didn't look safe. One of the sailors I didn't recognize studied us from the railing.

He may not understand English, so I switched to Danish and requested Captain Mikkel. The sailor didn't respond, so I asked for Uffe Petersen.

Albert stood on the gangplank ready to tackle it on his own.

"You better wait. I got in trouble boarding by myself."

Albert obediently walked back to the pier next to us.

"What language was that, Kat? Sounds complicated."

"Danish. The ship and crew are from Denmark. The captain speaks English very well, and I believe some of the others do as well."

"I hope so. I do not speak any Scandinavian."

"Danish," corrected Albert. "Some German words are the same."

"The Captain's name is Mikkel. An old Danish version of Michael."

"What about the other name?" Rosie tried to pronounce Uffe.

"Uffe is an old Danish name. I don't know what it would be in English. You don't hear it often."

"My name is also old. Henry II had a mistress named Rosamund. He was the King of England in the twelfth century. She had a bad end. Murdered by his wife, Eleanor of Aquitaine."

"Life was hard back then for women."

Rosie nodded. "Times are more civilized now. Kathryn is a powerful name. Henry VIII had three wives named Catherine, and the Empress of Russia was Catherine the Great."

"Sadly, no relation or I might be rich and could buy this ship."

We laughed. What was taking so long? Perhaps Mikkel didn't want to see me or wouldn't let us board.

We went to see the bow, or front of the ship, and I pointed to the wooden point. "The bowsprit."

I touched the intricate carvings on the side and admired the ornate name, *Anne Kristine*. The figurehead resembled a beautiful mermaid with long blonde hair. A man passing by stopped by to ask Albert a question and Rosie stood next to him.

While I had a moment alone, I whispered an apology for complaining about the decrepit conditions onboard. "Sorry, *Anne Kristine*. Now I know it's not your fault. You are perfect for 1862." I patted her side. "I know you can do this. Get me to Hong Kong and back to my own time. Thank you."

Albert and Rosie stood behind me. "Are you thanking the ship?"

"Yes, I suppose I am. We have a long voyage ahead."

"Is that *Anne* or *Kristine*?" Albert pointed to her bare breasts.

"The one on the left is *Anne*, and the right is *Kristine*." I laughed at his silly, inappropriate joke. "In Danish, the 'e' at the end of a word is pronounced like an 'a.' Sounds like *Anna Kristina* in English."

"Whoever she is, she needs a proper camise." Rosie made clucking sounds as if embarrassed on her behalf.

"She wouldn't be able to swim fast enough in that, and she has a long way to go."

I caressed the side of the ship to reassure our wooden vessel that she was beautiful unchanged. My aquamarine ring sparkled in the sunlight a brilliant shade of blue.

"She is amazing." If updated, she would be a perfect dream ship.

"Exquisite workmanship," Albert said. "I have always longed to experience the wind and a sense of flying from aboard a square-rigged clipper."

"Not quite flying, but it is amazing. Lots of sails and speed on a three-master." I pointed to a smaller ship in the harbor to compare. "That ship over there is a schooner-style clipper. Only a two-master."

"You are a knowledgeable ship enthusiast." Albert grinned.

"I did ... I mean I do find them fascinating. I would like to know more." I swallowed hard remembering how I first thought she was so old and in need of an update. "She was built in 1852. Only ten years old and a young girl."

Rosie didn't look impressed and switched topics. "Your ring is beautiful." She took my hand to see it up close.

"Thanks. I bought it in Denmark before I left. The stone is an aquamarine."

"Matches your shawl."

I twirled around showing off the captain's gift. "The captain told me mariners wore or carried aquamarine to guarantee a safe journey. It symbolizes protection and serenity."

"In that case, I have some shopping to do." Rosie giggled.

Uffe called to me, waved, and hurried down the gangway.

I hugged him overcome with emotion. His body was as stiff as one of the tall masts.

"Uffe, this is Rosie and Albert. They are your new passengers. Can we visit?" Uffe didn't answer, so perhaps this was against the rules. "Is the captain on board?"

Uffe answered frowning, "N-n-no E-E-English."

I tapped my head at being so forgetful. I apologized to Uffe and repeated everything in Danish.

Uffe said in Danish, "Welcome aboard. The c-c-captain and first officer just left. Shall I wake Oskar?"

"No need. Let him sleep. We just want to look around."

I translated what he said for Albert and Rosie. "You couldn't ask for a better cabin attendant."

Albert asked, "Is he our cabin boy?"

"He is. A great guy. I prefer to call him a cabin attendant. He works so hard and while he is young and a boy, it sounds insulting."

Albert and Rosie both agreed that term was better.

Uffe escorted me up the gangway and afterward, did the same for Rosie. Albert insisted he could manage alone and followed them up.

Uffe showed us their passenger cabins and my old box was still the same in its ever-present brown. A positive sign I could re-board the ship. This time brown caramel candies and a chocolate milkshake came to mind.

Albert and Rosie were happy with the cabins despite no electricity or plumbing. We admired the dining room and stopped by the galley to say hello to Simon. He kneaded bread but wiped off his hands for introductions.

Simon spoke some English but stumbled over a few words, so I translated. I complimented his cooking skills, and Simon's face glowed with pride.

"How is little Esperanza, the cat?"

"Right here, waiting for you." He pointed to a little box under the table where she slept.

"I love cats." Rosie reached down to pet her.

"Essie got special permission from the captain to stay." Even with her white speck of bad luck, she was still on board.

"Glad to hear it. The cat is luckier than me." I slunk down on my knee to pet her soft fur and peeked up at Simon. "I changed my mind about the journey. I want to be back on board again, but the captain isn't sure. Essie was smart never to get off. Right girl?" I buried my face against her soft fur to stop worrying.

Simon took my hand to help me up. I yearned for a warm welcome with open arms, but he was lukewarm. Simon started to say something, but stopped, and said goodbye.

We admired the view of the town and what really was Southampton.

"We should get back to the inn." I hated to linger since we had not seen Captain Mikkel.

Before we left, I stopped to make amends with Uffe.

"Uffe, I changed my mind. I want to continue to Hong Kong. If the captain will let me. I promise no more complaints about the ship. The ship is beautiful, and you are an excellent cabin attendant."

"I wish for you to return, my friend Kat."

I hugged Uffe goodbye. He accepted it but was still stiff. I told the truth. Compared to all the vessels in the harbor and for her time-period, *Anne Kristine* was beautiful.

22 ~ Girl Talk

On our way back to the inn, we walked through town instead of along the waterfront. The streets were muddy from yesterday's rain, and the wooden sidewalks crowded, so we often walked single file.

Shops were open with sales clerks beckoning us to come inside, but we couldn't stop. I swore to Mikkel I'd stay at the hotel, and he might be looking for me. Visiting the ship to see him was one thing but not wandering around town.

Rosie and Albert walked close behind me while I tried to remember the way back to our inn.

"Stop, please. Doesn't afternoon tea sound lovely?" Rosie stood in front of a Victorian café.

The tea shop was charming like an old grandmother in a frilly flowered apron. We blocked the sidewalk, so we moved to a nearby alleyway.

"I really should get back first to tell the captain."

I could ask one of the young boys standing around to send a message. But what if they didn't go to the right hotel or find him? Plus, I had no money to pay them. A cell phone sure would come in handy.

"Are you not feeling peckish?" Rosie said.

"Peckish?" Albert repeated the strange word.

"Hungry. Tea ends in half an hour, so we must stop now. Furthermore, there is nothing to do at the inn."

"I don't want the captain to worry about me." This might jeopardize getting back on board.

"He is not your husband or your jailer. How could he object? Just what I need, another crotchety old man. We went to see him. He must not be that concerned."

"I know, but he doesn't know I'm here with you."

"I will tell the worried captain your safe whereabouts," Albert said. "Moreover, I prefer to relax at the inn before dinner."

"I wanted all three of us to have tea. We must stick together." Rosie reached for Albert's hand and groaned.

Albert must have sensed her anxiety. "A grand time awaits us on our voyage in many fascinating ports of call."

Rosie wiped away a stray tear. "The three of us must protect each other."

Albert nodded. "Precisely what Alexandre Dumas suggested in his novel. We should 'never fear quarrels but seek adventures.'"

"The Three Musketeers?" Who could forget the story of the feisty trio? "All for one, and one for all."

Rosie finished the quote. "United we stand. Divided we fall."

We placed our palms on top of each other's hands entering a grave pact. I liked my newfound friends and travel companions but were they trustworthy?

"A brief separation. I promise to inform the captain." Albert tilted his hat goodbye and walked off.

Rosie grabbed my hand, pleased. "We shall miss our dear Albert. But we shall force ourselves to make the best of it."

"Sure. But I don't have any money with me. Can I borrow some and pay you back later?"

"Of course, what else are friends for?"

Once seated, we ordered the last remaining plate of warm scones with traditional clotted cream and a pot of Earl Grey tea to share.

Afternoon tea was a must every time I visited England. If we were wearing jeans, I could be back in 2016 in an old-world tea shop.

After one bite Rosie stretched back and closed her eyes. "Thank goodness for Anna Maria, the Duchess of Bedford."

"Who?" I muttered while chewing on a scone.

"The woman who originated this glorious tradition. She had a healthy appetite like me. Her doctor suggested it after some fainting spells. A dear friend of the Queen, but she passed on five years ago." Rosie wiped some ginger jam off her fingers. "So many things you Yanks do not know."

I regretted not knowing more about the history of the 1860s. To stay more informed, I would study the newspapers as if assigned to a secret research project.

Rosie liked to chat and kept the conversation going. "Today there are too many single women and not enough marriageable men. And now in America, you shall face the same problem. Many of your men are at war and will die."

"Yeah, I guess so." It was so strange knowing the Civil War raged, and I couldn't do anything about it.

"Have you read, *Why Are Women Redundant*?"

"No, the title sounds dumb."

"The essay received extensive publicity. The author, W.R. Greg, said, 'Single women are living an independent but incomplete existence.'"

"How wonderful. I suppose W.R. is a man?"

"Yes. Mr. Greg was critical of men who refused to settle down and marry. As a governess, I shall remain independent and support myself."

"I work too. In Finance in New York. Best not to depend on anyone."

"Many of the women from the finer families in England are unable to marry well. They cannot maintain their way of life without their usual luxuries: maids, servants, fine crystal, lace, and so on."

"We will be fine without that stuff."

"Yes, we will. But many married women and widows I know miss those days."

"Not me. I prefer being independent. People often let you down. I'm never getting married."

"Never?"

"Nope. Been there, done that."

"Been where?" Her eyes were large and intense.

"An old saying. Means I'm not interested."

I could tell she wanted to know more. "My husband died of cancer over a year ago. I went through all the official stages of grief - denial, anger, bargaining, depression, and acceptance."

"In time, you shall reconsider and remarry."

I shook my head. "Last week I found out he had planned to leave me. If he hadn't had incurable cancer, I would be divorced. And, right before I left home, I had some miserable dates."

"Poor girl." Rosie patted my hand.

"Oh, I'm fine. Every day it gets easier. Now I don't miss him so much." She didn't look like she believed me. "I'm not anti-men. My goal is to be more like them. To not commit to anyone and date around."

This concept must be too modern and avant-garde for Rosie. Even for me, but I must adapt and learn from my mistakes.

Rosie poured me another cup of Earl Grey. "Any children?"

"No. Didn't really try. A long story."

"I want children very much."

"You are so young. I am sure it will work out."

Rosie picked up the teapot to refill her cup. "A most civilized tradition. One I shall miss in Hong Kong."

"Hong Kong also has this tradition."

"Do you think so?"

"Oh, yes. Most definitely." I knew they did. I had been to Hong Kong and had afternoon tea at a British-style hotel there. But I stopped. Don't lie, but don't elaborate to avoid unnecessary questions.

"Well, it shall be a long journey. I am so glad we can travel together."

Having friends around like Rosie and Albert will make all the difference.

She said, "Have you been to Bath?"

"The spa town?"

"Yes, Jane Austen lived there. One of my regrets. I never visited Bath."

"It is on my travel wish list. Perhaps you can visit when you return."

"Return? It's not likely I will ever ..." Rosie looked out in space and drifted off.

"Never?"

"It is a long and expensive journey. I might return one day. If I marry and my husband chooses to do so. But I expect neither."

"Any man would be lucky to have you."

She smiled and pulled out a small leather case with a photo and passed it to me. "My parents." Rosie's eyes teared up, and she gazed down at her purse.

The older woman had dark hair parted in the middle and pulled behind her head resembling Rosie. Her father had a full beard, broad nose, and dark eyes. Both looked stern and unfriendly.

"Your photo looks old."

"Oh no, taken a few months ago. An ambrotype image and keepsake. I may never see them again." She sniffled.

I might never see mine again either, but I refused to cry before it was definite. "I am sure things will work out. You will see them again eventually."

"Yes, perhaps." She wiped her eyes with a handkerchief and forced a smile. "Enough with the tears. Do you have one of your family?"

My smartphone inside my stored luggage in Copenhagen had hundreds of photos. "No, I left them in Denmark, but I regret it. My parents live in Texas where I grew up, and my only sibling, a brother, is dead."

"Texas? Fascinating, you must tell me all about it."

I wanted to stick with the truth but realized my mistake. How likely would I live on the East Coast while my parents lived in Texas? "Sure, on the ship, I'll tell you more."

"I accepted this teaching position because of some difficulties in my prior position."

She leaned towards me so only I would hear her confession. I'd had my share of challenges working on Wall Street in New York City. We could compare horror stories.

"I do not believe in flogging students. Children are physically and often brutally reprimanded. None are spared."

"What happened?"

"I refused to pick up the ferule. The supposed cornerstone of a sound education."

"Ferule?"

"A flat ruler with a widened end or a cowhide whip. Take your pick. I refused both."

"How cruel."

"The school could not discipline my refusal per se. They made my life unbearable with snide comments and looks. I could bear it no longer. I marched to the deacon's office and resigned. So here I am. Sallying off to be a governess in the untamed Far East."

"Wow. Quite a story. I am proud of you. You didn't back down despite everything."

Rosie fidgeted with her hands.

"Do you know your new employer?" I took airplanes and

instant travel for granted. She was brave to leave her country and everything she knew behind.

"I knew his wife in school for many years but never met her husband nor the children. They settled there, and teachers are in demand. He is a bank manager and wants a proper English woman to raise his children. I shall do my utmost to comply."

"A bank? Which one?"

"The British Orient Bank."

I sunk down in my chair at a loss for words. That bank, nicknamed BOB, took the honor of being my last employer before I ventured out on my own with an internal audit consulting business. BOB was the start of so much trouble.

I had stumbled upon old notebooks while cleaning out the audit department's file room. Some coded journals referred to an account dating back to the 1850s and the despicable opium business. The account was actively used to launder drug money and miscoded, so none of these transactions were subject to surveillance.

The investigation got so risky the FBI and CIA were involved. We faced death threats. Right before I left home, friends cautioned me against stepping foot in Hong Kong again. I had planned to either disembark at an earlier port or stay in the airport before catching my flight home to avoid it. Now all bets were off.

Rosie interrupted my awful trip down opium memory lane. "Perhaps they can loan you some money? If you need it when we arrive."

Money didn't bother me but arriving in Hong Kong in 1862 during the rebellious opium days did. But first, I had to get there. "Yeah, maybe."

They owed me big time, but I'd never collect, and that would be the last place I'd go to borrow or exchange money. That bank and their money laundering drug customers placed a curse of death on so many innocent people.

Rosie changed the subject, and we chatted about the same topics I talked with my girlfriends about in New York. Happier subjects like fashion, food, and books. Rosie was lively and spirited and the ideal travel girlfriend. If I had been born in the nineteenth century, perhaps I would be more like her.

She paid the bill while I promised to reimburse her for everything after I spoke with the captain.

"Nonsense. Not only is that man your keeper, but he is also your banker. And not a generous one at that. I trust he has some redeeming qualities."

"He isn't so bad. Domineering and protective since he's burdened with so much responsibility. He has this 'I'm in control' charm. Somehow, it's hard to dislike him. Plus, he is terribly attractive."

"Being pleasing to look at does not hurt. But I prefer agreeable qualities that last such as sense, taste, manners, and position."

She winked and took my arm as we left the shop. "I never married but have read so much about married life and men. Women are much smarter. We can compare notes on our journey."

My ideas and track-record hadn't worked out so well. Could nineteenth century female wisdom do the trick?

23 ~ *Kicking Back*

On our walk back to the inn, Rosie and I passed an art gallery with impressive paintings in the window. We stopped to admire them.

I was dying to go inside. "Can we check this shop out for a minute?"

Rosie, always ready for an adventure, agreed. The two rooms overflowed with art. Paintings hid the walls with many crammed against each other on the floor.

I crouched down to look at some up close. This can't be. A painting by Édouard Manet casually placed on the floor? French impressionist's paintings are in the best museums and owned by billionaires. I stood so close I could touch the frame.

One of my hobbies was guessing the right artist at museums before reading the sign. Having toured so many art museums, with impressionism my favorite, I was often right. This painting must be merely a well-made copy.

Another painting of a woman and a dog had an artist's signature that resembled G. Courbet. Was this Gustave Courbet? Impossible.

I glanced out the shop's front window. The sun would soon set, and we would be wandering around in the dark. We must leave soon to walk back to our inn.

A third painting called out for a closer look. A full-length portrait of a woman in white was signed by Whistler with the date 1861. I had seen similar ones at a museum, but these can't be authentic.

With regrets, we left the shop. The gallery closed for the day, and it was unlikely I would ever return. Not that it mattered. I had no money.

The urge to confide in someone overcame me, and Rosie was the only person available. "Those paintings were extraordinary. If you could afford to buy one, you will be very wealthy someday."

She laughed. "I agreed to pay for tea, but not to purchase your artwork. You require either a rich husband or an admirer."

"Or both." In all seriousness, I could ask Mikkel. The ship could use some art on the walls, but he wouldn't want them. They must be clever reproductions for local buyers. And if they were real, these delicate paintings might not survive a voyage to Hong Kong.

I stopped when I recognized the same kitschy outfit in a shop window. Signs were missing from half of the streets, and it was that shadowy, dim period before sunset.

"Rosie, are we walking in circles? I think we're lost." My sense of direction was terrible.

We went into a small grocery shop for directions to our inn. The man's accent was strong, but he knew our hotel. He created a small map on a sheet of paper and walked outside pointing directions. But his series of rights and lefts on streets and unmarked alleyways were impossible to follow.

Our busy and safe street turned into a quiet, dark lane with buildings hiding the setting sun. Behind us, some shabbily clothed men were watching us. Whenever we stopped to check the map under a streetlight, they slowed down.

"I don't want to scare you, but I think we're being followed. Hold your handbag close to your chest." I showed her how I carried mine. Not that I had anything valuable, but her purse had money and family remembrances.

We continued at a quicker pace and turned to our right. This road led to a dead-end and was an enormous mistake. Behind us, the men were closing in.

"Can you run if we need to?"

Rosie said she could.

We crossed to a small passageway and had to turn back, but the men did the same thing and faced us. They were young and lean, while we wore long dresses that made running difficult.

I hated to stop, but I didn't see a way out.

One of the men said, "Little ladies, can you help us out?"

"No, we can't. We don't have any extra money." I didn't mind helping the homeless but not under pressure.

I took Rosie's arm and crossed over to the middle of the small pathway to get past them.

We hurried to slip by to safety. I avoided eye contact to

discourage them. Even from a distance, they reeked, and their clothes were filthy.

"Let me rephrase that. You will help us out. Give me your handbags."

"No!" I let go of Rosie's arm. "Now Rosie." She hesitated, so I pushed her. "Run. I'll catch up."

The man cocked his head at my uncommon accent. The other man seized my left arm and tried to snatch my handbag, but I jerked it away.

From my years of kickboxing training, I swung my right arm and heard a cracking noise when my elbow hit the man's head. The other man reached for me, but I kicked as hard as I could and hit something, but I didn't stop to check. Without any hesitation, I ran after Rosie screaming for help.

Rosie talked to a man in a suit and pointed in my direction. As expected, the two men didn't bother following us when they saw Rosie with a respectable man.

"Thank God you are unhurt. The kindhearted Mr. Jones offered to escort us to our hotel."

We walked along with our friendly escort. This time even Rosie was quiet, but she answered his questions.

My heart raced after the confrontation. The sun had set, and footpaths off to the side were pitch-black. A few minutes later our inn appeared from around a corner. We thanked Mr. Jones and hurried up the front steps eager to get back to our safe zone.

Inside the front door, Mikkel sat in the lobby reading the paper, and I told Rosie to go ahead.

"Hello, I'm back."

Mikkel shook his head. His eyes flashed in anger.

I sunk down on the sofa next to him. "I stopped with my friend Rosie for tea. It's a tradition here. Didn't you get the message?"

"No. Kind of you to trouble yourself. Did you forget we agreed you would stay here? And your clothes are torn."

The man must have torn my sleeve when he clutched my arm. "Oh, it is. I can fix that." A minor problem after escaping from those two men.

Rosie collected her key from the front desk and stood nearby waiting to talk to me.

I wanted to introduce her to the captain. But Mikkel was fuming and ignored us both by reading the paper. Where was Albert, and why didn't he notify the captain?

"I owe Rosie some money for afternoon tea. Can I borrow a few pounds?"

Mikkel sighed, took out some coins, and handed me some to give her. "Is this sufficient?"

Rosie nodded and rolled her eyes. "Shall I see you at dinner, Kat?"

Mikkel said rudely, "No, we have other plans."

"See you tomorrow, Rosie." She said goodbye and disappeared upstairs to her room. I longed to follow her lead, but another lecture was imminent.

"The hotel staff suggested a suitable women's lodging for you here in Southampton. I found you a ship bound for New York in the springtime. The crossing is not so treacherous at that time, and they won't call in Bermuda. That's a dangerous island now with the war and secretive trade with the Confederate rebels."

"Mikkel, please. I must go with you to Hong Kong. I promise I won't complain or be any trouble."

"You said your uppermost desire was to return home. Hong Kong is the opposite direction. This is all for the best."

After the physical fight outside, I lacked the energy to argue.

"Whilst the refund will not allow for frequent new attire or fancy tea in cafés, the sum due shall be sufficient for you to live modestly."

I shook my head and struggled to come up with a sensible argument. I had to get back on his ship, not another one.

"Who are your new friends that you brought on the ship today?" His crew's update traveled fast.

"Rosie and Albert?"

"Yes, those two."

"Your new passengers for Hong Kong."

"On my ship? No, that cannot be. My passengers are two men, not a married couple."

"They aren't married. Rosie and Albert are friends. I met them at the hotel today."

"There must be some mistake. I will look at the documents and confirm with my agent." Mikkel was brusque and snippy.

"Please change for dinner. I reserved a private room here. We shall first meet in the salon."

I had to know how much time I had left to convince him. "When are we, I mean the ship, leaving?"

"Tomorrow, but that is not your concern. You are staying here. I shall arrange for your transfer to your new accommodations beforehand."

I trudged upstairs to my room full of disappointment. The men in the alley should have put me out of my misery. I didn't see a weapon, but they could have strangled me with their bare hands. All that trouble with only my almost empty purse and Rosie's handbag to show for it.

I regretted leaving the hotel. Mikkel might have forgiven me. I had less than twenty-four hours to convince him I'm sane and trustworthy. While I paced about inside my hotel room, I stared at the floor for an idea. However, I only found useless dust bunnies.

Besides the alley confrontation and argument with Mikkel, it was a fantastic afternoon. The best one so far. Albert and Rosie will help me. A surge of hope warmed me from the inside out. My two Musketeer friends won't let me down.

24 ~ Howdy Texas

In the formal salon, I joined Albert and Rosie.

"Did his mood improve?" Rosie said.

"No, he won't let me back on board, and you're leaving tomorrow."

"We shall hide you. The ship is certainly big enough. Right, Albert?"

Albert knew this was unwelcome news but forced a smile.

"Albert, did you give him the message about tea? He said he didn't get it."

"The hotel staff said he was out, but I left a note for him at the front desk. I shall go and inquire."

Rosie squeezed my hand. "Do not fret, Kat. He is an old cow. I will speak to him. And if space is an issue, you may share my cabin."

"Very kind of you to offer." But I frowned doubting her plan would work. Getting my ass kicked off at the first port would not be fun.

"You look pretty with my hairpins. You shall charm them all with your artistic style."

"Thanks, Rosie. I'm far from artistic or talented when it comes to fashion." Her elegant pins and hairstyle suggestions helped, but my goal was never to be a fashionista.

"Not artistic, my dear. I should say unconventional. So American - refreshing, bold, and enlightened."

My outfit was virtually the same as hers. Barring the odd clashing colors, I looked the same as everyone else. I wanted to blend in and had nothing else to wear. My hairstyle twisted into a bun resembled all the other women around town as part of my quest to fit in.

Rosie's outfit was a wild mix of plaid with mismatched colors. Last night other women wore similar dresses, so it must be in fashion now. I never kept up with trends or what was in style. My wardrobe included what I liked from the sale rack.

My preference for no-frill solid colors was not popular with other women. Tonight, I dressed up in a gold-colored silk evening gown with the aquamarine necklace and bracelet to match my ring.

"I should go talk to the captain, but I would rather stay here with you."

Mikkel and his First Mate Lars were speaking with a stout older blond-haired man. Could he be a new passenger taking my old cabin?

"We shall wait for Albert."

I nodded to delay the inevitable. "By the way, the captain insists he has two male passengers, not a woman and a man. But if you can wait to confront him, I'd appreciate it."

Rosie frowned at such stupidity. "I brought the documents to prove it. All paid for so that cannot be the tyrant's excuse."

Albert joined us again with a smile. "They said they delivered the message to Captain Madsen's room. I don't understand why he didn't receive it. Is he here?"

I nodded and pointed out Captain Mikkel. "The tall, thin one."

"I shall clear this up at once. Perhaps it will help your case."

Albert made a fast beeline to talk to him.

Rosie and I watched the four men get introduced and shake hands. Albert asked him something. The shorter blond man pulled a piece of paper from his pocket and gave it to Mikkel. Mikkel read the note, spoke to Albert, and clapped him on the back.

Albert waved for us to join them. Rosie led the way, and I trailed behind.

"My apologies, Kat. I have received the note you went for tea. Better late than never." He grinned, so I hoped that meant all was forgiven and forgotten.

Mikkel introduced us to his friend, Captain Matson, from Sweden. So that explained the mix-up. The odds were uncanny. Two captains, one Danish and one Swedish, with almost identical last names.

"Captain Matson will take you to New York City next April."

"Thank you, Captain Matson. Appreciate it, but I must be on the *Anne Kristine* bound for Hong Kong."

"My dear, you donned my colors. Blue and yellow for

Sweden." Captain Matson winked at Mikkel teasing him since the Danish colors were red and white. "Hong Kong is a long and dangerous journey for a young woman alone."

"I am making that exact journey, and it is not too perilous for me. And, I need a friend along." Rosie was indignant and spoke loudly to get their attention.

"You? Are you R.A. Styles?" Mikkel didn't sound thrilled with the possibility.

"Here in the flesh. Or did you expect Robert?" She laughed. "I am your passenger, Miss Rosamund Agatha Styles."

"My apologies, Mrs. Styles. I understood from my agent you were a man."

"As you can see, I am not. And it is Miss Styles."

"My apologies Miss Styles." From the captain's body language and tone whoever booked her on his ship was in hot water.

"You should know, Kat is perfectly adept at protecting herself. You should have seen her today."

"It was nothing much. Where are you from in Sweden, Captain Matson?" I was desperate to change the conversation.

Mikkel ignored me. "Please resume, Miss Styles,"

I motioned to Rosie to stop. But she didn't notice. Her eyes and body language were animated, and I feared she would tell him everything.

Rosie said, "Kat can explain better than I."

Mikkel glanced at me for a second and cleared his throat. "Miss Styles, please tell us your version of what happened today." His words were evenly measured and tense.

"Two ruffians tried to steal our handbags. Kat sensed they were following us and calmly instructed me as to what I should do."

"She did?" Mikkel moved closer to hear more details.

"Yes, I held my handbag here in front of me as she said and prepared to run."

"And did you?"

"Oh yes. The robbers threatened us. Kat flew into a rage. I ran to safety as she instructed, and she … well, I didn't see the conclusion."

"What did you do, Kat?" Captain Matson tongue flicked against his plump lips. "This is better than Dickens."

I frowned at Rosie and shook my head to indicate this was a huge mistake. She lifted her shoulders with a weak grin apologizing.

They kept waiting, so I said, "Not a big deal. Some men were following us and tried to steal our purses. I objected, and they stopped. Nothing much more to it."

Rosie said, "She's much too modest. Screamed and fought them like a Johnny Reb. She has this uncensored intrepid spirit. Not at all weak."

Albert and Rosie smiled, but Mikkel was upset. Millie's suggestion for me to fit in and disappear into the background had backfired. Our escape had turned into a major snafu, and the type of spectacle Mikkel hated.

I needed a drink and searched for a waiter. "I just convinced them not to bother us."

"How did you convince them?" Albert pursed his lips for the mystifying details.

What the hell? I was proud of my years of training and kickboxing skills. "I hit one in the head with my elbow and kicked the other."

"Afterward, Kat ran and joined me." Rosie expressive face made it more damaging. Dramatic storytelling must come easily with all her teaching experience. "In the meantime, I found a kind gentleman to escort us back to the hotel."

Despite their surprise and shock, I was proud of how we handled it.

"After all she has Texan genes. I feel safer already."

Mikkel rubbed his beard. "Texas? You said you were from New York City."

His views on the Civil War and slavery were clear, and I didn't want to be associated with the rebel south. "I am, but I grew up in Texas. My parents live there. But they aren't Confederates or slaveholders. They're liberals."

"So, you see Captain Mikkel, she is brave and an asset to have aboard." Rosie beamed as if she closed the Kat versus the Captain legal case, and her arguments won.

Mikkel didn't comment and looked upset. I got a nagging feeling she lost my case.

Captain Matson tapped my back. "Jolly well done."

Albert beamed impressed with our feat. "God watches over

drunks, fools, and children. We shall have to add bold women to the mix."

Others echoed similar comments. Even Lars, the first mate, but Mikkel touched his chest as if he had indigestion.

"I couldn't be prouder of my new best friend," Rosie said.

"But, you see, it is just as I feared." Mikkel looked at the others ignoring me. "She is wholly unsuitable for the voyage and will put us all at risk. I must decline her passage on my ship."

"You cannot do that. I am begging you." Rosie wailed with such emotion that it surprised and touched me.

"I can, and I will." Mikkel refused to bend.

"Albert, tell him." Rosie grabbed his arm as if he was a student that needed reminding.

"What?" Albert scratched his head trying to remember.

"About us. You know Dumas and the Musketeers." Rosie had switched tactics again.

"Very well. Captain Mikkel, we made a pact today. The three of us vowed to look after each other. Like the Three Musketeers."

"Makes no difference if you were appointed by Saint Elmo, the patron saint of mariners. With regret, my decision is final. Kathryn made it very clear. She shall not be compelled to board my second-rate floating amalgamation of wood."

I focused on the hotel's carpet embarrassed. I had insulted the ship on more than one occasion.

Mikkel turned away ignoring Rosie to respond to a hotel employee.

Rosie said to the rest of the group, "Seamen are known to be difficult. Marco Polo said, 'a man who sails the seas is disqualified from acting as a witness or guarantor.' We will make him see reason."

Lars knew him the best and snickered.

Mikkel made a face as if he had overheard Rosie's insults. "The other passenger, Niels Hviid, is not yet here. But dinner awaits. Shall we?"

Mikkel put his hand on my shoulder to guide us towards our private room. Before we left, he said to the Swedish captain, "Interested in joining us, Svend? Our mysterious passenger, believed to be a man, has not arrived. We possess an empty seat at the table."

"A kind offer but I am engaged this evening. Tomorrow, I shall see you at the Rushmeres."

The Swede's absence at dinner tonight was a plus. He presented another obstacle to re-boarding Mikkel's ship, and I didn't like the way he ogled my necklace and what happened to be right beneath it.

25 ~ Give Me Another Good Reason

The dining table was set for six with one empty seat. Captain Mikkel and First Officer Lars sat at either end with Rosie, Albert, and I sandwiched in between.

Mikkel said, "A few minutes ago, I was informed that we have experienced significant delays in the receipt of our cargo. But we shall depart promptly the day after tomorrow. With favorable winds, we should recover the lost time."

No one seemed to care, and the delay provided me with another bonus day to convince him. Empowered by my new friends, I was eager for our dinner party. I would be on my best behavior. This should get me back in the captain's good graces. But Captain Mikkel's silence and reserve made me uneasy.

Albert broke the silence. "How did the ship come to be named the *Anne Kristine*?"

Mikkel said, "The ship is named after my wife, Anne, and my mother, Kristine."

"Are they in Denmark?" Rosie asked.

"Yes, in the churchyard."

"Sorry to hear that, Captain Mikkel." Rosie frowned.

Albert tried again. "Kat, did you enjoy your visit to Southampton?"

I hesitated. He assumed this was my first visit. I wanted to say fabulous, and ignore the dying horse, the underage working kids, sad-looking hungry people, the night at the asylum, and all the other problems.

Mikkel said, "Kat has had a trying visit here so far. One she will likely not forget for some time."

Albert and Rosie murmured their concern. I avoided mentioning the sordid details about my stay in the asylum or trip to the hospital. I couldn't dredge up and discuss that when I was so powerless to do anything.

Mikkel rubbed his beard. "We came across a horse and wagon on High Street. The poor beast had reached the end of its natural life. The wagon's contents tossed about and spread along the street. The coachman tried to whip the dying horse back to work. Kat flung herself down on the animal as if to bring it back to life. She scolded the man in front of the crowd. I retrieved her from the scene before an insurgency."

What? Would the evil coachman have whipped me? He made me sound like a complete fool and exaggerated the situation. As if people were going to riot in the streets. They should, not for me, but for dying horse.

Rosie said, "Hear, hear. Someone should stand up for the weak."

I had one ally, and Albert grinned and winked. Mikkel's witty remark backfired.

The waiter served an aperitif, and the appetizer *parfait de foie gras*. I had seen this on menus in France but never ordered it since the geese were force fed to get a swollen liver. Reluctantly, I took a small bite.

"Captain Mikkel, please expound on why I can travel to Hong Kong and Kat may not." Rosie was anything but subtle.

He scrutinized her after finishing his *foie gras* and cleared his throat looking annoyed with her directness.

"It cannot be solely because she is a female," she said.

After a brief knock at the door, a hotel employee ushered in a dark-haired man with a flashy smile and intense eyes.

"My sincere apologies for being late, but it appears you have only just begun." Niels Hviid circled the table and insisted we stay seated while he made introductions and shook hands with each of us. He introduced himself as Niels Hviid to the captain and Lars, but as Niels White to the rest of us.

"Is your name Hviid or White?" I asked.

"Hviid. I use White here in England. Explaining a silent H and a double I which sounds like an E is nothing but trouble. And, conveniently, Hviid means white in English. If only I had a common name like Hansen or Jensen."

"My last name is Jensen. Want to trade?" I had contemplated erasing the memory of my husband and changing my name back to Carlson, my maiden name. After twenty years of Jensen, all the explanations and legal documents didn't seem worth it. I frowned remembering my quandary.

Niels laughed. "My apologies, Madam Hviid. You are

anything but common." He eyed me again as if trying to read my mind.

"Mr. White, you arrived in the nick of time." Rosie lifted her aperitif and made a toast, "To women."

"To wives and sweethearts," Niels said. Under his breath, he added, "Who cares if they ever meet?"

Encouraged by Rosie, everyone lifted their glasses and sipped.

Rosie put down her glass eager to continue. "Captain Mikkel, I must hear all reasons. Three, you said."

"Three reasons in regard to what?" Niels raised his eyebrows.

"Why poor Kat is not allowed back aboard." Rosie shook her head as if this made no sense at all.

"As your captain with responsibility, not just for the journey but the crew and everyone aboard, I maintain my reasons."

"Which are?" Rosie pressed on refusing to give up.

Mikkel rubbed his chin and paused deep in thought. "I do not believe Kat would appreciate having these reasons discussed openly."

Did he plan to tell them about the insane asylum? If he did, Rosie and Albert would want nothing more to do with me.

I downed my aperitif for courage. "I don't mind. Go ahead." I had to know what mistakes were so inexcusable. Rosie or Albert might change his mind.

Mikkel told the waiter to serve the next course. "Very well. Kathryn disregarded my instructions on no less than two occasions and did not adapt to life at sea as required."

"Please provide the details," Rosie said. If I ever had to be on trial, I would want Rosie to represent me. She was relentless.

"Kathryn was under my strict instructions to the contrary but left her cabin during a severe storm. She was in grave danger and was nearly washed overboard."

He had stopped calling me Kat, my nickname. This didn't bode well.

"I felt ill. The thunderstorm stopped, and the sea was peaceful. I thought it had ended and went outside for a breath of fresh air."

"Very understandable," Rosie said. "What else?"

"May we recommence this conversation after dinner?"

"I see no reason to delay." She insisted like a no-nonsense school teacher.

The next course was a bland vegetable soup. I sensed the tension grow between Mikkel and Rosie, but she pressed on with her questioning.

"Today, Kat left the hotel whilst under my direct instructions to stay. She swore to stay." He tapped his fingers on the table for emphasis.

"I met Rosie and Albert here. Since they are your passengers, I took them to tour the ship on such a pretty day. I planned to meet you there. On the way back, Rosie and I stopped for afternoon tea, but Albert promised to tell you."

"I talked her into it, so that is all my fault. Am I also barred from boarding the ship?" Rosie emphasized by resting her hands on the table.

Even Albert offered, "Also my fault. Kat wanted to come back. She was concerned. But I assured her I would tell you that she was with Rosie, and all was well."

Mikkel shook his head. "You don't understand. Kat has been ill. She hit her head in the gale."

"Please stop with that. I am one hundred percent fine." I wanted to jump around and yell to prove it but remained seated.

"I am a physician and a trained surgeon if that is of any benefit." Niels sat next to me and touched my arm.

I stiffened remembering Dr. Johnson and Dr. Fitzpatrick. Instinctively, I leaned from Niels closer to Mikkel.

"What about the third reason?" Another point for Rosie. She was keeping track.

"The third?" Mikkel thought for a moment. He could mention my confusion over 1862, and the night I spent in the loony bin. Or when I pressed him to tell me his real date of birth. If he did, they would all agree. I should stay behind and go home.

"She did not attend our church service. On the Sabbath, she stayed in her cabin."

"What? When?" Now wasn't the time to mention I was agnostic and rarely attended church.

"The day before we docked in Southampton."

With nothing much to do on board, I never got up early so I would have slept through it. "I didn't know it was Sunday, and no one invited me."

Niels cleared his throat. "If church-going is an issue, I shouldn't be permitted to board. Attending church is a complete waste of time. In my most humble opinion."

"You see, Captain Mikkel. All your arguments were countered with rational explanations."

"I am responsible and must do what I believe is best for everyone involved. For Kathryn's sake, she must return to her home in America."

"Captain Mikkel, isn't your ship *Anne Kristine,* a woman? In need of female companionship?"

Mikkel shook his head. "Kat dislikes the ship." He turned to me. "Didn't you tell Simon she resembled a floating dump and a mouse trap not worthy of a cat?"

I couldn't help but grimace. Other complaints were worse but said in the privacy of my cabin.

He continued his rant. "Kathryn called her a subpar wooden crate. I wish to spare her the trial of living 'in an uncivilized manner,' as she described it."

"After the storm, I got depressed, and I was lonely without any other passengers. I didn't mean it. The *Anne Kristine* is a beautiful ship."

"Regardless. It is unsafe for Kathryn." Mikkel's tally of reasons continued, and I had lost count.

"For some reason, it is safe for me, but not for Kat?" Rosie probed deeper as if opening a wound.

"It is a miracle we didn't lose her overboard."

"The ship, the *Anne Kristine*, watched over her. Another significant reason to permit her to return."

Mikkel glared back at her but stayed silent.

"If you don't allow Kat to re-board, mark my words, you shall face the wrath of *Anne Kristine*."

"Now, hear this Rosamund Styles. You may not speak in that manner. *Anne Kristine* is mine. I know her better than anyone."

"Well, I refuse to board without Kat. It is too risky for me. Albert? Niels? Is it worth the risk to you?"

Albert hesitated, but Rosie would never forgive him if he

didn't try. "With all due respect, Captain Mikkel, I do wish Kat could join us. I must agree with Rosamund."

Rosie glared at Niels waiting for his support, while he sipped his wine.

"I am not superstitious. You may never meet a more thorough disbeliever in the cosmos." Niels waved his hand in the air as if to threaten whatever spirits might be lingering nearby. "I may be swayed by other reasons. But not because a ship has human emotions and controls our destiny. It, or if you prefer, she, is simply a floating vessel, nothing more."

Mikkel rolled his eyes. "Will I never hear the end of this? There are sailor superstitions, and I must consider my crew. All my men have had a hard lot in life, and their well-being is important to me."

"Thanks, Rosie. His mind is made up." I appreciated her efforts, but his mood was hostile, and I wanted her to stop.

Rosie clearly wasn't a quitter. "It is simple mathematics. Two negatives multiplied equal a positive. Ergo, two women together on a ship are positive." If she had a chalkboard, I could imagine her illustrating a complicated mathematical formula to support this position.

"One negative plus another negative is a bigger negative," Albert, the engineer, said.

"This is not elementary addition, Albert." Rosie's voice bubbled with rage and frustration.

The conversation around the dinner table became subdued. The mood remained so tense even a sharp knife couldn't cut it.

Mikkel stood and winced as if in pain. "If you will excuse me." At the door, he said, "I will rejoin our dinner soon. If this is still a topic of discussion, I shall be obliged to reconsider the entire passenger list."

26 ~ Money Makes the World Go Round

With Mikkel absent and the arguments over, the mood around the table slowly lightened. Rosie reached over patting my hand to comfort me.

To change the subject, I made light conversation with Niels while Rosie and Albert chatted. Niels complimented my evening gown and refilled my wine glass. He flirted, and I enjoyed the unusual dark-haired Dane's attention, a welcome distraction from my dilemma.

When our main course arrived, Mikkel returned. A typical English meal was on the menu: roast beef with Yorkshire pudding, potatoes, and green peas. The meat was overcooked, but the horseradish sauce helped.

I focused on eating my piece of beef. I wanted to believe they treated and slaughtered the poor cow humanely, but this was doubtful with so many hungry people. I should become a vegetarian, but I had already lost weight. Edible salads and vegetables were rare.

We ignored Mikkel and Lars, the inflexible tyrants, seated at each end of the table. Mikkel focused on his meal and ate without speaking. He looked exhausted from arguing and perhaps from speaking in English so much.

"Why are you going to Hong Kong?" I asked Niels.

"I am a surgeon and trained in Paris with the very best. They are in great demand in the Orient, and it is quite lucrative."

"Are you French?"

"No. I am a Dane, but I lived in Germany and France for many years. I adore variation." He sipped his wine and appraised me. "Why does an American woman fancy a voyage to Hong Kong alone?"

I shifted in my seat uncomfortable with lying. "My uncle is there, and I wanted an adventure."

"I sympathize with your predicament. We may yet be able to convince the captain. Your girlfriend rammed him into a corner, so he fought back." Niels motioned with his wine glass at Rosie.

Niels pressed near with his face close enough to touch mine. I could feel his warm breath on my neck. "We have some time to convince him. If we put our heads together."

Mikkel tapped me on my shoulder to get my attention. "If you still desire, I will take you on my next voyage to Hong Kong. But you must recover your health first." He spoke so low no one else could hear his sympathetic offer.

"Thank you. How wonderful. When?"

"Next year. August or September. Do not tell the others. I cannot be hounded any further."

My heart sunk. I couldn't wait here a year. What would I do in England without money or a job? What would happen when the ship reached Hong Kong without me? Max and the travel agency might give up, and I would never get back home.

Dessert was a platter of chocolates with coffee, port wine, and brandy. I had lost my appetite and declined the liquor. I wanted to be alone and think about how I would survive and make a living here in 1862. Rosie might help me find a temporary teaching position.

My gut ached from the constant stress. I had contemplated dropping to my knees to beg him. My pride and upbringing in San Antonio, the site of the famous no-surrender Alamo, stopped me. "Good night everyone. Please enjoy the dessert. It's been a long and difficult day."

I made brief eye contact with Mikkel. "I promise to stay here." Where else could I go? This had to be one of my lowest moments with no money or hope.

Rosie appeared heartbroken mirroring my feelings. But I wanted to escape and burrow under the safety of my bed's comforter. "Don't worry. I'll manage." I forced a weak smile, more of a grimace. "I will figure things out."

"Kat, please wait. We –" A loud knock interrupted Rosie.

A breathless man wearing a suit explained he was a courier from London. "An urgent delivery direct from London."

Mikkel reached for it, but the man said, "Pardon me, sir. I must personally hand deliver this to Kathryn Jensen."

"That's me. I am Kathryn Jensen." I signed for it, thanked the man, and took the pouch. I hesitated for a second before ripping it open. I made a wish this didn't unleash Pandora from her box. Although what could be worse than right now?

Easy. A school teacher trapped in 1862.

Two envelopes were stuck inside the pouch. One envelope had my name on it, and the other was for Captain Mikkel Kløve Madsen.

I passed him his envelope and considered leaving to read my letter in private. Everyone watched eager to know what was inside, and I couldn't wait either.

I ripped open the envelope and stood under a wall sconce to read the typed message.

> *Dearest Kathryn,*
>
> *I was dismayed to hear your voyage does not meet your expectations. I must urge you to continue to Hong Kong. I am notifying the captain of the same. The unfortunate circumstances regarding 1862 and 2016 will unravel. I shall try to send you messages from time to time. The office insisted I tell you we are all rooting for you. Just don't put down a tree root.*
> *Your Uncle MAX*
>
> *P.S. As a token of our sincere apologies, we transferred £10,000 funds, a full refund, to a bank in Southampton.*
>
> *P.P.S. Your wallet and passport are safe and will await your arrival in Hong Kong.*

After reading the letter twice, I turned my back to the group and stuffed it into my bodice for safekeeping. I didn't bring a handbag, and my dress lacked pockets. I couldn't let the others read it and ask questions about 2016 that I couldn't answer.

I grinned at Rosie while the captain read his letter. I ached to jump and scream for joy but contained myself. He didn't like being backed into a corner, and Uncle Max did that.

These funds reimbursed me for the entire cost of the trip, but the cost no longer mattered. I just wanted to get back on the ship and home. Despite whatever happened, at least I had some money to manage through this mess.

Mikkel folded the letter with care and thrust it inside his jacket. "Your uncle made a convincing argument. Against my better judgment, you may board my ship and disembark at another scheduled port. Or if you wish, the final port of call."

"Oh, thank you, Captain Mikkel. I promise I won't be a burden. You won't regret it." I strode over to his chair and delivered an awkward embrace touching his shoulders.

Captain Mikkel said a polite goodnight to everyone. "Kathryn, in the morning I shall take you to the local bank as your uncle requested." He stood slowly as if lifting a heavyweight. His train accident injuries must be worse than he admitted.

After Mikkel and Lars left, Rosie jumped up and hugged me squealing with joy at the turnaround. "What did your uncle say? I cannot wait to meet him."

"I don't know exactly. My uncle arranged my trip and must have reminded the captain. He sent me some spending money."

"Your uncle has considerable influence." Albert stood and clasped my hand smiling at the turnaround, and I hugged him.

"You sure know how to argue, Rosie. I am so glad I met you today. And you, Albert. Thank you."

Niels walked between us. "What about me?"

I was on top of the world after being allowed back on board. Even better, I had spending money. With some reservations, I embraced Niels. He held me tightly. On auto-pilot, I stood back in surprise while he ruffled his hair and smirked.

The waiter showed up and looked confused.

Albert said, "A bottle of your best champagne. Laurent-Perrier, if available. We deserve it." He turned back to us. "Such a stressful dinner! I trust this shall not be a regular style of dinner conversation. My poor digestion could not bear it."

Rosie jabbed him in his middle. "I was certain these complications would vanish. This was the right decision from the start. The captain refused to show any weakness, but wisely switched sails."

"Rosie, tomorrow I will have some money again. My own money. We need to do some shopping. Travel preparations."

"My pleasure. I brought my sewing machine, and we can obtain some trim for your dresses."

"Trim?"

"Lace and ribbons. I can decorate your plain dresses."

Not what I had in mind, remembering the ugly brown ribbons in the trash can. "What about a piano for the ship?"

"Kat, you are too extravagant."

"No promises. Only if I can afford it."

Money gave me control and more choices. I savored the taste of cash and what it could buy while ignoring the desserts on the table.

I bit my lip worried about the hours until we were at sea imagining setbacks. Would Max's strange letter cause problems? The paper dug into my skin reminding me. I could toss it into the corner fireplace with a log burning.

Before I decided what to do with Max's message, a hotel employee burst in with a well-dressed woman behind him.

She headed straight to Niels and confronted him in a mixture of French and broken English. The only French I understood was *diable* or devil. Whatever had happened, she was furious with Niels.

Niels took the woman by the arm escorting her out the door. Before leaving, he turned back to say goodnight.

"My sincere apologies but, as always, there exists another urgent medical issue. I shall join you in a toast later, Kat. *Au revoir*."

Albert laughed. "Damn. This dinner was unusual compared to back home in Prague."

"Usual good or bad?" I asked.

"Bad in the beginning, but excellent now."

Rosie and I laughed. The waiter reappeared with our well-deserved bottle of champagne, filled our glasses, and we made a toast.

"To Kat." Rosie grinned.

"And the *Anne Kristine*," Albert said.

"To the four of us, including our ship. I am so lucky to have you two."

27 ~ *Roguish Sherry*

After dinner, I flung myself across my bed and pulled out my letter from Max. I read it three times committing it to memory, but I didn't want to destroy it. This letter proved I was sane and heading home.

Someone knocked on my door. I stuffed the letter back into its hiding spot and felt my heart pound through the paper.

While I stretched my aching back, I answered the door hoping for a more personalized apology from Mikkel. Maybe his mood had improved, and we could pick up from the night before.

"Oh, it's you."

Niels rested against the doorframe with a bottle of sherry and two glasses in his hands.

"Yes, me. Were you expecting someone else? Saint Nicholas perhaps or the obstinate Captain Mikkel?

"Of course not, but it's really late."

"Still early." He glanced at his pocket watch. "Kat, dear. I hold in my hands an outstanding bottle of French sherry. Imported by my very own person. A shame not to share what is left with you. After all, I was cheated out of the champagne celebration."

I hesitated and blocked the door with my foot.

"I was under the impression you sought friendship with all the passengers. My mistake." He stood in the doorway but prepared to leave.

"Oh, all right. One quick drink." The French sherry did look like a perfect ending to a stressful day.

Niels sat down on the overstuffed Victorian sofa, the size of a loveseat, and patted a spot next to him.

After I squeezed in with my full skirt, he opened the sherry and filled our glasses.

"A superb bottle of France's best. You will never know the lengths I took to procure this brand and transport it here. But sharing the remainder with you is worth the vexation."

This must be the best sherry in the world. I let the liquid sit on my tongue to taste what must be otherworldly. He had exaggerated. Nothing tasted that unusual or special to go through all that hassle.

I was curious about his mysterious visitor. "What happened with that woman?"

"Oh, nothing, a minor misunderstanding. An irritation I'm now rid of, and another worthy reason to go to sea. Enjoy another sip of my fine sherry."

Niels refilled our glasses to the rim, and I tried not to spill it.

"I must confess. I smuggled it here. Something alluring about the forbidden. The taste is better. Do you not agree?"

"No, not really." Breaking the law made me nervous, especially now.

Niels got up to put the bottle on the table next to my money. He sat down again, and with all the extra material, sat on my skirt. He must have noticed, but he didn't apologize or move. Even without the hoop, my skirt spilled out around me, but I didn't want to push him away. He fascinated me like an exotic animal.

"Another blessing, I shall be accompanied not just by one attractive woman, but a second young governess." He clinked his glass against mine. "Perhaps she shall provide private lessons aboard."

"Lessons from Rosie? You are devilish."

I struggled to stand, but I couldn't with him sitting on my dress. With my free hand, I nudged him away, but he refused to budge.

"Take your expensive contraband and go visit her. She is one floor up."

Besides, I shouldn't get involved with anyone. Things were too complicated. Niels oozed charm like Matteo, the Italian doctor I dated in New York City.

"Ah, just a joke. Do you not favor old Niels? Let us toast our upcoming journey."

We clinked our glasses and sipped. The French liquor had a smooth finish and coated my throat. But tonight, I'd had more than enough with the aperitif, wine, champagne, and now sherry.

"What would you toast to Kat?"

A second later, I blurted out. "Returning home in one piece."

"Interesting. Do you mean to return as just one person and not as two? Without a husband or child?"

While charming, Niels was overly attentive. His nails were perfect as if manicured, and his hands were soft and clean. His skin smelled masculine and musky.

"Something like that." I wasn't about to get into my life story or plans.

His teeth were so white they reminded me of TV commercials for whitening treatments. Most people had stained and dingy teeth here if they still had them.

"How are your teeth so white?"

"Kissing beautiful woman helps. And avoiding tobacco."

He eyed my chest. A tiny corner of my letter was visible from my bodice.

"What happened to your arm?" He gently fingered the swollen bruised area.

"I was bled."

"Bleeding is bad business for your health. Refuse it at all costs. Notwithstanding what everyone thinks, nothing beneficial ever comes of it." He examined my injuries and kissed the worst slowly moving up my arms.

"I know, but there was no choice in the matter." I didn't want to go into more details or remember it. "What would you toast?"

"Hmm. What shall it be?" He slid closer to me. I could smell his cologne while he kissed my neck. "To find my second piece."

I couldn't move and didn't want to. I enjoyed being at the center of his attention.

Our eyes met, and he kissed me, first softly, and harder as if I was his lifeline to some other world.

"Stop. I can't breathe."

"I shall breathe for you." He continued his kisses, but they were fast and light pecks while he moved down my neck to my chest.

His wavy dark hair was irresistible, and I laced my fingers through it. He had an angry red mark on his neck, and when I touched it, he jerked away. "Did that hurt?"

"No. You caught me unaware. Minor accident." He resumed kissing me and rearranged my dress. "I shall be fine in another day or so."

I settled back into the plump sofa enjoying his attention.

Outside some metal cans crashed and glass shattered. A dog barked causing a chain reaction among the other canines which turned into a yelping chorus. Foreign sounding men swore and hollered at the noisy dogs.

Niels stopped kissing me and cocked his head. He hurried over to the window and opened it to listen. He put his fingers to his lips motioning I shouldn't speak.

After less than a minute, he shut the window. "Sorry to share unwelcome news, Kat dear. The time has come for me to leave. Nevertheless, we shall have many more evenings together. Tomorrow, the next day, and the next, etcetera."

"What happened outside? Are they coming to arrest you?"

His eyes widened in surprise. "A little *commediene*?" He laughed tapping my nose. "*Non, non, mon chéri.*"

"You should leave." I didn't like his smug attitude.

"Pleasant dreams, dear Kat." He licked his lips and narrowed his eyes.

I stood up to push him out the door. If he planned to be my gigolo at sea, he would be deeply disappointed.

"You do not mind if I borrow a few bills, do you? With all the money from your rich uncle, you shall not miss this. And, I will repay you. You shall be more than satisfied, my dear."

Before I could answer, he scooped up some of my British pound notes and stuffed them into his pocket.

A smile crossed my lips since he would soon find out they were worthless. Whoever he offered them to would toss him on his ass into a dirty street for using counterfeit bills.

I opened the door ready to kick him out. He stunned me by kissing me and reached into my bodice snatching my letter.

Bumping against him, I tried to steal it back, but Niels held it out of my reach. "Niels, I'll scream, and you will be forced to give it back."

I lunged for it again and shouted as loud as I could. "No!"

Niels put his hand over my mouth, so I bit his finger. He cried out in pain but didn't remove his hand, shifted his position, and held me so tight I could barely breathe. He wasn't much taller than me but powerful and pure muscle. "My dear, do you want everyone to know we are here together and alone? The captain may change his mind yet again and forbid you on his ship."

I nodded I understood. Niels withdrew his hand to inspect it.

"I am astonished you did not break the skin. I merely want to stay informed. This is a long voyage, and I do not relish so many secrets. I shall return your precious letter tomorrow."

He took his hat and slammed the door on his way out.

I wanted to run after him, but my hair hung loose, and my chemise was partially unbuttoned. If someone saw me in the hallway that would be scandalous.

So, I stayed in my room and locked the door without my valuable letter and fifteen British pounds poorer. After seeing what prices were in the shops today, I estimated fifteen pounds was worth about five-hundred dollars.

I shuddered at the memory of my twenty-four hours in the looney bin, remembering Millie, Maxi, and all the other women stuck there. Be careful. Trust absolutely no one.

Niels left behind his empty bottle of sherry. I complained to the bottle, "Damn it. Why didn't I destroy the letter?"

I poured the last few drops into my glass and swallowed it. Just as well, I don't need any more liquor. Tomorrow will be hectic.

I rubbed my bare feet on the worn rug, slowly undressed, and critiqued the room. It might get a two-star rating compared to the no-star rating for my box on the ship.

A painting of a bucolic English village scene was on the wall. In real life from recent experience, the village would be smelly and dirty, and the poverty would be overwhelming.

I slipped on a silk nightgown, brushed my teeth, and splashed water on my face. If only the ship were more like this with carpets and artwork. As I dried my face, the idea hit me. Why can't the cabin be more like this room? With money, I could renovate it like the shows on TV. At the end of the voyage, it would be a goodbye gift.

I found a notepad and began a shopping list. I had to be quick with just one day left. With money, I could rescue Millie and help the other women.

I lay in bed trying to sleep and forget about the letter. I focused on the retail therapy ahead, and all the useful things I could get during a shopping spree. Department stores didn't exist making my plan more challenging. I estimated a minimum of ten different shops to visit.

Rosie will help me. With real money to spend, I could make the journey more enjoyable for both of us. I was ecstatic. Even that thief Niels couldn't get me down.

Whoever said that money couldn't buy happiness was wrong and hadn't spent the night in a madhouse. I was beyond happy at the power it would yield.

My plans wouldn't let me drift off to sleep. Too energized, I abandoned the battle and turned on the light again to add more items to my to-do list.

A sentence from a favorite children's story came to mind. "Oh, the places you'll go."

You could say that again. But I must be more careful. One night in a madhouse was plenty. Don't trust anyone unless their name happens to be Millie or Rosie.

28 ~ *In Pounds We Trust*

Despite waking up exhausted, I dressed quickly to claim my cash courtesy of Max before it disappeared. Ten thousand pounds meant the world to me. And in 1862, it would be worth so much more.

I went to the breakfast room for coffee and Mikkel, but I only recognized Niels.

"Where is my letter? Give it back. Now."

"Good morning, my dear. Can a starving man not consume his breakfast without being put upon?"

"No, I want it now." I stood next to him and smacked his shoulder.

"Ow. That hurt. In the appropriate time." He drank some coffee and tapped the chair next to him for me to sit, but I remained standing.

"If you were a gentleman, you wouldn't have stolen it."

"What is it worth to you?"

"Worth? Is this blackmail?" I checked around for someone to help me. "You are exactly what that woman said last night."

Niels shrugged his shoulders as if innocent and played dumb.

"She called you a devil. Now you devil, give me back my letter."

"Circumstances have changed, my dear. Your well-to-do uncle distributed quite a sum. How much is his letter worth? A few hundred pounds seems fair."

He snapped his fingers for emphasis, and the waiter reappeared at his elbow nervous he had done something wrong, but Niels waved him away. "Consider it a loan. I will pay you back. I know what you like."

"I'm not giving or loaning you anything. You already stole fifteen pounds."

I punched him harder and nudged his arm. His coffee spilled on his plate, and the thick brown liquid seeped into his toast ruining it. Served him right.

Niels seized my wrists holding me captive. Other diners in

the room watched us.

"Just a minor spat, folks."

I froze in surprise. My former boyfriend, Charlie, had used those precise words when we fought at the airport. But Charlie was wealthy and would never be this rude. He was the one who gave me his leftover cash from a recent trip to London.

"Let me go. I just want my letter."

From behind me, a man's gruff voice said, "Release her, this instant."

Niels let me go. "All her fault. She initiated this."

I rubbed my aching wrists and turned to thank my rescuer, but Mikkel glared at both of us.

"Captain Mikkel, he stole my letter from my uncle. He refuses to give it back to me."

"Niels, do you possess her letter?"

"For safekeeping. It is in my room." Niels flagged a waitperson to bring him another cup of coffee.

"Go and retrieve it. At once." Mikkel was back in his element barking out commands, and luckily, this one was for my benefit.

Niels acted annoyed but didn't argue. The captain could bar him from boarding as well. Niels left griping about me acting like a crazy woman.

Mikkel and I sat down, and he put his newspaper on the table. The server poured steaming hot coffee into our cups and handed us some menus.

"I wouldn't be surprised if Niels is another quack." I had to destroy whatever influence he might have over the captain.

"Quack?"

"Not a real doctor or surgeon. Last night after you left, a French woman came in yelling for Niels Blanc. She dragged him off."

After we gave the waiter our breakfast order, Mikkel scanned the paper but didn't say anything.

"Who in the world has so many different names? Niels Hviid, Blanc, or White. Take your pick."

He peered over his paper at me. "I certainly expect aboard my ship, and the remaining time here, the two of you will act like adults, not children. I do not have time to mediate petty squabbles."

I took the front section after he set it aside to get up to speed on what was happening in 1862. My knowledge of European history was weak. Politics and wars disgusted me, but I had to be prepared for questions.

The front page of the Southampton paper mentioned the railway accident. Half of the passengers died, and many were seriously injured. I caught my breath. Mikkel must be in significant pain but hiding it. No wonder he stood and walked as if carrying a bag of concrete.

"The train accident sounds awful. You could have died."

"Yes. Horrific."

"Then where would I be? Left to rot in the asylum."

He knit his brow with an expression of concern and sadness. "I am glad I left you there regardless of how much you disliked it. You might not be here today."

"Did people die near you?"

Mikkel nodded but refused to elaborate.

The traditional English breakfast arrived with eggs, sausage, a tomato slice, and brown beans. The dark red-brown colored sausage was suspect. Just the idea of blood pudding sausages made me sick. I jabbed it with my fork and plopped it on Mikkel's plate without asking.

This tiny gesture resulted in his dazzling smile. I longed to give him another dozen to wallow in his approval.

His newspaper gave me an idea of how to turn things around for Millie and the other trapped women. Although, I would need help. I took some paper from my handbag and wrote a brief request for Albert and Rosie. I was eager to get to the bank and start my lengthy to-do list and my plan.

Niels, the thief, may have left to rob a bank since he was gone so long. When he finally showed up, he waved my letter out of my reach teasing me.

"Captain Mikkel, you should read this." Niels unfolded my letter and dropped it in front of him.

Mikkel took the letter, folded it without reading it, and gave it back to me.

"This is a private letter from her uncle. I will not read it unless Kathryn wishes me to. You should respect her privacy."

I stuck the letter in my handbag, but at my first opportunity,

I would burn it to a crisp. If Mikkel changed his mind, it would be gone, and Niels or anyone else couldn't steal it. Knowing that Max and the travel agency were looking out for me had to be enough.

I went back to my room to grab my new coat. In the lobby, I dropped off my messages for Albert and Rosie.

Niels and Mikkel sat together chatting. "May I join you?" I asked.

"Please sit." He motioned to a chair next to him. "Since Niels is a doctor, I told him about your predicament. Your health may be in jeopardy from the stay at the hospital yesterday."

Niels grinned and nodded. "I must do an examination. That facility is known for diseases which can be contagious. I would hate for Kat to become ill aboard the ship and spread the infection to others."

Niels was too inquisitive. I wanted to explain I took some antibiotics. But did they exist in 1862? "I feel fine. I'm strong and healthy."

"Vicious and painful diseases fester within those walls. Smallpox, flu, tuberculosis, malaria, measles, cholera –"

"Very well. Take Rosie to accompany you. Niels must conduct his medical examination today. If you need medicine, today is the time to arrange for it."

If Mikkel regretted taking me to the damn loony bin and putting me at risk, he didn't show it. Niels smirked at how things were going along with his plan.

I pleaded with Mikkel to leave, eager to get away from Niels and delay another worthless medical examination.

~~~

After waiting ten never-ending minutes, I couldn't sit still any longer. I stood to admire the English landscape paintings on the wall. These were not fake, but the best they could afford. This reception hall aimed to impress wealthy customers in the venerable and famous Bering's Bank & Trust.

I considered urging Mikkel to transfer my money to another bank, but my funds were safe for a few months in 1862. They went bankrupt in the 1990s after being hit with a lethal trading scandal in Singapore. Their financial meltdown shocked the entire world, including the Queen of England who also had funds there.

If they had paid attention to their internal auditors, they might have survived. The audit reports warned them of the trading issues and the potential for financial losses. No one predicted they would be so significant and lead to their demise.

"My letter mentioned ten thousand pounds. Is that worth a lot?"

"Your uncle must be exceptionally fond of you. A woman may live free from financial concerns on five hundred a year."

"Oh, great. Quite a sum." Mikkel may have overvalued it and not factored in inflation. I refused to count on anything until some real cash was in my hands.

"It will make a respectable dowry when you marry with extra for trifles, clothes, and such."

I was speechless. A dowry for marriage? Giving it to a man or getting married was the last thing I would do.

"I am astounded we heard back from your uncle so soon. What do you propose to do with this sudden windfall?

"What else? Spend it."

"Be cautious with your funds. People may try to take advantage of you."

Like Niels, he meant. I wanted to boast that my account in New York City had over a million dollars, and it better be there waiting when I return. My nest egg of blood, sweat, and tears money, all legal, gained from frugal living, and steady investing over the years.

"I want Esperanza, the cat, to stay on board. I know there is a silly superstition about her minuscule spot of white fur. I will cover her expenses and anything else."

"You do not need to buy favors. Simply ask me. Simon and I have already agreed on this matter. Save your money for more sensible expenditures."

Mikkel pulled a newspaper out of his briefcase and opened it so forcefully he nearly ripped it. I counted the decorative floor tiles under the plush rug desperate for our long wait to end.

Finally, a man in an expensive suit, who must be the manager, greeted us. "The paperwork is in order. We merely need your signatures."

In his plush office, he handed us the documents and showed us where to sign. I read over the new account documentation, thrilled at seeing it official and in writing.

The banker asked Mikkel to sign a set of documents. "Were you given some money?" I asked.

"Your uncle provided an additional thousand pounds upon your safe arrival in Hong Kong. When we arrive, I shall have access to the funds."

Now I understood why he agreed to take me back. Money talks loud and clear, but at least it worked.

I debated how much money to withdraw today. "How will I access my money while abroad? I don't intend to be back in Southampton."

The greedy financier would keep all my money if I never returned. He fished out a pamphlet listing their branches around the world. They were in all the far-reaching British territories: Gibraltar, South Africa, India, and Hong Kong.

Mikkel said, "We shall stop in Cape Town. You may obtain more funds there."

I estimated two weeks and didn't want to run out of money beforehand. The banker suggested I get authorized checks to cash in ports without a bank branch. I calculated spending a third to half and saving half in case Hong Kong didn't go as planned.

"All right. I want four checks in five hundred-pound increments to –"

"So much?" Mikkel said in a rush.

"Just in case. I want to get a few things for my cabin while we are in Southampton. What's the best way to buy things?"

The banker said, "You may carry currency with you, but I do not advise it. A better method is to authorize payment at the stores with your account number. Shopkeepers will sell you whatever you require, obtain their funds from the bank, and deliver your purchases."

"All right. I want one thousand in cash."

"One thousand? No, no, no. You cannot carry so much on your person. It is much too perilous," Mikkel said.

"I must agree with Captain Madsen, Mrs. Jensen. There are many rogue types, and it would be unsafe. Potentially life-threatening."

I remembered the men yesterday. "All right five hund–"

Mikkel interrupted me. "Sir. Give her two hundred. More than she requires today."

I got my cash, and we shook hands. Following Mikkel outside, I ran the numbers in my head. Spend a thousand in Southampton, three thousand more in ports along the way, and another thousand in Hong Kong. I would keep half in reserve in case I didn't get home.

If I did return home, I couldn't claim any money left in this account. The bank didn't even exist in 2016. I told Mikkel I needed to ask the bank manager another question and ran back to his office.

The financier stood in the corridor.

"I want to assign beneficiaries to my account."

He groaned as if I was his absolute worst customer but escorted me back to his office.

"I have been told many times it is a long and dangerous journey." I glared at him, and at last, he supplied me with the designated papers.

I jotted down a couple of names, and for their addresses gave *Anne Kristine,* the name of the ship. The form accepted up to four beneficiaries. I chewed on the end of my pen considering my options.

"Oh, whatever." I wrote down two more names. If all went as planned, they would each receive a thousand pounds or more. Officially, I would be declared missing or dead but safely back home. At least, my leftover funds could go to my friends.

Mikkel leaned against a wall smoking a cigarette in the sunshine. "All resolved?"

"Yes, all done. Are you feeling all right today?"

"Sore but healing. Much to do today before we set sail."

"Can I help?"

"No, enjoy your last day in England. Quite a sum is burning a hole in your pocketbook. Do be more careful today."

"I will. Rosie wants to go shopping, and we will drag Albert along with us. No one will bother us. Can I borrow Uffe and Henrik for a few hours?"

"To carry your packages, I suppose?"

I nodded, but that was not the reason. They would carry their own purchases. "What does the crew like?"

"Like?"

"To eat, drink, or have on board?"

"Any self-respecting sailor would say, 'ale, some spirits, and a first-rate piece of meat.'"

"Perfect. I'll have it delivered to the ship."

"What?" He rubbed his beard while his blue eyes sparkled in the sunlight distracting me.

"I want to buy them something. A small token of my appreciation."

"No, Kat. The crew is my responsibility, not yours."

"I want to do this. The guys I've met have been kind to me. Especially Uffe, Henrik, and Simon. And I'm bound to get to know them all when we are underway."

"Do as you want, but do not be extravagant. Those funds are for your benefit."

By spending some money, a pittance in the overall scheme of things, I could smooth over potential problems if they were worried about having women on board. With two long months before me, I would need all the friends I could get.

29 ~ *Undercover Success*

As expected, my new best friends, Albert and Rosie, waited in the lobby for me.

"We got your message. How can we help?" Rosie was bursting with excitement about our secret mission.

I directed them to a private room, laid out my plans, and asked if they would help me. Without any hesitation, they both consented. Real friends don't need bribes.

In the buggy on the way to the lunatic asylum, I answered their questions. This carriage had seen better days and bumped along. The cracked leather seat pinched my leg, so I sat close to Rosie.

My stomach complained, not from hunger but nervousness, at the idea of returning to the prison-like psychiatric hospital. What if something went wrong, and I had to stay? I would miss the ship's departure ruining my plans.

"Perhaps we shouldn't do this? It might be too risky."

The coach began the long drive up towards the entrance. Today was sunny, so it resembled a magnificent manor house and not so threatening.

"Nonsense. Our pleasure." Rosie squeezed my hand, and Albert echoed his support.

Albert opened the massive door leading into the gothic-styled reception area.

"Impressive." Rosie was in awe as I had been when I first saw the building's interior.

Albert's mouth hung open while he gaped at the ornate architecture. This fancy lobby represented only pain and suffering.

Some visitors and staff crowded around, but I didn't recognize anyone. I walked up to the area where Mikkel had spoken with someone to admit me.

A dark-haired woman sat behind a desk. "May I help you, Madam?"

"We are here to see Dr. Davies. His friend, Dr. Niels White, arranged an appointment this morning. It's critical we see him as soon as possible." To avoid using a name they might recognize, I used my maiden name, Kathryn Carlson.

She left to check. I worried the doctor was booked solid, but luck was with us. "Dr. Davies is unaware of this appointment but shall see you momentarily."

"Did Niels set this up?" Rosie asked.

"No, but he knew who was in charge. I am still not convinced he isn't a phony."

"A what?"

Before I could explain, the woman returned. We trailed behind her down the narrow hall where I had been dragged against my will. I swallowed hard and let Albert lead the way.

After brief pleasantries and introductions with Dr. Davies, a plump and bald administrator, I took control and pulled out a pen and notebook to look more official.

"Dr. Davies, I am Ms. Carlson, an investigative journalist with the *Washington Post* in the United States of America. Mr. Bittner is from the world-renowned German conglomerate *Springer Publishing*. Miss Styles is a freelance writer for the London publication *The News of the World* among others."

"What has this to do with the Hampshire Asylum?" Dr. Davies shifted his ample girth, and his chair creaked in despair.

"We were tasked with a joint investigation into the quality and condition of all asylums. You must be aware of the problem. We have received many complaints. So many that my publisher urged us to do the unthinkable."

"Unthinkable?" The doctor bent forward as I had longed for, but angry creaks from his chair complained at the shifting burden.

"Yes. Unthinkable. A colleague recently spent one day and one night to investigate the conditions here. Undercover, of course, so no one knew her true purpose."

"I see."

"I am to report back her results and –"

The doctor stood. "I suppose you want payment of some sort."

"No, but the appalling conditions must improve at once. Today. The residents need proper food, warm and clean clothes, decent beds with quality blankets, and something to do, books to read."

"I see." He stroked his beard considering this.

"Shameful. Their oversight and treatment should be what you would provide to a dear family member." Rosie, the experienced lecturer, chastised him.

"And with medical treatments to help them. Nothing compulsory like bleedings," Albert said.

"Well, that can be organized." He stood and walked to the door eager to get rid of us.

"Dr. Davies, to ensure you've complied with our requests, we shall send another person undercover to investigate. If conditions have not improved, we shall publicize this atrocity. My publisher promised to keep Abe and Vic informed. If necessary, they will force changes."

"Abe and Vic?"

"President Abraham Lincoln and your very own Queen Victoria."

His eyes widened in surprise. "Yes, of course."

The doctor opened the door and called his secretary. "If nothing further, I shall begin to initiate the improvements without delay."

"*Gut*," Albert said from deep down, and we echoed his approval in English.

"One more request. I would like to see a patient. Mrs. Millicent Phillips." I wanted to ask about Maxi, but since I didn't know her real name, I would find Millie first.

He told his secretary to look for her and excused himself practically running away.

To save time, I told the secretary, "I believe she's in room 12 in the B wing." I took out an envelope stuffed with my new cash. To get Millie released, money might pave the way to help her reach her cottage or another place to stay.

I thanked my journalist pals for helping me.

"Our meeting went well. I am proud of you, Kat." Rosie smiled.

"Very glad to help. I hope Dr. Davies is true to his word." Albert sighed and looked unconvinced.

A few minutes later his secretary walked in with a report in her hand. "Millicent Phillips was released last night."

"Released? To who? Where?"

The secretary thumbed through the paperwork. "Her son, Edgar, collected her."

"Is there a forwarding address?"

We waited while she left to get it. I debated asking her about Maxine. Without a real first name or last name, the odds were against me. If she quizzed an employee, they might recognize me, and our persuasive game with Dr. Davies would end. If discovered, the three of us could face harsh consequences.

Albert and Rosie lingered, but I could tell they were ready to leave. A doctor talked to someone outside the doorway. His voice was familiar, and I froze terrified.

Dr. Fitzpatrick poked his red head into our room asking for Dr. Davies. I turned to hide my face, and Albert told him to look in the next room.

The secretary came back and rattled off an address in London.

My hands shook while I jotted it in my notebook. I would stay in touch with Millie and send her a letter and money. She could help Maxi and the others.

If I ever returned to England, finding Millie was at the top of my to-do list.

~~~

The three musketeers, turned investigative journalists, celebrated our success in our getaway horse carriage on the way to our ship. We acted out the meeting and made fun of Dr. Davies and how he shook when it dawned on him the real purpose of our visit.

Albert was convinced we had scared him but not optimistic about lasting change. "I wonder how much he would have paid us?"

"Not enough. That place is disgusting. I hope he spends lots of money improving it."

"I have heard stories about them. They are all vile and need investigating. And that quote, Kat. Impeccably done. Who in the world calls our Queen Victoria Vic?"

"Oh, I don't know. I made it up."

Rosie laughed so hard she began to cry.

I wanted to buy them lunch but needed to tackle my to-do list. The first item, new clothes for Uffe and Henrik might take extra time if it's like buying a woman's coat.

When we reached the ship, a sailor I didn't know approached. I introduced myself and shook hands. He didn't speak English, so I switched to Danish and translated for Rosie and Albert.

"Can you ask Uffe and Henrik to come down to meet us? We have some shopping to do. The captain said it was fine."

"Why are you taking those men shopping? To carry your purchases?" Albert said.

"Oh, no. Our cabin attendants need clothes that fit."

"I have my sewing machine. I could help with repairs," Rosie said smiling.

"Thanks, but they need something new. While we're here and I have some money, I want to buy them some new clothes in their size. A gift for services rendered."

Simon walked down the gangway and stopped to say hello.

"You are just the person, I wanted to see." He had a heavy bucket with him, put it down on the pier, and rubbed his sore palms together.

"Glad to have you back aboard, Kat. The ship has been quiet without you."

I laughed. "Well, it might get louder with my girlfriend." I pointed at Rosie.

"Me? I'm as quiet as a church mouse." Rosie batted her eyes looking shy.

"What's in the bucket?"

"Our slush fund for a tannery up the street."

"Isn't a slush fund slang for extra money?"

"Exactly. Some extra money for the ship's cook." He raised the lid to show me. "Fat from the bottom of the barrel."

I nodded. "I want to buy the crew a gift for being so helpful on the journey from Denmark. I will introduce myself to everyone when I'm back on board."

He paused as if uncertain and didn't respond.

"Captain Mikkel mentioned the crew likes ale, spirits, and meat. Can you get them liquor, beer, and a local specialty like prime rib with Yorkshire pudding? For tonight's dinner, if you can."

I took a wad of cash from my purse and pulled out a ten-pound note.

"Is this enough so everyone can have a special dinner? One you don't have to cook?"

"He eyed the bill I handed him. I tried to recall how many sailors there were and estimated a minimum of twenty. I shoved into his hands another ten-pound note. "Is this enough?"

"This covers our food budget for a month."

"Well, fine. My contribution to eat something out of the ordinary and thank the crew for all their hard work."

Rosie watched the transaction. "You are so generous."

"In the U.S., we have a saying. Money is like manure. You have to spread it around."

She grinned. "Our English philosopher, Francis Bacon, would agree. He said, 'Money is like muck, not good unless spread.'"

Simon shook his head in amazement, chuckled, and said a polite goodbye.

I called after him. "Don't forget little Essie. Please give her some steak leftovers."

30 ~ *One Leg at a Time*

After a short walk into town, Albert found the men's clothing store equipped with tailors. Uffe and Henrik refused to enter arguing the shop was for fine gentlemen. I feared our two young men would return to the ship or hide in town if I went inside to ask. Rosie abandoned us for a shop next door selling fabric and trim for sewing projects, so I sent Albert inside.

After five minutes, my patience and shopping time was running out. After getting Uffe and Henrik to promise not to leave, I walked inside and found Albert reading the paper.

"What is going on? Where's the tailor?"

Albert pointed to a doorway obscured by a curtain.

"This is ridiculous. We don't have unlimited time to wait." I marched over there and pulled aside the fabric hanging in the doorway. A man stood on short pedestal partially clothed. Another man, who must be the tailor, with fabrics swatches in his hands and a measuring tape hanging around his neck, was measuring him for a suit.

They both froze as if under a magic spell. The man on the pedestal wore white underclothes, so he was not completely naked. A shame though. He stayed fit and was in excellent shape.

Albert stood next to me and tapped my shoulder to get my attention, but I ignored him.

The tailor said, "Madam, please, some privacy."

"Excuse me, but we are in a hurry. Can you make suits for two young men? I need them today."

The tailor said, "I am almost finished here. Send them in."

"Well, there's a slight problem. They refuse to come in."

"Refuse?" The tailor scratched his head but avoided poking himself. He wore wristbands covered with pins and needles.

His customer stepped down from the pedestal, turned his back to me, and pulled on his pants. He said, "This suit fabric is fine. Please help the young lady."

I nodded my thanks to him. The tailor and Albert followed me outside to see Uffe and Henrik.

"These young men need new clothes." I showed him how Uffe's sleeves and pants were too long and rolled up.

After the tailor scrutinized Henrik and Uffe for one whole second, he shook his head. They did resemble street urchins and not the smart and wealthy young men riding in carriages. When he finally spoke, he said, "Exceedingly irregular."

"I have the cash. My friends will look great in some new clothes."

The tailor ignored me and went back inside his shop shaking his head. I was embarrassed on their behalf. At least he didn't lock the door.

Even without understanding English, they recognized the insult, and I didn't know what to say or do. Uffe remained silent, but Henrik said, "Kat, we want to go back to the ship."

The customer who had been standing on the pedestal came outside and joined our little group adding to the confusion on the narrow sidewalk. He asked Albert, "What is wrong?"

I had to take charge. "That man, the tailor, is a snob. He refused to help, and we are paying customers."

The golden-haired man said, "Madam, please permit me to assist. My name is Gustav Wallström."

In the sunlight, he had the aura of a movie star, but better, since he stood right here. Speechless, I wished he had shown up yesterday when I needed him. Some God from above must have dropped him from the sky to help me.

Gustav took my shock as agreement and spoke to Henrik and Uffe in what sounded like Swedish or Norwegian.

They spoke rapidly to Gustav, explained who they were, and the pitiful spot they were in.

Henrik said, "She insisted against our will to buy both of us a new outfit. Clothes we do not want or need."

Gustav nodded and understood them. Norwegian, Swedish, and Danish languages weren't that hard for Scandinavians to understand. Finnish was completely different.

Gustav's blue eyes searched my face as if he recognized me. He wouldn't since I would remember a guy like this. He switched to English, "I know of a more suitable shop to take them not far from here. Where my crew goes shopping. I am also a seafarer." Gustav's accent was lyrical and more sing-song than Danish with its guttural sounds.

"Perfect. Lead the way." I was ready to escape from outside this offensive shop.

Albert had an appointment with a barber but reminded Rosie and me of our dinner engagement tonight. The captain had arranged a special dinner with one of his wealthy patrons. But not having a watch or smartphone made it challenging to keep track of the time.

Rosie and I strolled with our new friend, the Swedish officer, to a cheaper shopping block off High Street. Rosie stood outside the casual clothing shop to prevent the boys from running off while Gustav and I explained to the clerks what we wanted. These staff knew how to treat customers and were eager to help us.

"You can come in now," I said to our reserved and shy cabin attendants.

While the tailor measured them with Gustav's help, Rosie and I admired all the different fabrics piled up in the store.

After the measurements were done, I explained to the tailor, "They need several suits in the thicker fabric since it gets cold on the water. In hot weather, people use lighter colors like beige."

"Uffe, do you want light blue or light brown for Hong Kong?" He liked blue, so I instructed the tailor to make a second in light blue for them both.

"Madam Kat." Uffe had stopped stuttering, so whatever bothered him must not be too bad, but then he stopped.

"Sit down here, Uffe and tell me whatever it is."

"T-T-This is very kind of you, but I should not accept. My clothes will be finer than the men aboard and ..."

"Will they be angry with you?"

"Y-y-yes."

"Sir," I asked the old tailor who stood nearby listening but not understanding a word of our Danish conversation. "Do you have clothes for more sailors? Pre-made to buy now? There are about twenty men on board, I believe."

"We have some clothes pre-sewn which only require minor adjustments." He put a few on the counter and showed us the unfinished hems for the pants and sleeves.

Uffe and Henrik conferred and approved the plan. My sewing skills were nothing to rave about, but Rosie offered to make the alterations. With Gustav's aid, we negotiated a better deal with the tailors.

Uffe thanked me and didn't step back when I hugged him goodbye.

The sales clerks packed the clothes for delivery to the ship, and I calculated the bill envious of their new pants. My legs nearly froze on the way to England.

"Rosie, I'm getting a pair of trousers? Do you want one?"

"What?"

"Yesterday Albert said the famous global traveler, Ida Pfeiffer from Austria, wore trousers under her dresses in the 1830s. Why can't we?" I pulled from the pile an unhemmed navy-blue pair of pants about my size.

Rosie laughed and selected a matching pair holding it to her waist.

Gustav chuckled when he realized these pants were for us. "Quite fashionable."

If it was acceptable for an officer and gentleman like Gustav, it had to be okay with Captain Mikkel. And unless he looked under our skirts, he would never know.

31 ~ *Shop Until You Fall Over*

"Oh, Rosie, isn't this fun?"

She giggled agreeing. "Who said money is the root of all evil?"

"Not my Uncle Max."

"I cannot wait to meet him. To thank him, of course."

I froze caught off guard. Mentioning Max, the computer, was not really lying. "Me too."

Gustav had to return to his ship, and I hated to say goodbye to our Swedish lifesaver. We turned down his kind offer to tour his Swedish steamer. Our shopping spree was amusing but time-consuming.

I had spent a ton of money to prepare for the tough journey looming ahead. We bought a piano and some smaller musical instruments as part of Rosie's knack for bargaining. Some of the crew might like to play the assortment of flutes, horns, and fiddles.

We stopped at a bookseller and grabbed up some children's books to help Uffe learn English, and some serialized stories republished as books that Rosie wanted.

Inside the chemist, an old-fashioned pharmacy, we mulled over every toiletry they had in stock. We overloaded our baskets with a hefty assortment of soaps, hair tonics, gargling oils, cherry toothpaste, eye water, and beauty creams. I gathered some oddities including cod liver oil for irregularity, stomach bitters, fig syrups, skin creams called *frostillas*, and seltzers.

The labels, etched in glass, were hard to read. Since money was no longer an issue, Rosie and I agreed it was better to be safe with extras than miserable without. They didn't stock liquid hair shampoo and conditioner, but Rosie found what she called hair soaps.

Rosie handed me a bottle of weight loss medicine. "What is your opinion? I hate being called a pudding bag."

Simon would qualify but not Rosie. She wasn't so overweight.

I scanned the label's suspicious sounding ingredients and gave it back to her. "Bad idea, Rosie."

"I do not want you to purchase it for me."

"It is not the money. Some of this stuff is poisonous. Like arsenic."

She held on still trying to decide.

"I cannot lose you. You are my new best friend. We are sure to hit some rough weather, and you'll be seasick. A fast weight loss cure."

She didn't look convinced and held on to it. "And the food on the ship is okay but not great. Just don't tell Simon, the chef."

I stopped at a prominent display of Worcestershire sauce and laughed at the site of the familiar steak sauce in a pharmacy. The paper wrapped bottles had glass stoppers instead of lids. The sign claimed this rich digestive seasoned meat and would make your hair grow thick and beautiful. The ingredients included barley malt vinegar, spirit vinegar, molasses, sugar, salt, anchovies, tamarind extract, onions, and garlic. I threw a handful of bottles into my heavy basket.

At the register behind the cashier, some greenish-brown skulls gaped back at me.

"Are those real?" I pointed to the skulls while the clerk calculated my bill. They must be a fake Halloween leftover.

"Yes, Madam. Authentic human skulls. We sell the green moss."

"You sell what?"

She took one out of the glass case behind her and plopped it on the counter. With her pen, she touched the moss growing on the skull near the empty eye sockets. "Cures nosebleeds. Insert moss into the nostrils."

Stepping back, I bumped into a stranger waiting behind me. Apologizing, I shook my head in surprise. I would use a handkerchief if this was their solution.

I paid the bill and had to trust my purchases would reach the ship before we left. We couldn't carry it all. Time was running out with more stores to visit.

Rosie lingered outside waiting. She dabbed her eyes with a hankie.

"Are you feeling all right?"

"Yes." Except her voice told me the opposite.

"What's wrong?"

"Sometimes I am overcome with fear. I have never been to sea. The storms and seasickness scare me. I do not know if I will manage."

"Of course, you can. Really, it's not so bad. You get a stomach ache, but sometimes you can still eat. And the captain knows all this sailing business. He will protect and help us."

I straightened my back and stood taller to look braver. Some of Rosie's dark hair fell loose into her eyes, and she smoothed it back behind a hairpin.

"Please don't worry, Rosie. We have more of my uncle's money to spend."

"Have you not spent more than enough?"

"Oh, no. We have a couple of hundred to spend."

"Two-hundred?" She choked. "That much? In one day?"

"Well, maybe not all, but some more. Let's see how it goes."

"That is such a vast sum to comprehend. My new position pays only one-hundred-thirty pounds sterling a year. Our tea yesterday cost less than a pound."

She shouldn't be embarrassed about her salary. Women's wages lagged what a man earned even in 2016.

"I am saving some." I wanted to downplay my sudden fortune. "But if I don't spend it, my uncle may take what's left."

"Take it back?" She frowned. "We must, therefore, put it to use. Are you not famished?"

We stopped at a food stall for a quick bite. Rosie suggested the eel pies since they were fast and filling. She ordered a couple baked in puff pastry. We ate them standing next to other hungry customers and shared a bottle of local ale.

The smell of the freshly baked pies overwhelmed the street smells of rotten trash and urine. I had eaten smoked eel in sushi but never like this. Few of my friends back home would ever try it. But this meal was a perfect Anthony Bourdain moment and hit the spot.

~~~

"Do you think Albert would like this?"

I held up a medium-size landscape painting of snowy mountains and a lake with small fishing boats to show Rosie.

"This might be a pleasant reminder of his home in Czechia, the Czech Republic."

"Where? Albert is from Bohemia on the Continent."

"Oh, right I mean Bohemia." Bohemia became part of Czechoslovakia in the twentieth century. My great-grandfather immigrated from Bohemia to Texas in the 1850s.

Strange to know that he was alive at this exact moment. I imagined meeting him and what I would say. 'You don't know me, but I'm your great-granddaughter.' Even I would think that person was crazy.

The song, *Bohemian Rhapsody*, by Queen had nothing to do with the country of Bohemia. Some lyrics echoed in my head. Is this the real life or just fantasy? I blinked several times to force myself back to the here and now.

Rosie assessed the painting. "Very agreeable. This artwork must be expensive."

We were back at the art gallery we visited yesterday to see what I could afford. *Anne Kristine* needed freshening up with a woman's touch.

"Pick one you like."

"Me?"

"Not you. The woman standing behind you."

She turned around to check, and I giggled.

"Yes, you." I didn't look up trying to see as many paintings as possible. From earlier negotiations, I had learned to pick some out, get a quote, bargain for a lower price or freebies, and have them delivered to the ship.

Plenty of money remained, but I had misplaced my shopping list. Visiting all these small shops was exhausting. Whatever I had forgotten must wait for Vigo, the next port of call.

If I were a rash investor and gambler, I would spend all my money on art. But if the art was worthless and I was stuck in 1862, I would be penniless again. The set of paintings I bought, imitation or not, might not even survive the journey to Hong Kong.

Rain started falling, and we waited at the shop to get a carriage ride to the inn. We could afford to travel in style. Just like in New York City, finding a cab in rainy weather was almost impossible.

Despite sending most of our purchases to the ship, I carried around two items I had to have: the pair of pants and a thick wool sweater.

We were way behind schedule, but I tried to be patient. With so much cash, walking back was too daring even for me. A lot of suspicious looking men wandered around town, but they were most likely down on their luck. From what I had heard, taking a bath was a luxury and a weekly affair at best. Showers didn't seem to exist.

Finally, we climbed into a rundown carriage with an old pony. The small horse, drenched from the rain, looked pitiful. I planned to tip generously with instructions to buy extra oats for the wet pony.

Rosie said, "I'm relieved we didn't attempt an outing to Chawton today."

"Chawton?"

"Albert and I talked about going to see Jane's last home. She lived in a cottage on her brother's estate. In Hampshire County not far from that hospital we visited."

We referred to Jane Austen as Jane, as if we knew her. "I always wanted to see that museum."

"Museum? A grand idea. The cottage is still used by the family."

Accidentally I had discussed the future again. The museum must have opened after 1862. Rosie didn't seem to notice my faux pas. If she did, she could add it to her list of weird Yank sayings or Kat-isms as she called it once.

Rosie would be pleased to know Jane Austen lives on in 2016 with not just her books but movies and TV mini-series. An international fan club exists with members called Janeites. But the zombie riff on *Pride and Prejudice* would upset her.

"It is called a cottage but quite spacious. I could joyfully live the rest of my days there."

Rosie would make a great roommate. If I couldn't get back home and she didn't get married, we could share a place. Being around her made 1862 almost bearable.

The rain slapped down on our carriage and became a torrential downpour. Our crudely-made coach swayed and swung to the right, balanced on two wheels on one side, slammed down with a thud, and a sudden stop.

Rosie fell on top of me and into my lap.

"Almighty God!" Rosie grabbed her skirts, shrieked some more, and slid back to her side.

I cursed under my breath and stuck my head out the cloth window covering into the rain. "What happened?"

The driver howled in anger at the drenched pony. He shouted above the downpour, "Not your concern!" And more politely, "Madam, a minor problem."

I slid over to the other side to see what happened. Our driver stood behind us and pushed a wheel.

"Are we stuck?" I called out.

"Yes, it seems so." Like a flat tire, we had to get the wheel moving again.

"Rosie, what happens now? Will someone help get us out?" The shops around us closed at dusk, and no one walked by during this deluge.

She shrugged her shoulders. "We shall be delayed and tardy for dinner." Her voice cracked from stress.

I jiggled the latch, opened the door, and climbed out into the rain. We couldn't be late.

The driver dug muddy debris away from the wheel with a small hand shovel. With the nonstop rain, this was a losing battle. We could be stuck here for hours.

"Can't we just push?" I asked.

"Push?" He shook his head. "No, we shall be fixed set and set upon again."

Whatever that meant. I searched for something to put under the wheel to keep it from sinking in the mud. The rain rolled off my bonnet, across my neck, and down my back under my wet coat. I collected a piece of wood and some straw from the side of the road.

Our irate driver insisted I get back in, but I pulled my dress above my knees and knelt to put these items under the wheel for traction.

"I will push. You coax the pony forward."

He didn't look happy but did what I suggested. Following orders from a woman must be a novel and undesirable concept. Without my help, he wouldn't get another customer anytime soon. And from his rank smell and old clothes, he needed many more to survive.

"Ready?" I shouted as loud as I could above the howling rain.

"Aye."

The whip cracked in the air and hit the pony's flanks. I winced imagining the pain and pushed with all my might to make it stop.

The wheel spun around so fast I couldn't stay upright. I slid onto my knees, and one slammed against a buried cobblestone. My palms kept me from falling face first into the mud.

After recovering from what happened, I ran after the carriage now in the middle of the street where the ground was wet but firm.

He stopped the pony, and I wiped my dirty hands on the front of my ruined outfit and climbed inside. Rosie, for once, didn't comment on my appearance. What was important was making it back in time. Clean dresses waited in my room but getting through the lobby unnoticed would be a challenge.

32 ~ *Funny Money*

When our banged-up pony cart arrived at the inn, I considered finding a back door. But if they were locked, this would cause further delays.

"Rosie, I'm following right behind you. If all goes well, no one will notice."

She nodded, but I missed her cheery self. The mud on my dress reeked of urine, feces, and unidentified trash.

As we hurried through the lobby, Mikkel and Lars saw us. I told Rosie to go on, and she slipped by without a second glance.

Mikkel inspected me from head to toe and shook his head. "Did you swim in the mud to get here?"

I shook my head. "I fell." I counted on some sympathy, but it was a lost cause.

His mood was as expected, angry. "Lars and I must leave momentarily. Albert and Niels will escort you and Rosie, but do not waste time. We have dinner invitations at Lord Rushmere's estate. You shall be dreadfully tardy."

"Sorry. I will hurry."

"I shall arrange to have the hotel's laundress clean your attire. They might be able to salvage it. Such a shame ruining your new coat. Furthermore, don a proper gown. The red one is becoming. And beforehand, adjust your hair." He inspected my head. "Good lord. You have mud there too. You must wash in depth."

I wanted to suggest I could skip this formal dinner, but he strode off. People in the lobby stared at my dirty clothes and wet hair. On my way to the stairs, I passed Niels, ignored his snide comments, and ran upstairs. The captain could still change his mind. I can manage one last dinner party in Southampton.

Back in the sanctuary of my room, my reflection in the mirror was shocking. Mud smeared my face and coated strands of hair.

Immediately, I turned on the water to fill the tub, but the

water pressure was weak. I lay out my fanciest evening gown and stripped off my clothes when someone knocked at the door. To avoid getting mud on my single clean white towel, I used my dirty clothing as a shield.

"Yes?" I called from behind the locked door.

Niels said, "Kat, give me your dirty clothes. I shall see they get cleaned."

"I am not dressed. Please come back in fifteen minutes."

"Kat, the captain instructed me to do this immediately. Hand them over."

"I will turn them in myself."

"I had to make specific arrangements with the laundress, and she is waiting. Unless you prefer not following the captain's orders and cleaning them yourself."

"Fine. Wait a moment."

"Have you forgotten? I am not just a doctor but a surgeon so there is very little I have not seen. All afternoon I passed the time here to conduct your medical examination. Now it must be done tomorrow on the ship."

Unless I was unconscious or died that would never happen, but I lacked the time and energy to argue. Wrapped in the thin towel, I opened the door a crack to hand Niels my muddy clothes and ruined coat. But he forced his way into my room.

"We need to talk." He eyed my bare legs. If I hadn't been so filthy, I would have hidden under the bedspread.

"Not now. You can't stay here." I tried to push him away. "Leave so I can take a bath."

"I can wait."

"Fine. I can wait too, and we will be even later. What will the captain say about that?"

The sound of splashing water came from the bathroom. I ran and turned off the faucet to stop the overflow onto the floor. A corner of the small carpet in the bathroom was soaked.

"See what you made me do. Get out now."

He picked my purse off the carpet and rifled through it looking for cash. "Quite a pretty penny."

"You thief."

"A miserly twenty pounds. I promise to repay you, Kat. We shall discuss this later. On the way to the Rushmere's manor."

He snatched some bills from my purse, stuffed them in his

pocket, and left with my dirty clothes held at arm's distance.

I locked the door to prevent further interruptions. After draining some of the water, I climbed into the lukewarm water, scrubbed hard, and sprang into my petticoats and fancy gown in a flash.

Now Niels owed me thirty-five pounds. If he didn't repay me soon, I would complain to the captain. Fortunately, I had spent or hidden most of my cash.

Without a blow-dryer, I parted my wet hair down the middle, instead of on the left, and twisted it into a bun higher on my head to dress up a bit. My fringy bangs had grown out, and with some hairpins, they might stay hidden from view.

Makeup wasn't a customary practice, but for a fancy dinner, it was mandatory for me. I swiped on some black mascara. A quick spritz of Italian perfume and my aquamarine jewelry finished the job.

I stood back to survey the results still longing to skip this formal dinner. Far from sexy, I was at least clean. Unfortunately, this was a rare occurrence for most of the people I'd seen. After reassuring the strange woman in the mirror with, "This is as good as it gets," I flew down the stairs to the lobby.

~~~

Albert and Rosie took an earlier coach, so I was stuck waiting for the next carriage with my least favorite person.

Niels said, "Where is your coat?"

He touched my arm covered by a thin black sweater. Since I wasn't walking, I could manage without a coat. My cover-up shielded my cleavage, and the pale bruises on my arms from the bloodletting.

"Have you already forgotten? You took it."

"You have no other? And with wet hair?"

I shook my head. I'd sent the borrowed cape back to the ship.

"Curious woman." He heaved a loud sigh. "Wait here. I shall loan you one. Free of charge because, unlike others I know, I am generous."

A few minutes later, he returned with a creamy beige-colored coat. He helped me put it on. The soft wool felt luxurious.

I smiled. The sleeves were too long, but Rosie could alter them for me later.

"From a rich client in Paris. Do not get any budding ideas. I am not gifting it to you."

Our carriage arrived, and we settled in the privacy of a small, but plush two-person coach called a hansom cab.

"You now owe me thirty-five pounds. I expect to be repaid before our next port of call with five more in interest." In case he was dense and couldn't add. "Forty pounds total."

A lamp dangled inside the coach, and he pulled out two bills from his wallet. "Here's your fifteen pounds back without interest. Now I only owe you twenty. Funny money. A game you like to play?"

I reached for the bills, but he held them out of my range. "I don't know what you're talking about."

I watched the lamp hoping it was secure. After the adventure just an hour before, I worried about a fire hazard.

"Who is that lady on the note?" He waved my bills in front of my face.

"What lady?"

Niels pointed to the woman wearing a crown on my ten-pound note.

"Queen Elizabeth," I blurted out before realizing my mistake.

"Queen Elizabeth the first does not look like that in any of the paintings I have seen to date. And this bill clearly says E II R."

"How am I supposed to know about British royalty? I got this money as a goodbye gift."

Niels grunted but didn't accept my explanations.

"I swear it was a gift. From Charles Richmond in New York City. He visited England recently on business and gave me this money."

"A very generous gift."

"Not so much." He double-crossed me, and I played a sympathy card. "We dated, but it didn't end well."

"Surely you do not expect me to believe that nonsense? I demand an honest answer. The back makes no sense. How do you explain this?" He handed me the bill.

On the flip-side of the ten-pound note in shouting capitals

stood *The Bank of England*.

"I don't see anything unusual. A red hummingbird, yellow flowers, and Charles Darwin."

"Nothing out of the norm?"

"Nope."

I grabbed my money back not wanting Niels to keep it. In modern-day Hong Kong, I could spend it when my 1860 currency was worthless.

Niels seized my arm and snatched it back.

"Right here under his name, Charles Darwin, 1809 to 1882. How does the Bank of England know he will die twenty years hence? Do they have a crystal ball?"

"How should I know? It must be a stupid printing mistake. Ask them."

Our conversation stopped. This should put an end to it, but a gnawing feeling in my gut told me otherwise.

33 ~ Traveler Beware

Our hansom cab turned into a gated entrance with an impressive brick mansion at the end of the cobblestone road. The ride took a half-hour, so Southampton was far away.

"Welcome to Hampshire Hall," a uniformed man said in the hallway. "Lord Rushmere was delayed at the harbor but should arrive momentarily."

All this rush for nothing. Inside a lavish reception room, Rosie stood by the doorway and introduced us to Miss Harriet Rushmere and Miss Adele Rushmere. To circumvent excess formality all night, I suggested we use our first names, and they agreed. Harriet was about Rosie's age, and Adele much younger, about fifteen.

We chatted about our dresses and girly stuff. Niels rolled his eyes at our boring conversation and strode off in a huff. Rosie, Harriet, and Adele moved to a seating area in the vast room. Rosie touched the seat next to her and invited me to join them.

"I would love to, Rosie. In a moment."

Niels marched towards Mikkel, and I shadowed behind worried he would tell the captain about my weird money.

Albert and Mikkel were intent on a game of chess with Lars watching.

Niels said something I couldn't hear to Mikkel.

"Patience, Niels. I am trying to win this match." Mikkel moved his queen and noticed me. "Ah, here she is. From wallowing in the mud to this opulence." He waved his hands highlighting our sumptuous surroundings.

Since he complimented the room and not my transformation, I couldn't resist a comeback. "So, I wasn't late after all." But this was a spectacular room. The entire house could be a museum.

The chess game continued, and I watched as they made their moves.

Albert leaned forward. "Checkmate."

"Damn. I shall have my revenge at sea." Mikkel sounded

angry but grinned teasing him.

Albert laughed. "My pleasure, but alas, there you shall have the advantage."

Mikkel signaled to some chairs on the other side of the room. "Kat, we should talk."

I ambled behind him hoping the lord of the manor would arrive and save me from another scolding. I sat on a plush sofa, and Mikkel surprised me by sitting right next to me.

"Now, I understand having so much money to spend for one day before we leave must be exciting. But I must mandate that you be punctual. Always. On our journey, there will be many seaports. We cannot wait or search for you. No one knew where you were today."

"Rosie accompanied me. Today was different. The rain and the carriage –"

"Stop. With you, there is always an excuse. You strain my patience. You cannot run wild like an animal doing whatever you want. This must cease."

A wild animal? Such a strange thing to say. "I apologize, Mikkel. I didn't intend to worry you."

"These are treacherous times. You are no longer at home protected by your friends and family. Your sense of adventure and foolish bravery will go too far. Heed my warning."

A cold shiver went down my back. I wanted to shake off Mikkel's bad omens.

"I must forbid you from wandering around town with Rosie. You should have a male escort always. An officer from the ship, or Albert or Niels, to look after you."

"Niels? Oh no, he is a troublemaker."

"A respected surgeon? You did not appear as we agreed for his medical examination. He is a well-trained doctor concerned with your best interests."

"My interests? By stealing my letter and my money?"

"Kat, please attempt to pacify him."

Pacify him? He should pacify me, Besides, who in the world says words like pacify?

Mikkel misunderstood my silence and stood, "Good. That matter is settled." Mikkel walked away. Worst of all, he headed in Niels' direction.

I followed him after accepting a welcome aperitif from a

formally dressed waiter. After a day like today, I deserved a few drinks.

While admiring two portraits on the wall nearby, I listened in on their conversation.

Niels said, "She is not who she appears to be."

"Why do you suspect this?" Mikkel asked.

"The letter from her uncle for one. It is a farce written in such a singular manner. She also has money that is peculiar and worthless. Everything she says and does is strange. Why is she on this journey? Nothing interests her apart from arriving there."

Mikkel glanced up and noticed me, but I turned away to eye a landscape painting. Rosie stood next to me making it more difficult to focus.

Mikkel continued his conversation with Niels. "I have corresponded with her uncle several times. He is eccentric but deposited ample funds for her benefit. He must favor his niece, and Kat wishes to continue the voyage. I cannot abandon her in England against her uncle's wishes."

Rosie said something about the paintings of Queen Victoria and the love of her life, her first cousin the German Prince Albert. I would have been interested but missed overhearing what Niels blabbed about.

Mikkel said, "She had a minor head injury and is confused. Two doctors examined her. She is headstrong, and a few minutes ago we discussed this. She knows this was unacceptable and will not put anyone at risk. You may perform your examination tomorrow on the ship. If she requires more medicine, Vigo is nearby."

"Head injury? On top of her night at the facility permeated with diseases? Captain, I have done my duty and am no longer responsible. You know the consequences. Notwithstanding her unique charm and uncle's influence, having an ill passenger puts us all at risk."

"Very well. I will take this into consideration."

I wanted to convince Mikkel I was in good health. How without admitting I spied on his private conversation?

A uniformed servant opened the double doors and in walked Lord and Lady Rushmere of the manor house. Behind them, stood the Swedish Captain Svend Matson with his First Mate

Gustav Wallström.

Gustav grinned and waved hello. My mood brightened at the sight of him. Gustav would be the perfect advertisement for Sweden with his blue eyes and golden hair matching the national flag. He smiled so often his face must hurt.

Now I was glad I wore my best outfit. My burgundy-colored evening gown was custom-made, and the most expensive outfit I had ever owned. I sent a silent word of thanks to my one-time boyfriend, Greg, for buying it.

A gong echoed throughout the mansion, and I chatted with Gustav while they guided us into the dining room. I couldn't help comparing my surroundings to the TV series *Downton Abbey* and how the nobility lived in country estates during the nineteenth century.

Even with the mud and delays, I was thrilled about this dinner. I could spend a few more hours with my favorite young Swede, avoid Niels, and prove to Mikkel that I was perfectly fine.

~~~

Somehow, my reactions were slower than usual. What should I expect after pushing a wheel out of the mud just a few hours ago? That was the only logical excuse I could find. Whenever you are dealing with snakes like Niels, they quickly slither into small spaces and hide.

When a flustered Lady Rushmere announced where we should seat, I was sandwiched in between Gustav and Niels. Like an old chain around my leg, I dreaded being so close to Niels for what might be hours and wanted to switch with Rosie.

Niels offered to help with my napkin, but I snatched it from him. After all his tricks. I turned to Gustav, my well-mannered and charming dinner companion.

A beautiful chandelier with lit candles hung low over the dinner table. More candles, stationed along the walls, produced a romantic glow. Everyone looked ten years younger after only one drink, a plus with dim lighting.

Harriet was about thirty and the same age as Rosie. Now that I shaved off so many years, I was close to their age. My years of sunscreen, healthy eating, and working out at the gym had paid off.

People aged fast here. Life was hard, and the food quality inferior. I felt like I had aged years just over the past few days. By the time I reached Hong Kong, I might qualify for old lady hag status.

The expensive china and abundance of silverware helped me ignore these worries. Our meal should be top-notch with all the forks and knives lined up.

Rosie sat across from me. She said, "Jane, please help us." She blinked at me. "Ready?"

I nodded. "You start."

She enjoyed communicating with her favorite author, Jane Austen, and had done this earlier today.

"It is a truth universally acknowledged …"

This was my cue. "That a single man in possession of a good fortune …"

Rosie winked, but before she could finish the opening line of Jane Austen's *Pride and Prejudice*, Harriet chimed in. "Must be in want of a wife."

The three of us giggled. Being the only formerly married woman, apart from the married Lady Rushmere, I couldn't resist adding. "Been there; done that. Your turn. You can have them."

Harriet, Rosie, and I burst out laughing even though this probably wasn't proper.

Gustav was unfamiliar with Jane Austen. So, I explained how she wrote books that will live forever. He smiled and said he understood. Gustav didn't lecture like Mikkel or act untrustworthy and devilish like Niels. His voice was softer and less gruff. Being so handsome didn't hurt either.

We had Sweden in common. My grandfather immigrated to the U.S. from Göteborg, a major port city, and Gustav's hometown. He kept insisting we must have a family or an acquaintance connection.

Adele, the teenager, sat across from Gustav. I tried to bring her into our conversation, but she acted shy and tongue-tied.

Niels said, "Albert, why did the three of you visit Hampshire County's Lunatic Asylum and impersonate newspaper reporters? My associate, Dr. Davies, found your visit highly unusual. Kathryn pried his name from me this morning at breakfast."

Albert looked uneasy suddenly on the spot in front of everyone. "We were there to ask some questions and share our suggestions."

Lord Rushmere raised his eyebrows. He had bushy sideburns with a clean-shaven chin, like many of the upper-class British men I'd seen around town. "A triumvirate of three?" He laughed. "I shall mind my P's and Q's."

Since this was my plan and responsibility, I assumed the lead. "Niels, your friend runs a despicable place. It deserves a thorough investigation." We took a risk and did something extraordinary but necessary.

This dinner was the complete opposite of what those poor women endured every night. "The conditions there are appalling, and someone should do something about it."

"Dr. Davies is no friend of mine. I have seen patients there, and it is foul. To be avoided at all costs." Niels narrowed his eyes as if he knew much more but didn't mention my overnight forced visit.

"We only tried to convince him to make some improvements for the patients. If he won't, it should be closed down."

Niels looked confused. Dr. Davies must not have told him the full story. "If he acts, the medical establishment would be in your debt. Your true identities were not revealed by me."

Rosie and Albert nodded. Without knowing everything, they must have guessed I stayed there. How else would I have known Millie and wanted to go there?

"Such an expression of *noblesse oblige* is to be admired." Adele raised her glass as if to salute me.

I didn't know what that term meant but assumed it was a compliment. Niels took this as another opportunity to flaunt his French language skills and embarrass me. "A noble obligation. The privileged often feel obliged to behave with nobility and generosity to those less fortunate. Such as those residing in a lunatic asylum."

I raised my glass and smiled at Adele while ignoring Niels. I still didn't trust him. He could have ruined everything if he told Dr. Davies the truth about us.

Niels whispered in my ear how he could teach me French 101 or something insulting like that while at sea. Under the table, his hand landed much too casually on my leg.

Overcome with a destructive urge to fight back and stab him with my cocktail fork, I made an excuse and found my way to the restroom. I needed a moment of peace to prevent doing something unladylike that I might regret.

When I returned, the waiters were serving a set of appetizers from ornate silver platters. Rosie was telling everyone about our beautiful ship. She raved on and on about our home for the next few months. Mikkel and Lars looked pleased with her compliments.

Harriet said, "Kathryn, you departed from Denmark. How was the crossing to England?"

Everyone watched and waited. I didn't want to scare Rosie or upset Mikkel but had to be honest. "Fine. We did run into a storm though. One rough night, but not so bad."

"Like camping on an old boat. Isn't that how you described it?" Mikkel boomed from the other end of the table.

"Well, it was different. My first voyage on a clipper ship." To not scare Rosie, I didn't add it was the worst seasickness I had ever experienced.

"We encountered a severe gale. They present their grim and turbulent faces on occasion." Mikkel smirked trying to make light of it.

"Ah, yes. I also experienced seasickness and have ridden through many rough swells. More than once I feared my mortal remains would be committed to the deep." Lord Rushmere puffed out his chest, proud to have survived.

The waves tossed our ship like a toy, but I couldn't scare Rosie.

"How strong according to Beaufort's scale?" Lord Rushmere asked. "Over the Atlantic, I once experienced an eight with winds at thirty-five knots."

Mikkel said, "Much more wicked. Over forty-five knots, so a nine approaching ten."

Rosie's face turned white, and Albert looked away as if reconsidering how much adventure he wanted. Niels licked his lips as if relishing the danger.

Mikkel must have noticed he might lose two passengers before they even boarded. "Gales are not unexpected in the North Sea. The rest of our journey should be calmer."

The high ranking of our thunderstorm frightened me, and I swallowed hard hoping never to experience another one like it.

"That storm was considerable. Mrs. Jensen is hardy and reminiscent of many of her compatriots." Lord Rushmere appeared to admire my ability to survive such a storm.

"Yes, she is. Nine lives like a cat."

My nickname might bring me some luck. I could use eight lives in reserve for this trip.

"Horrid, my dear Lord Rushmere." Lady Rushmere referred to him in by his formal title which struck me as strange for a wife. No one had called him by his first name. "Pray, do not leave us here and venture across the Atlantic again. I worried so during your brief seafaring venture today."

"I shall not cross the oceans anytime soon, my dear." Lord Rushmere covered his wife's hand with his as if she was a lovesick simpleton. "I had a pleasant but long day in the harbor with our Swedish Captain Matson." He grinned. "The engines refused to start, so we waited for a tug. However, steam is the future. We must embrace it."

"Are you ladies prepared to embark on such a long voyage?" Lord Rushmere directed his question to Rosie and me.

Not waiting for our response, Mikkel took charge. "I have tried to convince Kathryn to return home to America. Her foremost desire when we disembarked in Southampton. But she changed her mind, and her uncle insists. My hands are tied."

"We sail to New York in the spring. A safer and shorter route." Svend offered his services again.

"Excellent idea," Gustav shouted. He shifted in his seat and tilted his body towards mine. "We could take you with us, Kathryn. Our pleasure."

"Thank you, but my mind is made up. My uncle is waiting. I must get to Hong Kong. Rosie and I will have fun together."

Harriet asked Rosie and me, "Are you not worried about shipwrecks? Absolutely horrid what happened to Miss Ann Saunders."

I had never heard of Miss Saunders, but Rosie said, "The book she wrote is as tragic as the title."

"Many extenuating factors caused that calamity. Ships are much safer now." Swedish Captain Matson stressed the here and now. "Wintertime journeys across the Atlantic include the hazard of freezing temperatures and ice. Kathryn should wait to cross in the spring."

"There are other dangers such as being held captive. Like Horace Holden thirty years ago." Her Ladyship rapped her fingers on the table. "I shall never permit Harriet or Adele to go on such a hazardous journey."

Svend said, "Captain Madsen, despite being a Dane, is an expert seafarer. I would place my wife and daughters aboard his ship with no hesitation at all." Mikkel nodded in appreciation.

Mikkel must have lost at least one passenger or sailor to the deep. But why bring this up? None of us would dare board the ship. Two lifeboats were on board, but we needed at least four. Plus, the crew climbed to the top of the masts without wearing harnesses or having safety nets under them.

My internal auditing job focused on evaluating risk management procedures and finding ways to minimize risk, wherever possible. Without a doubt, this wasn't going to be the vacation I planned. Risks were everywhere I looked.

34 ~ Channeling Jane

"Mrs. Jensen, did your ancestors fight against us in the American Revolution?" Lord Rushmere kept calling me by last name, but I let it go. The conversation stopped when he spoke, and they waited for my response. His accent was strong, but he must be referring to the Revolutionary War less than one hundred years ago.

"I believe I do. General James Newsome was my ancestor. A Revolutionary War captain in Georgia."

"We have a cousin named Newsome, Henry Newsome. Perhaps we are related." Harriet spoke rapidly. The likelihood that she was a distant cousin was improbable.

Before I could answer, she fired off another question. "Do you know your English ancestors? After all, you are country of immigrants, and many are British."

"His parents or grandparents were from somewhere east of Blackpool. I heard about some trouble with Cromwell which may have been the motivating factor to emigrate. I can't remember the details." Whatever I had learned was online in my family tree. Captain Newsome was likely since many DNA matches shared his last name.

"Fascinating. I should like to meet my American cousins. I must give you our address." Harriet grinned as if we were now united as long-lost cousins. "And please tell us about Asia, a mystical land, indeed. You are a brave woman to venture so far."

"Smart to leave the States during their crisis," Lord Rushmere said. "My southern business associates call it the war for southern liberty against northern aggression. Rebels fight on both sides." He winked as we shared a secret.

"If only the fools had not fought so dearly for independence merely a hundred years ago," Lady Rushmere said. "If they had been sensible and remained part of the Empire, slavery would have been peacefully outlawed thirty years ago."

"Doubtful," said Lord Rushmere. "The South's cotton and tobacco are needed here. Slave labor is the best method. No other economical way exists to bring it forth."

"Entirely dreadful. Those poor people." Adele leaned forward her innocent face illuminated by the candlelight.

"Need I remind you, Adele. Your cotton is from the Confederacy. Your fancy dresses may be Chinese silk, but what of your undergarments?"

"Yes, papa," Adele said. Her face turned red. Mentioning anyone's underwear in public would do that.

"I should never have named my daughter Harriet if I had known Harriet Beecher Stowe would be the focus of so much attention from such an inflammatory book. President Lincoln claimed it was the impetus for this dreadful war." Lord Rushmere rapped his hand on the table as if he would smack the famous author on the knuckles.

Harriet frowned either at her father or the comparison to the famous author of the novel *Uncle Tom's Cabin*. I would be proud to share her name.

"Poor Mrs. Stowe envisioned freedom for the slaves but not in America. They would only be free in Canada, Africa, or the afterlife," Rosie said.

She did? I was curious but could ask her later. This topic launched the men into a discussion of the Civil War, slavery, President Lincoln, the rebels, and the Federals. Weird, they don't know how it ends.

Mikkel said, "The Fugitive Slave Act mandated that everyone in the United States, no matter their belief, support slavery. Apart from her book, this law fanned the fire, and I am greatly troubled the Southern rebels may prevail."

I had to reassure him. "Things will change. President Lincoln and the Union will win. The turnaround takes place in Pennsylvania at Gettysburg."

The conversation came to a sudden stop, and everyone stared at me. The war didn't end until 1865, so Gettysburg must not have occurred yet.

"Well, that's my best guess." I didn't want to sound eccentric by predicting the future.

No one said anything for a few moments, but Albert came to my rescue. "Kathryn is right. The North will prevail. However, the states may reunite without an end to this miserable business."

Mikkel and the others talked about the brutality of slavery, and the conversation shifted away from my prediction.

"A legal question exists as to whether the southern states may secede. If the North can impose or force a union," Albert said.

"Of course, they can. The captain of a ship has complete control and responsibility. It's the same for an elected President. We will unite as one country again without slavery. Trust me." I had been reckless again and took another sip of wine for courage. Niels scrutinized me as if I was a Martian.

Albert said, "Even so, President Lincoln denied the war is about slavery."

I clamped my mouth shut to not mention the Emancipation Proclamation. Lincoln didn't issue this until after the war began, and it must have happened after 1862.

Lord Rushmere shook his head. "I hate to differ, but I must. My colleagues and I are betting on the Confederacy. We own Confederate bonds and trade rifles for cotton and tobacco through Bermuda."

"A brutal trade," Mikkel said. "My brother has a plantation in the Danish West Indies. I will never forget the site of the auctions there and in New Orleans. Men, women, and children chained together for sale. Their clothing ripped away to show their strength with scars riddling their bodies. Their treatment was inhumane."

Everyone stopped eating, and Mikkel apologized for disrupting the dinner and bringing up such atrocities.

"Not at all," Lord Rushmere said. "Life is difficult for many. No need to hide it. I have also traveled in the United States, the north, and the south, and have seen the colored folk and negroes. If I were one, I would rather take a chance on having an owner support me, if only to protect his investment. A free negro in the north risks dying of illness or starvation."

"Please, my dear." Her Ladyship wore an expression of pure horror at his implication.

He waved her off as if an insect landed on his expensive jacket and stared at the men around the table one by one. "Next time you smoke tobacco or wear cotton, recall where the best is grown and how it must be picked."

I couldn't listen to this cruel justification for slavery any longer. "It doesn't mean the cotton or tobacco has to be hand-picked by slaves. They could be free, hired as employees, and paid an honest wage."

"We have an abolitionist, perhaps more, in our company." Lord Rushmere regarded me as if he wanted to plan a suitable punishment. Would he send me and the others to our room without dinner?

"Kathryn and I have found a topic of mutual agreement," Mikkel said.

Rosie and I blinked at each other in wonder. After all our arguing with him, I wanted to give her a high five hand slap.

"I trust you have no objection to carrying my fabrics produced with Confederate cotton aboard your ship, Captain Madsen?" Lord Rushmere glared at poor Mikkel.

"No, sir. I will take your fabrics. I draw the line against the transport of slaves or arms for war. If I did not take some fruits from slavery, I would have an empty ship."

"Your conscious shall be light carrying my gin. I can assure you it was produced here in England without any slave labor."

Ten to one he paid his gin-making employees starvation wages to afford a richly furnished house and servants who at this moment hovered near his elbow. The idea that his money came from the toil of slaves made me ill. But I couldn't leave and risk my passage to Hong Kong.

His Lordship's waiters, another form of slavery, brought in our next dish.

"I learned all I need to know about men and relationships from Jane Austen." Rosie enjoyed explaining how life-changing these books meant to her.

I was grateful for a change in topics. "But Jane never got married. How would she really know?"

Niels snorted. "Precisely. As if I should learn to be a surgeon from reading a book by someone with a peculiar notion of becoming a genuine doctor."

Niels' rude interruption was unwelcome.

"Not quite that bad," I reassured her, but Rosie acted offended.

"She had several affairs of the heart. How else could she write so clearly? Men will never understand." Tough Rosie was back and in fine form.

Harriet was also a fan. "I do believe she rejected one proposal of matrimony, and there may have been others. Her writing was her true love."

Niels sighed and rolled his eyes. "Miss Austen will have you believe that to sell –"

I interrupted Niels. "Keep quiet if you can't say anything polite about Jane Austen. And where's your French tart or whoever from last night?"

His face turned pink. "Miss Austen's novels abound with female delusions. Such a pity. Not like a great Shakespeare tragedy or the accomplished American Edgar Allan Poe."

I turned to Gustav to ignore Niels, but he was hungry for attention and tapped me on my shoulder.

"If you must know about the French woman. She was upset over a medical emergency with her mother-in-law."

"What happened?"

"Alas, she is very ill. Nothing to be done as I suspected."

"Sorry."

"Why should you be sorry? If that is the reason, you must be sorry for every minute of every day. Someone is always dying."

People like Niels drove people like me to drink. I took a sip of wine and turned to Gustav. If only they could trade places on the ship, but Gustav had a job. If there had been more time, I would have asked Uncle Max to switch Lars for Gustav.

When the waiter served our soup, Niels refused to be quiet. "My favorite novel is Victor Hugo's *Les Misérables*. Rich with history and drama. An epic masterpiece. Hugo's a true visionary living in exile on the Channel Islands. Have you read it, Kathryn?"

I shook my head. I had only seen the musical and movie version.

"I could loan it to you. Alas, it is an original in French. And you cannot read French, can you? Such a pity for those uneducated foreigners." He touched my arm in sympathy.

A sharp knife waited on near my left hand for the main course. It took extreme willpower to not threaten Niels with it.

"I have read *Les Misérables* and highly recommend it," Harriet said.

"You have?" Lady Rushmere sounded disturbed. Niels was a scoundrel, and the book's subject matter was intense.

"Does the cat have your tongue, Kat?" Niels accentuated my nickname. "I shall be pleased to translate it for you whilst at sea."

"I am going to be busy with Rosie, I mean Rosamund. We have plans."

"What mischief will keep the two of you occupied for months?" Niels waved his hand in the air as if we were fools.

"School." I omitted the undecided details.

Rosie cleared her throat. "Kathryn and I will teach the crew English. Those who want to learn."

Mikkel's knife fell on the table making a loud clatter. "My seamen will attend school?" He laughed. "They are much too busy with their duties and maritime school."

"Which is much more appropriate," said Niels happy to destroy our plans. "Furthermore, you do not speak proper English. You speak American, and your Danish is flawed."

The table's polite chit-chat stopped.

"Did I say I would teach them Danish? No, I did not. Perhaps, Dr. White, you should stay here and get your ears examined by a real doctor."

Harriet giggled, and Adele looked shocked at our sparring contest. Their mother bestowed a disapproving look.

Gustav said, "Danish is a difficult language. Much harder than Swedish. I often have trouble understanding it. I admire Kathryn and any English speaker for attempting it."

"What else do you expect from a Swede?" Niels rolled his eyes.

Gustav frowned. "You must insert potatoes here to speak Danish." He opened his mouth illustrating where he would put them, and everyone laughed. "Say something in Danish, Lars."

First Officer Lars hesitated, made eye contact with Captain Mikkel for his okay, and didn't proceed until he had the nod. In guttural Danish, he said, "I am honored to be here tonight. Your home is magnificent. Thank you for your kind invitation."

Gustav recited Lars' exact words in Swedish. He reminded me of the hilarious Swedish chef on *The Muppet Show*. His funny expressions and sing-song voiced lightened the mood, and most of the group laughed. Everyone but the Danes since he had poked fun at their mother tongue.

Mikkel said, "Kathryn's Danish is fine. Few foreigners attempt to say anything beyond good morning and thank you."

"*God day og tak*," I said translating for everyone. "I know my Danish is far from perfect. I can't pronounce the ø sound deep in my throat as Lars so expertly demonstrated."

"A school is quite an undertaking," her Ladyship said.

"Most of the crew only speak Danish, and in all these upcoming ports English is more useful." I took a sip of my beverage. "Rosamund is a trained teacher, and I will help. If they have time and want to, we will make it fun and easy."

"Kind of you both," Adele said.

"I would attend" Upbeat Gustav came through again.

"A fine idea," said Svend. "All Scandinavians should know how to speak basic English or American. Small difference."

"Quite right." Naturally, his Lordship supported the English-speaking empire that spanned the globe.

"Do they speak some German?" Albert asked.

Mikkel shook his head, "Very little, but the officers can help translate. Niels, did you not live in Germany?"

Niels nodded. "But I prefer French." Typical Niels had to be difficult.

Mikkel shrugged his shoulders outvoted. "I suppose English classes would not cause a problem. If they have the time."

Rosie rolled her eyes. "We have our work cut out for us, Kathryn. Preferable to being idle."

I raised my glass and caught Rosie's eye. We made a silent toast to whatever would happen in our makeshift classroom.

Our discussion stopped with the arrival of our next dish, and the conversation dispersed into small groups around the table. Gustav and I talked about his life in Sweden. He was great at small talk and told me funny stories about his childhood.

Adele cleared her throat as if preparing to make a speech. "Nothing is so painful to the human mind as a great and sudden change."

"Is that another quote from *Frankenstein*?" Harriet shook her head. "Just horrid."

"Oh, I like *Frankenstein*." The movie, I was about to add.

"My favorite book. *Frankenstein; or, The Modern Prometheus* by Mary Shelley." Adele gleamed with pride as if she was the co-author.

"Finally, a sensible young girl who does not fawn over Miss Austen," Niels said. "But I hate to disappoint you, Miss Adele. It is medically impossible to build a man from cadavers. They have tried. I am a surgeon, so I know."

"I like the idea. It is so unusual and daring."

"The idea of creating a man from dead body parts is ludicrous," Niels said, not giving up.

"Niels, you of all people should keep an open mind. Medical miracles and strange things happen all the time," I said.

"Perhaps to you two, but not to the rest of us."

Under the table, Niels rapped his hand on my thigh as if trying to discipline a wayward child. I grabbed Niels hand under the table and jerked back his fingers.

"If this really occurred, she should have set the book in Paris," Niels said through clenched teeth while he pulled his hand and fingers free. "The only medical school in the world which utilizes corpses. I can testify to that."

"Say what you like. I do not care. I love that book." Adele's head shook, and her curls bounced loose.

Rosie looked nervous, and her voice shook. "If I die on the voyage, please lock my coffin in a metal cage. I am deadly troubled by resurrectionists."

"What's that?" I asked.

"Body-snatchers and grave-robbers," said Harriet with an evil smirk as if she would do such a thing.

"Harriet, Adele, young ladies should not talk about such matters," Lady Rushmere said.

Harriet rolled her eyes as if used to her mother's complaints.

Lord Rushmere said, "Adele, we've spoken about this. You do not love such a book. Reserve it for worthy books like the Bible."

Her mother wrung her hands and shook her head. "Adele, you must not bring that vile rubbish about monsters and that abhorrent Frankenstein into our home. Your father and I forbid it."

Adele looked humiliated and had my complete sympathy. Her public scolding was excessive for something so silly.

But Adele bounced back undeterred. "Victor Frankenstein is a doctor, not a monster."

Lady Rushmere shook her head tired of the verbal volleyball. "Regardless. That Mary Shelley. A disgrace to her family, his family, God, and everything sacred. Everyone sighed a collective relief when she breathed her last."

"What happened? Did she murder someone?"

"In a sense, yes. Miss Mary Wollstonecraft Godwin eloped with Percy Shelley. His pregnant wife was so distraught she drowned herself."

Harriet said, "Her body was found by the Serpentine river in London's Hyde Park. She left a suicide note."

"Oh, how awful. I didn't know."

Her Ladyship shook her head. "Of course not, you are an American."

A bell chimed, and this time I was grateful to escape the wrath of Lady Rushmere.

35 ~ Not My Kind of Turkey

Lord Rushmere rang the bell for the next course. Waiters rushed in carrying a Thanksgiving-style turkey on a massive platter. Unfortunately, they started with me, and the server said, "White or dark meat?"

The turkey was so intact and real, I considered requesting the fish or vegetarian meal option. Mikkel didn't seem thrilled with my comments on Frankenstein, so I knew not to embarrass him further.

"White, the breast, please," I said as politely as possible.

Adele and Harriet giggled, and Rosie shook her head slowly to signal me.

What was so funny? The waiters put a generous slice of meat on my plate. When they reached Gustav after serving the ladies, he asked for white and whispered to me, "I also like it the best."

When the platter reached Niels, he said, "American women. Direct and to the point. Protocol be damned. I prefer dark meat. A leg and thigh, if you will."

More nervous giggles erupted from the ladies. Was it off-limits to mention breasts or legs? Sitting up straight, I frowned at his rude implication.

Mikkel said, "Shall I remind my passengers we are not ruffians? This is a superb dinner my Lord and Ladyship. One we shall remember fondly, whilst we are at sea and far from such a magnificent feast."

I cut the meat and chewed a small piece of turkey. The meat had a strange texture and milky taste.

"What type of meat is this?" I asked Gustav.

Gustav shook his head, uncertain.

"I declare there is no enjoyment like eating," Rosie said. "Borrowed from dear Jane's *Pride and Prejudice*. Except she said 'reading' not 'eating.'"

Harriet echoed her agreement eating swiftly.

Adele moved the meat around her plate with her fork not eating much. "I wish we did not serve peafowl. Such beautiful creatures."

I asked Adele, "Do you mean peacocks?"

She looked downcast. "Males are peacocks, and females are peahens. Both are peafowl."

I choked and dropped my fork with a clink against the delicate china. Once a beautiful male peacock in France had put on a private show for the wrong type of female. The romantic Frenchie rotated, lifted, and shook his feathers for an audience of one ordinary human with no peahens in sight.

I grabbed my wine glass and gulped some Bordeaux wine to wash away the taste. His courtship ritual, known as train-rattling, mesmerized me as planned, and I fell in love. I couldn't bear to eat one.

"Adele, you always complain about their constant screeching. One fewer noisemaker." Harriet chided her little sister as if this happened often.

After an uncomfortable pause, Captain Matson changed the subject. "Kathryn, you should sail to America on my ship. Gustav and I would be pleased to welcome you aboard. We leave for the warmth of the Mediterranean in a few days. Gibraltar is lovely this time of year."

Gustav put his fork and knife down as if on high alert. But it must be my overactive imagination.

"Gibraltar sounds great, but I must get to Hong Kong. My uncle, dear Uncle Max, is waiting."

"Gustav shall have his own ship next year. I am pleased with his skills," Lord Rushmere said.

"How did you happen to meet Gustav?" Captain Matson asked.

I hesitated not wanting to mention he was standing in his underwear when I first saw him. My friends at home would laugh, but this would shock and horrify them.

Gustav was unfazed. "She wanted to acquire some men's clothes. She was –"

I touched his hand to apologize for interrupting. "We met at a tailor on High Street. Albert brought Rosie and me. We took our cabin attendants there to buy them a new set of clothes."

"Yes, and it all worked out beautifully. Not at that shop, but a more casual one on the side street. You know the one, Svend. Where our crew bargains for their clothes."

"Have you tried on your new trousers?" Gustav asked me quietly, but Adele overheard him.

"Did you buy men's trousers?" Adele's eyes grew with excitement, and she repeated this loud enough for everyone to hear.

"Um, yes. For under my skirts like Ida Pfeiffer, the famous Austrian explorer."

"How wonderfully brave of you," Adele said.

I focused on eating some potatoes. "Albert suggested it."

Albert shrugged his shoulders. "I mentioned Mrs. Pfeiffer but did not recommend it."

Everyone stopped eating to look at him.

Mikkel sat back in his chair with a thud. "I regret to say sporting trousers is quite unremarkable. Kathryn is fond of dressing like a boy."

Mikkel stood and excused himself. As he left the room, I considered chasing after him to apologize. But that would be unladylike, and he adhered to strict protocols. I shifted in my seat still wedged between Niels, the snake, and Gustav, a charmer.

Everything I did to fit in turned out to be a mistake. Tears welled up, and I dabbed at them with my napkin. I willed them to disappear and clenched my fists under the table with my nails digging into my palm. "Buck up," I said under my breath, "You can handle this."

Gustav noticed I was upset. He touched my shoulder to cheer me up while whispering some encouragement. "Do not fret. He is a gruff old man, but I have heard excellent reports from his crew."

"Women clad in pantaloons is most peculiar. Nevertheless, I shall delight in viewing something beyond relentless waves." Niels smirked.

Rosie piped in. "I bought a pair of trousers, too. The weather can be dreadful on the water. You shall not see them since they will be under our dresses. What was that saying you told me today about being stoic?"

"Keep calm and carry on?"

"Yes, that one. Lovely. We shall keep calm and carry on. Do you concur, Albert?"

Albert nodded and looked apologetic.

Mikkel returned to the table. His bruises had faded and were almost unnoticeable, but he didn't look well. During the discussion of slavery, his tanned face had turned pale. He can't afford to be ill with our long and risky journey ahead.

The conversation shifted to ships, voyages, journeys, storms, and back again. My heart wasn't into the chit-chat. Hong Kong couldn't come soon enough.

A stray strand of Gustav's blond hair came loose and lay on his shoulder glittering in sharp contrast to his dark suit.

I pulled it from his dinner jacket and dropped it on the floor. "Thank you, my dear."

"You are most welcome, my dear Gustav." I joked back. Despite my worries, I enjoyed his attention.

Adele gawked as if we had kissed.

Gustav laughed and reached under the table for my hand. Mesmerized by the candelabra with five candles flickering across from me, I needed breathing room and excused myself, letting go of Gustav's hand.

On my way back to the dinner party, I stopped to admire each painting in the hallway. My purchases today would have fit right in.

I heard my name whispered and dreaded Niels with another dirty trick. But Gustav poked his head from behind a massive mahogany cabinet and gestured. I tiptoed to him relieved, but with a nagging feeling. This was a risky move.

"Kat, please return to the States with us. On our ship."

"I can't stay. I don't know anyone here in England."

"I shall be in the port of Southampton every month or so. We could get to know each other better."

"Sorry." I shook my head. "Even if I wanted to, I really can't."

I turned to leave, but he took my hand and kissed it. "Please, Kat. Reconsider."

I delivered a quick peck on his cheek, but he turned his head and kissed me on the lips. Gustav placed his hands on my shoulders as if I was fragile.

"Ah, Gustav," a man said. Immediately I stepped away from his embrace.

Captain Matson, Gustav's boss, marched toward us. He spoke in rapid Swedish to Gustav. I understood pieces of it since Swedish and Danish had many similar words. Svend scolded him for carrying on in the hallway.

Gustav apologized, and I strolled back to the dining room. The servants waited to clear the table while the men stood around chatting.

"Pardon me, gentlemen. I am not fond of cigar smoke and shall attempt to keep the ladies' company." Niels bowed in my direction.

I ignored him. Not just tonight, but for the next two months or however long it took.

Gustav also made some vague apologies to join the ladies, but Captain Matson wouldn't allow it.

Even if Gustav somehow traded places with Lars, I couldn't fall in love. A long-distance romance was one thing, but this would only lead to disaster.

The women drifted in pairs back to the salon where we gathered before dinner, and the men went to the library to smoke. I sat next to Harriet. Her high-neckline and expensive jewelry protected her like armor. Her dark hair, almost black, was pulled tight into a flawless chignon.

Harriet asked, "How do you spend your time in New York City?

"I work most of the time." I almost mentioned my gym workouts, but that might be a strange pastime for women.

"And for pleasure?"

"For fun, I see friends, go to the theatre, museums, and out for dinner. Lots to choose from in New York City."

"What kind of work are you engaged in?"

"Finance and Wall Street business stuff."

"Are you a secretary?" Harriet continued to grill me, but I didn't mind. I wanted them to know women could have other career options.

"No. I ran my own consulting company for two years. But I closed it right before I left. Beforehand, I was a senior vice president for a bank."

Harriet's eyes widened in surprise, but before she could speak, Adele beat her to it. "Do you have a position or fiancé waiting for you in Hong Kong?"

"No. I am not planning to get married again. When I get back home to New York, I will find another job."

"A professional woman not pursuing a rich man. How marvelous." Adele wore a sly grin when our eyes met.

"Kathryn, you are young and should reconsider marriage and family." Lady Rushmere sneered as if she was a marriage counselor. "Gentlemen will be disappointed, my dear."

"Oh no, not again. Whoever it is, is better off with someone else."

Niels listened to our conversation. If he had any plans to marry me for my money, he should forget it.

Her Ladyship, as chief matron, shifted in her seat uncomfortably at my independent streak. "Let them arrive at that conclusion after the marriage, Kathryn."

I bit my lip refusing to agree, so she focused on another target. "Niels, what are your plans in Hong Kong?"

"They are in dire need of surgeons. Nothing holds me here, so I am off to make my fortune."

"What of your family?" Moving across the world alone for a job must be rare in her immediate circle.

"They are prosperous and content in Denmark."

"Have you been in England long, Dr. White?" Harriet asked.

"About a year. Excuse me, ladies, whilst I take this opportunity to inspect your collection of impressive art."

Niels walked to the far end of the room and inspected a painting up close and at a distance as if he contemplated buying it. An unlikely event considering his financial situation. He couldn't even afford the oil paint unless I lent him more cash.

Lady Rushmere excused herself to join Niels and show off her art.

Rosie, Adele, Harriet, and I breathed a collective sigh when they left and giggled. Our laughter grew until it was loud and unrestrained from deep in our bellies. Looking at each other and trying to stop just made it intensify. The four of us, all single women, left alone refused to remain demure and polite.

Whatever the reason for our laugh attack, I enjoyed the short break from this male-dominated society overloaded with harsh judgments and rules. Even if it only lasted for a few precious minutes.

36 ~ *Golden Grotto*

"Please call me, Kat."

Adele and Harriet meowed in response pleased to use my nickname. All this formality wore me down.

Rosie joined in and insisted on her nickname too.

Adele giggled. "I prefer Dellie."

Harriet frowned. "I yearned for a nickname for years. Harry does not work well."

"I would go with that. Men have it much easier," I said. In 1862, they certainly did.

"I do not have a husband to object, so perhaps I shall." Harriet's lighthearted response surprised me since she hid behind a haughty demeanor.

Our conversation shifted to books, music, theatre, and current events in England. I was at a loss to contribute much but enjoyed hearing them talk about their life. Harriet and Dellie led such different lifestyles. My friends at home would never believe this dinner party. I could barely imagine it, and I was here.

"Rosie, what happened to Ann Saunders?"

She fumbled around at a loss for words.

"The woman and the shipwreck mentioned at dinner." I prompted her in case she forgot.

"I am baffled how you chose to take this voyage but missed that infamous story. Miss Saunders was an Englishwoman who crossed the Atlantic for Canada forty years ago. Her ship ran into all sorts of troubles." Rosie looked away not saying more.

"Most of the men died, and they turned to cannibalism to survive. Miss Saunders helped with the dead. The captain said she had more strength than most of the men." Harriet acted as if she was discussing something casual like the weather.

Rosie's face turned white. "I shall return shortly."

Dellie offered to escort her, but she turned her down. I wanted to follow Rosie to make sure she was all right, but I couldn't resist hearing more gory details.

Harriet took my hand eager to fill me in on the tragedy. "Her book tells what happened, but it requires a strong constitution to read. Miss Saunders cut and cleaned the dead bodies herself. As soon as they stopped breathing, they drained their blood for the others to drink. When the survivors were rescued, over half had perished. They only survived by living off the dead. Even her fiancé succumbed."

"How awful." My overstuffed stomach ached at the tragic situation. "Was that legal?"

She nodded. "The custom of the sea and sometimes the sole way to survive."

This disgusting possibility had never occurred to me. Yet, plane crash survivors in the Andes back in the 1970s turned to cannibalism. This still happened.

"I should remind you, Kat. Do not imbibe salt water or urine. It will make you foolish." Harriet tapped the arm of her chair. "If you do, you will go stark raving mad and die."

"Drinking urine?" The idea sickened me, and I had to escape. An artistic tapestry across the room beckoned. I made a feeble excuse to avoid experiencing more of Miss Sanders' miserable adventure.

Adele followed me and took my hand. "Please forgive my sister, Harriet. She has no patience for an imaginary monster but is utterly fascinated by gruesome true-life events."

"Thanks, Dellie. I'm fine. Better to be prepared."

"I shall pray for you, Rosie, and Gustav. All of you at sea. Will you write to me? I fear I shall never make such a grand voyage. I should like to hear about the pleasantries and far off ports."

"I would be happy to do that." Except for Millie, I had no one else to write to, unless I needed more help from Uncle Max.

After seeing the artwork, Dellie offered to show me around upstairs. We invited Rosie, who had recovered her natural skin tone, but she and Harriet were busy discussing their favorite topic, Jane Austen.

At least, they had switched to a better topic. Harriet was cruel to remind Rosie of those grisly details written about by Miss Saunders. But a female survivalist with those skills would be useful. An event like that was out of my league.

Inside Dellie's bedroom, I admired a painting of a mermaid. "This looks like the figurehead on our ship, the *Anne Kristine*."

"I should like to see your vessel. Perhaps I can convince Papa to take me there before you depart."

"Please do, but you must like early mornings. We are supposed to leave port by nine."

She wrinkled her nose at the distasteful idea of getting up so early. My thoughts exactly, but I couldn't wait.

"If you like mermaids, you must see the shell grotto. We must go outdoors to see it."

We slipped off our hoop skirts and pinned our outer skirts high to keep them from dragging in the dirt. I followed Dellie downstairs, through their enormous kitchen, to the back door. A servant girl helped us put on fur-lined hooded cloaks.

Adele took a lantern and passed another to me. "The grotto is small and magical at night."

We wandered along a narrow stone path through their formal landscaped gardens. Adele stopped to show me some evergreens. "Our latest addition. Monkey puzzler trees. Have you seen them before?

We stopped, and I admired them. "Those trees look odd. Why are they called monkey puzzlers?"

"A nickname. The trees shall grow tall with long trunks and branches at the top. Difficult for a monkey to figure out how to climb them. Hence, a monkey puzzle."

"Cute." I laughed. "Never heard of them."

"I cannot remember their Latin name. They arrived from the South American continent. The garden is my mother's pride and my father's joy. You must visit during the daytime to see the gardens. They are exquisite and well known in these parts."

"I would like that." But secretly, I couldn't bear a future trapped in 1862.

"We have three female monkey puzzler trees competing for the attention of one male. Like at our dinner party tonight," Dellie said.

"What do you mean?"

"In twenty to thirty years, the monkey puzzlers should bear seeds. Tree offspring." Dellie snickered as if this topic was off-limits. "Females trees must be patient. What Harriet, and now I, must endure. One suitable man surrounded by three anxious women."

Rosie had also complained about the lack of men to marry. "You aren't a tree, Dellie. If you want to get married, I am sure you will. Any man would be lucky to have you, so don't stress about that."

"Do you have feelings for Gustav?"

"Feelings?" I rubbed my arms feeling the chill from standing still unsure how to respond.

A "who-who" from an owl interrupted the eerie silence. "Do you have a zoo with monkeys here too?"

"No, not yet," Dellie said chuckling. I wished they didn't own peacocks either.

"I apologize I should not have pried into your personal affairs." She marched ahead. After watching her for a minute, I ran to catch up. Monkey puzzlers might be harmless, but I didn't want to lose sight of her in the trees.

The grotto hid at the base of an outcropping of rocks. Dellie jiggled the key in a timber door cut to fit the oddly shaped entry.

"I like Gustav a lot. He is charming. But he has his ship, and I have mine. After tonight I'll never see him again."

She stopped to look at me. "Gustav is truly delightful and so attentive. Your heart must be heavy with sadness. Every broken heart leaves a permanent crack behind."

I was far from heartbroken but didn't want to sound callous. I debated explaining why. My weird story wasn't a novel like *Frankenstein*. Young Dellie had enough on her mind.

The door creaked open, and she disappeared. I ducked my head and followed her. Our lanterns illuminated thousands of shells that glistened in this fantasy cave world.

Dellie shut the door behind us. Shells were everywhere; even on the ceiling.

"The lady of the house loved the ocean and built this over a hundred years ago."

I raised my lantern to eye level and dragged my finger across a few shells. "This place is amazing. How did she do this?"

"She had them glued with a clay concoction made with

urine and blood. Not from humans though."

"Oh, how gross." I pulled my hand away from the shells, regretted touching them, and longed for some hand sanitizer.

"Foul but it holds."

"Miss Adele, are you there?" We heard a voice calling from the garden.

"My apologies. That is Henry. I shall return. Sit here, if you like." She patted an overstuffed chair with space for two draped with blankets.

The intricately placed shells formed pictures, and I read a shell-based story. The artist had designed elaborate borders too. After five minutes, I sat on the sofa and wrapped the soft wool covering around my shoulders to stay warm while I waited.

Adele opened the door again.

I stood up to greet her. "I can see why you like to come here. It's beautiful."

Except it was not Adele. In the dim light from the flickering lamp, a much taller person wearing pants snuck into the grotto.

"Adele could not return. Her mother needed her. I offered to fetch you," Gustav said.

"Oh, thanks. Have you ever seen a shell grotto?"

"No. Extraordinary indeed. I have always wanted to see one." He raised his lantern to see the shells and whistled his appreciation.

I turned towards him, and our metal lanterns clinked together. "Oh, the glass. We could have broken them." A fire would spread in a flash with the straw scattered on the ground.

Gustav put his lantern on the ground and sat on the settee. "Come and sit here next to me."

I hesitated since I should go back to the party. But a few minutes wouldn't hurt anyone.

"Kat, I wanted to tell you all night how much I enjoyed seeing you again. Sitting next to you. This has been the most pleasant night of my life."

"Oh, yes. Nice."

"More than nice, I trust." His breath warmed my neck, and I kissed him on the cheek.

He moved closer. The chair creaked while he kissed me

passionately.

"We should go." In between his tender kisses, I tried to resist and be sensible. "The others will be waiting."

After another minute, I reminded him of his boss. "Captain Matson." Not to mention my Captain Madsen. I couldn't risk this. Mikkel could still bar me from boarding, and I shuddered at the mere suggestion.

Gustav rubbed my arms and held me tighter, misinterpreting why I shivered.

I nestled into his arms safe and warm.

"Please, not yet. We have been given a special moment to spend together."

The shells flickered around us, and I had to agree. The magical grotto with a guy like Gustav was enchanting.

~~~

Back inside the manor house, I stopped in Dellie's room for my hoop skirt and smoothed my clothes and hair. I joined the others in the salon and sat in a chair next to the unpopular Harriet. I needed some distance from Gustav after our *ménage à deux* in the sensational grotto.

"Where have you been hiding?" Niels said. "Frolicking in the muck again?"

I had crossed my legs, and one shoe peeked out from under my skirt with mud covering the toe. I didn't like being under such scrutiny and gave him my most hostile look.

Niels tapped me on the shoulder and pointed at my foot as if I was an idiot. If I weren't in such polite company and on my best behavior, I would have taken off my shoe and thrown it at him.

"If you must know, Adele showed me their shell grotto. And for your information, those happen to be located outside in the garden." None of the other women crossed their legs, so I shifted around and put both feet on the floor.

Adele heard her name. "Kat saw the grotto, and Gustav wanted to see my stamp collection." Adele grinned and winked at me. She must have planned it and even had an excuse ready.

Gustav didn't say anything. Lying didn't seem his style.

Harriet, in competition with her younger sister, said, "Would you like to see my coin collection, Gustav?"

Gustav turned her down politely, but Niels said, "I most certainly would."

Harriet stood, and sticky-fingers Niels said, "Shall I follow you?"

"Certainly not. I shall bring the collection downstairs."

Harriet was too well-trained to allow a man into her bedroom and especially not a scoundrel like Niels. But she would miss out if she never visited the family's grotto with a special someone.

Niels hid his disappointment, but I was relieved. He might be desperate and steal some of her coins. If any went missing while we were here, it would cause an uproar.

A bottle of Plymouth gin with a full-rigged sailing ship on the label sat on the table. It reminded me of the naughty Norwegian aquavit that got me here in the first place. This gin must be part of our cargo to Hong Kong.

Lord Rushmere said, "You must try my English gin. Created from the purest water in England and a blend of seven exotic botanicals. We shall have a quick toast before dessert."

To prevent a hangover, I turned him down. What if I overslept and missed the departure? But all the men and even Rosie took a glassful.

Lord Rushmere said to Mikkel, "Give my regards to Lord Harrington in Hong Kong. Provide him with an extra case of gin with my compliments."

Mikkel pledged he would, and his Lordship clapped Mikkel on the back as if they were old friends. Over cigars, they must have patched up their disagreements on slavery. Or Mikkel could act along with the best of them.

"Do you know Lord Harrington?" Rosie asked Lord Rushmere.

"An old friend from my early days at school."

"Such a small world. Lord Harrington is my new employer. I shall be their governess."

"Splendid. Do give the Harringtons my best."

"Of course, I shall most willingly," Rosie said.

The servants carried in trays laden with desserts and a glass bowl teeming with layers of cream, fruit, and cake.

"Matilda makes the best trifle in England," Lady Rushmere said. "Kathryn, you will never taste such perfection in

America."

"How can I resist? Thank you, Matilda."

Matilda bobbed her head and handed me a generous serving.

I took a bite. "Packs a punch," I said teasing her Ladyship. The sugary sweetness lost the battle against the infused liquor.

"The sherry. Matilda has a heavy hand, but now I cannot imagine it made alternatively. Does it meet your expectations?" Lady Rushmere paused for my response.

Winning me over shouldn't matter. "The very best I've ever had." I couldn't recall ever eating this and smiled at Matilda energized from the sugar rush.

Harriet started to play some classical music on the grand piano filling the corner of the salon. Only Rosie and I paid attention, and Harriet had real talent.

Adele asked if I could play, and I told her a little. I planned to stay under the radar and far from their intimidating piano.

She urged me to play, and Rosie joined in and begged. "You must play for us! You promised."

"I did?"

"When we first met at the inn."

This would be humiliating. With my napkin, I wiped the last of the sugary dessert from my lips. The sherry, disguised as a trifle, had softened my resolve.

My eyes met Gustav's reliving his warm embrace and kisses in the grotto. I had money, friends, and an exciting journey before me. Contentment spread out like my full skirt.

Rosie brought me back to my current dilemma, to play or not to play, by taking my hand to coax me.

"Kat procured a piano for the journey. I would not be surprised if she is an accomplished pianist in addition to a prosperous businesswoman."

Harriet finished playing, and I headed her way fueled with liquor and determination. When Rosie heard how poorly I played, she wouldn't be so adamant about not accepting the piano as a gift.

"Bach?" I asked Harriet as we passed by.

She rolled her eyes as if that was the dumbest question imaginable. "The Johann Gottlieb Goldberg Variations. They were intended for the harpsichord, but I do my best."

"You are talented, Harriet."

Her eyes narrowed as if preparing to strike, but she only hissed a warning, "I do not give a fig. I never perform for them. Only for my own enjoyment. You should do the same, Kat."

"Right. Thanks, Harry. I will."

She grinned at her nickname and squeezed my arm signaling her appreciation. Her 'I don't care' words amazed me. Sadly, tonight few paid any attention to her deserving musical skills.

I sat on the cushioned bench and adjusted the seat closer to the keyboard and pedals. Under my breath, I said, "She was spot-on. Art should please the artist."

This piano was first-rate and the exact opposite of the one in the mental institution. My fingertips slid across the glossy and perfectly made ivory keys. How could I follow someone so talented? They will hate my lousy playing, and my singing isn't much better.

I slid down the bench to join the group again, but Rosie stopped me. "Please, Kat. Just one song. I promise to go next."

While the gifted Harriet was snubbed, I had an audience before I even began. Probably curious to see what damage a rough and uncultured Yank from the Divided States would do to their piano.

Fine. I sat tall to channel Carole King one more time. I caught Gustav watching me, felt his encouragement, and contemplated the pristine, intimidating keyboard. Even though my performance would never compare, I could add more feeling. Harriet's played like she ate, spoke, and dressed - stiff and deliberate.

I played a few chords and *The Pink Panther* movie theme for a warm up. I got out the kinks, sang, and improvised what I could remember of Carole King's song *Will You Still Love Me Tomorrow*.

Music needed passion even if you hit a wrong note. That was the best advice I ever received courtesy of my talented brother Keith. By playing music they had never heard, I could escape the worst of it.

I finished the piece, rested my hands in my lap, and scanned the room. Our refined group did not applaud or cheer. Carole King might not have appreciated my efforts either, but I'd scored high on my personal rating scale.

Rosie sat next to me, and Adele and Harriet stood by the piano's open lid watching me as if mesmerized.

Rosie said, "A beautiful song. One more, please."

"Okay, one more, and then your turn." For my finale, I was bold. "This is dedicated to Dellie, Harry, and Rosie." A song to support the unmarried women and loosen their bonds.

I played the risqué song; *You Make Me Feel Like a Natural Woman.* I sensed some tension in the high-class air. This reaction was perfect. I focused on playing the right keys and not harming Carole King's legacy. I imagined Lady Rushmere gasping at the suggestiveness of the lyrics.

When the song ended, Rosie and Dellie clapped and pulled me back to the present. Gustav had joined our group and cheered. Even Harriet congratulated me.

Mikkel and his Lordship were involved in an intense discussion and, to my relief, were not paying any attention to me.

Niels looked as if he was still trying to figure out which planet I was from. Svend and Lars, both happily married with children back home, looked uncomfortable.

Gustav stood behind me. "Bravo. You are magnificent."

Adele gushed with compliments. "Those are the most beautiful songs I have ever heard."

"Quite unusual." Lady Rushmere inspected her fingernails not making eye contact.

Like Harriet, I didn't care. My performance tonight hit my all-time best, and that was enough for me.

37 ~ *Greed's Not Good*

I expected an overpacked Volkswagen beetle experience while we rode in the carriage back to the hotel. All the other carriages I'd ridden in were small and maxed out with four passengers. But we were living the life of the rich and famous. The way the Rushmeres lived every day.

Lord Rushmere had insisted we return to town in his spacious Clarence harnessed with two muscle-bound stallions. Lars and Gustav rode in the smaller hansom carriage directly to their ships in port.

Rosie and I sat next to each other. The men granted us extra space for our full skirts, and out of politeness, they didn't sit so close to women. We had more leeway and whispered a private conversation. The ride was so smooth like a limousine and the perfect ending to the dinner party.

I recalled my bittersweet goodbye with Gustav, and his tireless attempts to convince me to stay and sail on their ship. He reaffirmed that nice guys do exist. Worst case, if I am stuck here permanently, I will return to England to see Millie and Dellie and find Gustav.

As if Rosie could read my mind, she said, "Good company is always worth seeking."

"Another Jane-ism?"

"*Northanger Abbey*."

"I am going to have to reread them all."

"Not a problem at all. Jane's entire repertoire is coming with us."

The heavy Clarence bumped along with what must be a very rough patch, so all conversation stopped.

When the men were preoccupied, Rosie said, "Agreeable family, the Rushmeres."

"Yeah, if you like that sort of thing. Too oppressive for me."

"Ah, life with the nobility."

"All the women talked about was shopping and Leeds. Kirkgate market with five hundred shops, and the glass dome for foul weather. I suppose it would be better than messy High

Street today."

"Such a fun diversion when we told them about our carriage escapade."

"You think so?" Rosie didn't laugh when we nearly fell over.

"Oh, yes. Your cleverness got the wheel free. Adele was awestruck, and I am so impressed." Rosie squeezed my hand.

"It wasn't much. We were in a hurry." I clenched my jaw. We may not be so lucky again.

"Delightful young women. A shame to not see them again."

"Put in on the wish list, Rosie. Tuesday market shopping day in Leeds with Harry and Dellie. Maybe they'll treat us."

"I am sure they would. They have plenty to spend. Lord Rushmere is one of the wealthiest businessmen in England with his valuable mills in Lancashire. If he can keep getting southern cotton through the blockade via Bermuda."

"Yeah, I suppose so." Serves him right to lose every dollar he invested in Confederate bonds. But I hoped this wouldn't hurt his daughters.

"Dellie was smitten with Gustav until you flicked hair from his shoulder."

"They made a big deal about it."

"That was a very personal gesture. We are much too proper and stiff."

"Well, now I know never to do that again."

"You are Dellie's role model for life. I shall not be surprised if she marries a Yank, but one who looks like Gustav. Did you hear Harriet wanted Mikkel to stay another day?"

Mikkel must have heard his name. "What?"

"Harriet wanted you to stay another day."

"She has tried that before." He looked embarrassed.

"Are you not interested?" Rosie pressed for an answer while he withdrew back into the corner of our spacious cab.

"No." He shrugged his shoulders while Niels said something derogatory about Harriet's appearance that made the men laugh. They soon turned their backs and ignored us again.

Rosie said, "Her parents would never approve of it. Not a marriage to a lowly sea captain. Wedding poor gentry with a title is more fitting. Furthermore, he is not British. Do you remember how they treated Captain Wentworth in Jane Austen's *Persuasion*?"

"Vaguely. Such a shame. Harriet looked older than Lady Rushmere."

"Lady Rushmere is not her mother. Harriet is the child from his first marriage, and her mother died. His second wife is Adele's mum. Harriet resembles her father with the Rushmere's unattractive square jaw. Dellie resembles her mother and will have abundant suitors in a few years."

"I guess you are right." Poor Harriet. She wasn't beautiful but far from ugly. A makeover with more attractive clothes, a better hairstyle, and some makeup would do wonders.

"Harriet has an older brother. He will follow in his father's footsteps as the next Baron. I got a sense he was a black sheep."

"Poor guy. I hope not as black as Frankenstein's monster. They hated him." I curled my fingers around my face and made a growling noise.

Niels heard me and cocked his head. "See Mikkel. She is surely losing it. Entirely lost without her sweet Swede. Assuming she ever had him."

Svend gasped when Niels referred to Gustav, his first mate. Probably alarmed at the possible loss of his number one employee to a renegade American.

"If anyone's losing it, it's you. Niels is a thief and a scoundrel, Captain Mikkel. He stole my letter and now my money."

"Must I remind you, Kat, you have your letter. Or did you misplace it again? Furthermore, it was not theft, simply a short-term loan."

"Well, interest has increased because of your rudeness tonight. Now it's an extra ten pounds payable at our first port of call. What's our next stop again?"

"Vigo, Spain," Albert said. "Easy to remember. We go to Vigo."

"Cute. So, Niels, if you must sell something or build something to sell, like Frankenstein's monster, you better hop to it."

Niels glared back. "How does one respond to someone like that? Albert, she listens to you. Please talk some sense into her."

Mikkel frowned. "A dinner party with the two of you is like being in the jungle with bickering primates."

His frustration killed all conversation, but it was just as well since we reached our destination. As I climbed out of the Clarence, I tripped and nearly fell from exhaustion, but Albert caught my elbow steadying me.

Mikkel requested we gather inside the lobby for an announcement before we separate for the night. "You must be fully packed and ready to leave the hotel at 0700 hours in the morning. I reserved additional carriages and wagons. Barring any emergencies," and he looked at me briefly, "we shall set sail by 0800 hours. The hotel staff will deliver breakfast to your room at 0600 hours."

Rosie sighed at such an early morning departure. For me, the earlier, the better. I couldn't wait to get away before anything else went wrong.

When I received my room key from the front desk, Niels said to Mikkel, "I will be ready in ten minutes."

"Ready for what?" I asked Niels.

Niels rolled his eyes. "You are much too curious for your own good."

"Better than being too annoying for your own good."

"My, she fights back. I must conduct a thorough examination tomorrow to find out why you are so extraordinary." He reached to reposition some of my hair hanging loose on my shoulders, but I moved away.

"You can't examine me. You will never understand me." I took off his expensive coat and handed it to him.

He chuckled and moved closer. "Perhaps you are right." He shook his head. "You may keep my precious coat. I should hate for you to get pneumonia and need my doctoring whilst underway. Although you must promise not to wear it the next time you decide to wallow in the mud."

I ignored his rudeness and held his gift close to me, glad to keep it.

Niels stroked his coat still clenched in my hands as if it was his favorite pet. "Like you, it needs tailoring to fit. We shall have plenty of time in the months to come."

Albert and Rosie were halfway across the lobby. I gathered

my long skirt in my hands and ran to catch up with them. Behind me, Niels laughed.

"Are you going out again?" I asked Albert.

"I am calling it a night. They are meeting young Edward Rushmere for some entertainment. The son and heir who missed our dinner tonight." Albert yawned and bid us a fond goodnight.

I asked Rosie, "Why weren't we invited?"

"Entertainment is a code word for whiskey and women." She checked to confirm no one was nearby. "From what I have been told, those ladies do not wear trousers, or much at all, at those bawdy-houses."

"You mean prostitutes at a brothel?"

She nodded. I shook my head visualizing Mikkel, Svend, and Niels bar hopping and chasing women.

"Poor ladies. Great to know my loan to Niels has such a valuable purpose. I should raise the interest rate again."

"I cannot believe how bold and uncouth he acted tonight."

"I can. Men like Niels think the world revolves around them."

~~~

Safely inside my room, I pulled off my detested hoop and petticoats and rested on my bed for a moment. The floor moved as if I was at sea. I should have passed on the after-dinner liquor.

His Lordship had personally filled the glasses. "Bushmills whiskey, the world's oldest distillery from the thirteenth century. The only item of value from winning the Battle of Culloden."

I had to honor the Scots and morn their devastating loss. Not just their lives but much of their culture was destroyed after that battle.

I must have drifted off since I woke up in my velvet gown. I removed my jewelry and hair clips and put on my nightgown. I will miss this soft bed and a real bathroom, even without a shower. Our hotels in the other ports may not be this upscale.

A sharp rap sounded at my door, and I tiptoed there to listen.

"Who it is?" It must be the middle of the night wishing I had bought a watch or clock today.

A muffled sound came from the hallway.

"Gustav?" I debated what to do. If I invited him in getting him out wouldn't be easy. I must refuse and stay on course for Hong Kong.

Someone snorted indicating a dirty trick.

"Is that you, Niels?"

"So, my dear Kat. No reunion tonight with desirable Gustav? You should know, I rectified your situation with the captain. Assured him of your health and well-being. You are such a worthy opponent. Cannot bear to leave you behind, dear Kat."

"No luck with the ladies?" I couldn't resist teasing him.

"Let me in, and I shall answer all your questions. And, we have a minor misunderstanding between us I should clarify." He jiggled the doorknob trying to open it.

"You can clarify from there."

"Oh, my dear. I am here for you. The only lady for me." He slurred his words and must be intoxicated gushing over with fake compliments.

"Yeah, right. Go to bed, Niels. Tomorrow's a busy day."

"For this slave, if there be any cunning cruelty that can torment him much and hold him long, it shall be his."

"What in the world are you talking about?"

"Lodovico from *Othello*. I saw your book on Shakespeare, and I assumed you –"

A man from out in the hallway said, "Can you leave the lady in peace? And the rest of us? Go sow your troubles elsewhere."

Niels said in a lower voice, "Another fiver, at a minimum, please. I shall explain later. You have ample funds, and I need your help."

"What do you need all this money for?"

"I had a few debts that required settlement. My income lags the cost to manage a suitable lifestyle. I promise to repay you generously."

"I guess you're not familiar with Shakespeare's *Hamlet*. Neither a borrower nor a lender be."

"I know. I know. For loan oft loses both itself and friend and borrowing dulls the edge of husbandry."

"You need to budget. Live within your means. I cannot be

your banker."

"I know. The money is not for me but to help a friend. She is in severe need, and I must reach her tonight."

What sort of severe need? To spend the night with a penniless prostitute? I picked up my purse and thumbed through my remaining cash. I had a five-pound note. In fact, I had several. I often donated five-dollar gift cards for a meal at McDonald's to the homeless. I folded two five-pound bills together debating how much to give him.

"You shall live to regret your selfish greed. *Adieu*."

Niels must have grown tired of waiting. Before I could respond or slide the money under the door, his footsteps thundered down the hallway as he stormed off. I pondered opening the door and running after him. Except I was wearing my nightgown and didn't want to wrestle with him. He was likely lying or exaggerating again.

While I lay in bed, Niels' comments about being selfish kept me awake. I tried to be generous. I bought so many gifts and distributed coins to needy kids all day today. But this represented just a fraction of my money, and I could have done more.

Would I regret my actions and this voyage? More than he would ever know. But I will make the best of it and reach my final port of call.

38 ~ Boarding All Boxes

Before the courtesy wake-up knock at the door, I lay in bed paralyzed with anxiety. I ached, not from a hangover, but from that combination of fear and desire.

That familiar feeling, I experienced every time I climbed the ladders to the high diving board at the local pool. The thrill of the freefall and watery plunge always scared me, but I loved it. To relax, I tightened and relaxed my body starting with my feet and moving upward.

At last, the hotel maid knocked on my door removing me from my trance. She delivered my breakfast tray and returned with my dress, petticoats, and coat from yesterday.

"My apologies, Mrs. Jensen. Your apparel is still damp. The laundress was unable to remove all the mud stains." She pointed to a tiny hint of brown remaining on the hem of the skirt and coat.

"This is great. So much better than I expected. Thank you." I pressed a generous one-pound tip into her hand.

She was so dazed at the tip, she backed into the tray, but I caught it before it hit the ground.

After she left, I sipped my coffee and took a bite of bread to calm my nerves.

Niels stinging comment at being selfish would not disappear. On my last day in Hong Kong, I will distribute all my funds to the poor. In every port, I resolved to try to help all those less fortunate.

Someone knocked at my door. I expected to see the maid again, but Mikkel waited dressed in his dark blue captain uniform. His eyes were red, and I waved him in.

He noticed my messy room but didn't make a snide comment. What did he expect? I was in the middle of packing. He walked over to my chair as if to sit down but stopped. My new trousers hung on the back of the chair ready to pack.

"I only have one pair which I will wear underneath my dress when it's cold. No one will ever know."

"I suppose I should expect some changes with my first

modern passenger. I wore dresses once. As all young boys do. I must admit I prefer wearing trousers."

I sat on the edge of my bed curious why he made this unexpected visit.

"Albert told me what you did to help those women. I did not know the doctors treated the women so despicably. Honorable of you to help them. Even if your actions were devious."

Last night, I heard the police would have hauled us off for an unpleasant interrogation. But I was proud. If we had rescued Millie and Maxi, it would have been perfect.

"Are you positive you want to leave with us today?"

"Yes, for the thousandth time. Did Niels put you up to this?"

"Niels raises some valid concerns. Our voyage is long and perilous. The journey to America is much easier. And, I must warn you. Mariners are a superstitious lot. When you fell in the storm, there was much talk about it. In particular, your strange clothes."

He rubbed his forehead, reached for the pitcher of water, and poured himself a glass. "To stop them from thinking the worst, we placed the small black cat in your cabin when you were unconscious. The cat would sense evil and if so, would shun you. As I predicted, the cat enjoyed your companionship."

"The cat?" They believed adorable little Esperanza could tell them this?

He nodded. "Notwithstanding the strong report from the doctor, some of the crew hold doubts."

"About me? Do they all feel that way? Do Uffe and Henrik?"

"No, they would like you aboard. If you desire it."

The other sailors were polite but aloof. I rarely had an opportunity to meet them and few chances for them to get to know me. They were either rushing around working or downstairs in the hold.

"You are the captain. Don't you decide? You said I could go. I promise I will disembark in Hong Kong and won't be any trouble."

"And you shall. Once you become acquainted with the rest of the crew, all shall be resolved."

That settled it. As soon as can, I will find Stefan and thank him for saving my life. If Simon bought them a delicious meal with my contribution that may have won over some of them.

Mikkel inspected my breakfast tray again.

"If you're hungry, help yourself. I don't have a 'hair of the dog' cure."

"Dog cure?" He wiped his face with his sleeve and chuckled. "Not a cat cure?"

"No, cats are smart and wouldn't need one. That's what we call it in the United States. A special drink with alcohol to cure a hangover."

"Thank you, but no. I had ample last night. I shall be fine with fresh air."

Mikkel grimaced. "Excuse me." He ran to the bathroom. The sound of vomiting came from behind the door. The toilet flushed, and water ran in the sink. When he exited my bathroom, his face was pink with his hair damp by his forehead.

"All better now?"

"Pardon me. I shall be in good health on my ship." He smirked, and I grinned back.

Last night he may have spent time in the arms of a woman. Despite that disappointing image, I wished him a speedy recovery. He needed to be top notch to sail our way out of here.

I stood ready for him to leave to complete my packing, but he didn't move.

"There is something important I must discuss with you."

I braced myself for terrible news. Did Niels jinx me?

"Svend's first mate, Gustav Wallström –"

"What about him?"

Mikkel gazed out the window. "Gustav found me last night, and we stayed up until dawn. He is quite taken with you."

"I barely know him. He is only a friend."

"Regardless, he cares very deeply."

I started to argue.

"Hear me out, please. Gustav will command his own ship next year. He is a respectable and amenable young man. He would like to court you. If you leave today, you will not see him for a year or longer. If you change your mind again, it will be difficult to return. Other ports do not provide the frequent passage and ease of Southampton."

"You shouldn't be concerned about that. I am not getting off your ship for Gustav or anyone else."

He cocked his head. "You appeared rather smitten last night."

"Gustav is a great guy. He is easy to talk to, but I hardly know him." My recent dating fiascos were proof of how wrong first impressions can be. "I am not looking for someone to marry."

Mikkel didn't look convinced.

"My marriage didn't end well. My husband planned to leave me before he got sick. So, you see, I doubt I will ever marry again." One passionate night in a grotto with Gustav wouldn't alter that.

Mikkel touched my shoulder. "My apologies. Marriage can be quite pleasant and a righteous reward. But with a sailor, even a captain, the time apart and uncertainty add further hardships."

What else is new? Hardship follows me everywhere, but I stayed quiet.

"If you can, enlighten him gently. Gustav shall be on the *Anne Kristine* this morning to speak to you."

After Mikkel left, I gazed out the window. Explaining to Gustav why I can't marry him would be easy. Countless good reasons danced before me. But this was an ego-boosting problem to have. He must be twenty years younger than me and so charming. I wished I could take a selfie of the two of us to show my friends if I get back home. I reminded myself: not if, when.

I finished stuffing everything into the carpet bags while humming the song *Don't Worry, Be Happy* and went downstairs to join the others. I couldn't imagine marrying a sailor. Traveling for business was one thing, but living on a ship for years? Or waiting for him to show up? Nope, not happening, ever.

Outside, Rosie, Albert, and I milled around by the carriages waiting. Luggage, trunks, and crates obscured the roofs of the carriages with the overflow packed into added wagons.

Mikkel joined us. "Has anyone seen Niels this morning?"

None of us had, and Mikkel swore under his breath.

"Albert, please go inside, make inquiries, and check his room. I shall take the ladies to the ship and send Lars to collect you both."

As far as I was concerned, good riddance. Niels was on his own. I was eager to get to the ship. My purchases from yesterday were waiting with only an hour or two to stash them away.

~~~

My butter pecan colored cabin was a mess. Both trunks were open, buried under clothes, and in complete disarray. Uffe followed with my carpet bags and stashed them inside. I slammed the door shut behind me to check on my deliveries. Unpacking and straightening up had to wait.

Deliveries piled up with stacks of wooden boxes including some marked from the pharmacy and clothing shop outside my cabin. A temporary narrow walkway slithered among the barrels and boxes of goods waiting for storage in the hold. Large crates waited on the pier for the nets to haul them on board.

With four passengers boarding, chaos was an understatement. The experienced crew rushed around but didn't seem overly stressed. They must be accustomed to this happening at every port of call.

Heavy crates stood outside my cabin from the liquor store chock-full of wine, champagne, and other mysterious liquors I couldn't resist. Stinky cheese wafted from one of my boxes, and I had to deliver it to the cold box in the galley.

I passed Uffe a small crate, and I carried a variety of local cheese including Stilton, one of my favorites. The food purveyor also sold me some jams, jellies, and chutneys that would add more zing to the menu. Simon should welcome these contributions and make his menu planning easier.

On the way to the galley, I passed a few unfamiliar sailors. I didn't want to slow down, but one of them stopped to speak to me.

"Thank you, Madam Jensen, for the special dinner. The others asked that I thank you on their behalf until we leave port. Later, they shall have an opportunity to thank you properly."

"I hope everyone liked it."

I shifted the box to one arm and shook hands with him. "Please call me Kat. Short for Kathryn or Katrine in Danish."

"I am Stefan, and he is Peter."

Stefan and I shook hands. I extended my hand to Peter, but he shuffled his feet and stared at his shoes. He slumped down, and his body seemed to shrink from nerves.

"Apologies, Kat. Peter does not shake hands."

From Stefan's left hand a sparkle of steel glinted. Under his long sleeve, he had a metal hook. I looked back at Stefan's face to hide my surprise.

"Oh, no problem at all. Some people don't do that to avoid germs and getting sick."

"Getting sick? No, he just never does."

I shifted the box and glanced back at Uffe. He had put his crate down, so I did too.

"Totally fine, Peter." I offered him my best smile even if he couldn't see it.

"Are you the Stefan who rescued me in the thunderstorm?"

"Yes, Kat."

"I wanted to thank you and never got a chance. You were so brave and saved my life. I do appreciate it." I tacked on the Danish expression *tusind tak* which meant a thousand thanks. He must think I'm a self-centered ingrate when I never bothered to thank him.

"Sorry. I must run. Crazy now."

"Crazy?" Stefan asked looking worried.

"Oh, not me. Today is crazy. I bought so much stuff and must oversee all these deliveries before we leave. We'll talk later."

Stefan nodded, and Peter caught my eye for a second but looked away as if upset. They walked off in a hurry. Peter may be superstitious, but I could win him over later.

How impressive that Stefan managed to save me with only one hand and a hook. My admiration for the captain grew tenfold if he willingly hired injured and handicapped employees. Mikkel had said several times his boys were different and deserving but never explained how or why.

Uffe and I gathered up our boxes again. In the galley, crates, cans, bottles, and bags of food surrounded Simon. I put my container on the deck since the table overflowed with purchases.

After a quick greeting, I said, "I bought some cheese and jams for everyone including the crew. Maybe you can use them?"

He accepted the box and loaded it on top of some crates on the table. "Kind of you, again. Thank you."

"Sorry to be a bother, but I also bought some liquor. A few cases are by my cabin. Can I stash them somewhere?"

"I will find you a storage place in the hold. Uffe can bring them around."

Simon took a clay container off a shelf and shook out some notes and coins and handed them to me. "You were too kind."

I stepped back and shook my head. "No need to repay me. The money was a gift for an exceptional meal for everyone. Why didn't you spend it all?" I should have ordered the meal.

"The meal was superb, but the funds were too generous." Simon put the money on the table.

Mikkel walked into the galley and saw us standing over the money. "Are you turning into a moneylender, Kat?"

"No, this was for a crew dinner." This was my money. If I wanted to give it all away, I should be free to do so.

"What crew dinner?" Mikkel asked in a hurry.

Simon shrugged his shoulders.

"Never mind. Simon, explain this later. Kat, Gustav is here and wishes to see you. He is waiting in the salon."

"Not now, sorry. I have deliveries to see to."

I headed out to search for my paintings, piano, and other expensive deliveries.

Mikkel said, "Stop."

I froze and turned around. My instinct was to question or disregard dumb commands. Except I should try to follow the captain's rules whenever possible.

"All that can wait." Mikkel escorted me to the salon door. "You must not summarily dismiss him. Consider his proposition sensibly. It is much safer for you to remain here."

"Here?"

"In England, or for that matter, America."

"Not that again. Fine. I will meet with Gustav one last time."

I inhaled and pushed open the salon's door ready to face my overly sweet Swede.

39 ~ A Fair Trade

"May I write to you, and will you write to me?" He stared at me while making notes in a leather-bound notebook.

"Sure, Gustav. But it takes so long to send letters back and forth."

"Packet ships for mail are surprisingly fast. You may write to me via the ship at these ports. I have listed the estimated dates. And here is my sister's address in Göteborg. She handles my post."

I took his detailed handwritten note. "These dresses are so impractical." Without any pockets or a purse with me, I stuffed it in the only safe place I could find, my bodice.

He grinned. "My address is lucky to be so near your heart. Please Kat, give me your address in America." Gustav turned to a clean page in his notebook and handed me his pen.

I debated making up an address in case someone like Niels saw it and used it against me. But they had to be familiar with New York City to know shacks and pig farms once blanketed parts of the Upper West Side of Manhattan in 1862. How fantastic if Gustav's letter did somehow arrive. As rare as receiving a love note in a bottle one-hundred and fifty years later.

I wrote down my real address leaving off the zip code. "Gustav, you should find another girl. Someone more your age. She will be the luckiest woman in the world."

"I shall wait one year, or until you write and tell me otherwise. Your uncle in Hong Kong may have plans for you."

"Uncle? Oh, that guy. No way!"

He smiled but looked unconvinced. Gustav kept trying to talk me into staying in England while making notes in his book.

Uffe knocked at the door. Gustav stood and greeted young Uffe like a dear friend.

Worried about what he had jotted down about me, I snuck a glance at his open notebook left on the table to see what he had written. He had made an ink sketch of my face. His quick drawing of me was uncanny.

I gazed at Gustav trying to understand what such an attractive and wonderful guy saw in me. His only flaw was being too persistent. Our relationship, even in 1862, would never work. He was too young and lived on a steamship.

He was isolated and surrounded by men. That was the only plausible reason women weren't standing in line waiting for him. Single ladies hadn't discovered him, and when they did, he sailed away.

"Madam Kat, your piano and musical instruments are here. What are we to do with them?" Uffe asked.

"Put them here in the salon for now. Can you ask Rosie where she would like them?"

Uffe hesitated. "I can't speak to her."

"Oh, right."

I said to Gustav, "Uffe doesn't speak much English. I need to find Rosie. Do you want to come with me?"

Gustav cleared his throat. "I shall wait by the gangway for you." He must feel second-rate behind the priority of a musical instrument.

~~~

After getting the piano and instruments settled with Rosie and Uffe, I went in search of my Swedish officer and gentleman. The morning haze had burned off, and the sun brought a welcome layer of warmth. But the ship wouldn't be leaving on time contrary to Mikkel's plans.

I joined Gustav by the railing, and we gazed at the busy dock below. An oversized crate was transferred from a wagon into a complicated set of nets to load onto our vessel.

A man in a refined business suit stood next to the crate, shouted, and swore. "Look here. Careful! These contents are exceedingly fragile."

The sailors sweated and traded off turning a metal crank to lift the crate in the air and swing it onto the ship's deck. I held my breath when it got close to the railing. The worried man ran up the gangway while he watched the crate.

"My Great Lord Jesus Christ. Would you swing your mother about like that?" The red-faced man wiped sweat from his forehead with a handkerchief.

Did the container hold something fragile like a live animal?

He stood under the net unconcerned that the giant container might fall on him.

The sailors may not have understood English, but they got the gist of his concerns and were more cautious.

Once it landed, he said, "Thank God. If there is any damage, you shall hear from my superiors."

Some sailors lingered nearby curious about the contents of this mysterious crate.

Mikkel approached the man. They chatted, but I couldn't distinguish their words. The man pulled out some paperwork for his review.

Mikkel called me, but I hesitated. I hadn't ordered anything fragile like a live animal. Mikkel waved me over impatiently.

"Mrs. Kathryn Jensen?" The man read from his papers.

"Yes." I wiped my hands on my dress and shook hands with him.

"Your artwork. But we must inspect it first. Those barbarians were apt to harm it. With any luck, it is minor and only the frames."

Mikkel said, "Be quick about this inspection. We are leaving in a half-hour. The tugs will arrive soon to take us to the channel."

"Since time is of the essence, we shall reduce the price for any damage."

Four sailors each took a corner and moved the heavy crate to the salon. The man had special tools he spread out to open the container with Uffe's help. Since this would take time, I went to find Gustav and say goodbye.

Gustav stood on the bridge with Lars looking at some charts and maps, and what must be the first leg of our journey. Both first mates were clad in navy-blue suits. Last night, they were sharp in formal attire, but in uniform, they stood out from the others and looked handsome.

"There she is. The lady with the peculiar crate." Lars said, and we all laughed.

"As if they were loading a mountain lion. Just some paintings. What an ordeal."

Gustav took my arm, and we walked over to the railing behind the cabins and near a lifeboat. The quiet shoreline on the opposite side of the pier was soothing.

"Kat, by next year I will oversee a ship. Not like this. A steamer, and the ship of the future."

"How exciting. I am happy for you."

"I know you do not want to wait or make a promise."

We had gone over all this in the salon. I should be cruel and tell Gustav he isn't my type and end it. Except I couldn't, he was an unbelievably sweet guy, just like Niels had said.

He clasped my hand. "Are you familiar with the word *gantlet*?"

"Do you mean gauntlet? Going through something hard to get to the end?" Too familiar; this trip was a gauntlet.

"It is from two old Swedish words, *gata* and *lopp*, meaning lane and course. I shall remain on a *gantlet* with you in my thoughts."

"Oh, Gustav, don't do that. It's unlikely I will ever come back here."

"I shall wait a year. If you don't send word by the end of 1863, I will know the answer."

"On the day I reach Hong Kong, I will send word."

"Thank you, Kat. I will pray for your safe voyage, and if you desire, your return. Swedes live a life of *lagom*?"

"*Lar-gum*?"

"Another Swedish word but harder to translate. *Lagom är bäst. Lagom* is best." He caressed my flyaway hair. "It means that we live in moderation and keep our expectations in balance. We possess enough."

"Not a bad idea." I should adopt this mindset to reduce future disappointments.

"It would be easier if you would remain here in England." He sighed, indicating he was resigned to my departure.

A sailor gave Gustav a message. Gustav read it and crumbled it into his fist. "I must return to my ship and bid you farewell, my dear. Svend demands my presence within the hour."

"I wish you all the best." I hugged him goodbye. His arms were strong, and he smelled soapy fresh with a hint of cologne. For a moment I hesitated unwilling to release him. "If you do write me a letter, please send me a sketch. Your portrait to remember you."

"A portrait of me?"

"Like the one you made of me today."

He grinned. "I shall be honored to do so."

After I let him go, he said, "Please be careful. That doctor, Niels Hviid, is untrustworthy." He checked around as if someone might be listening. "The old man, he is …"

"Old man? Who?"

Gustav laughed. "No one told you? Seafarers are citizens of a maritime world ruled by King Neptune. We have own language, customs, and culture. You shall learn it on the seas."

"And heavily superstitious."

He nodded looking out at the water. "An old man is a captain. Yours is well liked by his motley crew of mariners, but he is …"

"What?" I strained to concentrate disrupted with the memory of the famous rock band, Mötley Crüe's popular concert finale song *Home Sweet Home*. The song about nostalgia for home hit hard. I ached to sing out part of the chorus, *I'm on my way*.

His brilliant blue eyes looked serious. "From what I have heard, his sailors will readily risk their lives for him. I admire him and should like to do the same thing if I could afford it."

"Do what?"

"My dear Kat, I fear there is no time to explain, and I lack all the answers. You shall discover that and more on your voyage." He took my hand and kissed it. "You should know that Svend told me your captain fears you."

"Fears me? But he said he wasn't superstitious."

"All mariners are superstitious. As inescapable as the salt water that permeates our blood. Please be careful. You can trust Lars Hansen, your first mate. He assured me he will watch over you."

Gustav pulled a small gold ring off his little finger. "I would like you to accept this. For our friendship."

"Oh, no, Gustav. I can't. That looks expensive. Save it for your wife."

He shook his head, and his blond hair glistened in the sun. "Please take this, *min älskling*."

Älskling sounded about the same in Danish and meant darling. He loosened a top button and pulled over his head a silver necklace with a small black cross."

Gustav held the chain dangling in the breeze, but I kept my hands at my side. "I am not anti-Christian but not a strong believer. I have never worn a cross."

"This is not a cross. It is an ankh with a handle. See here." He outlined the big loop on top of the cross. "It symbolizes life and good luck. It is not Christian, but ancient Egyptian."

I hesitated not wanting to accept it.

"Please wear it. This will keep you safe."

"You should keep it. Especially when you get promoted. Captain Mikkel has lectured me about this. Captains are responsible for everything all the time. Even the weather."

He shook his head. "I know, but I insist, Kat."

"You are a kind man. I wish we'd had more time together. You deserve a woman to make you happier than you ever dreamed."

He clutched his necklace in his hand with the ankh dangling under his fist and gazed across the water. I kissed his cheek, but he pulled me to him and put his hands on my hair kissing me on the lips. His lips tasted of salt, but also something exotic like a sweet mango.

I hugged Gustav goodbye and ran back to my cabin before I changed my mind. Even though the ship remained tied to the pier and wasn't moving, I stumbled on the way while I coached myself. Think with your head. You met him yesterday. You don't believe in getting married. And most of all, you don't belong here.

The man in the salon had unwrapped my paintings. I tried to stop thinking about Gustav.

The art dealer had kept them wrapped in protective quilts and showed each one to me individually. We went through them while he crossed each one off the list. A few of the frames were slightly damaged in the corner, but nothing some spackling and paint couldn't fix.

I signed the invoice and jotted down my new account number. The deliveryman could take every cent in my account if so inclined. My thoughts were on Gustav, not money, so I didn't bother negotiating for a higher discount.

I walked back to my cabin to sort out the mess.

Uffe said, "Carpet delivery, Madam Kat. Did you buy magic carpets? My mother told me tales about them."

I laughed remembering the magic carpet ride at Disneyland. "I did. In case we decide to fly around the ship."

Uffe took my hand. But something pulled me back to the pier. "I will return in ten minutes, Uffe."

Gustav was halfway down the gangway to the pier. His head hung low as if suffering. An ache in my chest made me reconsider. Was I too cruel?

"Wait, Gustav," I yelled to stop him. He smiled with too much anticipation. "I want to give you something."

I ran to the salon, grabbed a painting of a ship with a vibrant sunset, and hurried back to the gangway. My personal favorite which reminded me of the masterpieces by the famous British artist J.M.W. Turner.

Gustav smiled as he sprinted back up to meet me.

"Here." I panted breathing hard from the workout. "I hope you like it. I will trade it for your necklace. If you still want to."

He whistled admiring the painting and took off his ankh necklace. I squeezed the chain tightly, and we hugged a final emotional goodbye in front of the observant crew.

"I shall treasure it always," he said. "And when we meet again, I shall have your portrait painted."

"Mine? Oh, Gustav." He said when not if, and I couldn't find the right parting words.

A true romantic, he sang a few lines from last night's Carole King song. "Will you still love me tomorrow? I know I will."

40 ~ More Men in Blue

I leaned against the railing to watch Gustav walk away with my painting and exchanged a final wave goodbye.

Someone tapped me on the shoulder, and I turned around expecting Uffe to bring me back down and hurry me along.

Mikkel's voice rang out above the commotion. "Kathryn, these men need to speak to you."

"Men?" Whenever he called me Kathryn, instead of Kat, I feared trouble.

I turned in such a rush, my heel caught in my extra-long petticoats without a hoop skirt. The momentum thrust me forward as if diving into a pool or doing an uncharacteristic gymnastic flip on land.

A wall of a blue with a line of brass towered in front of me. I tried to stop myself, but my head slammed against it. The wall fell with a distinct groan and the hiss of air. Thankfully, the wall felt soft, and my head, while jolted, didn't hurt. I had landed on a layer of grape jelly.

Someone grabbed my arms pulling me to my feet. I stood dazed and confused.

The wall of blue was a heavyset man and not a peanut butter and jelly sandwich. The man I toppled sat on the deck, and another man huddled over him. The other man was smaller in girth but identically dressed in a blue suit with a strip of brass buttons. He helped him to his feet.

I came to my senses and hurried over to him. "I am so sorry. Are you hurt?"

I stood by horrified, but Mikkel had a funny grin on his face as if trying not to laugh.

The fallen man brushed off his suit and dusted off his hands. "I am fine, young lady. But you must be more careful." His strong accent clipped his words, and he was winded from his fall. "Particularly on a ship. Someone could be knocked overboard and drown."

"Yes, I know. My long dress got wrapped around, and my heel caught –"

"Let us join the others to resolve your plight," Mikkel said to avoid wasting time. I followed him while the other two men walked behind me.

Albert and Rosie sat around the table waiting for us. Once seated, Mikkel made the introductions. "These police officers are searching for Niels White. Has anyone seen him? His hotel room and cabin are empty, and his belongings have not arrived."

We told the police we last saw him at the hotel after the dinner party. Mikkel explained how Niels had joined some of the others for festivities but left early.

"And none of you have heard from him since? No messages?" The younger police officer, who I avoided knocking over, grilled each of us.

"He contacted me. He came to my room," I said.

"Ah ha, I knew it." The police officer I toppled licked his lips as if going in for the kill.

"He did? You let him in your room?" Mikkel said in disbelief.

"I didn't let him in. We spoke through the door, and he left. He didn't say where. I'm surprised he isn't here."

"At what time did this occur?" The younger police officer jotted down information in his notebook. After so many years as an internal auditor, I usually asked the questions. I would respond honestly without anything extra.

"Late last night or early this morning. I don't own a watch, so I'm not sure." Women wore watches hidden in their pockets, and I regretted not buying one. It was on the top of my shopping list for Vigo.

"Why didn't you let him in?" The older officer took over the questioning.

"He wanted ... I mean it was late. I was tired." I didn't want to explain how we argued all the time.

"So, he only wanted to come inside your room?" The police officer squinted and appraised me like a piece of property wondering why he would bother. Today I was a mess after not getting enough sleep, rushing around with the boxes, and pleading with Gustav.

"No, he wanted to borrow some money." I pressed my lips together with regret. If they saw my odd currency, it would raise too many questions.

The police officers scrutinized me. The old one took off his hat and wiped his head with his handkerchief as if this would help him understand this new twist. I squirmed, wishing I could run and hide.

"Kathryn loaned him a small sum a few days ago," Mikkel said. "How much was it?"

"Fifteen pounds, but he promised to repay me with interest."

"What did he need this new loan for?"

"I don't know exactly. Niels said he needed it for a friend."

"How much did he ask for last night?"

"Five."

"Five pounds? In addition to the fifteen?" Mikkel shook his head. "That fool."

"I didn't give him any money. He left before I could put it under the door."

"Anything else you can recall? Facts we should know?" The snide police officer pursed his lips studying me.

"I hope he's all right." Niels was annoying, but this inquiry was nerve-wracking.

"You did more than anyone would expect. His proper home is with all the other debtors at the Marshalsea," Mikkel said.

"Where is that?"

"A prison for those with unpaid debts across from London Bridge," Rosie said. "Charles Dickens' family lived there. But it has closed. Today Niels would be sent to the Queen's Prison."

"For being in debt?" I asked. Movies based on Dickens' novels showed how tough life was back then which was now. Bankruptcy, forgiveness, and a clean slate were almost impossible.

"Regardless. You must live within your means." Rosie had clearly heard this too many times.

"Odd fellow, but a pleasant enough chap," Albert said. "A skilled surgeon from what I heard about town. I wonder how he got himself into such debt."

Students borrow a mountain of debt to cover outrageous college costs. "Perhaps his debts were related to his training in Paris to be a surgeon. Medical school can be expensive."

The questions directed to me ended, so I had a few of my

own. "What did Niels do? Forgery?" To send two men to find him, he must be in serious trouble.

"No, murder. If you happen upon the rogue or hear from him, let us know at once."

Rosie gasped, and Albert said, "My word."

Mikkel's reacted with pure anger. "Search the ship again. I want him removed."

The younger police officer said, "This voyage must be costly. Did he pay for the entire journey?"

Mikkel's eyes narrowed. "No, he has not paid a shilling. Niels received a discount in exchange for his medical skills. He pledged to pay a deposit upon boarding the ship."

"Is that typical?"

"No, Niels argued he had substantial funds guaranteed. He vowed to settle his account in full before we left Europe."

"How did you meet him?"

"He contacted my shipping agent. I know nothing more than his name and occupation. I can give you their address in London. Doubtful you will obtain more information there. They refer names, and I decide."

"You do not confirm references?" The police officers shook their heads as if they were dealing with a foreign imbecile.

"For my mariners, I make inquiries, but not for passengers. My ship rarely carries them. Niels is a fellow Dane who I supposed was trustworthy. I can assure you. Thorough investigations will be done on everyone in the future." Mikkel spoke fast in a clipped tone.

The police officers and Mikkel stood, and Mikkel consulted his pocket watch. "All this has caused a major delay. We must set sail in thirty minutes. I will free up some men to assist with the search."

The police officers must be wrong. I disliked Niels, but he didn't seem to be the murdering type.

Rosie and Albert shook their heads, and we left for some fresh air. If they found Niels, I didn't want to see him arrested and dragged off the ship.

The younger and more easygoing officer stood by the railing and lit a cigarette. It was now or never. I approached him cautiously to avoid another collision. "Who is the person?"

"The person?"

How could he be so dense? "The person Niels may have murdered?"

"Ah, it's not a question of *may*." He exhaled a thin trail of smoke and flicked some ashes into a small metal jar on the ground. "We possess an eyewitness and a dead body."

"What if it was an accident? He is a doctor and a surgeon, you know."

"Not for me to decide. The courts, under the authority of the Mayor of Southampton and Her Majesty, do so." At least, Niels wouldn't rot in prison without a trial.

"Who it was? The person who died?"

The police officer pulled out his notebook and flicked through some pages. Mikkel strode our direction with a couple of sailors in tow, so he had to hurry.

I glanced down at the warrant. The name I dreaded was halfway down. Millicent Phillips died early this morning. Cause unknown. Niels White, alias Niels Hviid, alias Niels Blanc, is the prime suspect. Reported by her son, the Earl of Montford, Edgar Phillips.

"Is she the victim?" I asked in disbelief.

"Dowager Countess Phillips. First name Millicent. She expired at her son's estate at approximately three this morning."

"Oh," I groaned unable to speak.

Mikkel interrupted us. "Ready?"

"Yes, sir. This ship has a lot of nooks and crannies. With your crew's help, we shall find the devil. Good day, Madam." He tipped his hat farewell. I slammed against a wall and slumped down wanting to cry and scream in agony.

Poor, dear Millie is gone forever. Somehow the news she was a countess didn't shock me and didn't matter. The scoundrel Niels killed her. How in God's name did that happen?

41 ~ Arresting Developments

Uffe pulled on my sleeve and brought me back to the real world. "Kat, the paintings and carpets. We m-must move them from the salon."

"Oh, right." I was pleased Uffe dropped the Madam habit and grateful for a temporary distraction from Millie.

Uffe and I each carried a framed picture over to Rosie and Albert. Rosie kept insisting it was overly generous, but she was ecstatic.

The painting she selected was bright and filled with flowers adding much-needed color to her dreary cabin. We had agreed that color therapy was essential to support our health and well-being.

Albert accepted my gift of a European mountain and lake landscape painting. He was astonished and speechless for a minute and hugged me. "A perfect reminder of Bohemia." Albert shook Uffe's hand so intensely that his shoulder shook.

Rosie and Albert were busy stashing belongings and sending whatever they could to the hold. They had a ton of belongings but understandable for such a long-term move. I would fill an eighteen-wheeler the next time I moved.

Uffe waited to help me carry the oversized painting to Mikkel. I admired it one last time and enclosed it back into the protective covering. It would be a shame if this one got damaged. I splurged to give him something memorable as an apology for everything I had put him through. And for all the mistakes, I was bound to make in the future.

We set the heavy painting against Mikkel's door to rest. I knocked but predicted he was elsewhere busy with tasks before leaving port.

I planned to prop it up against his door with a box, but the captain yelled, "Enter." Mikkel sat in his adjoining room working on his logbooks and referring to charts. "Did they locate Niels?"

"I don't know."

"What do you have there?" Maps and a few small pictures

decorated the walls of his office, but his bedroom had an empty wall large enough. A pity since I would never see it again.

"A gift for you."

"Kat, I told you to save your funds and not fritter them away."

"A small token of my appreciation. And an apology for all my mistakes." Plus, for those inevitable future blunders that are bound to happen.

I waited for Mikkel to remove the wrapping and be impressed. But he continued writing in his logbook.

When he realized we were waiting, he said, "Thank you. I suppose your portrait or some such nonsense from a down-on-his-luck impoverished artist."

"Not quite." I laughed at the idea of commissioning my dull portrait.

He didn't look up again. "Kat, I apologize. I must complete this paperwork. Leave it against that wall. I shall see to it later."

After Uffe and I left, I regretted my generosity. "If the captain doesn't like it, I will find someone else who wants it or sell it." If I could bring it back to the United States with me, I would. The painting reminded me of another spectacular Turner.

"He will like it. It is the most beautiful painting ever made of a ship. He reveres the sea." That settled it. Uffe gets it, but I'll wait to tell him when Mikkel rejects it.

We dragged the tightly rolled rugs to my cabin. The narrow runners would cover the cold timber floors when I got out of bed. Three rugs fit inside my cabin, but I had three more.

I told Uffe to take one, but he refused. He had never had a carpet. After I threatened to give it to another sailor, Uffe finally agreed.

We stuffed the remaining carpets under my bed. I could give the extras to Rosie and Albert.

The wool rugs were thick and plush. I sat on one and sunk my fingers into the soft wool.

"Sit here for a minute."

Uffe kneeled unsure about sitting cross-legged on the floor.

"This is like a magical carpet."

A weird noise came from my armoire. Something or someone was in my cabin.

"Did you hear that sound?"

He shut his eyes to listen, but the sound was gone. "Perhaps death-watches?"

"Death? What in the world do you mean?"

"A name for b-b-beetles that infest timber and make clicking sounds. Death omens."

He must be one of the superstitious sailors. "Nonsense. No wonder we hear odd sounds with all the commotion outside. Must be from out on the deck or the hold." All these new boxes and crates were bound to bang against each other on a rocking ship.

Mice might have snuck inside my deliveries. Every surface on the ship shone from all the mopping and polishing by the crew, but the pier and streets in Southampton were filthy.

"A fine carpet. Very soft." Uffe said still kneeling.

"Sit here right behind me and close your eyes. Where would you like to go?"

"Go? I don't know."

"I know this is silly, but it's fun to imagine."

Another slightly muffled bump sounded.

"Did you hear that? Wait here."

I stood, opened my armoire, and moved things around to check, but saw only my clothes.

"Oh, never mind." But I would avoid walking around barefoot just in case. I sat back down next to Uffe. "Close your eyes. That will help. Where would you fly if you could?"

"B-but I can't fly."

"Just imagine."

A sharp knock rang out from the door, and before I could uncross my legs and get up, Mikkel opened the unlocked door and saw us sitting on my new rugs. "Is everything all right?"

"Yeah. We were playing around," I said.

Uffe stood and extended his hand to help me up.

"A game?" Mikkel looked surprised.

"Yep, a carpet ride. Maybe we'll invite you next time."

Uffe looked uncomfortable caught acting childish in front of his boss. He left the room taking his rolled-up carpet with him.

Mikkel snickered. "Perhaps another time. I must thank you for the magnificent painting of a beautiful ship. I insist on reimbursing you."

"Oh no. No need. Glad you like it. Much prettier than my portrait."

"I would never say that."

"No, but it's the truth. I apologize for all those rude comments about the ship. *Anne Kristine* is beautiful, and I am lucky to be here. I want to start over."

"Nothing would please me more. I shall try to be more attentive to the concerns of the fairer sex."

I giggled. "Not sure how fair I am."

"My tongue will tell the anger of my heart, or else my heart concealing it will break."

"Shakespeare again?" I had to read the book of his plays to keep up.

"*The Taming of the Shrew*. Katherine is always arguing with Hortensio. Please tell me when you are angry or upset. A long voyage awaits us. If we communicate our concerns, we may prevent misunderstandings."

"Sure, but I hope it's unnecessary. I know you and the ship's rules better now."

He looked embarrassed. "I must go to the bridge. Do you wish to watch our departure?"

"I wouldn't miss it for the world." Although nothing would compare to that magical first late-night departure from Denmark.

"I shall send word."

I stayed in my cabin to avoid witnessing when they found Niels and arrested him. If he saw me, he might try to bring me down with him and scream out a final threat.

I sat on my bed and hugged my pillow. Millie is dead and gone. I held her gift, the spiritual book, close to my chest and traced her name on the book's inscription by the author. "Oh, Millie. I am so sorry. I was too late to help you."

She was ill when I left, and somehow Niels killed her. I shut my eyes, but tears rolled down my cheeks. If only I had been there earlier.

Two sailors in the designated search party knocked at my door to look for Niels. I let them in and brushed my tears away. They were polite and didn't stare. Everyone had seen me with Gustav and must think my tears were for the handsome Swede.

The searchers were thorough and opened the door to the armoire and dropped to their knees to look under the bed. My little box had few hiding spots, so it took less than a minute. Niels must not be on the ship. Only a fool would hide where he was supposed to be.

I couldn't shed more tears, so I started sorting the boxes, crates, and clothes. After a few minutes, I abandoned the task and lay on my bed staring at the ceiling. People were talking outside, and someone knocked on my door.

Uffe said, "The police officers need to talk to you again."

I followed Uffe to the dining room where the captain argued with them. "He is not on my ship. My men would have discovered him."

"Indeed. Dr. White remains a fugitive from justice," the older officer said, while he beckoned for me to sit. "Mrs. Jensen, since you were the last person to talk to him, we require your aid."

"I am not sure how I can help you."

"Let me be the judge of that." He snapped back. "Where is Dr. White?"

"Now? I have no clue."

"Come now, be honest. You planned this elaborate scheme. You both knew the deceased."

"With Niels? Millie Phillips was a friend. I wanted to help her."

"Some help. My belief: you met the woman and realized she was wealthy. You met your fellow passenger, Niels White. Together you hatched this plan to murder her and abscond with her money."

"No, that is crazy. I would never do something like that." I shook my head in horror.

Mikkel studied the police. "Madam Jensen is telling the truth. I insist my ship, with every officer, crew, and passenger, except Niels White, be allowed to leave at once. Our harbor escort has waited for some time now."

"Mrs. Jensen must return to the station for further questioning."

"What? No, I must stay here. I did nothing wrong." The words were painful since my throat tightened in panic.

"Where is your ship's destination, Captain Madsen?" The younger police officer said.

"Vigo, Spain."

"Once she is cleared of any wrongdoing, she may rejoin the ship there."

"Impossible. We shall be in Vigo a short day or so, and afterward, depart for the Canaries. This ship is swift, and another would never reach us in time."

"Is there another way?" My voice sounded odd.

The police officers insisted on some privacy to discuss their options.

In shock, my feet felt numb, and I couldn't stand after this turn of events. Mikkel helped me from my chair, but outside the dining room, my legs lost their strength, and I slumped to the deck.

Mikkel scooped me up in his arms, carried me to the salon, and placed me on the sofa as if I was a child.

Albert stood so quickly the pages of his newspaper scattered. "My goodness. What is the matter?"

Mikkel explained their new demands.

"Was that the woman you tried to find and help at the hospital?" Albert asked.

I nodded.

"Why would Kat do this if she plotted a murder? A logical, sane person would avoid the lunatic asylum to stay clear of any investigation. Captain, I must explain this to the authorities."

"Then you must explain how you impersonated a journalist. A crime in their eyes," Mikkel said.

"I would gladly take that risk. It cannot be as grave as a murder charge. Kat, do you agree?"

I couldn't speak while trying to absorb what happened, but I nodded.

Mikkel said, "Make your best attempt."

Albert left in a hurry, and Mikkel touched my arm to console me. "That devil. If I ever see him again, he shall pay dearly for this."

"I still can't believe he would do this. Of all people, Millie.

Everyone loved her." More tears escaped while I remembered my compassionate and friendly roommate.

"People are not always who they seem to be."

Lars strode into the salon. "Captain, the harbor pilot wishes to speak with you. He cannot wait much longer with his schedule today."

Mikkel hesitated, so I said, "I promise to wait here."

I wanted to curl up into a ball and hide somewhere on the ship. But when they found me, they would conclude I was guilty. Since I'm innocent, I will wait here. I bit my lip thinking about their life-threatening, or even worse, life-ending jail.

Albert's abandoned newspaper offered a welcome diversion, and I skimmed the news. My hands shook as I read yesterday's date, Thursday, November 13, 1862.

News reports covered the United States and the status of the Civil War. The paper described a three-day gunboat battle in Bayou Teche, a Louisiana waterway and the death of two Brigadier Generals. Charles Davis Jameson for the Union, who died at the age of thirty-five, and John Bordenave Villepique for the Confederacy's lost cause. He was only thirty-two.

What a waste. We should have remained part of the United Kingdom if we could have outlawed slavery peacefully in the 1830s. Slavery should never have existed. My hands stopped shaking from anger. Re-enactments of wars took place on battlefields throughout the United States. At least I was on a ship and not stuck in a war.

The last tidbit from the no longer United States concerned the patent for a machine gun in Indianapolis by Dr. Richard Gatling. More unwelcome news: a faster way to shoot people. Local news coverage focused on happier times including society weddings and parties in Southampton and London. The articles included unusual details. Everyone in attendance, what they wore, and even the food they ate, was described.

"Kat, great news."

I dropped the paper in anticipation. Albert stood grinning with Mikkel beside him.

"I explained the situation with Rosie's help," Albert said. "We documented the facts in an affidavit, a legal statement of facts, and signed it. If you agree, sign it to clear your name."

I followed them back to the dining room. Rosie, my defacto lawyer, known as a barrister in England, chatted with the police officers.

"Everything, the misunderstanding, has been clarified," she said, beaming at us. "That Niels, such a prig and so superior to the rest of us. He took advantage of Kat's honesty and goodness."

The old policeman said, "We still find these circumstances unusual. You must cease any journalist career until you secure true employment if that is your choice of profession. However, with these collaborating statements from Mr. Bittner and Miss Styles, we shall accept the signed declaration of facts."

The young police officer frowned unable to hide his disappointment.

A handwritten sheet of paper explained our attempt to free Millicent Phillips from the Hampshire County Asylum. Rosie and Albert had both signed at the bottom of the page.

"Fine." I grabbed the pen and signed.

"Another document for you to confirm." The old police officer slid across another paper and looked sympathetic. "Took my family weeks to remove my auntie from that revolting establishment. Months before she was herself again."

The second paper explained that I had never colluded with Dr. Niels White, alias Niels Hviid, alias Niels Blanc, to defraud or harm anyone. I dipped the pen in the inkwell, signed, and slid it back.

"If evidence arises to the contrary, we will require your hasty return and reappearance. Provided we apprehend Dr. White for the trial, we may require your testimony."

I nodded. How would this work from half a world away? Another reason to escape the nineteenth century.

Mikkel stood. "If you will excuse us, gentlemen. Unless you would like to disembark in Vigo."

The police officers laughed. The older one said, "We best be going. My wife would skin me alive if I am tardy for dinner."

Albert and Rosie stayed with me, and I thanked them for

saving my life.

"Do not mention it, Kat. Three Musketeers stick together. Remember?" Rosie said. "Those men were vulgar imbeciles. How they solve any crimes, with such a limited mental capacity, is beyond my comprehension."

"I can't believe all this happened. I will never forgive Niels. Millie didn't feel well but to die so suddenly."

"Doubtful, we shall ever see him again," Albert said.

"We should never have trusted him. A *bon vivant* living beyond his means and badgering poor Kat," Rosie said.

"What if Niels is not guilty? Doctors do lose patients." Albert looked circumspect. "At least, my knowledge of elementary police procedures came in handy."

"How did you know what to do?" I was curious since he was an engineer.

"My brother is a regional police superintendent. We often talk about crimes. Who and why."

"I always think about means, motive, and opportunity. Requires all three."

"Furthermore, you were completely innocent of all three," Rosie said.

Niels had the means and an opportunity, but was her money that strong of a motive? Her son controlled almost everything.

I was beyond grateful for my new friends. Even Mikkel helped rescue me. With their help, I avoided testing whether innocent until proven guilty, beyond a reasonable doubt, existed in 1862. Another narrow close-call that could have ended badly.

42 ~ A Golden Goodbye

The ship swayed and rocked as if eager to leave, and I hurried out to see our departure from port. A steam-powered tugboat pulled us out toward the channel. The crew couldn't hoist the sails until we left the narrow inlet of rivers and were further from Southampton.

I tried to stop thinking about leaving Millie behind and not attending her funeral. Out on the deck surrounded by living and breathing people, I was on my way. What Millie had urged me to do.

The channel's rolling blue-green waves lapped against our ship. A slapping sound echoed off the timber hull like a centuries-old maritime greeting. In less than an hour, we will be out in the channel with no turning back. Like the mermaid figurehead on the bow of the vessel, I focused straight ahead. I licked my chapped lips already tasting a hint of salt.

Captain Mikkel stood next to me and put his hand on my arm. "I shall do everything in my power to ensure a safe and comfortable journey. This morning I sent a personal request to King Neptune to be more compassionate."

I studied his face in amazement with such kind words. "I am determined to enjoy this. Planning to adjust my personal sails for whatever comes our way."

Instead of typically scanning the horizon and the surrounding water, his eyes met mine, and he grinned. "I am relieved to hear you say so. And for your benefit, navigational lessons shall begin early tomorrow morning."

I groaned teasing him. "Just when I thought I could sleep in and start my vacation."

A sailor approached. "Ah, Captain, Sir, pardon. The tug is setting us free shortly."

"Yes, of course." He excused himself and hurried over to the bridge.

The ship's canvas waited as if ready to go on stage and perform. Each of the differently sized sails had a unique name. With three masts, how they remembered them all and kept track was astonishing.

In the months ahead, I planned to advance from the inexperienced landlubber category. With the first part of my voyage behind me, I was no longer a first-timer called a greenhorn.

As we cut through the water, we left Niels further behind. If he was smart, he stood on another ship bound for Denmark or France, or he was already hiding in London.

The tugboat cut us loose to steam back to Southampton while our crew hoisted the waiting canvas in a fast but skillful synchronized series of movements.

Would this old ship make it all the way to Hong Kong? In 1862, we were vulnerable without standard modern emergency equipment like radios and radar. Helicopter evacuations were impossible, and any rescue at sea would be difficult. Tomorrow, I'd schedule a similar cruise industry mandatory evacuation drill.

Rays of sunlight snuck in and out from behind the clouds. Albert and Rosie joined me to watch our departure and see the sails now flying overhead. I smiled at the cream-colored canvas above me. Like old friends, they helped me escape from my troubles in Southampton.

The coast of France neared, and First Officer Lars pointed out Cherbourg, a busy port on a peninsula, jutting out into the Channel toward England. He handed us a spyglass, a shiny brass telescope, to see the coastline.

Ten years ago, I toured Normandy between Cherbourg and Le Havre and visited many World War II memorial sites. I borrowed the spyglass to see the shoreline. Under my breath, I said, "At least this isn't D-Day. We don't have to scale a cliff or fear being shot by Germans."

"What did you say?" Rosie was taking notes on the journey to tell her students in Hong Kong and family back home.

"Just remembering a famous battle. The Germans …" I stopped realizing my mistake. Rule number one: Don't bring up anything after 1862.

"Germans? What did they do now?" Albert had made it clear several times he was from Bohemia and not Germany, but Bohemians spoke German. Even his French sounded harsh.

"Oh, nothing. A novel I read about a war." My prearranged standard excuse if I accidentally referred to the future. No matter how hard I tried, events and ideas from the past one hundred and fifty years were bound to slip out.

"The book was about American soldiers, including a group of Texans, wet and cold after the boat ride from England. They scaled massive rocky cliffs. Over there in Pointe du Hoc." I pointed to a vague area near the French beaches named Utah and Omaha during World War II.

No one said anything, so I continued. "The book said how the odds were against them. The Germans had strong defenses and pelleted them with bullets and bombs. Even though half died, the others reached the top, and their sacrifice and bravery helped win the war." I was proud of their skills and bravery in fighting the Nazis.

"How dreadful, but so brave." Rosie looked wistful.

"I should like to read a book about that battle in Pointe du Hoc," Albert said.

"I would give it to you, but I didn't bring it with me."

"Pointe du Hoc? Have you been there?" Mikkel stood behind us.

Rosie shook her head. "Southampton is my furthest venture from home. Have you visited France, Kat?"

I nodded hating to lie. "Yes, years ago."

"We shall not pass nearby. I can show you our route on the charts if you wish," Mikkel said.

Albert clapped his hands. "*Wunderbar*. That would be excellent."

Rosie took Albert's arm to stroll over to see the navigational plans.

Mikkel offered me his hand and led us to the chart room on the bridge filled with maps. He slowed his stride, and I walked next to him. He acted relaxed and pleased for once. "This shall be the voyage of a lifetime."

I smiled. More than enough for my lifetime, but I didn't want to be rude and annoy him.

He pointed out the route to Vigo, Spain, and mentioned some sites we would pass along the way.

Lars interrupted to discuss more pressing matters, so I wandered to the railing and gazed at the water. After everything that had happened today, I needed some time alone to reflect.

Uffe tapped me on the shoulder and gave me a small box tied with a red ribbon.

I unwrapped the gift surprised and wondered what Mikkel had bought me. Inside the box, I removed a beautiful ring with an enormous yellow stone. This gemstone resembled yellow quartz and reflected the light from the sun.

I put the ring on and was about to find Mikkel to thank him when a small piece of paper fell out of the box. Uffe retrieved it before it blew into the water. The note's scrawling handwriting was hard to decipher.

> *Dearest Kat,*
> *A yellow diamond to match your lovely blonde hair and to our adventure ahead.*
> *Yours faithfully,*
> *Niels*
> *P.S. I am innocent!*

I read the note twice unwilling to believe this ring was from Niels. Yellow diamonds cost a fortune, and he was always broke. Looking up, I expected to see him strut confidently in my direction at any moment. I pulled my coat tighter as if preparing for battle. Could he still be here? How did he evade the police and the crew's thorough search?

"Uffe, who gave this to you?"

"A man presented it to the sailor over there. The man told him to give it to you when you were alone. He had to work, so he asked me for help." The sailor Uffe pointed to was preparing to hoist more sailcloth under Mikkel's watchful eye. Further questions had to wait.

I scanned the area again but didn't see Niels. The yellow stone sparkled in the sunlight as if sending a weird SOS. The money I had loaned him was minuscule compared to the value of this ring. Knowing Niels, it was another trick and a fake. I stuffed the ring back in the box along with the note.

"Uffe, can you please put this in my cabin?"

I searched the blue ocean for an answer. If Niels killed my good friend Millie, this ring would be a painful memory. I contemplated running after Uffe and tossing the box into the waves.

But Niels didn't strike me as a cold-hearted killer. Albert believed he was innocent and, as it often happens, lost a patient. Rosie, the governess turned role-playing attorney, deemed him guilty. I was stuck in the middle.

The ports ahead may be more dangerous than Southampton, and this ring might be useful as a bargaining chip. If I had to use it, I would thank Millie, not Niels.

Rosie tapped me on the shoulder, and I turned desperate for any distraction. She surprised me with a hug.

"I overheard Mikkel tell Albert you are melancholy about leaving Gustav. Blue like your dress, I suppose. I didn't realize you had such a close relationship."

"With Gustav? Oh no. Wonderful guy and charming. Trust me; he's better off without me. I keep thinking about Millie and those poor women in the asylum."

"Well, you achieved what you could. Shall we join the others? The trousers were an excellent idea." She pulled up her hem to show me a few inches of her new pants.

"Glad you like them. I forgot to put mine on."

"Female ingenuity to the rescue."

Rosie took my hand, and we strolled to the bridge where Mikkel and Lars monitored the ship's progress.

Albert stood around and chatted with the officers when they had a free moment. He was visibly in awe and impressed with all the sails.

These old clipper ships were truly exceptional. Today's departure was impressive but not as magical as when we passed by Kronborg, Hamlet's castle, in the moonlight.

Uffe stood ready with a bottle of champagne and six flutes.

Albert popped the cork, but I insisted on pouring the golden bubbly into each glass.

"Who is the sixth goblet for?" Captain Mikkel asked without mentioning Niels. If they discovered him on board, I'd heard the captain would throw Niels in the brig below deck to rot until we reached Vigo.

"Where are you, Uffe?" I glanced behind me and tugged Uffe by the arm into our circle. For once, he didn't argue that he couldn't or wouldn't. Uffe's stuttering was becoming less frequent.

"A fine-looking suit," Rosie said, complementing Uffe's new outfit. Not a fashion statement, but at least his clothes weren't three sizes too large.

Uffe didn't understand what she said, so I translated it to Danish. He impressed us both by thanking her in English.

Mikkel stared at Uffe's clothes and asked him to turn around like a model. I expected some snide comment, but instead, he chuckled. "Kat spent more money, I presume."

"We need a toast," Albert said looking at me.

"To being at home in the world." Rosie smiled. "I borrowed that saying from *Persuasion.* Jane's last published novel when Anne Elliott goes to sea."

"To being at home on the gorgeous and strong *Anne Kristine.*" I wanted to make her one of us.

We raised our glasses, but with the rocking of the ship, we didn't try to clink them. The bubbly tasted smooth, not bitter as I feared when I bought it.

Mikkel threw back his head and drank his champagne in one gulp while keeping a watchful eye on the crew. "The officers, crew, and I shall do our best to provide a pleasurable voyage. You must excuse Lars and me. *Anne Kristine* is a demanding mistress, and this channel requires our close attention."

Lars carried a brass megaphone called a speaking-trumpet. He communicated to the sailors positioned high overhead in the rigging with it, and they unfurled more canvas to speed our journey.

Albert said, "This is perfect, and exactly what I envisioned. But our goblets need replenishment. Never fear, I shall remedy that minor problem."

If only he was right, and the only problem was running out of champagne. But we faced a long, challenging journey into a vast blueness, and a deep menacing unknown surrounded us.

I sipped my champagne, optimistic the alcohol would dissolve the fears swirling in my stomach. Losing Millie and leaving Gustav didn't make it any easier.

How did this happen? I still couldn't believe boarding a ship could send someone into the past. But I had to accept it. Continuing to deny my new reality was a complete waste of time. The sparkling champagne bubbled reminding me to focus on the here and now.

In Denmark, a fortune teller warned me of severe hardships on this voyage. I had contemplated canceling, but he said, "This is your destiny." And, now it's my only way home. At least, he also had encouraging words. "Your determination will see you through."

Albert reappeared with Oskar, our nocturnal second mate, and another bottle of champagne. Oskar wore a broad-brimmed hat tied around his neck to protect his fair skin. Without sunglasses, which didn't exist in 1862, he squinted in the bright sunshine. His dark green eyes reminded me of deep ocean water.

Oskar yawned, unused to daytime duties, and gave me a courteous welcome. "I refused to miss this. A magnificent day, indeed. I always knew you would return."

He stared at my Egyptian good luck necklace. I twirled the ankh in my fingers while mentally wishing Gustav a safe journey without it. "You did?"

"Certainly. A little someone whispered in my ear." He threw his head back laughing and readjusted his hat.

"Really? You're kidding."

He smiled but wouldn't explain.

"Who told you?"

"A sorcerer never reveals his sources." Oskar winked and teased me.

In return, I gave him a light punch on the arm.

He smiled. "I will reveal one secret. You shall remain with us until Hong Kong."

I hoped so and laughed knowing I had plenty of time at sea to extract a full confession.

Albert filled my glass with the last of the dazzling golden champagne. Surrounded by friends and in good spirits, we had another round of toasts filled with upbeat wishes.

My glass remained half-full of cheerful dancing bubbles. The depressing, gloomy blueness I had experienced on this voyage switched over to optimism and sunny happiness. Nothing would stop me this time.

~ ~ ~

The End

~ ~ ~

About the Author

Karen Stensgaard is the author of the novel *Aquavit*, the first book in the Aquamarine Sea series. She grew up in San Antonio, Texas and after high school graduation, was a foreign exchange student in Denmark. After completing her MBA in Texas, she moved to San Francisco and through a series of unexpected twists became a bank examiner and later an internal auditor consultant. Karen moved to New York City and held many senior audit positions at financial firms. She lives in Philadelphia with her husband and two rescued cats.

To find out more about this book and stay up to date on new ones, visit her website blog on karenstensgaard.com. Sign up for updates or join her Facebook Novelist page. On Pinterest, she has created boards which visualize key characters and some scenes. Karen also blogs about her travels, libraries, and other fun topics on her website.

If you enjoyed reading *Aquavit* or *Blueness*, please share the word with your friends. Send feedback to me or even better, post an online book review on Goodreads, Amazon, or another site. Your support is incredibly valuable in today's busy world.

Let's stay connected on social media!

 Karenstensgaard.com

 @karenstenzy

    Karenstensgaard

Q & A with the Author

Why the fascination with time travel into the past?
Before I moved to New York City, I lived in old Victorian and Edwardian houses in San Francisco, California. Any building that survived the 1906 earthquake qualified for a badge of honor. I often fantasized about wandering around San Francisco to see how life was before the city-changing quake. I would stick out dressed in jeans and needed to be invisible or wear something from that time-period. Luckily, it never happened since I didn't have anything from the early twentieth century in my closet!

The voyage takes place on a clipper ship in 1860. Why?
Clipper ships were sleek, fast, beautiful, and the story had to take place when they existed. After the completion of the Suez Canal in 1869, the popularity of sailing vessels without steam engines went into a slow decline. The Star Clipper cruise line uses clipper ships except they are equipped with generators and motors. The trade-off includes excellent bathrooms and electricity. Kat would love those ships!

Kat speaks Danish on the ship. How did you learn this language?
I learned Danish when I was an exchange student to Denmark. I wanted to blend in some of my knowledge of Danish culture into my novels. The seafaring life has a long and close relationship with many Danes. The crew and officers on the ship speak Danish to Kat Jensen, the main character. Because this can become a burden to read, I included only a few keywords with a quick translation to provide a flavor.

Is there a message in your book you want readers to grasp?
Be brave, embrace life, and never give up on your dreams. Try to enjoy your journey, not just waiting to get to your destination. Blueness, or feeling blue, is unavoidable, but optimism will usually win out with the help of your friends.

What are you working on now?
I jumped ahead a year for a modern-day financial thriller featuring Kat Jensen and more of her adventures. But additional books in the *Aquamarine Sea Series* are outlined and planned. If you have a preference, send me an email to tell me which type of story you prefer. You can contact me via karenstensgaard.com or through the usual social media sites.

~~~

Book Club Discussion Topics

Spoiler Alert!

In honor of arriving in Southampton, England, enhance your discussion with a tasting of British ale and Stilton and other English cheese. Surprisingly, beer often brings out the flavors in cheese better than wine. Cheers, or as Captain Mikkel would say, *skål*.

1. Kat finds out her adventure at sea isn't what she expected. Is she making the right decision to continue to Hong Kong? What would you do?
2. Kat gets involved with three men: Captain Mikkel, Niels, and Gustav. She doesn't have much luck with these men either. Has she done the right thing? What's your opinion of these guys?
3. When Kat arrives at the lunatic asylum, she starts to give up. Millie and Maxi are spiritual and encourage her to be more optimistic. Do you think Kat changed after meeting them?
4. Do you trust Kat's new friends and fellow passengers, Rosie and Albert? Discuss reasons you do and don't.
5. What do you think happened to Dr. Niels White?

~~~

www.ingramcontent.com/pod-product-compliance
Lightning Source LLC
Chambersburg PA
CBHW031942130726
47905CB00002BA/464